COME AS YOU ARE

COME AS YOU ARE

AMY J. FETZER

BRAVA

KENSINGTON PUBLISHING CORP.
http://www.kensingtonbooks.com

BRAVA BOOKS are published by

Kensington Publishing Corp.
850 Third Avenue
New York, NY 10022

All Kensington titles, imprints and distributed lines are available at special quantity discounts for bulk purchases for sales promotion, premiums, fund-raising, educational or institutional use.

Special book excerpts or customized printings can also be created to fit specific needs. For details, write or phone the office of the Kensington Special Sales Manager: Kensington Publishing Corp., 850 Third Avenue, New York, NY 10022. Attn. Special Sales Department. Phone: 1-800-221-2647.

Brava and the B logo Reg. U.S. Pat. & TM Off.

ISBN-13: 978-0-7582-1657-1
ISBN-10: 0-7582-1657-2

First Kensington Trade Paperback Printing: December 2007
10 9 8 7 6 5 4 3 2 1

Printed in the United States of America

Dedicated to Maureen Child

Thanks for always *being in my corner.*
—*Amy*

One

It was supposed to be an easy retrieval. Pickup and delivery.

Now they were FedEx with assault rifles and hauling ass.

The door of the speeding chopper thrown open, Logan hung onto the *oh shit* strap and sighted through high-powered binoculars on a ship, that up until eight minutes ago, was dead in the water.

With no answering hail or a distress signal, the luxurious 140-foot killing machine at top speed was rudderless, cutting through the surf and kicking up boiling waves. Effectively thwarting any asinine attempt to board her. *That would be me*, Logan thought, holding on as he glanced at the radar. Closing in on Cuban waters.

"I thought this thing could do over a hundred?" Wind battered his face, nearly knocking off his headphones.

"We'd use up too much fuel," Sebastian said. "It's a long way back to land."

Logan threw him a look and words died.

"Christ. Hold on," Sebastian warned. "Going postal."

Logan gripped the strap as Sebastian pushed the chopper to its limits, the force slamming him against the interior. *I really need to learn how to fly,* he thought, bringing the binoculars into position again.

"We've got bad guys," Logan said as two figures appeared in the passageway, then moved to the stern. "With scuba tanks." Logan quickly zoomed in on their faces as one man looked up, his smile vicious, seconds before he pulled on his mask and executed the backward fall into the sea. *He had something in his hand.*

Below the chopper, a 43-foot turbine Scarab speedboat slowed long enough for an Interpol agent suited in minimal dive gear to drop into the water and search. It was useless, the targets already deep, their bubbles churning with the waves. Logan focused on the yacht closing in on Cuban waters.

"No sign of the divers," Max said, watching out the opposite side. "No pickup boat near enough, either. A hundred miles out in shark-infested waters?"

"He's got help." Anchored under the ocean had to be a propulsion torpedo. Or worse, a submarine. What any of it had to do with a privately owned yacht wasn't a concern. Their job was to find it and bring it back to port—but not from inside Cuban territory.

That bad taste in his mouth was quickly going sour, and Logan turned away from the open door, reaching for the harness.

"What do—? You can't be serious, man," Max said. "It's got to be going 40 knots."

"I don't see we have much choice." Logan slipped into the harness. "If anyone's got a flash, clue me in now." Strapped and locked in, he clipped the cable, then pulled on a helmet.

"It's suicide," Sebastian said with resigned calm. "The wind speed alone will push you back fifty feet."

"Then drop me on the bow."

"Let Interpol blow it out of the water before we get near Cuba," Sebastian said. "They take protecting their waters very seriously."

Logan didn't look up as he snapped his gun into the holster. "We aren't being paid to destroy it, or do you have this month's payments handy?"

"I'm on welfare," Max groused, and reluctantly manned the winch. "You really think anyone's still alive?"

Logan leaned out as Sebastian shifted the chopper to the right and ahead. He knew what he'd find. Nothing. Seven people were onboard the yacht when it left a Miami port. Five crew including the captain, and only two passengers.

Logan shifted to the edge of the chopper, his feet braced on the door treads. The wind snapped at his jumpsuit, loosening his footing.

"I can't get any closer, the yacht's too erratic," Sebastian said. "We have more company." To his right, a black screen screamed the demarcation of international waters and blips coming toward it. "A Cuban Navy ship and it just launched four attack boats." They couldn't be seen on the horizon yet, but they were moving fast.

"Interpol is ready to fire!" Max yelled, launching between the seats and grabbing the radio.

The Scarab wasn't manned with rockets, but while one boat circled for the attackers, on the other, an agent stood at the prow and lifted a shoulder-mounted stinger into position. Logan could see Riley aboard the Scarab, his weapon drawn on the agent to stop him.

Max called frantically over the radio, then looked back at Logan. "Not yet, not yet!"

But Logan was already sliding over the side.

Max hit the winch, lowering him. "He's got a death wish, I swear," he muttered, then into the radio repeated, "Interpol, stand down! Cuban forces approaching."

Sebastian angled the chopper to the left, swinging Logan like a pendulum and putting him within a few yards of the yacht, but the sea and the boat's erratic speed hampered him. Dropping Logan on a boat that was already going nearly 50 miles an hour covered a lot of distance. By the time Logan reached the yacht, it would already have gone past. Sebastian had to get in low, and avoid the antenna and satellite dish on top that would hit the chopper skids or impale Logan before he landed.

Then they didn't have to worry about it.

The yacht took its direction from the current and Logan saw his chance evaporating. He hit the clip release and dropped on the roof of the bridge, the impact sending him tumbling down the sloped surface, across the windshield. He grabbed for anything to stop himself. The satellite dish broke off in his hand seconds before he crashed into some deck chairs. *Man, I really don't want to bounce.* The force snatched the choice. He was airborne, smacking into the bow railing. The rail broke away on impact, and he scrambled to grip the flagpole and latched on. For a couple seconds, he stopped, then the pole bent, and he went over the side like wet fish.

He caught the twisted metal with one hand, the sudden stop nearly tearing his arm from the socket. He dangled for a moment, beaten like a banner against the side of the yacht. He could hear Max through the radio in his helmet but couldn't understand anything beyond the noise of splitting waves. If he fell, he'd be crushed under the ship or chewed by the propellers.

He strained his muscles to pull his legs up to the deck, but the metal started to tear. He risked drawing his gun and fired two shots at the Plexiglas portal, then jammed his foot in the rim, pushed up for a better grip and hoisted himself over the side. He fell to the wet wood floor. The chopper hovered.

"The Commies are coming, and the Scarabs are approaching from your east, armed till that yacht reaches the marker, then we're all fair game," Sebastian said into his helmet radio. "Gitmo Bay went on alert and Cuba is not answering our hail."

Guantanamo Bay Marine base. Well, crap. Start a pissing contest with the Cuban Navy over this? He pushed off the floor and hurried to the bridge, throwing open the door. The collision sirens blared in the empty bridge as he rushed to the wheel. The throttle controls were smashed and at full speed. He pulled them back, knowing it was useless, then hit the emergency engine stop. No response.

Oh, you knew what you were doing, you bastard. He didn't

look up, didn't want to see the attack boats speeding toward him, and rushed around to the computer console, typing. Nothing responded. The ship was still traveling at incredible speeds and she had full tanks. Logan dropped to the floor and rolled under the console, pulling wires.

"Cutter, come in, come in."

"I'm here," Logan said and then gave them a rundown. "I'm trying to get into the computers and stop the engines."

"You're half a mile from a marker. ETA less than four minutes."

Great, nothing like a little more pressure.

Logan disabled one computer. Whoever did this had destroyed the steering controls but not the engine operations. Logan disconnected the computer from the main console, then leapt to his feet, tapping keys again. The engines roared high and he smelled burning oil. It's going to explode, he thought, and take anything within five hundred yards down with it.

He cut the circuits to the engineering and emptied the fuel into the sea. Not environmentally correct, but let the tree huggers deal with that. He went to the wheel and tried turning it, but the craft refused to budge. The engines weren't cutting off, too much fuel in the system still, and he raced back to the computer and blew the ballast on the right side. The ship listed dangerously, and started turning away from the marker and Cuban ship, but only slightly. They'd still collide.

The steering was gone, the throttle high and damaged—he couldn't stop it. There was no connection between the operating computers and the engines.

He left the bridge and ran down the curved stairwell to the belly of the ship. The LCD panels were lit up, the horn blaring a warning of the oncoming collision. Yet the entire access panel was smashed and smoking. He followed the computer wires from the panels to the electronic console, then yanked a handful of wires. Nothing.

"Well, shit," he muttered and went to the electrical panel, flipped it open and reached to switch off circuits and found them smashed and melted in the ON position. "Gimme a break here!" Rushing topside and back to the bridge, Logan's view filled with the Cuban naval ships, as big as the yacht but faster and heavily armed. While the Cuban ship recognized the oncoming collision and made to turn, a few thousand tons of steel didn't skip on the water. He blew more ballast, nearly capsizing the yacht as it tipped sharply to the side.

"Cutter, get off that thing!" Sebastian shouted in his ear mic.

"It's too late."

Logan braced himself. Impact in five . . . four . . . three . . . two . . . The gray steel hull of the ship filled the windshield as the stern hull impacted with the prow, scraping its sides. The megaton ship pushed the yacht aside like a bath toy, throwing Logan across the bridge as the yacht rocked violently, nearly on its side, and took on water.

"Oh, hell no. You're *not* sinking with me aboard!"

Hanging onto the door, Logan struggled to reach the ballast door's switch, using shelves and cabinet doors to pull himself toward his target. He slammed his fist down on the switch, unloading the left side. He couldn't tell if it worked, the impact still propelling the rudderless yacht sideways.

The vessel shuddered violently, engines choked. "Come on, you steel bastard, just die!"

The fuel finally spent from the engine's chambers, the craft started to slow and almost righted itself. She still had a drunken tilt to her, yet was seaworthy. Oily smoke curled up from below decks into the pilothouse. The ship bobbed on the waves.

"Cutter, Cutter!" Sebastian shouted his call sign over the frequencies.

"I'm here." Logan yanked at his helmet strap, then winced when Max whistled.

"Jesus, you're lucky," Max said. "The Cubans are standing down. Guantanamo Bay must have gotten through. The other ship is banged but above the waterline."

"They'll probably bill us." Logan didn't exhale a breath before the engines blew, bearings ricocheting inside the hull like a pinball machine. Exploding parts hit the floor under his feet. He tried dropping anchor but even that failed. At least it was clear of the other ships, he thought, as he removed his helmet and pushed his fingers through his hair before he fixed the transmitter in his ear and adjusted the mic.

Then he smelled it. The familiar scent of death. He looked around the bridge, just noticing the blood splatters. Everywhere.

"Max, get down here. Tell Interpol we'll need a video camera."

It wasn't until he left the bridge on the leeward side that he realized it wasn't water that made it slippery, but blood.

The ocean's depth squeezed on his lungs, yet his air flowed freely as the propulsion torpedo dragged him through the water. He felt the pitch of the sea, the jolt of ships colliding, and smiled around his regulator. The impact shuddered through the water, scattering sea life in all directions, but he experienced only a ripple. He held tight to the torpedo as it pulled him toward the fishing boat anchored two miles away.

The agents and whoever was in the chopper wouldn't find anything he didn't want them to find. He'd made sure of it. His orders were clear.

No evidence to follow.

He checked his watch, the digital readout counting down.

Drawing his weapon, Logan moved forward. The evidence of someone being dragged was obvious. A victim's handprints, like claw marks to keep from going over the side, smeared the passageway and rails. The chopper hovered overhead as Max lowered to the vessel, dropped and rolled. He hurried to Logan as Interpol's Scarab pulled alongside. Logan let down the emergency rope ladder and agents boarded.

The two agents, Brewer and Medina from the South American offices, were chasing sea pirates when Dragon One asked for assistance. Three vessels had been attacked recently, so they were more than happy to lend a hand.

"I'm past the fail-safe mark," Sebastian said over the radio. "I've got to return for fuel."

Logan waved and Sebastian rocked the chopper before he headed toward land.

"We'll take belowdecks. Crews' quarters," Medina said, handing a compact video camera to Max, then sighting through another, he made a general sweep of the area. After synchronizing radio frequencies, they moved off.

"It's slippery, so watch it," Logan said. "I didn't notice blood belowdecks, but then, I wasn't looking for it."

Brewer nodded, his expression grim and angry.

In the aft of the ship were the staterooms, galley and dining/living room. Logan and Max circled the deck, sections of polished wood still gleaming with fresh wax, others stained red with blood. A massacre.

They entered the main stateroom. Long, wide doors were open to the elements, and Logan kicked aside towels and lotion bottles, ignoring the padded chaises about to topple into the sea. The sun brightened across the deep maroon sofas, the wood tables and a wet bar. In inclement weather, the doors would slide closed and seal the passengers in a warm cocoon. Not this time.

Logan and Max passed through the main cabin and headed toward the private staterooms as the agents scoured the belly of the craft into the engine rooms. Logan could hear them tearing open anything suspicious, the destruction rising through the dying ship. Max trailed him with a small video camera, his weapon drawn. But Logan knew there was no threat. No reason to hope. They cleared each cabin and were outside the main stateroom when the agents joined them.

"There's no one here. They put up a fight. There's a lot of that." Medina gestured to the blood splatters.

Logan recognized the pattern. Point-blank range in the head. An execution. He nodded and entered the main cabin.

His aim faltered, something inside him crushing his lungs when he saw the wedding gown hung on the door.

"Oh man." His gaze snapped around the cabin. A bride's frothy veil and a pair of man's shoes and jacket lay tossed in the corner. The cabin was a shambles, yet like most ships, everything with weight was bolted down, including the bed, wide-screen TV and its components. The bed linens were tangled, body depressions still visible, a bottle of champagne up-ended into a silver bucket now tipped on its side on the floor.

"There's still ice in it." Max nudged the bucket, and watery ice melted into the carpet.

"The TV is still on," Logan said. "I couldn't cut the electricity."

"They run on battery," Max explained. "Separate from the engines." He stepped to go look, but Medina stopped him.

"I'll cut the power," Medina said as Brewer spoke into the radio to his home base.

Logan scowled at him.

"It's international waters, and now a mass murder."

Logan nodded and moved around the large stateroom, searching for identification, careful not to disturb more than was necessary. Max picked up the TV remote and pushed PLAY, the screen blinked on, the video from the wedding playing. Logan heard him groan with sympathy and glanced briefly. The wedding videographer was going from table to table and recording best wishes from the guests. He looked away, his gaze traveling over the cabin. Why? Was there anything of value other than the ship itself?

"If it was pirates," Logan said, "then why not keep the vessel? Why kill them all and crash the ship?"

"A cover-up?" Max asked, still watching the video. "Yachts aren't built for speed, and you know how I like a good conspiracy theory."

"Turn that off," Logan snapped as he hunted for the passports.

"Not yet, look at this. I'd swear that was your dad."

Logan turned sharply, his gaze narrowing on the screen.

Max froze the frame, then backed it up. Logan moved closer, a hard chill pulling on his skin. His mom was there, laughing with his father. Instantly, he turned up the volume and heard his father say, "Like a daughter to me."

"Oh, Jesus," Logan whispered, then started rifling through the drawers like a wild man.

Medina reached to stop him, but Max stepped in the path. He rewound the DVD to visions of the bride just as Logan found the passports. For a heartbeat, he stared at the identification, then sank to the edge of the bed, his throat closing tightly.

Oh God, no. He handed over the passports to Brewer and muttered, "Cassandra Furman. Twenty-three." He rubbed his face, then stared at the wedding video. "I remember when she was born."

Logan let the memory slide through his mind; the little dark haired girl who lived up the road, pampered from the moment she arrived. A fiery temper and rebellious, Cassie was the belle of the county—and raised on a two hundred year old plantation. Just like him. About fifteen years senior to her, he'd left home when she was still a child, but remembered little Cassie sitting on the side of the long, oak-lined drive, waving a small flag, her face peering over a poster welcoming him back from Desert Storm. She had a crush on him then, and he'd adored her, but he hadn't seen her much since she was in high school. His eyes burned as he looked at the dainty wedding gown, knowing this would destroy so many families.

"They're from South Carolina. I'll give you the information you'll need for contact. No, when you do, call me, I'll do it." He shot off the bed, his fists clenched.

He wanted to pound something. Max went to pat his shoulder, then thought better of it.

A horn blasted, and they rushed to the side of the craft. The second Scarab pulled alongside, a body in a dive suit lay in the bottom of the speedboat. Riley pointed accusingly at the agents. There wasn't much left of the diver. They'd apparently shot the dive tank and the body was a grisly mess, an arm missing. One down, one to go. He watched the horizon in the false hope that the diver would surface. If the bastard had a rebreather, no telling where he'd turn up. Logan never got a good look at the tanks, but that smile he'd remember until he died. Or till he killed him.

He pushed away from the rail.

"Logan, we need to split. Interpol has to handle it now. We can't do anything more."

He would, alone. "Board the Scarab, I'll be right back." Logan turned back into the luxurious cabin, and after he'd handed over the passports to Medina, he ejected the DVD out of the player and slipped it in his vest pocket. He held his hand over it for a moment, bitter rage welling inside him. Then just as quickly, he pushed it aside to search the cabin once more with Brewer. Mentally, Logan fitted the light dust rings to the bric-a-brac scattered on the floor. He picked up a couple of pieces, positioning them into place. The diver had something in his hand when he went over the side. Like a small jar or a cup. But most of what was here was either broken beyond recognition or near its original position. So what did he take? What was worth the lives of seven people?

Squatting, he flipped up the bed skirt, and shined his flashlight into the darkness. Nothing. Not even dust. He straightened, then started to leave the cabin when his attention caught the alarm clock. It was still running.

"Didn't you cut the power?"

Brewer kept inventorying the cabin. "Medina did, yes."

"You're sure?" Max said the cabins' electrical ran on batteries, but . . . Logan grabbed the end table, pulling at it, but it was bolted to the floor. Then he lightly grasped the cord, following it to the wall. He pushed a chair aside.

It wasn't plugged in.

He let go and stepped back. "Oh, Christ. We gotta bail." Brewer frowned over his shoulder, but Logan grabbed a handful of his shirt and pulled. "Bomb!"

The two men rushed to the upper deck, shouting as Logan

ran for the bow. He didn't stop and dove, arching his body to get far away from the ship.

The blast erupted, sending him head over ass twice before he hit the water. The impact stunned him, pain screaming through his skin as he sank deep, the pressure pushing on his skull, his ears, and the underwater vibration shaking his brain. He swam away from the explosion, arms digging into the water. A shudder echoed in the depths, the sea warming quickly, the force of the blast pushing him along. He prayed the team had gotten clear.

His lungs strained, pinpoints of light fracturing in his eyes, and he dove deeper, debris raining like missiles. Shrapnel clipped his shoulder, and he flinched, losing precious air, but the debris kept falling, dropping like stones and kicking up silt. His body wanted air, now, and he struggled for the surface in wide, hard sweeps, releasing increments of air until he didn't have any more. He shot out of the water, then bobbed, sucking in a lungful. He whipped around, searching for the Scarab boats. The pair were circling the arena around the yacht ablaze like a Viking ship sent to Valhalla. That was too close.

Without fuel in her tanks, the explosion wasn't as bad as it could be, but the bomb leveled the first two decks including the pilothouse. The *Sea Empress* looked as if it had been attacked by a can opener, thick metal peeled back and tattered. There goes any chance of getting paid.

He waved and a Scarab headed toward him. One was damaged, the tear in the hull just barely above the waterline so they had to take it slow. Max leaned and reached out for him, and Logan grasped his forearm, then rolled into the boat.

But not before he glimpsed the white wedding gown floating nearby, the lacy arms torn and outstretched before it sank under the sea.

Inside the Pentagon
Months later

General Joseph McGill didn't earn his three stars without hearing a lot of carefully worded bullshit. This time the pile was getting deep, and considering his company, it was almost natural for them to color information. Just not this brightly.

He'd been acting Deputy Director of the CIA Special Operations for less than a month, something he'd lobbied against till the Secretary of Defense ordered him into the position. McGill thought the SOD wanted to shake things up, scare some people. A recent intelligence leak to the press had him clamping on his people so hard their necks hurt. But that would have been an easy job. McGill wasn't certain the President was aware of this meeting, or who was covering their ass and what for. But his number one target was less than ten feet from him.

On the other side of the long conference table, Elizabeth Jacobs sat erect, her spine stiff, eyebrows high with indignation. At forty-eight, the sharp red suit and carefully applied makeup was just a smoke screen. She was a cobra who was off the map when it came to understanding how special operations worked. To her, they were all expendable. Oh, she'd bemoan the loss of a service member, but that didn't stop her from pushing to send more into a dangerous situation. She was the tactical director on a mission that had failed miserably. Even stripped of her clearance and control, she couldn't stop behaving like an operative in the field. Everyone was an asset and expendable. Including her.

It turned his stomach to look at her.

"Are you suggesting I leave this to the good ol' boys, General?"

There's a reason I wear three stars, cupcake.

With a light shove, he pushed the folder to the center of the table. "Your strategy was deeply flawed. You should have aborted at the first shot fired. You went forward with bad Intel, people are dead. Now you want to leave him there?"

"He understood the consequences and, while regrettable, he knew the dice before he rolled them. You've read the data, the psych reports. He was more than willing to take this assignment."

"At your behest."

"I'm paid to get the job *done,* General, and my career speaks for itself."

He scoffed. "I've read it. It's pretty shaky in some spots, even before this." He flicked a hand at the two-inch-thick file between them.

Her expression turned as snotty as a rebellious teenager cornered by a parent as she said, "Operations always have kinks that must be dealt with in a matter of seconds. I did what needed to be done. And frankly, I wasn't aware that you had full authority over the matter."

Seated around the room, men sat back collectively and attention shifted to the Secretary of Defense.

"Liz."

She looked at the Secretary, her skin reddening as if she just remembered his presence.

"While this was initially your operation . . ."

Her shoulders tensed, too smart not to know she was being stiffed out.

"It's not anymore," he added. "Ensuring that our man is brought home is our only consideration now."

"Then a clean sweep is wiser."

The SOD tilted his head. "You're not being asked to participate, you're being ordered to turn all remaining documentation over to the general." He stood and she rose slowly. "Today."

She didn't look anywhere but at the Secretary. "Sir, I must argue your decision. I'm prepared to return and rectify this problem myself."

"That's not an option." He nodded to somewhere behind her and a young man moved to her side.

He didn't touch her; they'd allow her the dignity of that.

She showed nothing. Not a flicker in her expression nor twitch in her body.

She's a cool customer, McGill thought.

"We'll discuss your future after the holiday."

She only nodded and with her escort, left the room.

The Secretary looked at McGill. "End this, tie it off. Go outside if you have to. The U.S. can never be implicated. Never. With the present state of unfriendly attitudes from this country's leader, we have to come away clean or the consequences will be insurmountable."

McGill saw the stress on his friend's face, how he'd aged in the last four years. It wasn't a job he wanted, ever. Right now, he wasn't liking this one, either.

"Joe, it's your game," the Secretary pressed.

McGill looked down at the files. He hated cleaning up his country's messes.

Too often, we've become our own worst enemy.

Two

South Carolina

Logan stared out the window of his house, watching the helicopter lower to the lawn, its blades stirring up the live oaks and palm trees, and gobbling half the flowers like an alien craft sucking up victims.

I'm not gonna like this.

Within moments, General Joseph McGill, a man he respected, climbed out of a plain black chopper. He'd wanted to speak to the team. ASAP. Although McGill gave nothing away as to the reason, he'd been overly polite. A three-star didn't have to be nice to anyone except the President.

Logan sipped his beer as the general headed to the sidewalk, a memory shadowing; Cassie on her bike, reaming him for sulking like an "ol' sour puss." His lips curved. She'd been right. Around then, he was just about everyone's pain in the ass.

His smile fell, her bloody handprints making a comeback in his mind.

Justice, that's all she'd want. But Logan was thinking; *severely avenged.* This was too cleverly done to be anything less than a much larger operation than two men. Not with the total annihilation of the ship and witnesses. Pirates, my ass. They would have raped the ship clean and sunk it. It was too big and slow for the speed they needed.

What was in his hand? flickered like a taunt. He was still waiting for the inventory of the ship's contents down to the cellophane-wrapped toothbrushes. It was the only way they'd be able to tell if whatever the diver took came from the crew or guests, or the ship itself. He rubbed the back of his neck for a moment. That attack was Mach 1 overkill.

Directly behind him on a desk once owned by Robert E. Lee, a laptop computer ran through photos, searching for a match from his admittedly vague composite of the killer. His partner, nearly blown in pieces by the exploding tank had a handprint. The time in the water and the explosion left little evidence for forensics, but Interpol's face match gave them Felix Carona, Aymara Indian, born in Venezuela and once a captain in its Army. He'd been discharged with full honors, and like Dragon One, worked for the private sector. Though morally, there was no comparison. Carona and a few of his buddies had been linked to more than one assassination of anyone in power who opposed President Gutierrez's "communal socialist" philosophy. Well executed and no witnesses.

Where have I heard that before?

He pinched the bridge of his nose. Scrape it as clean as they wanted, he could still smell it.

"It's got to be serious shit for McGill to come himself, without his aides," Max said from somewhere behind him.

Or his security, Logan thought. "Time to find out."

Logan moved away from the window, taking his beer and heading to the door. He opened it before McGill met the sidewalk. In jeans, loafers and a polo shirt, he looked more like his own father than a man who commanded thousands.

"What?" Logan asked. "You couldn't hop a cab?"

"Too slow. Thanks for meeting me."

"It's good to listen to the wise men once in a while."

"I wish someone would."

That didn't sound good.

McGill shook his hand and stepped inside. The chopper lifted off behind him, a few thousand in landscaping going with it.

"Want a beer?" Max approached, holding out a cold one.

"Hell yes." McGill took the longneck bottle and stepped farther inside, sipping. "Nice place, Commander."

Dragon One had an unofficial headquarters above Sebastian's restaurant, the Craw Daddy in New Orleans, so Logan wasn't home often. He'd reacquainted himself with the four-bedroom house in the past days, filled with items that evoked a story. Probably why he didn't hang around. Some stories should just fade away.

"It's just Logan," he said, and gestured to a chair. "You want to hire us." Why else would he be there?

Joe McGill should have remembered he'd get right to the point. Logan Chambliss wasn't one to waste time with pleasantries. Just like the rest of the team members. Dragon One was efficient and morally stronger than most teams because they'd all been so royally screwed by their own government. They'd been tested in fire and survived. It could have easily gone the other way. "Yes, we do."

"We?"

"The Department of Defense."

"That's a big place." Logan sat back, shrugging. "You've got field CIA or Spec Ops at your fingertips, so it's something dirty." Logan glanced at Max and smothered a smile when he started humming the theme from *Mission Impossible*. "Why aren't you sending them?"

McGill shifted in the chair. He'd practiced this moment. It's how he remained diplomatic when a bunch of self-important senators made him want to smack their heads together. But this was different. They had a problem that couldn't be rectified through legal or diplomatic channels. "We did. They didn't come back."

Logan scowled. "Then the price just doubled."

"Tripled," Riley said loud enough for McGill to hear. "I've already died for one mission, I'm not doing it again." On crutches, Riley limped into the room, munching on a sandwich and using his bad arm to do it.

Logan gave him his well-honed doctor look, and Riley

rolled his eyes, yet lowered gingerly into a chair. The guy was in a coma a few months ago and had a long way to go still.

Logan focused on McGill. "You can understand why we don't want to even hear this."

"Hell, I wouldn't." McGill took a sip of beer, rolled the bottle between his hands. "I can tell you that without agreement, I stop here, and don't say—wait," he said when they grumbled. "Those are my orders. Now, this is what I can say—"

"The U.S. fucked up," Max said.

"Bluntly, yes. We got too involved. Do you recall the recent coup d'état in Venezuela?"

"Who doesn't?" Logan said. "It lasted two days and Gutierrez blamed the rebels. His troops killed a lot of innocent people, the Vice President was injured, and the general who supposedly helped stage the coup is still in power. So Gutierrez might be President, but his control isn't that strong."

McGill nodded, choosing his words carefully. "Before that, Vice President Garcia was a shoe-in for President and Gutierrez couldn't run again. The two have been on opposite sides often. So much that Garcia's opposition made him a target for pro-socialism supporters. He'd suffered two assassination attempts, one that killed his only brother. It put Garcia on a warpath for change, and within days the coup occurred. He was accused of instigating it."

"Gutierrez has considerable support from other countries," Sebastian said. "It won't be long before Venezuela is a new Cuba."

"So it's Communism versus democracy?" Max said. "I can live with that."

"I can't," Logan said, and they all looked at him. But his attention was on the general.

McGill looked grim and it was almost painful to say, "During the two-day coup, Garcia was shot and dragged away. No body. Witness stories are shaky—"

Logan put up his hand. "Wait a second." He searched his memory and recalled the recent pictures of the limo turned on its side, his security dead. "You mean all this time the government has behaved as if Garcia were found, wounded, but alive?"

"Yes."

"Then who the hell is in the Vice President's house?" Logan had seen him on TV a few days ago. A simple smile and wave for the crowds, nothing more.

"He's our man. Physically altered." McGill made a quick circle around his face. "He'd been severely injured fighting for his country and volunteered."

The room was so quiet, McGill looked up from the bottle. He finished off the last of the beer as he sat back and said, "Let it sink in. It doesn't get better."

Instantly Logan's mind filled with all sorts of ramifications. "This will mushroom out of control. An American in the power position in another country? It's a time bomb for war. Christ, this has to be one of the dumbest things the U.S. ever did in the name of liberty."

McGill's features pulled taut, his shoulders shifting like a gamecock with his feathers ruffled. He might agree, but he didn't voice it. "So you understand we need to act quickly."

"Without Garcia to put back in his place, it's impossible. Why did the U.S. do this?"

"It's classified."

"There's the door, sir." Logan's point was clear. Give them all the Intel or no deal.

McGill sighed, aware Dragon One was his last option. "Garcia came to us for protection, for himself and help for his country. He had evidence that Gutierrez was making secrets deals with the Chinese, and he kept the talks from his own cabinet and advisors. Why and the purpose behind the dialogues?" He shook his head and sat back in the stuffed chair. "We can speculate, but Garcia would not give up anything solid without agreement to help on his terms."

A wise decision, Logan thought.

"Our man was to assume the role, infiltrate all aspects to find the documented sources."

Logan eyed McGill suspiciously. "Did he?"

"Unfortunately, since the coup, and Gutierrez retaking power, his support is even stronger and he's clamped down hard on communications in every aspect. He blames the U.S. for instigating the coup. No. We didn't," he added at their scowls. "We've tried everything just short of a bullhorn but can't reach Ramos. He's wise enough not to risk being found out to confirm or contact."

All Logan heard was Ramos. Time stood still, a prickling racing through his blood. Old news, old anger, he thought.

"Paul Ramos?" Max asked, his expression darkening.

Now comes the tricky part, McGill thought.

Logan's gaze lifted slowly and met the general's. "You're really up shit creek or you would never have come to me."

"Commander Chambliss," he said, the address calling to his sense of duty. "I know there's bad blood between you two, but Ramos is an American."

Logan went perfectly still. "Let him fucking rot."

"We can't. This is *our* security at stake. We did this to help them keep democracy. Garcia orchestrated it to protect himself. We put an American in the role. If we could have found a Venezuelan, we would have, but there wasn't time. Corruption is rampant, and the attack came during the switch. Ramos was still recovering from his surgical wounds and it played right into Garcia being shot and critical."

"The President is still in power. Gutierrez is a showman more than a statesman," Riley said. "He likes the sound of his own voice, but his country's economy and security are in a coma."

"Which he's ignoring to make these deals."

"A snatch and grab on foreign soil at the home of a high ranking government official. He's second in command. That's a hairy deal," Max said. "So the question still is, why ask us?"

"Leaks. Your team is off the grid, and outside the usual channels."

Most of the time, Logan thought.

"The closer it gets to Washington, the more chance of leaks. I don't want to use CIA resources. This man is as under the wire as it gets. If the press gets wind of it, America will be everyone's target and we'll never be trusted again."

Logan spoke. "No. Too political."

"Don't you all have to agree?" McGill's gaze swept the other three men sitting around the living room. Their expressionless faces told him where he stood. "Where's Moore and Wyatt?"

"Unavailable." McGill didn't need to know details. Killian Moore was on loan to DEA in Colombia, using his alter ego of Dominic Cane to get into the cartel again. Sam Wyatt was probably on his ranch with Viva, or planning a wedding. Dragon One didn't need a full roster on every retrieval.

"I've read the reports, you know." McGill rose and faced Logan. He and Ramos had been SEALs at the same time, and while Logan left the Teams, Ramos was enlisted by the CIA.

"Mission debriefs don't tell everything, sir, and I couldn't care less if the man died, slow and agonizing."

Max straightened next to Sebastian. Riley swung his legs off the sofa. Battle lines, McGill thought.

"His failure to obey orders got civilians killed under my command," Logan said.

"You were cleared."

Logan's gaze jerked to McGill's. "I was there."

"Equal blame, isn't that right, Commander?" McGill knew Logan shouldered the responsibility because Ramos didn't. Ramos had a Top Gun attitude with deadly skills and while his career had been shady, it was McGill's duty to tie this off and bring him home. "The man has since paid with his face in Afghanistan last year. When this opportunity came, he'd just begun his plastic surgery to repair the damage."

"So a few implants and he volunteered to help? Or get the face of a powerful man and use it to his advantage?" Logan shook his head. "He cannot be trusted."

"Regardless, we need to get close enough for face-to-face

contact. We've seen what the press sees, just better angles. He doesn't look like he's recovering very well."

"You want a medical assessment, too?" Max blasted. "I see the only choice for *you*," he stressed, washing his hands of it, "is to get the *body* out. Assassinate him. Let them bury him like he's their Vice President."

McGill frowned at Max Renfield's macabre vehemence. "When they dress him for the funeral, something the family does, they will know. His face might look like Garcia, but the rest of him doesn't. We couldn't alter fingerprints or dental records, Garcia didn't have a single cavity."

"Wow a Crest boy, who knew," Max snarled. "Garcia is dead."

"But no body," McGill reminded him. "What if it turns up, no matter how decayed, when Ramos is in his place? It would be a disaster for Venezuela. The country is already polar without the rebels."

Add the drug and arms dealers who were locked at the hip with some members of the government and it made the entire concept dicey, but Logan didn't think that would matter.

"He sounds convincing," Sebastian said. Logan had forgotten about him sitting in the corner reading a book. "The thought of helping that bastard for even one second frosts my ass."

Logan kept his gaze on McGill. "You're withholding something, General—what?"

McGill's expression didn't change a fraction as he looked at Logan. "You know what I know."

Fine, I'll play the game for now, Logan thought. "What's your theory on why there's been no contact?"

"It could be any number of things. Found out and held prisoner, joined the dark side."

Logan stared him down. "Treason sounds right up his alley." With the Vice President's face, Ramos could do anything he wanted. So why wasn't he contacting McGill?

McGill understood his misgivings. But Elizabeth Jacobs had to have pressed Ramos long before this happened and did so without authorization. McGill hadn't been informed of that till his superiors dumped this in his lap. He really hated being CIA, and expected more to come back to bite him when he wasn't looking.

"If he's gone Commie, we have to remove him by force and that's tricky." Sebastian unfolded his long frame from the easy chair, leaning forward into the light. "We'd never know if he's crossed until we got in there."

"You're considering it?" McGill had been prepared to return to Washington without success.

Logan went to the rear of the house, then pushed through the French doors. The Carolina heat smacked him like a wet towel, the sun sizzling on the stone floor as he stepped onto the covered porch.

With a precision that cut to his soul, he hated Paul Ramos. Missions go wrong, that's a given. It wasn't that Ramos had made a supreme mistake, but that he never owned up to his part, letting Logan take the heat. Ramos's failure was nothing more than a show-off taking an unnecessary risk. *The op was secure, they had the package.* Logan stopped his memories cold, slamming a mental block over them. Hashing it over hadn't changed the fact that lives were lost.

He felt the general move up beside him and knew that brutal honesty was in order.

"Ask me to kill him, I'll do it. Don't ask me to risk this much to save his life."

"Logan," McGill said softly. "I'll watch your back, but no government in the world would believe we didn't have anything to do with this beyond supplying a face on a body."

The U.S., and mostly the government, would never survive this defamation, Logan thought, especially from its own people. He looked at the general. "You're certain that's all we did there, sir?"

Joe McGill looked into the eyes of a decorated SEAL veteran, a field surgeon and a man he admired, then he did as ordered.

He lied.

Tuvana-i-Tholo, Fiji

Orion was clear in the midnight sky as Bati warriors cast shadows across the white sand, tall bonfires undulating with the spins of the tribal dance. Tessa was enthralled and until the man at her side spoke, she was trapped in a different time.

"You know you're getting me hot all over in that getup."

Tessa didn't bother to look down at herself. She revealed more flesh than she'd shown her last lover, but wearing the traditional costume, a brightly painted *sulu* skirt, tattered at the hem, endeared her to the natives who weren't all that friendly to outsiders.

"It makes my job easier." She adjusted the material looped around her neck and wrapping her breasts.

"You just like giving me a hard-on that could crack coconuts."

She eyed him and thought, *Oh, yeah, I'm ready to strip and jump his bones with that line.* "Rein in the testosterone, will you?" Were all baby-faced photographers this horny? Or just the classless ones she got stuck with lately? "Don't," she said, putting out a hand when he started to lift his camera to focus. "You want to get us kicked off the island?"

Andrew frowned, lowering the Nikon, then noticed a few men looking his way. "Fine, love, but if I can't take pictures, then how are we going to get a film crew in here?"

"I'm not certain. Their chief is still a little wary. People don't visit this island except to take pictures and stare. Or for the surfing."

"Offer yourself in marriage. Or sacrifice. I promise, I'll get you out before they swing that hatchet." He nodded to the man holding the long pole topped with a metal blade so sharp it gleamed in the dark.

"Oh, Andy," she said in her best throaty whisper. "You say the sweetest things."

He cringed. He hated being called that. But Andrew Chaison Coppethwaite was too snotty British. He was anything but. Cute, in decent shape, he had a dry sense of humor and a nice butt, but off limits. Too young and she never involved herself with a colleague. Not that she had many. As a National Geographic Society location scout, she worked alone. When someone in the headquarters got a keen idea to do a show or a series on some obscure tribe or ruins, Tessa got all the fun. She was the first to arrive and scouted out more than location. She arranged everything from authorization from the local governments to hiring local guides and translators for the actual filming. In between and during, she got to do what she loved: travel, explore, dive, rock climb, even live with a tribe that modern culture just skipped past.

A mocha latte and i-Pod free zone.

"Need I remind you, we're on deadline."

"No, you are. Nothing goes ahead till I give the all clear."

Tessa understood his impatience. Andrew wanted to get back to his creature comforts—a running toilet, a shower and an occasional cigar. She couldn['t care less. Peeing outdoors, showering under a waterfall were just minor inconveniences compared with experiencing cultures that most people never knew existed and were still in the Dark Ages. It was tranquil. Crimes didn't exist here, no extremists trying to blow themselves up. No murderers or twisted sociopaths. Probably because the chief was the ruler and his justice was swift and very deadly. Then again, the islanders were the descendants of cannibals. Misbehave, and heads would roll, she thought, smiling.

Cannibalism wasn't a practice on the remote islands anymore—or so the Fijians told her—but then, most didn't get this close. She didn't take her gaze off the dance and the story told in wild gyrations. Acted out by several warriors, it dramatized the arrival of the Europeans and their subsequent deaths.

Bet they were tasty, too.

She loved her job. There wasn't so much as a telephone line on this island, a little difficult when her job required communication. Even now, she felt the weight of her satellite phone on the back of her skirt pulling it down and probably giving Andrew a good show of her butt, yet it was all she could do to conceal it. She didn't want to offend these people, but she wasn't willing to give up that much of her modern life. Help, if she needed it, was on the other end. Though it was days away. Sorta like paddling with your hands; she'd get there, just not swiftly.

A woman approached her with a broad wooden cup made from a coconut shell. Tessa had been through the ritual before, and she clapped once, clasped her hands, then took the cup. She drank the *yaqona* in a single mouthful before returning the cup to the woman, then clapped three times. "*Maca,*" she said.

The woman smiled approvingly, then offered the same cup to Andrew.

"Do as I did or you'll offend."

He obeyed, yet as the beautiful dark-skinned woman took back the cup, she eyed him from head to toe, not unkindly, before walking away.

"She loves me."

"Or she thinks you'll make a good Steak Tartare." Tessa patted his stomach and grinned at his horrified look.

A warrior gestured to her to join the dance with the women, and Tessa had seen enough to know the moves. She joined in, but not before handing her Sat phone to Andrew. "If my mom calls, ignore it."

A man answering her phone would just bring too many questions and her mom was in her "fix Tessa up with so and so's son" place again. People couldn't understand that she was perfectly content to live out of a backpack, travel and explore. How many times did a person get to shake booty with the descendants of cannibals?

As she slipped into the dance, Andrew hooked the phone on his belt and watched Tessa sway as if she were born to it. She stood out, not because of her hair or body, but because she was the only one not wiggling her bare breasts for the crowd. Damn shame.

She was about the most exciting woman he'd ever met, beyond that she was athletically fearless and drank up her surroundings like a sponge. He'd seen her hang from a cliff a thousand feet above rocky ground and be comfortable enough in her skill to actually *sleep,* a couple of ropes and a few carabiners the only things keeping her from being squashed on the rocks. That took guts, which he freely admitted he didn't have, but his job was catching it on film, enough that the producers could make a judgment call on location and content.

From the talk amongst the Society, she'd done the photography herself till it had taken negotiations to get her out of China last year. After the government ignored her NGS credentials and locked her in a women's prison, NGS insisted she have a partner. She didn't like it, and warned him the first day. *"Keep up, clam up, take the pictures. I'm not helpless, nor a piece of ass. You'll learn the other rules as we go."*

He preferred his women a little less intimidating, ones who thought of him as more than a camera flunky. The older-woman thing aside, he'd like to think a good shagging would change that, but the truth was, she was out of his league. Way out. There was something about her, a hawklike awareness of people and her surroundings that came with emotional baggage. As much as he had midnight fantasies about her, he wouldn't cross the line.

Andrew stepped back from the glow of the fires and lifted his camera, putting her in a frame. She avoided being photographed, insisting people didn't read the magazine or watch NGS shows to see a nobody in the wild. Yet as her arms lifted to the sky, willowy and tanned, he clicked off a few shots, then settled on the soft sand to watch Tessa Carlyle go native.

Aboard Dragon Six

Max dragged black duffel bags up the loading ramp and into the cargo jet. "We're doing this so you can beat the living shit out of him, right?"

Logan didn't glance up. "That's about it, yes."

"Just checking." Max cleared his throat, then added, "You don't think we should have a really stable moral ground to be standing on?"

"Not so much."

"McGill was lying, gagged so tight he was purple."

"He's desperate." Logan glanced back as he secured his medical gear inside the aircraft. "He's got a finger in the dike. Going outside assures no one in Washington would have the chance to leak it. So, of course, there's more to it."

"That's what scares me," Max said. "How did the first team die?"

Sebastian slipped a file in the pocket behind a seat, knuckling it. "It's in here. A two-man team. Videotape starts just as they move toward the VP's summer residence. Government troops were waiting for them. Ambushed before they got a foot on the property." The team straightened from their duties and looked at Sebastian. "They were betrayed."

By one of their own and Logan would bet his money on Ramos. Ramos knew there would be a rescue attempt. It was SOP, standard operating procedure. There was always a backup plan.

"It's in the file, all classified." Sebastian stepped into the cockpit. "McGill wasn't supposed to give us that."

"It's more bullshit," Logan said. "The man's holding out." Politically, the U.S. couldn't touch this, so it had to be worse than just getting Ramos out of the hot seat before a decayed body showed up. The jungle was a big place, ruins had been hidden for centuries, losing one body would be a snap. Ramos was there to do more and it went back to his intelligence and the source. The CIA.

"No outcry from Venezuela, or evidence of bodies, by the way."

"That would be admitting we were there."

The first team was CIA, highly trained with good Intel. Killed or captured, they were set up to fail.

Sebastian ran down his preflight checklist. "If they wanted,

Gutierrez could have used the men for propaganda and paraded them before the media and pushed his socialist cause along."

"Sure, but that would have made his business public." Logan shook his head. "They're covering their asses politically. Just like we are." He jerked on a strap. "No blame on their hands."

"But on the U.S. See how efficiently democracy works," Max said, finishing tying down the chopper, its blades collapsed inside the massive cargo jet. "Ramos knows the score, how it all works. He got promoted to CIA for a reason. Now he has anything he needs, the man's power and his wife. He's having a blast. Why would he want out?"

Max didn't expect a response and didn't get one. On some levels, they were all in agreement. Ramos was a problem that definitely needed to be solved.

"I want to know how's he keeping Mrs. Garcia happy." Riley stretched out on one of a row of chairs, flipping up the arms to set ice packs on various body parts.

"Eloisa del Garcia is never far from her husband's side and has a role in the government." Sebastian flipped switches and checked off his list. "She's an advocate of education, funding for restoration of ancient ruins. Programs for the Indians. Admirable, with lots of first lady potential."

Logan frowned. "She knows. A woman doesn't mistake her husband. Especially if they've had sex."

"They have separate bedrooms." After hooking his clipboard on the wall, Sebastian shook open the floor plan of Garcia's residence, then flicked the lock anchoring a table to the wall. "Separate wings, as a matter of fact."

"That never stopped me," Riley said, smiling with some old memory.

Sebastian spread the map on the narrow table. "The summer residence is five acres, corners a river that flows to the Amazon. The street side is a park and it's all heavily guarded."

"Ramos hasn't been seen in a couple of days, his condition reported as stable," Max said. "He's under wraps for a reason." He leaned over the map, pulling aside digital views and studying them. Square with a large courtyard in the center, it was the hacienda of a king. "This doesn't depict a man of the people, huh? I think Ramos was found out and Mrs. G is covering up for him."

Or *using him.* "If his cover was blown, we wouldn't see him at all, or they'd have taken the attack as an opportunity to just erase a problem. Max is right. Ramos is skilled and smart," Logan said, stepping away from the table and turning back to the gear. He hated to admit that Ramos was probably the best choice. "I know him. He studied Garcia before he went in. A portion of his throat and the underside of his left arm were burned in an operation eleven years ago, but not that much." He nodded to the man's picture taped inside the jet. "That looks good."

"I don't get you, Logan, how can you do this, risk all this? To kill him?"

"That would be the easy part," he said. Saving him wouldn't. He had good reason to walk away. He owed Ramos and America nothing. But as he clipped a carabiner, then tested the strap's strength, he thought he didn't want it to be personal.

Coming from careers of following orders, Dragon One ran itself on the individual side of everything. Opinion mattered, emotion counted. They didn't often take jobs to pay the bills but for a damn good reason. This time, it wasn't all that clear.

Paul Ramos was a dangerous stain lingering over national security, and Logan's life. *Yeah,* he thought. *It was personal.*

In the grass hut, Tessa felt the buzz of the satellite phone in her dreams. Go away, she thought. It had to be NGS headquarters. Interns never got the time difference right. Blindly, she reached for it and brought it close. She stirred enough to hit SEND.

"If this isn't Vin Diesel in tight biker pants, I'm hanging up."

"Tessa."

Her muscles froze, a lock on her joints that kept her on her side on the mat. Her breathing slowly increased. Humid air skipped between the gaps of the hut. The dark sky shadowed her surroundings as she pushed up on her elbow.

"I know you can hear me."

She recognized the voice, but the accent was all wrong. "I can," she said, her mouth drying up with each breath. Maybe she was mistaken? "Who is this?" She pushed back her hair and held it off her face.

"You said, if I ever needed help . . . to call you."

Oh please, no. She swallowed hard, fear gripping her throat. "I can't, you know I can't. Don't ask me."

The voice deepened an octave. "You owe me."

"Are you *threatening* me?"

"If it comes to that," he said. "But I don't have to, do I?"

No. And he knew it. The shock of hearing his voice fading, she'd known this moment would invade her perfect world and blow the hell out of it.

"You're a mean-ass son of a bitch," she snarled with a hatred she didn't recognize. "If I find you, I just might take you out of your own misery."

"Now that's the woman I remember."

Tessa cringed, pushing the feelings away, far away. God, make this a dream.

Across the hut, Andrew rolled over, frowning sleepily. "Tessa? Everything okay?"

She covered the phone. "Yes, bad timing, sorry. Go back to sleep."

She stood, shaking off the blanket before she left the shelter, stepping around snoring villagers and moving toward the shore. But he started talking fast, whispered, and that drove up her suspicions. She stopped to listen, detesting the sound of his voice and what it meant to her life.

Total ruin. Like worms after a storm, her ugly past crawled out from the darkness. Then the bastard set a deadline.

Three

The dark blue sedan sped across the airstrip toward the hangar. It was another ten minutes before it came to a halt. The driver remained inside as Nolan Deets left the vehicle. The rain spilled straight down, soft enough to soak everything as he walked across the concrete to the hangar doors. A few civilian workers milled at picnic tables beneath a steel overhang, the water running off and splashing on the ground so hard they were backed up against the walls, smoking and talking.

They each cast him a suspicious glance as he went to the door. A man in a black jumpsuit, cap and sunglasses blocked his path, and demanded ID.

Deets complied, then inclined his head to the workers. "If they don't have clearance, get them out of here."

The guard nodded, then stepped aside quickly and opened the door. The scrape of metal on metal rang in the yawning hangar and he stepped over the high threshold. Inside it was cold and damp, the smell of burned wood and scorched metal hanging heavily on the air.

Several people looked up, one man walking toward him, then stopped, nodding when he recognized him. The scientist returned to the long stretch of tables piled with evidence, scanners and computers for collection. At the far end, a lab was established, forensic technicians already working and, not to throw caution out the door, they wore hazmat gear.

In the center of the massive hangar, no fewer than a dozen men in black jumpsuits crawled over the yacht like leeches on infected skin. The forensic experts would pull anything that could be found, but Nolan wanted to see the damage for himself. He approached, removed his coat and tossed it on a chair beside a crate designated for collected evidence before he mounted the ladder running up the side of the ship. Once a beautiful luxury vessel, it was now nothing more than scrap, torn and twisted, yet no less imposing in dry dock and braced with massive timbers and steel scaffolding.

Nolan wasn't impressed. He could think of a dozen other ways to spend that kind of money than putting a house on the open sea. Yet when the Cuban Navy flexed its muscles on a civilian vessel carrying Americans, Homeland Security, FBI, CIA and the Coast Guard got involved. The National Security Agency was watching them all. When Americans turned up dead, everyone wanted justice.

Three other vessels like this had been seized in international waters by Interpol. What had led Nolan to this particular ship was not only the Americans who were brutally murdered, but that prior to being delivered to Miami for the bride and groom, the ship had docked to be serviced in China and boarded by officials. The Chinese weren't willing to share their dirty laundry with the U.S.—the murder being after the fact and having no consequence to the Chinese—but Nolan was still working on what had led them there. The other seized boats had made port on China's coast as well.

To him, it felt staged. The other boats were boarded and confiscated, so why risk another? Why try to sink it? The owner of the yacht was just that, the owner. Some software tycoon who rented it out through a broker to anyone who wanted to pay the ridiculous price to ride on the high seas in ultimate comfort. The ship carried people, and the cargo manifest was food and supplies for the honeymoon trip. It looked like a simple pirate attack, but the brutal murder and the bomb said otherwise. Pirates didn't hang around that long.

Interpol learned that pleasure boats were used to transport black market weapons and narcotics, but seizing the ships had given them nothing solid, except legal issues. Whoever was using the ships was off-loading cargo somewhere along the way.

He swung his leg over the twisted rail and dropped lightly to the deck.

Two men looked up, frowning, and Nolan showed his badge and turned away, snapping on latex gloves. One man handed him a pair of booties for his shoes, and he arched a brow.

"It's a mess down there, sir."

Nolan slipped them on. "What have you collected so far?"

"Bomb fragments. It was a big one, designed to sink it, but because the fuel was dumped prior to detonation, it stayed afloat. If your buddy hadn't been looking for it, it would have gone up in flames and sunk."

"They wanted no evidence at all."

"We have enough to know the rig and trigger." He showed him an alarm clock still in near-perfect condition, but because of the fire the wiring from the back had been reduced to a jellylike mass.

Nolan knew Logan Chambliss had been on this ship just before the explosion and why. In fact, he knew everything there was about Cassandra Furman-Layton, her groom and their connection to his college friend. They were all at the wrong place at the wrong time. He needed to learn something that would explain why.

Because nothing had been stolen—except lives.

Venezuela

Two things were hot buttons for her. Tell her what to do, then force her to do it. Tessa had let herself be used once before. She swore she never would again.

Yet, here she was.

Guilt was a nasty thing, she thought, and instead of pushing her anger aside, she kept it close, reveled in the outrage of someone blackmailing her for help. She relied on every smidge of it to propel herself as she bolted across the manicured grounds. Rapidly approaching the building, she used her speed as she jumped. Arms outstretched, Tessa sailed through the air like a black dart and gripped the decorative ledge above the first-floor window. Instantly, she snapped down her muscles, forcing herself to stop and not plow through the glass. She drew her legs up to slow her rocking, then hung straight to catch her breath.

She was dead center of the summer residence in the darkest section. It had windows straight to the top. Hanging like a rag, she glanced left and right for the patrols. They had precise movements, changing the guard every hour. She'd watched their predictability for a couple days with a group of reporters on the lawn across the street. It wasn't a government building, so no tours, no open house. The uninvited couldn't get past the door. And lately, no one came out.

The least the bastard could do was be *seen* so she could learn exactly where he was. He never called back and had blocked the number. He'd given her quick, short details to get to him, but he was a lying bastard, and could be setting her up. What Ramos was doing in the Vice President's summer residence opened a thousand questions and she didn't want to know the answers. Whatever he wanted, she had to do it. Being pulled back into her past to help a man who'd threatened to ruin her had so many double edges to the sword, she wanted it over with. But there were only two ways inside: hers and on the arm of someone powerful, but that brought attention to her. She wasn't going to come out of this stinking, so the cat burglar route was her only choice. Without rope and harness, it was a real pain.

With a chin-up, she drew herself up enough for leverage, then swung her leg to catch the ledge to stand. The hooded cat suit made movement easy. She gripped the ironwork, putting her toes in the carvings around the windows to scale higher. Below her, guards paced the circumference in a measured march. She bit back the urge to hum and kept moving past the second floor. If he was on the inside, he was in trouble and completely abandoned, or he wouldn't have contacted her. She wasn't useful anymore. There was so much going on here, she couldn't pin down which really made her more furious—that he threatened to expose her or that he was drawing her into something bigger. He was inside the Vice President's private residence, for pity sake. Just knowing what the U.S. was doing with this minor player was trouble.

I'm so getting fired for this.

The NGS didn't authorize her entrance into Venezuela and while backup was always good, she refused to bring anyone into a chapter of her life she wanted closed, and quickly. She'd thought it *was* closed. She neared the top, glancing down for the guards, then up to the open window she expected to be open. It was the only reason she went forward. Curiosity had nothing to do with it. Ending this pact with the Devil did.

She maneuvered to grasp the windowsill, then slipped neatly inside. She kept her back to the cool wall, with the curtains around her, then gently pushed them aside. There was a faint light from a few yards away on the right, and she edged the room, found the exits, then advanced. Encased in black, she blended and moved in short darts from darkness to the pithy black of the massive room. In a dance to avoid a shadow, she moved closer, then stopped, tucked near the drapes.

The light spilled from a small lamp on the desk and silhouetted the man sitting before it, his back to her.

"Very good, Tessa."

She cringed at the sound of his voice, the Latin accent odd

when she remembered a southwestern drawl. He turned in the chair, and she frowned, refusing to come out of the shadows. The light was near him. He'd have trouble seeing her, but she could see him.

Who is this man? Because it sure as hell wasn't Paul Ramos. The man she knew was cover-model material, around forty by now. This guy was closer to sixty, his cheeks scarred from bad skin.

"A shock, I know." He swept his fingers under a chin that was more square than she remembered. "Too many near-misses to be useful anymore, but all courtesy of our government. Certainly not a reward," he said, fingering the remaining scars. "A promotion."

To the CIA, she thought, noticing his accent fade with each word. "What is the company doing here?" The sound of her voice startled him, and he smiled. That's when she recognized the man beneath another's face. In the shape of his mouth, the chillingly dark eyes and the heavy brows over them.

"A long story you don't need to know."

No, she didn't. But he had to know she didn't have Intel resources anymore. It was pointless. "You're a perfect idiot, you know that?" The consequences of him being here, masquerading, were too big a political disaster for her to comprehend, and she didn't care. She'd trained herself not to or she could never have left so cleanly. "This won't work."

"It must." He looked her over with a feral threat. "We haven't much time." He held out a folded leather pouch. "Take this."

"Hell no. Come on, let's go." She tossed her thumbs toward the window. "Now."

"I'm not leaving."

"You bastard. You said you wanted out."

"I wanted *this* out." He held out the case again.

Her gaze flickered around the room and she smelled a trap. "Bring it to me."

Paul sighed and pushed out of the chair, grabbing a cane

before moving toward her, slow and unsteady. She understood why he wouldn't leave. He couldn't.

He stopped a couple feet from her, a pleasant smile on his lips. "I knew you'd get in here. You're still good."

"And you're a dirt bag. Wow, nothing's changed." She snatched the leather pouch and unrolled it. "What the heck is this?"

"Follow it. Figure it out and follow it. Whatever is at the end of it is vital."

She looked up, frowning. "You've gone nuts in here, is that it? Follow a map? Do I look like a treasure hunter? I can't do this. I have a life, and I'm not playing this game." She held it out and when he wouldn't take it, Tessa shoved it in his hands. They were cold and clammy and that forced her to look more closely. Dark circles under his eyes left him hollow, a hint of skeleton, his skin pale. His lips had a gray tinge to them.

"Why haven't they taken you out of here? *What* are you doing here?"

"If I could leave now, I would. Denmark stinks and, no, they don't know who I am."

Tessa shook her head as if it would make the pieces fall into place. "If you're playing Garcia, where's the real one?"

"Dead." He quickly explained the last assassination attempt during the coup, and the lack of a body. "This President spouts socialism, but his table is filled with some bad-ass Commu—"

"Like you give a damn."

"When it means staying alive, yes. Garcia and his supporters stand in the way, and I'm Garcia, the target." He pointed to his face and wobbled on the cane.

She frowned. "Have you seen a doctor?"

"I think the doctors did this to me."

"You're trapped, a hostage? Who'd do that to the Vice President?"

"Don't you read the papers? Take a number. Democracy is circling the rim here. Take that off," he snapped.

Tessa pulled off the black hood and met his gaze.

Paul Ramos stared into her icy-blue eyes and didn't have to see the rest of her. Her image was planted in his mind years ago; a body that was all curves, and an exotic look in sable hair and tanned skin. But it was her pale blue eyes that were arresting, intense light in sultry features.

He already regretted bringing her into this, but he was cornered on all sides and couldn't move freely. His only choice was calling the number that he'd recited like a bed-time chant, a reminder of his one decent act. Yet seeing her was like looking back on his shame.

"What's at the end of this?" She gripped the leather pouch.

"It was my wife's—his wife's," he said, leaning hard on the cane. "She's getting chummy with a lot of powerful peo-ple, too. Granted, her husband is like this"—he gestured to himself—"and she's filling in, but she's up to something."

"Up to something? Skulking in the shadows? Passing notes, what?" He was hallucinating. Eloisa Garcia was in her late fifties, well preserved and genuinely loved by the people. She reminded Tessa of Betty Crocker or Nancy Reagan with a fetish for handbags. But seeing him struggle to move, Tessa was realistic. She couldn't get him out. She stuffed the map in her small backpack, thinking that the wife of the VP creeping around her own house was just ridiculous. "What will you do?"

His features tightened as if he didn't expect her to care enough to ask. "Find out what's really going on and stop it."

The courageous hat didn't fit him well enough for that to have a shred of truth. "Why did you drag me into this again? We had a deal and you've broken it."

He looked repentant for about two seconds. "I'm cashing in the only chip I have left. Do this and we're done, forever, I swear."

"I don't trust you, so that means nothing."

Then behind him, she saw movement. She stepped back quickly as three men materialized from the far shadows in a circle behind Ramos. She watched through the sheer curtains. A hand over his mouth, a knife at his throat, and in seconds, he was gagged and secured.

The man in the center turned in her direction, aiming his gun. "Step out from the window, hands up."

Tessa held her hood, panic flooding through her. A bizarre sense of déjà vu engulfed her.

"Now."

She took a step forward, her eyes already burning with regret. Like the overlay in her memory, the new image pressed forward. He lifted thermal goggles to his forehead, his face and body hidden in Black Ops gear. Just like before. His gaze ripped over her and she saw it all in his eyes. Shock, dismay, then confusion.

His weapon lowered. "Tessa?"

In that instant, Ramos hit his heel on a floor alarm, setting it off. Tessa whipped her hair into the hood and slipped out of sight.

Logan headed after her, but Max grabbed his arm. "We've got to split."

Quickly, Logan cut Ramos's bond, yet stared into Garcia's face. It was uncanny.

"The whole family's here, how nice."

Ramos's shock was palatable and Logan recognized the oily smile. "We came for you, asshole. You blew it." Logan's anger exploded in his fist, one hit dead center of his nose. Ramos didn't move again and he started to heft him over his shoulder.

"No time, no time," Sebastian said into his headset, watching the doors. "We're blown."

"Finn? Finn? You get that?" Logan whispered Riley's call sign. "Abort. Cut all comms, all comms, bug out, now."

Reluctantly Logan left Ramos, rushed to the side of the room and checked the halls already filling with people. So the team moved to the only exit left. Logan opened the window and climbed out, scaling down the ironwork, going still when the searchlights splattered them in white relief. Waltzing from cover to cover, he tucked into the evergreen growing up the wall, waited for a pass of light, then slithered down the wall. He hit the ground running, Max and Sebastian flanking him, and they had a clear shot to the tree line. If they could get to the street . . .

Forty yards out, armed men swept in from all sides.

Logan stopped short, breathing hard, his hands up. "Well, crap."

Soldiers pushed assault rifles in their faces. The USA would not respond to their capture. They were on their own.

Two blocks and one street over, Riley Donovan tore off the headset, and put the SUV in gear, driving away from the residence. As he did, he shut down all communications and let the computer rest for a few blocks, then rebooted. The small laptop pinned to the dash glowed in the dark, and he switched frequencies, then pulled into a parking lot near a skyscraper and shut off the engine. He tipped the screen to lessen the glow, yet never took his eyes off the frequency line, open and waiting.

He wondered if he could hack into the security cameras, yet as he tried, two questions repeated. Who was Tessa? And what the hell was she doing in the private residence with Ramos?

McGill stood so fast his chair rolled back. The two other people in the room had seen that disaster happen. No one spoke, but ruination hung in the air. The night vision film rolled again and he watched, knowing it wouldn't change. Anger coiled in him. Ramos, he thought. McGill couldn't say for sure that Ramos hadn't recognized Chambliss before he set off that alarm, but it gave the woman enough time to escape, and trap the team.

"I want a digital of that woman."

"Cleaning it up now, sir."

*   *   *

Tessa righted a couple clay pots on the rooftop garden, then turned back to the edge. Going up instead of down put her in isolation and darkness. Well, partial darkness. Small eyeball lights plastered her shadow over the rim of crenulations that earned the nickname, the Citadel. She kept herself between the lights and through mini binoculars, watched as the three men were stripped of weapons. She held her breath when the troops yanked off the hoods.

Logan. It *was* him.

Good God, this was way up there on the weirdo meter.

Ramos with a new face, and then Logan here? Not good, not good at all. What was Ramos pulling her into? She suspected he'd set her up for that, but what the hell was with that leather thing? She could feel it against her stomach, tucked flat and sweaty. She winced as a soldier drove the butt of his rifle into the back of Logan's skull so hard he dropped to his knees. Oh, jeez, that had to hurt, she thought, and it was her fault. She didn't wonder why he was there. He was a SEAL and Ramos with a different, older face said a lot. Whatever it was, it was mega-classified. But when the soldiers forced the men back into the residence, she tried to speculate where they'd take them and how she could get in. The troops were crowding the area, congratulating themselves before leaving two guards standing post. The others left to check on their fake VP.

She lowered to the roof, her gaze flicking over the raised garden and seating area. An escape across a lighted lawn, what were they thinking? And just how did Logan get in? A HALO jump?

She hadn't heard a helicopter, and although the roof was the easiest route in, if that exposed risk was their retreat plan, it stunk. And so did hers, she thought, realizing she was trapped. As far as she could see, the only way off the roof was down through the residence already swarming with police.

This has been such a bad week, she thought, tipping her

head back. Dancing with natives already felt like months ago.

Shoulda never answered the phone.

On his knees, the back of Logan's head throbbed, his body stiffening against the next blow. It didn't come and he glanced to the side. Between the soldiers surrounding them, he saw a man striding across the lawn, shouting orders. A soldier yanked him to his feet, blood flowing warm on his neck as he forced Logan around.

At his feet, Max lay in a heap, moaning, and Sebastian didn't look up to speed either. Christ, what a fuckup. He was going to kill Ramos for blowing this.

He glanced to the side and saw a man pushing his way between the soldiers. A few moments later, someone jerked his head back. He stared into a pair of dark eyes and knew this wouldn't be pleasant. Within moments, the team was dragged into the residence, down two flights of stone stairs to what felt like a wine cellar. It was cooler, the corridors narrow, the baked walls crumbling as the soldier forced them below. Then three men circled them with weapons drawn as they cut their bonds.

One pulled open a door, then shoved Logan into a small room.

Logan turned sharply, his path blocked by a soldier who had to be a foot taller and wider. A good thing, since Max was slung over his shoulder. He levered him forward and Logan rushed to catch Max, but the giant dumped him on the stone floor. He flinched when Max's head bounced. Max groaned lowly, then went still. Logan knelt to check his wounds as Sebastian stumbled inside.

He caught the wall, then lowered to the floor. "What's with all the shoving?"

Logan tried to revive Max, rolling him over.

"Just kill me now," Max groaned.

"Keep your mouth shut next time. Though the German accent was clever."

"I've never been captured," Max said. "What do we do? Is there a course in this?"

"For Crissake," Logan said, backing off.

"A good pistol whipping is always fun," Max said as he tried to sit up and then just sank back on his elbow. He tested the cut on the back of his head, then pulled out a handkerchief and held it there. Sebastian rested his forearms on his knees. Logan lowered to the floor and cradled his skull, ignoring the blood dripping down his temple.

"Logan . . . up there—?" Max said quietly. "It was her, wasn't it?"

"I'm not sure." But he was. Some people you don't forget and Tessa was one of them. A half dozen feelings ricocheted inside him, but he couldn't focus. Because the last time he saw her, she was running with Ramos, seconds before an explosion that *killed* her.

Tessa pushed off the ground and moved away from the roof lights toward the seating area. She stepped over poles and canvas meant for shading and descended the stairwell. The landing was elaborate, a wide, curved staircase, slanted enough that it was effortless. Her escape plan wasn't contingent on Ramos's health. She'd planned to walk out of there with him. She stood at the door, listening to the voices on the other side. It wouldn't be long before they'd search up here.

She quickly stripped out of the skin suit. The tight spandex microfiber shrank down to nothing and she stuffed it in her pack, then unhooked the straps and changed it to look more like a purse. Doable. She stood and smoothed the skirt and scoop neck top that clung enough to be a distraction if she met up with anyone male. Expose the boobs and they don't see the face. She adjusted everything into its best display, thanking her grandma's heritage that she had enough to work with, then slipped on sandals.

The doorknob rattled and she thought, *I'm done*. Then she suddenly turned back to the furniture and sat on the patio sofa. Think, *think*.

When the men hurried up the staircase like a team of horses, she was posed and squinting in the dark. "Estavan? Is that you?" she asked in breathy Spanish. "I heard awful noises."

The guards lowered their weapons, thumbing on flashlights and gliding the beam over her. As decadently as she could muster, she slid off the couch and came toward them.

"What's wrong?" She stared between the men with her best dazed and confused look. "Estavan told me to wait here," she kept on in Spanish, referring to the Vice President.

The men smiled to themselves, one ordering another to escort her out, then arranged his men so she wouldn't be seen. Apparently, Estavan had been a naughty boy before. Oh, lucky me. Tessa paused by the oldest, looking him over like he was a Godiva chocolate before she followed the other men out. They took her down the servants' staircase, the halls void of anyone. A soldier gestured to the door down a corridor lined with storage rooms, and she smashed any urge to throw them a wink, and slipped outside.

Releasing a long breath, she hitched her bag on her shoulder and started putting as much distance behind herself as she could without running like hell. She was near the road when she glanced back. Guards lined the walkways near the entrance, yet there weren't many near the rear. She started to turn back to get inside and find the guys, but just as she took a few steps, she heard a sound like the slow beating of wings. The noise increased and helicopter lights speared through the trees. *Okay, not an option,* she thought, and turned away. She walked briskly toward the road.

She had to get out while she could. If they caught her with the leather map, life was over. She'd worked too hard to get hers back and keep it. She'd be damned if a bunch of stupid men would threaten it. But that wasn't getting Logan or Ramos out.

And now more people knew she was alive.

Paul Ramos felt hands on his shoulders, and he breathed through his mouth, his sinuses swollen shut. *Fucking Cham-*

bliss. Someone pressed an ice pack to his face. He grabbed it, glaring through stinging eyes. The room filled with soldiers, and he waved them off. "I'm fine," he said. "Look elsewhere."

Tessa was out, he was sure of it, and if not, he'd see her in a moment in handcuffs. But Chambliss? He hadn't been a SEAL for over ten years and the fact that Chambliss showed up told him someone powerful had him over a barrel. He liked the sound of that. But his next thought was, *Was he here to rescue me or kill me?*

CIA was desperate. He hadn't made contact but not for lack of trying. He didn't expect any help. Jacobs had made certain of that.

Since the failed coup, every phone and room in the residence was monitored. He'd found the surveillance equipment easily enough but hadn't learned who was monitoring it. The house security system cameras were unobstructed and obvious. These weren't. Chinese, and nearly invisible. With the help of a maid, he'd stolen Eloisa Garcia's satellite phone to contact Tessa. Neither U.S. central command nor CIA would accept the call because the number was blocked. Or they just couldn't believe it. Either way, he knew he was suspected of treason by now. His track record hadn't been stellar and they'd go with what they knew. To the CIA, he was over the fence, gone.

It would matter if Eloisa weren't misbehaving. *El Presidente* was a widower his first six months in office, and Eloisa del Garcia was the acting first lady. It gave her far too much power and two weeks with her was plenty. He pushed out of the chair and walked to the doorway, the entrance wide and leading to another room. The corridor between was broad enough to hold a banquet and in the vast room, the echoing beat of the helicopter blades alerted him. Garcia's wife was returning.

A guard came around the corner and stopped dead, lowering his weapon. Ramos took a few steps, his body not cooperating, and he saw the pity he'd grown to hate. He reached his hand out, and the man came to him, shouldering his weight.

I'm going to kill the fucking bitch.

As soon as he figured out how she was murdering him.

Diego Salazar devised a quick plan in the air, at his President's request.

Secure the residence, the Vice President, and any suspects. He didn't have to be told. It was his job to know. He'd ordered the pair of choppers to land simultaneously, and standing inside one, he waited till the other door opened, then quickly rushed to the other passengers and in the dark moved with them so that no one would recognize him, either. He hurried into the residence and flipped a quick, assuring nod to the woman before he took the servants' staircase to the second floor. As he climbed, he listened to reports over the transmitter.

Three men, no insignia, none had spoken. The alarm had come from the private quarters. "Is it secure?" he asked into the small microphone unseen in his ear. Confirmation and location came from the commander of the Presidential guards.

Satisfied with the safety of the Vice President, he entered the second floor, then turned to the right, running his hand along the chair rail trim till he felt the seam in the wall. He pressed and the wall sprang open. He slipped inside and closed the door.

The room was empty except for a bank of flat screens, each picture broken into quarters and showing the grounds and rooms. He removed his weapons before he sat in the chair and called up the security cameras. He replayed them, combing through the last hours. He had nothing on the men, the cameras blackened over before they were seen, yet before that, one lens caught movement near the windows.

He leaned closer, his finger running over the vague silhouette of a woman.

It seemed the Vice President had more than male visitors. Tapping the keys, he brought up the other cameras. He focused on the men. His best interrogators were working on the suspects. They'd only just started. He wouldn't view them in person. The less anyone saw of him, the better.

He opened the transmitters. "Stop, you'll kill them."

Instantly, the men obeyed, dragging them back to the cells, the same brigade used two thousand years ago by his Spanish ancestors.

Ramos hadn't made it out of the room when Eloisa came rushing toward him. As much as she would dare hurry, he thought. She snapped orders to the armed guard to bring a wheelchair and when he met up with her, he gave her his best forgive-me smile. The wheelchair appeared and he lowered into it. She dismissed the servants to wheel him herself. She wanted to keep an eye on him and while she should be asking what happened, she didn't.

When they were in one of the many living rooms, she closed the doors, then came to him. He stood. She froze in her steps, frowning. She hadn't expected him to be more than a jellyfish in the chair, and it made him think she was poisoning his food.

"You are feeling better?" she said, less pleased than curious.

"Aren't you going to ask what happened?"

"I have learned enough from the staff. All that matters is that you're unharmed."

"Where were you, *wife?*"

"Speaking with our President. I am acting as his first lady."

She was more than filling a role, he thought. She spent considerable time away, and while Garcia had influence, Ramos couldn't make it beyond the grounds before he'd pass out.

He advanced, smothering his amusement when she straightened her shoulders defensively. She was still a beautiful woman, he thought. When she was younger she was robust and wild, her roots were on the streets. She'd aged gracefully to deeply seductive. She understood her strength as a woman and he let himself appreciate her Rubenesque figure.

He stopped inches from her. "You reek of him."

She went still, her smooth brow wrinkling.

"Is he a good fuck?" he whispered in her ear like a lover's call.

She lifted her hand to slap him, but he caught it, smiling gently.

"Watch yourself, Estavan."

"What is it like keeping the widower and your husband happy?" He let her go, then turned toward the long sofa. "Perhaps Manny and I should discuss it." He sat, his hands on his cane. "We can't agree on policy, but in this, perhaps we could."

She came at him like a vulture swooping in. He was faster, catching her by the arms and holding her back. "No?" he asked.

"I am not unfaithful." She wrestled against him but he was stronger, for the moment. He didn't give a damn if she was screwing the entire army, but that she was spending more and more time with the President in Caracas, while he was trapped here, pathetically weak, said she had more control than the U.S. government had first thought.

He had to make it in her best interest to keep him alive. Blackmail had always done the trick before.

"Then you're willing to prove that?"

Her brow lifted. He could almost see the thoughts flying through her head. The first of which was, *"What will it get me?"* He didn't care. He took her mouth like a starving man.

She fought for control. It was game to her, a play for power, and she was very good at getting it. Her mouth teased him, and he drew her between his thighs. She came willingly, her smile soft in her beautifully elegant face, as his hand swept up the back of her thighs. He'd take back the power, like this, having her. Until his face was destroyed two years ago, he knew women and how to manipulate this one. He sought it for a means of escape, and while she used him, he returned it tenfold, torturing her with the only weapon he had left.

Before she killed him, he thought, as she pulled up her skirt and settled on his lap. He played the role of Latin lover. It wasn't an easy task, his hands moving slower than his brain. He was grateful for instincts and training, but that his entire life came down to screwing a woman to stay alive, was an incredible irony. She started working open his trousers, her dark eyes glittering with hungry anticipation. But his fingers were already under her clothes, between her thighs, stroking her.

If his behavior wasn't like her husband's, he'd tell her something syrupy like his brush with death made him appreciate what he had. She wouldn't care, distracted by her own desire, yet it would satisfy her ego. As Garcia, he was useful, and when he wasn't, he'd get a hero's funeral meant for another man—and destroy America in the process.

That alone was enough to push him to survive.

Logan had flashes of another time halfway around the world as they forced his head under water. Only then, it was into sand. How long had they been at this? It felt like an endless cycle from this room and back to the cell.

His hands bound behind him, he had no leverage, his skull in the bottom of the trough. Pinpricks of light burst behind his eyes, his lungs filled tight and pushing against fresh bruises. He'd reached the point that his body had stopped fighting for clean air, his blood pounding between his ears. He didn't struggle, didn't strain to pull upright. It wasted precious air to the brain.

The man yanked him up, Logan's hair blocking his vision already swimming with stars. I hate this part, he thought, and the soldier with the piercing eyes tipped his head back. In the corner of the room on top of an old refrigerator unit was a camera. Who's watching, he wondered, and where were his buddies? The last time he'd seen Max or Sebastian, they were face-down in a cell, bleeding.

They dunked him again and Logan wanted to go lax, pretend he was dead, but he was too deep inside for an escape and his buddies weren't with him. Three more times, the soldier shoved his head under water. Logan felt like he was back on a SERE training op, the instructors torturing them like this to see if they could break them.

Then, as if by mysterious command, it stopped. The soldier pulled him to his feet, and Logan stumbled against his captor, his weight pushing the man against the wall. Logan closed his hand over the man's knife and when he pushed Logan back, the blade came with him. Attacking was out of the question, but defense was another matter.

With a soldier behind him, Logan left the interrogation room and walked the corridor, his vision blurred from the strain of holding his breath. *I really should have cut down on those cigars,* he thought, still struggling to breathe easily. As they approached an open door, he glanced and intentionally stumbled to the ground, then pushed the knife into his boot. The soldier grabbed his hair, yanking his head back as he rattled off a few insults to Logan's mother. But he'd seen enough. More cameras, and in the room the men were tearing at their gear, and not just the load bearing vests, but using a small knife to rip the seams like a dressmaker. They'd come with minimal equipment, yet about ten grand in liquid body armor was now torn and bleeding the plastic mix on the floor. Good thing the GPS locator was in his boot heel. Expensive toys, and not one of them was saving their ass now.

Outside the cell, the soldier cut his bonds and with the cursory shove and kick, Logan staggered in and slid to the ground. He leaned against the stone wall, water dripping off his clothes. His thirst was so great, he let it drip into his mouth, then sucked the fabric of his shirt.

"All around it hasn't been a productive day, huh?" His head lolled to the side, and he could feel his heart beat in his teeth.

Wrapping his hands around Tessa's throat would be like morphine right now. She was easy to blame. But this was his fault. If they'd pulled Ramos out of there instantly, it would have been a clean break and they'd have been gone before the guards rotated for shift change. Out through the kitchen, then the laundry; Riley was to make the pickup in the laundry van.

Till Tessa. He didn't know whether to be happy she was alive or furious that it was all a lie at his expense. He'd mourned her, blamed himself for not keeping her safe, and now to find her still in the spy game and helping Ramos?

He almost couldn't comprehend it. Not from her.

He worked kinks out of his shoulders, then crawled to Sebastian, rolling him over and cursing the mess of his face. Logan was examining a cut over his eyebrow when he noticed something on the floor. Reaching into the corner piled with dirt, he found a small piece of fabric, a button still attached. He recognized the nonreflective button, then checked his own black clothes for a tear. There wasn't one and he held it out to Sebastian.

He checked his clothing, then shook his head. "I guess we're not the first guests."

Logan glanced around the cell, then gestured to the splatter on the wall. The blood stain was nearly black, old. The first team? Or some poor local?

Max rolled over. "What was I thinking?" he whispered.

"That you should shut the hell up?" Logan pocketed the button, then shifted to him, tipping his head toward the light. They went for the hot spots; nose, eyes and jaw, probably his kidneys, too.

"We aren't pretty anymore, so I don't think they plan to parade us for the press."

It would be a benefit to keep them well fed and clean, Logan thought, and took off his shirt and twisted it, holding the rope of wet cloth over Max. Water dripped, rinsing blood from his eyes, and he opened his mouth to catch some. They'd given them nothing except a good beating since they were captured. He glanced at his watch. Eighteen hours ago.

"God, McGill is going to be so pissed."

"Oh, he already is," Logan said. "We were videotaping."

"Great, a ringside seat to failure."

Logan pried at his wounds. "You need a couple stitches."

"How's Sebastian?"

"Pretty bad. I think they broke his fingers."

"Just my thumb," Sebastian said through gritted teeth as he forced himself upright.

Logan twisted the shirt again and gave what little water was left to Sebastian, then used the wet cloth to clean cuts. "They're looking for something. The troops stripped our gear down to the parts."

"There goes the budget," Max said.

"They're getting orders from someone," Sebastian said. "They have ear mics."

"I was so hoping for Third World electronics." Max finally sat up.

"Not a chance. This place is wired up like the White House."

Only Logan's gaze moved, indicating the camera secured to the corners. Their identities were compromised and although it would be very difficult for them to get a face or fingerprint match, parading them before the press was the least of their problems.

If they learned they were Americans, the U.S. was screwed.

Hours later, when the cell door scraped open and the guard held a jangle of leg irons, Logan knew—they were, too.

Four

A knock startled him and Eloisa quickly answered it, throwing the door wide. Sexually satisfied without removing a stitch, she was almost eager to be gone. It amused Ramos and warned him that she used him as well . . . enough to not notice he wasn't Garcia.

"I have a few questions," a deep voice said from beyond the door, and Ramos frowned.

Eloisa nodded and waved the man in, then looked back. "I'll leave you two," she said. Ramos caught the Cheshire cat smile she threw him before she disappeared.

The man stepped into the room and Ramos recognized him. Not from a past meeting but from a photo in Garcia's files. Diego Salazar. Ramos knew he was looking at his own counterpart. Highly trained and well funded, Salazar was deadly. Not in his skill but in his cunning use of power. If Garcia was to be believed, this man worked several sides of the box at once. He was in the hip pocket of the President, which meant his loyalty stretched to Eloisa. It was rumored he was once an advisor to Fidel, and was an intelligence officer.

Salazar would be his biggest opponent because he'd once served with Garcia. Ramos knew Garcia's enemies, and Salazar was one of them.

"Questions?" Ramos asked with authority. "Shouldn't you

be learning how they got past your men, Commander?" He didn't want this guy anywhere near Logan and his teammates.

"I will see to that personally, señor. What were you doing in here alone?"

"Reading."

"And you had no suspicion that these men would attack?"

"No, or I would be armed. Protection is your job, Salazar."

The man's features sharpened. The only sign the reprimand had hit the mark.

"If it were anyone else, I'd be dead."

Salazar opened his mouth and Ramos put up his hand. "Enough. Let me clarify it for you." He stood and, forcing an iron grip on his balance, he walked to behind his desk. He'd be damned if he'd let this man see him fall. "I was reading and they appeared from there." He pointed across the room to a set of doors he knew led to the roof. He assumed they came in that direction. It was the least patrolled. "No, I did not speak to them, and the moment I saw them, I hit the alarm."

"Wise, wise," Salazar said, rocking back on his heels. "They gave you that?" He indicated his swollen nose.

"Obviously."

Salazar wasn't ruffled and moved to the window, brushing back the curtains, then peering out to the grounds below. He studied it at length, and Ramos frowned. Salazar couldn't have seen her.

"Find out how they got in here, Commander. *Now.*"

Salazar glanced from under a lock of black hair, his smile almost fiendish as he straightened to attention. He did it slowly enough to be insubordinate and Ramos met his gaze, warning in every fiber. He wouldn't mince words with this man. He meant nothing to him and for a breath of time, Ramos thought, *Is that what I've become?*

"You have your orders."

"Yes, sir. I'll leave you to your . . . recuperation."

Ramos sat at the desk, shuffling papers, effectively dismissing him. He didn't look up as the man exited the room.

All his hope lay in Tessa getting cleanly away with the map. If Salazar had seen her, he'd hunt her, and the results wouldn't be pretty.

Eloisa threw off her suit jacket, tossing it to a servant as she hurried toward her rooms, cornering the halls. At her bedroom, she threw open the doors, striding briskly to the nightstand. She lifted the inlaid wooden box, then sitting on the bed, she drew it to her lap.

Gold and pearl dragons sprawled across the box and for an instant, she admired the puzzle within a picture, then glanced around at her own collection before coming back to her most prized. She pressed the eyes of the dragon, then swept her finger against the grain of the scales carved from mother-of-pearl. The head popped up, the claws springing from the sides of the box. She flicked them upward, then turned the box counterclockwise twice. She pulled the head and the box opened.

She stared down at the empty silk lining, her heartbeat increasing as a wash of heat swept her skin. She looked up, searching the room for anything disturbed. Everything was as she'd left it. Her maid wouldn't have attempted this, too stupid to understand the mechanisms. The only person who'd been in this room was her husband and he hated her puzzles. Enough that he'd banned them from the rest of the house. Anger boiled in her. It had been safe, under her control. Was this box a replica? she wondered briefly. She had the only one in existence that could have been copied.

She reversed her moves to close the box, then set it carefully back. Her hands shook as she realized what this meant. For her, for Venezuela.

There was a total news blackout on the assault, everything wiped away. For an attack on the private residence, the buzz was pretty low-key. Good that the world didn't need to know about it, and bad if no one pried, because then Logan and the others would just cease to exist. Tessa knew this was foolish, but she couldn't let them go to some prison. For hours, she'd sat in her car and watched the residence. A few of the reporters had remained, and she'd camped out with them on the lawn across the street, using her NGS credentials to chum up.

When figures finally appeared, being led to a black van, she'd had to get two sleeping men off her car to follow. The van was moving slowly and she pushed on the gas to catch up. The little VW screamed up the road, and she drove two streets over and parallel, thinking if she could get ahead of them, she'd have a great plan by the time she got there.

Man, she really missed the cannibals.

"Who are you?" Joe McGill held a cleaned-up photo of the woman that had been fed into the computers for a match. It wouldn't take long. She had a bewitching face and wouldn't be hard to spot. But the only people he could send after her, for the moment, didn't exist.

He glanced at the link to Dragon One. Dead air. They had intelligence only from the outside, from above. Satellite and thermal imaging. A cluster of thermal images put the team in the basement level of the estate next to the boiler room. That told McGill the area wasn't normally used as a prison. No one would put felons next to the one spot where they could blow the building back to the Incas.

He tossed the photo aside and watched the satellite reposition itself as another picked up the feed. There was a minute span where alignment gave them garbage between two screens, yet he watched it just the same. He asked for refreshed thermal, then was forced to wait till it narrowed the focus.

"Sir," Lorimer said, twisting in his chair. "They're no longer there."

McGill's features tightened. "Then where?" He looked at the screen as the satellite imagery peeled back layers, narrowing to the ground.

"Heading toward the jungle."

For no other reason than execution.

Tessa stopped the car on the side of the road, and let traffic pass by her. It shouldn't be this crowded, she thought, and left the car, moving to the front of the VW. She slipped her pack-turned-bag on her shoulder, then popped the hood, glancing up the road before she pulled out the tire and propped it against the car. She left the hood up and peered around it as the van came into view, a black earthworm on the long, sandy road. This was one of her dumber moves, but she had to help. It wasn't her fault they were caught and she escaped, but when the van started to head toward the Amazon, it scared her. There were undiscovered ruins all over this country. They could be executed in the jungle and never found.

Bending, she rolled the tire on the shoulder, away from the road. She was banking a lot on Logan because she could get the truck to stop, but overtaking soldiers with guns? Not up her alley. She didn't want to fight anyone. Logan was the strategy-first kind of guy. Tessa just did it. Right now, she felt stupid being out on the road this time of night and, despite the late hour, the air didn't move, the heat cloying. A cloud of gnats hovered under the single streetlight a good hundred yards away.

She tugged at the hem of her shorts, and damn if the little—preshrunk, my ass—things wouldn't get longer. She held the jack, prayed this worked and waited for the van.

She didn't get a chance to scream, the jack flying from her grasp when a gloved palm closed over her mouth.

The small jolts over the road made the ride painful. Woken after midnight and forced into the van, Logan had found small pleasure in just being still. There was some payback coming, he thought, and studied his surroundings. Three rows of seats in the van were separated by a narrow corridor between the chairs. Iron leg shackles were anchored to the floor, the chains jingling with the ride. The windows were painted black, and beyond the prisoner seats was a metal screen separating them from the driver and his backup.

Logan looked over at Max, who had an odd expression on his face, almost peaceful. A total lie, since he was concentrating. Logan didn't know if he was counting tire revolutions or if it had something to do with that quick glance at the sky before they climbed in, but there were times when Logan thought Max had memorized the Earth. He just waited.

"We're going away from the city."

"That can't be good."

Max stared up at the ceiling as if stargazing. "Orinoco," he said under his breath, then nudged the air with his chin. "Toward the river."

A soldier whipped around, and from the passenger seat aimed a gun and warned them to shut up. Logan nodded and shifted, using one toe to push the knife deeper into his boot. He tried not to rattle the shackles, bristling in the cuffs that were chained to his waist. The knife was useless if he couldn't wield it.

A fracture of light glinted off something and he glanced. Max held a pen and he quickly broke it apart.

Now we were getting somewhere.

Salazar sped up the recording, freezing it on the woman again. He ran his finger down the hazy silhouette of her body on the screen, but she was hooded. He hit PLAY and saw her pull it off, yet she remained in the shadows, her body turned just so. He tried another camera, on the far side of the room, the zoom-in distorting the picture. He worked the keyboard, cropping the photo, cleaning out the shadows and lighting her features.

He saw jawbone and her lips, but it was still unclear other than she had long hair. Lovely, he thought, though he didn't need to know why she was with his Vice President. Only that he wasn't surprised to see her. After that, the lenses went black.

She was gone, that much he accepted. He leaned in the chair and pulled up another stream of video. Part of him loathed himself for watching, for enjoying her abandon. She was straddling him on the sofa, bare to the waist, and the same skirt she'd smoothed over her knees earlier today was hiked high, exposing her. He watched, her hips gyrating and breasts bouncing.

His phone hummed against his chest and he answered it. "We have a problem."

Salazar turned away from the console. "I'm listening."

He catalogued his orders, already mentally breaking them down, but what surprised him was who was giving them.

"I want to be certain we're clear on the next steps."

He glanced at the video, smiling to himself. "You want them to disappear. They already have. To the hacienda."

Over the phone, he heard her soft intake of breath.

"I can work better there. In private."

"I cannot hear the details," she said sharply, then softer, "Get it back, Diego."

His name sounded good on her lips. "I will."

His gaze was still on the video and his body clenched when she tipped her head back and looked directly into the camera as she climaxed.

Beautiful.

He closed the phone, slipped it inside his tailored jacket and stood. Salazar understood his position, what was afforded him because he kept out of sight, and all confidences. Most didn't know he existed except by name. He preferred to watch, and slipped the CD from the security system, then erased any copy. He was keeping her privacy, he told himself, though few knew of this room's existence. It gave him delicious anonymity, kept any trail to him hidden and ensured his position in this administration. Beyond that, he'd follow the money, the power. As long as he was paid, he would do as ordered.

He opened his hand radio and contacted the driver. When there was no answer, he tried another frequency. He tapped the door. It sprang open and Salazar slipped out, then down the back staircase while demanding a response from the van of his prisoners. He hated repeating himself and changed frequencies.

Quickening his steps, he ordered the helicopter to the lawn.

Logan stared out the windshield at the woman in the middle of the road. The driver slammed on the brakes, throwing them forward. For several heartbeats, the guards just stared, then made a couple rude comments about the crazy woman, yet when a man followed after her, limping really, the guards left the truck, weapons drawn. Max immediately popped apart the pen and used the parts to work the locks.

"Was that Riley?" Sebastian asked, sitting forward.

"And Tessa." Chained, they could only watch.

She ran back, playing the role of hysterical female rather well, and neither guard noticed the nunchucks in her hand. She spun the wooden rods so quickly, Logan saw only the results. A crack to the head, the back slashes to the other's chin. Like glass, they broke and fell to the ground.

"Clearly, the woman is skilled," Sebastian said.

She certainly was, Logan thought. However, the woman he knew eleven years ago wouldn't have dared that alone.

"Another rule shot to hell," Tessa muttered, stuffing the nunchucks away before she searched them for keys. She kicked away the guards' weapons, then unlocked the door and yanked it open.

"Oh Christ, it *is* her," Max said.

Tessa smiled. "Underdog, here to save the day." She wiggled the keys in the air. "Go on, say it, you're glad to see me again." She met Logan's gaze, every cell in her body gone still as she waited for the reaming she deserved. But he just smiled, a delighted little sparkle in his eyes that went right to her soul.

"You've been a very bad girl."

She winked. "I thought that's what you liked about me." Then a man left the van and she frowned as he passed her. "Jeez, you guys look awful."

Logan snatched the keys. "Gee, thanks Tessa, and you don't look so bad for a walking corpse, either." Terrific, in fact, and he was still rocked to see her alive. He focused on springing the cuff. "Where's the guy who was chasing you?" Free, Logan handed the keys to Sebastian.

"Out cold on the ground. You might want to leave him to them." She inclined her head to the downed guards.

"Irish accent?" Logan eased out of the van, Sebastian behind him.

She frowned. "Yeah." Oh hell. Just then, a man hurried between them. "Him." She pointed.

"We gotta go," Riley said. "The van is hot."

"Defuse it." Logan said.

"You know each other?" she asked, glancing between the two.

"Until Daisy Duke here showed up," Riley said right over her words. "It would just blow the tire, like an accident. It's pressure sensitive and the van's sitting on it. And exploding on a stationary object with a gas tank . . ."

It would toss the van like a ball. "Good God, Riley, don't you think that was excessive?" Logan joined Max to collect weapons and communications gear.

"It's just a little charge," he defended.

Tessa stuck her head back inside the van. "Some guy's trying to contact the guards on tact 27."

Logan tuned the guard's radio and listened for a moment, then chambered a bullet. "We're getting company. Where's the truck?"

Riley gestured up the hill, walking stiffly as Sebastian caught the keys and ran to it. Logan pulled the unconscious guards off the road.

"I'm sorry," she said, alongside Riley. "I really am."

"I'm just glad it wasn't a nunchuck."

"I wanted to stop you, not kill you."

"The apology and kiss on the head was a nice touch," Riley said, introducing himself.

Tessa blushed. She'd never kneed a man in the groin and felt bad. But then, he shouldn't have scared the hell out of her.

"How do you know Logan?" he asked.

"It's complicated."

"Very." Logan was there, guiding her with him. "And if you two are through?"

She looked at him, dazed for a moment. God, it was so *good* to see him. Men always looked better with age, and Logan was no exception. After a decade or so, there were a few more lines, a couple of scars, but he hadn't changed. His dark hair was a bit longer, not the SEAL look she remembered, and like a pop flash in her mind, she had the image of her fingers pushing into that thick mop. A long time ago, she thought, then recognized his locked posture.

"Logan, I know this is a shock—"

"Not *now*."

Tessa had a sneaking suspicion *bitch* was mentally tagged to that.

But Logan didn't know what to feel, just looking at her blew the one horrible night into oblivion. He glanced, recognized her uncertainty and gave her a quick squeeze. Then he looked behind himself, to the sky. "Oh hell."

He heard it before he saw it. A glossy black helicopter swept in between the trees. Then Sebastian barreled down the hillside, the black SUV fishtailing across the road. Riley and Max headed for it.

"Split up!" Logan shouted as they climbed in the SUV. "Bug out the CP." He'd catch up when they didn't have so many soldiers climbing up their ass.

The chopper engine grew louder as it closed in. Logan pulled her with him toward her VW, threw down the hood and climbed in, then turned over the engine.

She was already beside him. "You can't outrun that chopper."

"I don't have to." He got out and leaned against the hood as if he had all the time in the world.

"Those guys are armed, you know that, right?"

"They'll think we're civilians."

The chopper lowered over the area, kicking up dirt and leaves in an opaque spin of debris. Then the door slid open.

"Logan. Let's go."

A man hopped out before the skids touched down, and two more followed, armed with assault rifles. Prisoner guards didn't carry more than a pistol. The leading man hurried forward, then froze when Logan aimed.

"You'd better be ready to shoot something—!"

"I'm trying. Hush, please." Logan realized the man wasn't looking at the weapon trained on him, but at Tessa. He fired. The van exploded, the charge ripping the tire off the rim and pushing the vehicle on its side.

"I don't believe you did that!" she said as he got in. "Cool move."

He threw it in gear and hit the gas. Dirt spit from the tires, and they shot forward, bouncing over the road. A secondary explosion rocked the darkness and she flinched, hunched, then twisted in the seat to see it tear through the side of the van, ripping metal like tissue and kicking the rear up. It landed on its roof.

"Do you always piss off the host before you leave a party?"

"When we don't have cover, and he knows this land better than we do, hell yes."

She couldn't argue that. "See, that's why you're the commando and I'm not."

Logan glanced in the side-view mirrors. "Damn, it didn't hurt the chopper."

"Wonderful, a few more deaths averted."

"I don't remember you being this whiny."

"It comes with age." She smiled to herself, and despite the danger felt only relief that he hadn't died on some operation in a Third World country in the name of democracy.

Suddenly, he slammed on the brakes, turned the wheel, throwing her against the side as he drove the car down an alley. They splashed through puddles, the little car struggling up a hillside. Once they crested it, he took his foot off the gas, coasting the car on its own power. He didn't check the streets, but the sky.

"We need to get out of sight." Deep, he thought, thinking like a wanted felon and doing the opposite.

She tapped him, pointed. "Under there."

Logan turned the wheel and slid the car beneath a blue tarp awning sandwiched next to a house. He shut off the engine.

"It might not start again," she said.

"We have to leave it. Come on." He got out.

She stood on the other side. "We lost them, we're okay."

He gave her a dry look over the top of the car. "You never were very good at this."

"That's why I left."

His expression darkened, and she came around the back of the car. "It was the *way* you did it."

"I had my reasons."

"Care to share them?"

"Not really." Not if she wanted her life back. She knew all this was a desperate attempt to recapture the moments before that call, and behave as if nothing had changed. But as she stared into his eyes, she knew nothing would be the same. It was cruel, but Logan wasn't ready to hear it. He'd never believe her. "I did my part, you're free to do whatever it was you were doing." She flicked her hand the way they'd come, then turned in the other direction.

"You're just all sorts of misbehaving lately, aren't you?" He swung her around with him in the other direction, walking the alley.

"Stop talking to me like I'm some kid, Chambliss, and why are we rushing?"

"To get out of sight."

"And why should I come with you? Jeez, Logan, slow down."

"Tessa," he said patiently, though she was practically running beside him. "They've chosen to hunt us instead of my team. They won't stop looking. There was surveillance in the house we didn't know about." Not to that extreme, Logan thought. Someone had a voyeuristic fetish. "They know our faces and they were looking for something."

Her insides seized.

"Now, I don't have a thing from Ramos, but you were already there. So what did he give you?"

She felt the clamminess of the leather tucked against her stomach and Tessa had two good reasons for not showing it to him. This was her problem, and he'd want to help. He was that kind of guy. Well . . . except maybe *now*.

"They don't have video of me. He told me where the cameras were located."

He scowled. Their pursuers' interest in her in particular said otherwise.

"I knew how to get to him, and it was easy. I studied the layout." She shrugged. "Somewhat. The plans are public record, the press knows his routine."

"Clever. You haven't been working the game?" But he knew the answer.

"Oh God, no. I'm a National Geographic Society location scout."

"No roots."

"I couldn't have any."

"Except him."

She blinked. "You're *jealous?*"

"Don't flatter yourself. I could have told you not to trust him. Or didn't I mention that before?"

"Now you're just being sarcastic," she said.

"But that doesn't tell me what he gave you."

"We talked."

"So then, what did he *tell* you?" Frustration laced his voice.

"Do you really want to get into this right now?"

"Just so you know," he said, taking her by the arm. "I'm not long on patience anymore."

"Yeah, well," she said. "You'd be surprised how stubborn I've gotten over the years."

He'd already noticed that difference in her and the irony of this struck him. She'd pretended to die, while Ramos, as Garcia, pretended to live.

His problem was that eleven years hadn't lessened her effect on him. He felt choked by it, and when he turned his head to look at her, he got the full impact of her pale, pleading eyes, the rich brown hair streaked with gold flowing wildly past her shoulders. Her skin still looked incredibly smooth, tanned, and his gaze slid to her throat, dove lower as rounded skin disappeared under the clingy neckline, the dark shorts exposing her muscled thighs.

She was still gorgeous in a kick-your-ass sorta way. More striking than delicate. Everything about her was vibrant, and very different from the woman who was shaking in her boots when she'd passed herself off as a Chechen courier and fast-talked her way around hired guns to access a faction leader. He frowned, dragging his gaze from her and staring at nothing in particular as he remembered her hand on his arm, as if she wanted human contact one last time before she faced the devils with AK-47s and bad attitudes.

That was then, he thought, and the longer he considered her orchestrated death, the more lies piled up. Her lies. She used him and, worse, Ramos was part of it. Yet Logan was the one who had suffered. Ten feet away was a woman he'd mourned. Jesus, he'd visited a gravesite with no one inside. He felt like a complete and utter fool. And while he wanted to hate her for it, his heart was screaming with joy.

She'd staged her death and hidden herself from the world

to protect herself. Although he planned on getting it out of her, he didn't think it was a good time to tell her he'd been wearing video equipment that night. A direct relay with no recording, so the Venezuelans didn't have it, yet even if the Vice President's security cameras didn't catch her on film, McGill did.

It wouldn't be long before the intelligence community knew she was alive. And for her sake, he hoped the *eyes only* classification kept her under wraps. Something had scared her into doing that and from the way she was behaving, it wasn't over.

As they moved, his hand on her wrist loosened, his fingers sliding to thread with hers. She clutched back and they raced away from the explosion still lighting the night sky.

Salazar jumped back into the chopper and ordered the pilot to lift off. Yet before they made air, a second explosion tore through the van. He cursed and took the controls, struggling to get the chopper above the heat and flames. The craft bucked in the sky, rocking right, and he stabilized, lifting higher. He called up reinforcements, blanketing the city with officers and closing roads. They would find the black truck while he searched for the couple.

He flew the helicopter over the city, using heat signatures to locate the green bug of a car. Then he turned over the controls to the pilot, watching between the land and the thermal monitor. He found it, lowering the chopper, and the blades kicked back the tarp. The rusted German car sat like a fat frog in the mist.

"Send a car right there," he ordered, then pulled off his headset and climbed between the seats. He reached for the cable and drew out a few feet before he clipped the hook on the cable and stuck his boot in the loop. Without missing a beat, he jumped. The pilot frantically hit the switch, then looked at the others. Two men gaped, the pilot only shrugged and held the craft still. As Salazar lowered to the ground, people peered through bleary windows, cracked open their doors, yet didn't step into the light. They knew better and went back to their small lives.

Salazar slipped his foot free and hung on, then dropped to the ground. The chopper lifted and he walked to the car, laying his hand on the hood. He jerked back, smoothing his scorched hand over his pants leg, then with a penlight checked the ground. The prints were faint and dusty, and he followed the logical path into the city, the stone walls hovering over him like sentinels. He'd never cared for the city, the musty smell, the drunks and dealers crowding the streets where children once played. A car with flashing lights headed toward him and he hailed them to stop. He ordered the men out, climbed in, then drove off. Pulling out his cell, he contacted a few men he trusted, ones who understood the kind of efficient discretion he needed.

This will be over before nightfall.

In the truck, Max grabbed the GPS tracker and turned it on. A green dot glowed, showing the beacon lodged in Logan's belt. "Logan's going in the other direction." He ducked to look at the sky. "Crap, the chopper's headed toward them, too."

"We can't help them, not if we don't get away," Sebastian said as they raced from the chaos. Knifing pain bled through his hand, numbing his fingers. "Riley," he said, "I hope you have some tricks planned." Sebastian pointed to the right, and several blocks down, they could see the spinning lights of the police coming toward them.

"Go to that store, there, with the red front," Riley said, pointing from the backseat.

Sebastian turned toward it and slid the SUV into the store parking lot.

"Wash it."

"Jesus, you don't want much, do you, gimp?"

"It's the best I could do with limited resources."

Sebastian left the truck and ran to the hose coiled on a rusty hook on the side of the building. He grabbed the bulk and uncoiled it toward the truck as Max turned on the water.

Sebastian shot the stream at the dark truck, washing away the paint and turning the black truck a hideous light blue.

"This is it? You really think this will work?" Sebastian asked, using his hands to loosen the paint.

"Anything's better than more torture," Max said, trying to spray the top. Within four minutes, they were back in the truck, dark watery paint sliding into the street. The radio snapped with Spanish, orders popping back and forth.

"The checkpoints and roadblocks are closing us off," Riley said.

"We need to go around," Max said, focused on the map.

"Back the way we came? No way."

"We don't have a choice," Max said. He adjusted the frequency on the radio, picking up the police. "They're closing in on them."

"We get to the CP first, agreed?" Sebastian asked, glancing in the rearview. He dropped his speed, the police vehicles closing in behind them, then blocking the streets.

Riley handed weapons over the seat.

"Max, get us out of here," Sebastian said when they faced a police cruiser barreling toward them.

"Stop," Max ordered.

"Hell no!"

"Pull over and stop," Max insisted and Sebastian obeyed, but not before he laid the pistol in his lap. The police car closed in behind them.

"Any more brilliant ideas?"

five

Overhead, the chopper moved back and forth in a grid, searchlights glaring randomly and making them stop and start, adding to their suspicious behavior.

Logan couldn't get a clear shot at it. Not that a .45 caliber round would do much damage. He was fast losing his last chance to bring Ramos home and cover up a mistake. Two teams had gone after the guy, and adding Tessa's incursion, it clearly defined Ramos's intentions to stay behind and do some damage. But for which side?

Logan saw two men under a streetlamp and steered clear. They looked directly at them, smoking lazily, yet didn't follow. When he saw another man, alone and two streets over, he wised up. "We have to get out of sight, *now*."

Tessa forced herself not to look. "Police?"

"Well, they aren't hiding themselves. Your eight o'clock."

Tessa had to think. If twelve o'clock was in front of her . . . She let her bag strap slip, then as she pulled it back up, she turned her head to the far left. "They're moving."

Logan used the shop fronts to look behind himself, but it wasn't good enough. He could feel them coming in closer. *They're narrowing the field and we have to get past it.* While he could see a couple men in the open, he felt more. "These guys aren't the guards. Someone else is running the show. They've got skills."

"What's the Venezuela version of the FBI?"

"This is a little darker, Spec Ops, maybe." Logan steered them away from the figures. "We need a new ride." They'd never make it out of the city on foot.

When Tessa moved closer to him, he offered her one of the guard's guns.

"No. I've broken so many NGS rules, I can't be an armed combatant."

Logan realized she hadn't actually fought anyone except Riley. The guards at the exchange never had a chance. "The nunchucks?" He fieldstripped one weapon, keeping the bullets and tossing the pieces in different spots as they walked.

"Self-defense. I learned in China. I was doing a layout trip for the Yangtze River and saw something I shouldn't have. I was rock climbing and by the time I reached the top, there were fifty soldiers and me."

They arrested her, he realized. "What did you see?"

"Hell if I know. I was taking panorama shots of the valley and river. They took my camera and film, so I never found out. I don't want to know. NGS got me out of a very nasty prison."

"How'd you work for them without a real ID?"

"I had one." She frowned, keeping up with him. "I didn't come to this decision lightly, you know."

"Not enough to sleep with me the night before."

She flushed, staring him down. He couldn't make her feel guilty over that one, rather spectacular night. It was another choice she didn't regret. "I couldn't stop my plan. It had already started. Timing was everything."

"Was I part of it?" Out of the corner of his eye, Logan saw opportunity and moved toward it.

"God, no. How can you ask that?"

"Easy." He strode up to a motorcycle and threw his leg over it. "You're not dead and I was pretty much the last person to see you alive." Except for Ramos.

She climbed on, wrapping her arms around his waist. "You're glad, though, aren't you?"

The little hitch in her voice snagged him and he patted her

hands. He was more than glad, their past was brief, ancient history and the woman he knew then—was not tucked behind him now. With the knife, he ripped out the ignition and used the blade to turn the engine over. It roared to life, and Logan gunned it.

"Faster," she shouted close to his ear, then looked behind herself. Three cars from the south, east and west, pulling behind them for a couple blocks, then splitting off again. Great. Synchronized bad guys. "They're trying to head us off." And succeeding.

Logan slowed the bike, then yelled, "Hold on" before he turned, low to the ground.

Tessa closed her eyes and clung, but he was in control, bringing the bike upright and turning them back the way they'd come. They headed toward the black police truck coming right for them. Neither slowed down.

She felt the rush, the fear, and could do nothing as the vehicles neared. Then at the last second, Logan turned the handlebars, only a fraction, and shot to the left onto the sidewalk, then back onto the road past the trucks.

"That was awesome!" She still had a death grip on him.

"We won't be doing it again."

Tessa risked a glance over her shoulder for the cars. They stopped short and tried to turn around. The helicopter was faster. "The chopper is turning!" She held on for the ride of her life.

Logan pushed the little motorcycle and concentrated on maneuvering through the longest straightaways, and she leaned with him, yet he couldn't see clearly ahead in the dark. Compensating for her weight on the back of the bike was getting tricky, and he was damn near out of gas. He had only one choice to make.

He headed toward the river, the chopper in his side mirrors, a shaky version of Dragon One's with a hell of a lot more armament. Seconds later, he tasted it as the chopper fired two streams of bullets, eating the road behind them. Logan gunned the engine harder and a few seconds later, he heard the scream of a rocket. The motorcycle ripped from beneath him and he was airborne—then falling fast.

Salazar cursed, a three point turn nearly impossible in the narrow streets. He spun the wheel, taking out trash cans and lampposts as he turned and sped toward the motorcycle and his targets. He ordered the chopper to fire, chasing them with a double line of bullets, but the man on the motorcycle held on as they headed toward a ravine.

"Stop them now! Fire, fire!" Salazar ordered into the radio.

The chopper shot ahead, and unloaded .50 caliber rounds behind the bike. The big cartridges chunked the ground, spraying dirt. Then the motorcycle tire blew, nearly tearing the metal hub in half and sending the machine ass up and forward. It sailed through the air, the couple thrown apart and dropping into the gully.

Salazar slammed on the brakes, his truck skidding to a stop on the edge of the ravine. He climbed out, signaled his team, and they spread out, flanking him as he slid down the embankment on the sides of his boots. The bike was on its nose, flames eating the exterior, already bubbling the paint. The men advanced, rifle muzzles sweeping back and forth in close combat grids. One forward, one covering.

At the bottom of the ravine, Salazar kicked logs and leaves, and when he crossed the creek and climbed the other side, he looked back. His dark gaze skipped over the land. *They're still here,* he thought, and ordered spotlights to comb the ground. He needed them alive. His interest wasn't in the man, but the woman, and the leather pouch Eloisa wanted back desperately enough that she had called him to hunt.

He glanced at his men. They shook their heads, and Salazar motioned them to continue. He wasn't leaving here without something. Even if it was a body. Thirty minutes more without success, Salazar stepped back, calling out a warning only seconds before he swept the gully with bullets at nine hundred rounds per minute.

Thirty seconds was overkill.

* * *

Logan dug his fingers into the ground to keep from flinching as the bullet ripped through the weeds around his head. His ears still vibrated with Tessa's scream. His body reeled from the impact and the hard roll down to the creek. His bones vibrated, the cushion of underbrush doing little to soften Murphy's Law. And in a split second of time, he felt wiped clean, then the hard rush of blood drove spikes of pain through muscle and cuts made themselves known. Cold water ran over his boots. He forced his breathing to slow, gaining enough control to think. He had no idea where she'd landed.

He heard footsteps move from his position and he opened his eyes, squinting in the dark. Above him, spears of light from the truck's headlights projected over the ravine, and silhouetted a swarm of men walking the gully and creek.

His gaze swept the area in a quick search, but it was too dark. Please be alive, he thought, and remembered praying for that when she was blown out to sea eleven years ago. After that shower of bullets, he'd hate to lose her—again—after losing her . . . Hell, he couldn't afford the therapy to figure that one out.

He moved and when he didn't draw attention, he pressed his luck, then rose up enough to quickly scan the area. She was likely nearer to them, and he reached for his gun. It was gone, and searching provided nothing except wet weeds and dead leaves. He went still again as the men splashed through the trickle of creek water, water droplets hitting him, and all Logan could see was a pair of boots in ankle-deep water. He held his breath. It would be over in a spew of bullets.

Where the hell was Tessa?

The impact pushed the air from her lungs and she thought, this is worse than falling down Kilimanjaro. She forced herself to move, to roll over, and keep rolling sideways. At least she thought it was, and she scrambled under the exposed roots of trees. Her head throbbed, her hands and knees scraped and burning. She brushed leaves and branches onto herself, leaving nothing exposed. In the back of her mind, she knew she was inside a potential snake nest, but consciousness was slipping.

Then she just didn't care.

Logan watched them, the morning sun beginning to rise and coating the men in a gray mist. Only his gaze shifted as the lead man moved through the ravine. He covered the entire area efficiently, but it was his hand signals and gestures that were familiar, engrained, and Logan realized, *We trained him*. The U.S. had loaned military instructors to train Venezuelan troops till Gutierrez was elected. He kicked them all out, trading them for Chinese. But they knew U.S. strategy, and while their training wasn't Spec Ops, he wasn't facing a slouch.

When the men retraced higher up the crevasse, Logan slowly rolled to the side, and rose to all fours, crabbing up the hill. He had to find Tessa. He moved in the shadows, picking up his hands and feet and placing them carefully. Sound echoed and bounced. His palm brushed something hard, and he closed his fingers around his gun, grateful for something in his favor. Hopefully, the magazine was still in it and he shifted to his side, stretching to look up at the trucks and men.

He extended his arms to aim. He needed a distraction, quickly and long enough to find Tessa and get the hell out of here. The chopper hovered, the men still searching. One man stood out against the headlights. Killing them would bring fast retaliation. He made his decision.

"Don't do that," she whispered.

Logan flinched, then glanced left. Three fingers wiggled in the leaves. He let out a breath, head down, then backed up and moved toward her. He slid into the cover of roots.

Logan held her tight. "Are you hurt?"

"My butt could use some ice."

Temptation won out and he palmed her behind. "I'll work on that."

"Ow, ow." She flopped on her back. "Can we call it a day now?"

"It just started." He smoothed his hands over her hair. "Open your eyes."

She did. "This is not turning out at all like I planned." Her lip quivered and Logan felt the knife of it somewhere in his chest.

"We'll be okay. But they won't give up. We have to get far away from here, quickly."

She grabbed his head and into his ear, whispered, "You say that like I didn't just fly off the back of a motorcycle."

Gunfire suddenly cut across the ground, and Logan held her head down, his body covering hers as bullets chunked near their position. They were no more than thirty feet from a man, the stench of flash burns from his weapon lingering on the steamy air. He wanted to look up. Wanted to see the face of the man barking orders. He heard voices, too soft to understand, then the chopper lifted, sweeping deep into the ravine, spinning debris and flattening grasses.

"Time's up." He came to his knees, aiming his weapon and unloaded into the chopper.

One bullet ricocheted off the bulletproof glass, the second hitting the hydraulics, a third increasing the damage. The chopper smoked, rocking violently. Logan pulled Tessa off the ground and backed away from the tottering machine.

"Jeez, I'm glad you're on our side," she muttered, then yanked him in another direction. "I know my way around. I've been here for days."

"I've been here a month." He swept his arm around her shoulder and pulled her away from the river.

"Oh well then, you win."

Together, they low-crawled up the opposite hillside, then she rose and veered into the creek. Behind them, the chopper tried to lift, men shouting and hailing gunfire over the ground. They had about a minute before those guys would shoot more, ask no questions. He pulled her through the ravine, splashing in calf-deep water under the canopy of trees. The chopper couldn't get off the ground and he heard the whine of it shutting down.

"Where are we going?"

"Need to know," was all he said.

He didn't trust her, she thought, and tried not to take offense. She had a lot of strikes against her.

They climbed out of the gully and hurried across a lot between two buildings, tall grasses hiding tires and discarded furniture. She pulled her hand free and kept up beside him. He only pointed to the right. A few yards ahead, the entire area changed. The stricken look of the dwellings gave way to renovated homes and shops with the influence of the conquistadors in iron and stucco.

Cars moved past them and they dodged a traffic circle and crossed to a two-story flat-front building. He concealed his gun before he went inside, and to the desk.

The woman was older and lovely, reminding Tessa of Sophia Loren. The lady displayed her assets well and from behind the counter, her gaze lowered over their muddy clothing.

"Señor? Did you get lost? In the woods?" She leaned over to inspect his feet, tsking at the muddy boots and giving them a terrific boob flash.

"We had a little accident, ma'am." He held out his hand.

She turned to a drawer, unlocked it and then gave him a zippered plastic envelope. Logan opened it and took out a key, then tucked the envelope under his arm before he turned to Tessa. He ushered her up the staircase. "Thirty minutes."

"We're not stopping?"

"Miles to go," Logan said, keyed the lock and pushed open the door.

Tessa stepped inside and glanced around the humble room. "Your tax dollars at work. I've had worse," she said, then went into the bathroom.

"The clock is ticking," he reminded as he checked the room's windows.

"And I have to pee." She shut the door.

It pays to plan, he thought, then from the envelope, emptied the money, a passport and a pistol with two magazines. He concealed it all, and while a cell phone would have been good, the less to find on him, the better. He dropped the guard's gun in the trash, and went to the bathroom door. He heard running water and tried the knob. A second later, he overtook the stairs and when he hit the last step, the older woman lurched back.

"You have misplaced her already, señor?"

He stopped short and looked at the woman. Her pretty features tightened.

Great, can't trust a paid asset anymore, he thought, throwing open the door. He bolted down the white painted porch to the side of the building. Jesus, she scaled the wall, he realized, then hurried down the street, pausing to search the windows of passing cabs, scaring the occupants. He pushed off a car to cross the traffic circle and ran, people lurched back, men started for him, and he glimpsed her as she turned a corner.

He bolted.

People wouldn't let him, and he forced his way into the congestion, making the corner. He spotted her again.

And at that moment, so did someone else.

Tessa heard her name and turned from the salon, the door half open. She should have kept going, yet she searched the area, and when she saw him, her shoulders drooped. She didn't try to outrun him, yet frowned at the desperate look on his face.

He reached her. "You don't know when to quit, do you?"

"That's what I was trying to do."

He gripped her arm, and didn't take a step when a bullet chipped the wall over his head. Logan ducked, searching the streets, and saw the silencer-enhanced gun an instant before the man fired two shots. One barely missed his throat; the second hit a man crossing in front of him, killing him instantly. The weight of the body fell against Logan and pushed Tessa into the salon. She tumbled across the threshold, the glass door slamming. One hairdresser rushed them, rattling that they weren't open, then saw the blood and took off. Logan rolled the dead man off him and scrambled into the shop.

"Oh God, that man!"

"I know."

She reached for him.

"He's dead. Christ, this guy isn't giving any slack." And didn't care who was in the line of fire. On his feet, Logan dragged Tessa off the floor and headed to the back, pushing open the door.

"Who is it? Who shot at us?"

He looked, then moved left, away from the gunfire. "Our little buddy from the ravine."

"How'd he find us?"

"Find *you*, Tessa. If you'd stayed put—" He glanced behind and saw a dark SUV heading toward them.

West of the river, they ran down a flat street, turning every couple of blocks around tobacco and cocoa warehouses. They moved fast, sporadically, and Logan ran between big steel buildings, then stopped at a random door and used the butt of his gun to break the rusted locks. He pushed her inside. Scraping metal shrieked as he slid the door closed. Tessa watched as he searched the warehouse, trying a rear door that was rusted shut. He judged the walls for a way out. She couldn't see one.

He posted himself beside the only eye level window, staring through the smudged glass. Neither spoke. He swiped at the blood on his face, then brushed his face across his shoulder. Briefly, he met her gaze.

"I guess waiting for you to trust me is out of the question." Disappointment laced his tone.

"It isn't a matter of trust, it's involvement. It's my problem." If he knew it all, he'd be trapped like her. He'd want to help, and after deceiving him so royally, she couldn't be crying wolf and whining about the repercussions.

"And bleeding over to mine."

Her chin lifted. "We sharing?"

"You owe me some answers first."

Her shoulders sank with resignation. He wasn't supposed to know. He was in a special job and couldn't afford to have his clearance revoked because of her. It sounded logical at the time, but right now, she couldn't stop drinking him in, her heart doing that crazy pounding when she was scared—scared he really did hate her. He was here, breathing, so near her, touchable. Tessa clenched her fists to keep from reaching out.

Logan Chambliss was her one regret.

"I've missed you," she said softly.

His gaze jerked to the window and he seemed to crumble, his shoulders sagging for just a moment, then like a tightening wire, the stiffness returned. He didn't say a word, his grip working the gun.

"Look at me."

Logan obeyed, so torn he could almost feel himself on some mental edge between rage and relief. "It was all a lie."

Sorrow glistened her pale eyes. "Oh, Logan, not all of it."

Logan sank like a stone, his defenses shot to hell. He shifted his gaze to hers and felt as if she were sitting on his lap, her presence more than physical. She stood rock-still, her breathing quick, and he saw fear in her eyes, a bit of pleading. He took a step, then another, and he was on her in a heartbeat, pulling her flush against him. He didn't have to seek, she was there and he took her mouth, then took more. His relief swelled and he unleashed it, his hands mapping her contours as the kiss turned raw, primitive. She was true hunger, and he hooked her knee, drew her leg up and ground into her softness. She thrust back, her tongue pushing between his lips and doing amazing things as her fingers sank into his hair. Oh yeah. She drew him into her, replaying his twenties and stealing away all doubt as her mouth molded savagely over his. The gun was still in his hand, and he slipped his finger from the trigger as he trapped her against the wall, her passion flooding over him. Up until this moment, he hadn't realized how dead he was inside. How deeply her death had affected him. *But it was staged.*

God, the consequences.

He tore his mouth from hers, and drew back suddenly, then he carefully laid his hands flat on the wall alongside her head. The gun clicked on the steel and doing anything with her was more dangerous than a loaded weapon. He couldn't resist her before, and now . . . His breathing labored with hers as he met her gaze.

"God, you can still kiss like nobody's business," she breathed, tipped forward for more.

His greediness for her weakened him and if he took what she offered they'd be in the sack first chance, and nothing accomplished except a climax. Not that some flaming monkey sex wasn't a good idea, but he needed information. Logan crushed down his desire, difficult with the crowd in his trousers, and pushed away. He went back to the window, watching cars move past and chanced opening the door to look for a chopper.

Seconds passed before he looked at her again. Narrow beams of sunlight spilled from roof cracks, and she crossed under it, dropped her bag on the floor, then scraped her hand through her hair. He wondered if she was as wrecked as he was.

"Why? Just tell me that much." Logan searched her face, the years barely spoken on her skin. He waited for a reason, an explanation, a goddamn lifeline, because he was ready to believe alien abduction right now.

"Isn't it obvious? I wanted out."

"They'd have let you go if you wanted," he said, disgusted, his gaze beyond the window. "You didn't have to do that."

She shook her head. "I tried, do you think I didn't try? I fell into that, Logan. Used because I fit the victim's description *one time.* Then there was another operation, and another."

"You could have gone above them for help." *Or come to*

me, he thought, then kicked the thought aside. They'd barely known each other then, other than the biblical.

She took up a position on the other side of the window, watching the opposite direction. "Oh, yes, I want to put myself up for scrutiny by the intelligence world because I want to leave it behind. No thank you."

"I never took you for a coward," he said.

She arched a brow. "Excuse me?"

"You didn't have the guts to get out, so you settled for everyone who cared about you mourning you. No, not a coward, just a self-absorbed user."

"Wow, honey, tell me how you really feel." She folded her arms, making her stand. "Back that memory up a bit, Chambliss. We worked together, what, three times? You had no idea what it was like for me. You got to prepare. You were trained. I wasn't. I'd be in the middle of an op before I could be briefed on the whole operation, trapped into doing what I was told, or blowing it and costing lives."

"That's how it works for the good guys."

She leveled him a sour look. "Get off that *really* high horse and come down here with the poor folk. We don't all get to have it in black and white. It never is, sailor boy. And the CIA doesn't always do the right thing."

He glanced at her. "Christ, you're a wiseass."

"Then, I was just young and scared."

What little Logan knew about her was on paper, long ago shredded and burned. They never got into backgrounds, homes; that was too personal and their knowledge of each other was in the moments of a mission. Except once. "Why didn't you say anything?"

Only her gaze shifted. "Duh? So *you* wouldn't have to *say* anything."

Logan's eyes narrowed. "To protect me? Jesus. I can take care of myself. If you had told me, maybe—"

"Don't go there." She took her attention off the goings-on out the window and put it on him. "We had one night, Logan. One. And we didn't do much talking as I recall."

His hard features softened. She was right about that, he thought, and by sheer will, kept the memory from bleeding into this moment.

Her gaze followed a dark car moving down the street, and she inched back from the bleary window. "If you hadn't coddled me through those operations, I would have never made it."

"You did fine, and I'd been through it before."

She leveled him with a bitter stare. "But I *hadn't*."

She had a point. He was trained. She'd been part of a couple operations with his team, usually something like being a lure to get quietly into a safe house for your latest splinter faction. Nothing too big. But she'd always been nervous, he recalled, triple-checking details. It was one of the things he'd admired about her. The ones who weren't scared made mistakes. Like Ramos.

The CIA didn't let you slip away, nor did the government, once you've served them in anything clandestine. Proof was him being pulled into cleaning up this mess. Hell, he'd left the SEALs and studied medicine to get away, and that he was hip-deep in the same muck again said he was one sick, twisted bastard. The only consolation was that the pay was better. He looked at Tessa.

Today, it was not enough.

He was still out to lunch on her story. She'd run first chance and she'd already staged the biggest lie of her life. Security was too fragile to have someone doing covert work who didn't want to be there. She was young and still new to it then, cutting her loose would have been the smart thing.

He met her gaze. So what did she know that pushed her to orchestrate her death? "Why so drastic?"

"It's classified."

Logan understood. There were missions he could never discuss. Yet when her hands trembled, and she kept pushing back her hair, he realized she was still scared.

"Don't ask more, please."

"Does it have anything to do with Ramos being here?" If it did, he needed to know it, screw classification.

"No. Nothing."

"Fair enough."

She looked up, a little stunned. "You're trusting me?"

He scoffed. "Not a chance. I'm respecting the classification."

"What brought you here to rescue Ramos?" she asked.

"What makes you think we were rescuing him?"

"If you weren't, it wouldn't take three of you," she said. "And I've seen you in action."

"Thanks, honey, I wanted to remember that," he said, and pushed away from the wall and crossed to the opposite side.

"What are you doing?"

"Looking for a way out that isn't facing the bad guys." He gestured to the window and she looked, catching the shadow of a man running left. Then he didn't have to hunt for a way out.

Bullets punctured through the steel, opening holes and streaming sunlight inside.

Tessa tried to get to him, but more gunfire sliced into the opposite wall, shattering the window and sending her into a dive. She grunted when she hit the floor, stayed still. Carefully, she lifted her head.

Logan searched through a crack in the corrugated wall. "He's counting on me firing back. I lost my magazine when that man fell on me. I have one left."

"Well, let's not expend those bullets unnecessarily."

Gunfire peppered the early morning and she realized they were shooting at all of the buildings. She crawled with her elbows, glass crushing under her arms, and Logan snapped her name like she was a puppy needing discipline. Then she peered out between a grouping of bullet holes.

"Christ," he muttered, then skirted the wall to her.

"We have an out, see that house on the hill?" She leaned so he could look.

"That's half a mile away."

"Yeah, well, that's your part, commando boy, I can get us in. It's secure." When he scowled, she said, "It's my hotel. Sorta. I know the guy who owns it."

A little spear of jealousy shot through Logan, but he didn't have the luxury. They needed to split before they were surrounded. Yet he couldn't see anyone, no more shooters, no cars. It made him more cautious.

"Go right, and at the end of this building, we cross and run behind into that little gully. Then once we cross that, it should put us near the road to the house."

"They'll be watching," she said. "I mean, I'm so tired of this, but trigger happy dude isn't willing to give up."

"We need to be smarter."

"Oh, well then, you shouldn't have invited me."

CIA Headquarters
Langley, Virginia

Elizabeth Jacobs had no hopes for after the holiday. The Fourth of July celebration would just rev up all that squeaky-clean patriotism and she would be sunk even deeper. She knew when to tie off an operation and she'd waited too long. She sipped her morning coffee, staring out the window. The parking lot wasn't a great view, half the spots empty for the long weekend that didn't start till tomorrow.

She turned away and one-handed, placed a few more personal items in the box. She wasn't in a hurry. Her escort had come and gone, taking everything on the operation days ago. Then the young little bastard copied, then erased her files all the way down to her personal e-mails. She felt stripped bare. She'd been allowed to clear the rest of her things out this morning, and now she sat at her desk to return the settings on the computer to the official version, then stood to freshen her coffee while she waited for them to incorporate. She reached to shut off the monitor and almost missed the ping. She drew back, staring at the little flag waving in the corner of the screen. A locked file had been accessed. *She'd* put the lock on it. She lowered into the chair again and worked the keyboard, trying to access enough data to know which file had been opened.

She glanced at the clock. Security would remove her from the building if she wasn't careful. She'd been allowed only this morning and because of the holiday, there was a skeleton crew working. They knew where everyone was, especially her, and only her position allowed her privacy. She dug through other systems to reach the archives.

Deceased employee records. She frowned. That's not necessary. Then she understood what was happening. Everything she'd worked on was being brought under question. She'd be damned if she let her reputation be destroyed without a fight. She did what had to be done, what others had wanted but were too damn political to make a stand.

The fact that it had failed wasn't a consideration to her. She had made a decision in a critical moment.

The image downloaded and as it clarified, she felt the iron bars of her nightmares clamp shut.

Then she heard her name and looked up.

"Ma'am?" the armed guard said not ten feet from her. "It's time to go."

She nodded, thinking, *The key just turned.*

The police car sped past them and Max grinned to himself. "We have new plates now, too."

Sebastian sent him a sour glance. "You two need to actually tell me the backup plan before they shoot." He pulled back onto the road.

"And give up a chance to look cool?" Max navigated him around the roadblocks, but it was another hour before they made it to the rental house, and Max was forced to put the GPS aside to load gear.

They broke down the command post in record time. Sebastian loaded the last of the gear as Riley smoothed a cloth pungent with ammonia and cleaned away fingerprints. Max gave the house a cursory last look before they piled into the truck. There were no sirens, no swath of police cars coming down the street. But there were enough roadblocks to dampen their success.

Sebastian took a side street to avoid the troops, and drove for three more blocks before they encountered another one. He turned before they spotted them, and he said, "We're boxed in. I'm open to suggestions."

"Something in a villa on a hilltop." Max took his face out of the GPS tracker long enough to program the one in the truck. "There," Max said, and Sebastian scowled, leaned deep into the windshield to see the hacienda on the hill.

"I can get the chopper up there," he said.

"There's a pad." Max was distracted by the marker. "They're moving fast and erratic."

"Anyone for aborting this and getting the hell out of here?" Riley asked from the backseat, his leg propped. He cracked open an ice pack and slapped it to his leg, then checked the load of his gun. He watched out the rear window.

"We haven't done the job."

"How long before they find us?" Riley asked. "Days? We have no chance of getting Ramos out of there now."

An even tone rang from the tracker. "They stopped. It stopped," Max said. Frowning, he turned up the police radio. Then he pulled the headphone jack free, and the sound filled the cab.

"My Spanish is lousy," Riley said.

"It's orders to capture her." Max looked up. "And kill him."

Six

Logan touched her shoulder, slid his hand down her arm to her hand. She squeezed it and tried to smile. "Stick close."

They were watching the exits, he assumed, and pulled on the bullet-torn metal, pushing it up, the sound scraping on the air. She made a *stop that* face and he threw it right back, then motioned to her. She wiggled through the gap, then stood against the wall till Logan joined her. The sun brightened by the minute and they hurried to the right. At the edge of the building, he stopped. Tessa moved up behind him, and he held her back.

"Army, nine o'clock, his back is turned." Logan instinctively looked elsewhere for more. "Go. Now."

She crossed the street, flattening against a cement brick building and glimpsed a soldier at the end of the street, holding an assault weapon. That didn't make the locals nervous? Then she noticed a woman slip back into her house, shades quickly drawn.

Logan snapped a quick look, then took off, crossing the road. He grabbed her hand as he ran past, taking her with him into the shallow gully. In the center, he held her still, then peered over the tall weeds. He patted her. "Okay, next leg."

She booked, Logan right behind her, climbing the hill. They ran down the barren street, pausing to check the distance and open area before going farther. It took them a half hour to go four blocks.

"We should come up on a service road behind it," she said.

Logan followed Tessa and didn't like giving over control or trusting her, but options were out of reach lately. Contacting the team was useless. Provided they hadn't been apprehended, they were moving the command post. Logan knew they just really wanted to leave the country. He'd never had a mission go belly-up so fast, and the reason was running beside him.

Over the rise, he saw a house that went on for blocks and faced the view of the river and mountains. They had to cross in the open to reach it.

"No time to think on how stupid this probably is," he said. "Up the hill, ready?"

Her gaze slid to his. "Sure. Race ya."

They ran, clawing up the slope and onto the service road. Logan turned to help her, but she was already beside him, crouched. They straightened together and Logan swept his arm around her waist as they briskly walked the service road. Without cover. Their destination came into view. The house alone had to cover an acre.

"Don't look," he said when she moved her head.

"I hate it when you do that," she whispered hotly, hunching against the urge to glance behind. "It's creepy."

He laughed, a low, Snidely Whiplash sound that made her smile and soften inside. *That* was the Logan she remembered. Tessa broke from him and ran to the gate, pressed a button and looked into the camera.

"Sorry to be so late, Ricco."

Logan had his back to her, watching the lawn and road.

"You don't look so good, señorita."

"Rough night. All my cuteness wore off. Open up, please." She waved to hurry him and immediately the gate started to open.

They slipped in as soon as it was wide enough, and Logan noticed the three pronged motion sensors lining the wall and low to the ground. Anyone coming over would set it off and probably with an explosive charge. "Christ, Tessa, who is this guy?" The two armed men on the top level instantly caught his attention.

"The owner—Armando? I met him on an expedition." When his look questioned, she said, "My field is the South Pacific, and during the monsoons, sometimes I join the scientific expeditions. I just handle the equipment." Her voice vibrated with their fast steps. "Anyone with a few grand can join the Explorer team for a couple weeks. This guy offered one of his many houses when I got here." She shrugged, glancing back for the cops. "It's as secure as it gets. He's a little paranoid."

An understatement, Logan thought, and when they reached the front, they heard cars and sirens advancing in the distance. Ricco opened the door.

"Is that for you, Señorita Tessa?" He motioned them inside.

"Yeah, my reputation is shot to hell." They crossed the threshold. "Don't tell your boss. He'll never invite me back."

Ricco smirked to himself, as if he'd seen worse. "Quickly."

Tessa felt Logan's hand on her back as they moved deeper into the house, then stopped. Ricco reset alarms, then said something into his radio. He focused on Logan, inspecting him, his gaze lingering on the weapon. Tessa glanced between the men, introducing them. Logan put out his hand, but the look he gave Ricco made her shiver. Like bulls in a pen, they assessed each other before Ricco nodded and shook, more out of respect than fear.

"Thank you." She looked at Logan, but he was inspecting the interior and not for its décor. She elbowed him. "Ease up. It's secure. Trust me."

Satisfied, he met her gaze. "After that stunt out the window?"

"I did it for you."

"Don't patronize me, Tessa. I'm older, not stupid."

Her heart clipped a beat at his tone, and she thought, *This day can't end soon enough for me.*

"Let's get cleaned up and eat something. Ricco makes the best *Carne Asada,*" she said loudly and heard a replying chuckle from somewhere in the house. Right now, Tessa would do anything to stall Logan, and led him into a massive bedroom, then moved past.

"I've got dibs on this bathroom. There's another down the hall. Make yourself at home. I think you might find some noncommando clothes in there." She flicked a hand toward the closet, dropped her bag, then hopped on one foot as she pulled off her boots.

Boots thunked to the floor, and Logan watched her go, his gaze on her slender back as she pulled her shirt off over her head. Then she disappeared from sight and a minute later, he heard the shower. Logan went to the door and opened it.

"Hey!" She whirled, covering herself with a towel.

Logan's gaze slid over her like warm wine and he enjoyed the curves and swells of her body. She had muscled legs like a Rockette, and from what he could see, some bruises that had to hurt. "You ran once."

"And promising not to will give me privacy?"

"You're the jungle girl, deal with it."

"Don't think I won't." She stepped into the hot shower, then she tossed the wet towel in his face.

He dragged it off, tempted to stay right there, but turned into the room. It belonged to a man, he thought, wondering how well she knew this Armando. The house had a lot of arched doorways, stucco and scrolly iron railings, but he was too damn tired to appreciate the architecture. The large bed shouted to him. Instead, he went to the bar, poured himself some bourbon, then tossed it back in one shot. It burned his throat and the warmth of the liquor made him feel every cut. One hell of a day.

He stared at the mirror-backed shelves, his dark shirt stained with blood. He stripped it off, searched the drawers for something to wear, then found the other bathroom and showered. Fifteen minutes later, he felt almost human, the first aid supplies under the sink helping that along. In borrowed jeans, he entered the suite.

He was sitting in a chair when she came out of the bathroom, dressed in fresh clothes with her hair wrapped in a towel. It made her features look tight and he watched her dig in her enormous bag for a comb and lipstick, then she did that ritual every woman practiced—applying makeup and judging herself in the mirror.

Tessa pushed the application stick back in the tube, tension spinning through her. He watched her every move. He didn't trust her and she couldn't blame him. She wasn't exactly a good citizen in his eyes.

A long stretch of silence reined between them and she swung toward him. "So . . . do you want to hear it or not?"

"I think I can figure it out. Ramos dragged you to the explosion that, I'm guessing, was rigged on the dock. He was injured, you were blown into the sea in little chunks."

He'd thought about it, she realized. How her last seconds were. Oh, God. "There was dive gear anchored under the docks. I dove to it, then swam up river for a mile or so before I came ashore."

"In the Danube River?"

He said it like he still couldn't believe she had the guts to do it. "At night too. I was terrified and got lost in Serbia, intentionally." She started braiding her hair, making a mess of it. "Nice place, once I got used to the gunfire." She gave up on the hair and threw it over her shoulder. "I became Lillian Richardson with all the documents to go with it." Ramos had gotten them for her. She'd never asked how.

"You never let on." Though he'd worked with her specifically only on a couple operations, she'd partnered with other teams.

"Living like I was going to die made some things unimportant."

Logan glimpsed a mischievous sparkle in her eyes and realized eleven years was behind that look. She wasn't the same person at all. Neither was he.

"I thought I was exceptionally clever, so I don't know how Ramos figured it out. Nor what he thought he'd gain by helping, except to blackmail me into coming back now." She wouldn't put it past him to use her as a trump card when things got tough for him. "If he's found out, he'll throw anything at them to keep the wolves back. I top the list. It may already be beyond that and it's why he was desperate enough to call me."

She still hadn't figured out how he got her satellite phone number or located her. Unless he'd been watching all this time. That creeped her out, but then, Ramos was a weird one.

"There was a full NCIS inquiry, with me as the star witness."

She stared wide-eyed. "Oh, Logan, I didn't know."

"Of course you didn't—you were *dead*."

"But Ramos—"

"He let me cook in an investigation."

"God. The last thing he said to me was that it would be fine, ruled an enemy attack."

"But you were *still dead*," he said through gritted teeth. "They investigated us, that one night." He left out that the CIA didn't paint a pretty picture of her, and he suspected it had something to do with why she wanted to leave so desperately. "I left the Navy a year later, and Ramos went on to become that." He inclined his head toward the residence miles away.

"Oh, man." She flopped back on the bed. Left the SEALs? It was his passion and he left? "I didn't know, I swear." Ramos betrayed Logan for her.

Tessa hated that her voice broke, that he could hear it, because she sounded disgustingly pitiful. But he had to know. He had to believe her. She sat up, pushing her hair off her face. "I'm so sorry, Logan, you shouldn't have been hurt. But I don't think it would have changed what I did. I didn't want to be covert, ever, and would have done anything not to be trading secrets in some dark alley. I don't want to look over my shoulder, or even have to. I can't live like that. Don't misunderstand me, I admire the people who can do it. I leaned on them like I leaned on you. I like thrills—hanging off a mountain or skydiving, that kind—and there's a big difference between an adrenaline rush and mind-numbing terror. I love my job and if the Company knew what I was doing for NGS, they'd try to use me, you know it."

"Oh, yeah," he said, and thought of his reasons for being here. CIA officers were dead or missing, an operative in the number two position in a foreign government, and now a dead woman resurrected?

"Wait, if you're not Navy or CIA, why are you and those guys here?" she asked.

"Hired."

Her eyes widened. "You? A mercenary?"

Logan opened his mouth, but nothing came out. He sighed. "Yes. Retrieval experts."

"That's just window dressing." She wasn't going to mention that from what she'd seen, they'd failed, but he probably blamed her for that. "What do you do?"

"Get stuff back," he said plainly.

"I was wrong, your humor hasn't improved that much."

He faced her. "Dragon One is for hire and, yes, sometimes we have to actually fight the bad guys. But we get paid shitloads of money because it's usually very dangerous."

Logan was a straight arrow, his convictions far stronger than hers, and he never had any doubt about what he was doing for his country. But a merc for hire? There had to be a catch. "It's the stuff no one else will do, huh?"

It was this time, he thought, and wondered how deep he could take her into his confidence. "Did you know Ramos was an imposter?" he asked.

Well, if that wasn't a "butt out," she wasn't as smart as she thought. "No, but the face was a shock. That goes way beyond the call of duty, 'cause he ain't pretty anymore."

"He lost some of his pretty-boy looks when you *died*."

Her expression soured. "Are you going to keep bringing that up? Because you need to get over it. Move on."

"Like you?"

"Well, yeah."

"Try living with the fact that someone you'd slept with was dead because of you."

She frowned, standing. "It wasn't your fault."

But Tessa knew from that look she'd never get past that "his team, his responsibility" thing. It was part of who he was. Ramos had disobeyed his orders for her. She didn't have room to argue.

"Did you even think of the ramifications?"

"I planned for them. No trace. I'm not stupid, I didn't do this to screw you. Blame me, fine. I can handle it, but now I just feel really guilty." She moved to him, her height putting her just below his eye level and she ducked close, into his circle. It was like stepping into the cool darkness. "You've been carrying this around, haven't you?"

His gaze narrowed and she got her answer.

"You were not responsible for *my* actions" she said. "My life, my choices."

Recent events only renewed her hatred for Ramos, and she thought of the pouch. That it was entirely possible he'd stolen it from the capitol didn't escape her great deductive reasoning, which should have had her seeing this as anything but a huge mistake with far-reaching effects.

Logan had already suffered because of her; she couldn't let that happen again. She couldn't tell him the why of it. There's only so much ugliness she was willing to share with anyone.

His hands suddenly gripped her hips, pulling her slowly against him. Tessa tipped her head, her lips a breath from his and she thought, *Oh goody, more.* His hands molded her spine, her hips, then swept over her rear, his finger sliding around the waistband of her shorts. Her stomach muscles flexed and she forgot about everything as he tipped his head toward her mouth, lingering, then he dipped his hand inside, his warm knuckles brushed her bare skin. He yanked. Tessa inhaled, the tear of the leather from her damp skin stinging.

He held the pouch. "I searched your bag. I knew it could only be in one other place."

Tessa fumed. "I should slap you."

Logan slid her a glance, the cold calculation in his eyes startling her before he turned back into the bedroom. "You should do a lot of things with me, Tessa, but that isn't one of them."

"Oh you wish, swabby." Tessa's words lacked power and she closed her eyes, her head *thunking* to the wall. She was almost glad that he'd found it.

"This is why Ramos wouldn't come with us."

She looked at him, then pushed away from the wall. "I thought he wanted out. But he wanted that out." She flicked at the leather. "If I could get inside, he could leave." She frowned. "He was using a cane and did you notice he looked pasty? But it's another man's face, so what do I know."

Logan had noticed Ramos was a bit sallow, but a medical assessment wasn't an option. Then there was the bloody nose he'd given him.

"He said he thought the doctors did that to him."

Logan scowled. "They wouldn't." Without speaking to Ramos, Logan couldn't catalogue symptoms to pinpoint his illness.

"Why not? Orders are orders."

"Because I'm a doctor and I wouldn't."

She stepped back. Whoa. "You've been busy, huh? No practice, big mortgage, little wife?"

"Dragon One is my practice, I rarely live in my house, and no." He met her gaze. "No wife."

Her lips twitched. "I'm glad we got that cleared up. Though how you can be a merc and doctor just escapes me."

"I save only the card-carrying good people," he said dryly, though resuscitating the same people he'd wounded in battle screwed over his ethics sometimes. He unfolded the leather in four directions. His brows rose sharply. "Good God."

Rows of symbols and words lined the page, and Logan recognized perhaps three symbols and those were from different cultures, one in Latin. The writing was on a single piece of thick paper, yet as he inspected it, he decided it was more leather, a frail, thin hide seamed to a leather backing.

"Someone went to a lot of trouble to make this," he said.

"I haven't had much chance to study it. It's written in hieroglyphics or something. There's some phrases printed, but not any language I recognize. Weird, huh? It's a mess of nothing."

"Where did he get it, whose is it? Garcia's? Or someone else? And what the hell does it have to do with anything? And foremost, why would he care?"

She slid her hand to his shoulder and Logan felt the warmth and calm. "From what I got, it's hers. His wife's. Garcia's, I mean."

"Why so elaborate?" He waved to the leather.

"He said that Garcia's wife was making plans, gaining control." It still didn't make sense. She was just the wife. But then, so was Princess Diana and look what she did for the world. "I think she arrived by helicopter that night, right after you guys were captured."

He swung around to look at her. "You stuck around? Are you crazy?"

"Call me reckless," she said, and did a game show shimmy. "What was I going to do? Leave you to the wolves?" She didn't let him comment and said, "Two choppers landed at the same time. They went out of their way to disguise who was on them. One was a woman." He scowled as she went to her bag, digging in it. "I might live out of a backpack, but I know good shoes when I see them. I didn't see a face, the best I had was my field binoculars and it was dark."

She rubbed something against her shirt and she put a small silver thimble on an empty shelf.

"What's that for?" he asked.

"Leave a gift and you'll be asked back. Armando will know what it means. They do it on the expeditions."

Logan watched her position it just so and thought again of the yacht. He was convinced that something had been left by a previous traveler and the diver knew it was on the boat to take. An easy front for smuggling lucrative items. He made a mental note to check the previous manifest and passenger lists, then turned back to the leather page.

"What makes you think it's a map?"

"What he said and the first symbols are Inca, journey, river." She pointed. "Then Luna god greets us all."

"The Amazon on a full moon night. Simple enough."

She nudged him. "It doesn't say night, and the Inca are not indigenous to this area. The Luna god *is* the full moon and the Amazon is farther south." The creepiest place on the planet, she thought, especially at night.

He studied it again. There was no pattern, no grouping of cultures. "You're right, this symbol is Latin for vision." He tapped it. "So the origin has nothing to do with it."

"Then each is a solitary meaning? To be read as a whole?"

"I don't have a clue. I wish I had my computer. I'd bet I could decipher this in a couple hours."

She went to her bag. "Call someone," she said and held out her satellite phone.

His features tightened. "Christ. Why didn't you mention you had that?"

"I was flying through the air with the greatest of ease?" She pressed it into his hand.

Logan immediately dialed the team, but the line was busy. He tried the break-in code to cut into the line, but it refused him. He gripped the document. "We'd have to scan this to make copies."

She pointed back over her shoulder. "There's an office full of stuff down the hall, but I will point out that computers are not my strong suit."

"They're mine."

She led him to the office. "I'd erase any trails." She pushed open the door and entered. "I don't know if this is linked to his companies, so I wouldn't send anything classified."

He tapped keys. "It's wireless. Excellent. I can get around it with a satellite link in your phone." He started unplugging cables.

"Do you recognize any of the symbols?" she asked.

"A couple."

"Show me which ones. It'll give us a start."

She went over to the machines to make a copy, then sat down and marked the symbols. Logan paused long enough to point out the three he recognized, then moved around the room, pulling a cable from the hard drive, linking it with the satellite phone and the scanner/fax machine. Obviously, he knew what he was doing. A geek commando doctor, she thought, amused. She didn't have a computer; the Sat phone did the job for her. She always needed immediate responses from NGS headquarters. In her packs, she had an MP3 player, but that's as far as it went with techno stuff.

"I'm sending it to my email account. Max can access it and load it." He stepped back and worked the keyboards standing up.

"You don't have much of a social life, do you?"

He looked at her, then shrugged, a little sheepish. "Not really."

Tessa moved closer, leaning to watch him become one with the computer. "You're not afraid of a trace or something?"

"No." He clicked stuff so fast she barely had a second to read it. "Searching the Net will take too long, and my system on the aircraft could decipher some of it."

"Aircraft? Then let's leave here."

"Not an option. Getting Ramos out is the mission and it's not done."

"Logan," she said reasonably. "I don't want to sound like a buzz kill, but he'll be surrounded now. He hasn't been seen in public lately, while *el Presidente* is accusing the U.S. of every atrocity on the planet. What do you think will happen?"

He didn't stop working as he said, "I don't care about politics. He has to come home, Tessa. Without anyone learning he's not the Vice President. Think of what this would do to America's image, our standing in the world."

That was the reason he took this assignment, she realized. "You're cleanup," she said, a hollowness in her tone that made him look at her.

"No." He straightened. He'd thought he could kill Ramos, but that was before he knew the truth—that somehow, Ramos had covered for her, been scarred so Tessa could escape a life she didn't want. "He can't die here." He told her McGill's reasons beyond the funeral, autopsy and dental.

Tessa sat on the edge of the desk, staring into space. "This will devastate the U.S."

He met her gaze. "Ramos knows his days are numbered, yet he refused his one chance to get out to give you that." He nudged the leather. "Wherever it leads, it's where we go."

"You aren't suggesting we figure it out and follow it, are you?"

"Not up for a treasure hunt?"

With the Venezuelan Secret Service after them, Tessa knew the last thing they'd find was a treasure.

Joe McGill pushed off the bed and swung his legs over the side. He rubbed his face and reached for the phone, speed dialing his wife. He wished he was home next to her, and when he ended the call, he pulled on his clothes and left the bedroom, then grabbed some coffee.

The house was like any other. A single level with below-average landscaping, and looking almost abandoned except for the satellite tower, a truck and the small chopper. The three bedroom, two bath house on a hundred acres of cornfields didn't get much use, and he headed to the cave, taking a small elevator to the windowless communications center two stories beneath the ground. While it was state of the art, it wasn't much for comfort. Without contact from Dragon

One, he wasn't going to complain. All he knew was, they weren't in the prison anymore.

He stepped off the two-man elevator, and his team flinched. "Nothing, sir."

"Go get some rest and chow, I'll watch it," he said. He felt guilty for leaving the post, even to sleep.

"Yes sir, let me explain how it—"

McGill put up a hand. "I got it." He'd been tracking troops before this kid was born. "Go."

Walker and Lorimer left and McGill sat before the console. Behind him the news played on a screen. He barely listened, his attention on the stream to the satellite link, waiting for it to connect.

He wouldn't think the worst until he had proof, and this entire operation floated on the flimsiest evidence of all.

A beep startled them and Tessa looked up, frowning, then went to the intercom on the wall and pressed CALL. "Ricco, I thought you'd be asleep." Though the sun was up and shining.

"Forgive me, señorita, but we have visitors."

Tessa snapped a look at Logan. "What kind?"

"*Policía.*"

Logan sprang from the chair and brushed back the drapes. A dark green helicopter lowered to his eye level.

"Down! Down!" He grabbed the map off the scanner and dropped. Men fast-roped from the helicopter and a voice over a loudspeaker warned that they were surrounded. He pushed her flat to the carpeted floor just before bullets shattered the windows and ripped through the wall behind them. Two canisters lobbed through the broken glass, and he covered her face, buried his in her back as it popped. The flash grenade burst with light, then a second charge sent smoke and heat boiling through the house, eating air and multiplying till it spread over and up, then exited out the windows. Curtains caught fire.

Logan covered his mouth and looked up, squinting through the haze.

"God, I am so tired of being shot at!"

"Annoying, isn't it?" He nodded ahead.

She rolled to her stomach, crawled with him to the hall, then toward the staircase. "Why aren't the extinguishers going off?" Before she finished, a white gas blasted out of reservoirs in the ceiling, the cool spray dousing the fires with a slow hiss.

"Señorita?" she heard several times. Ricco.

"Ricco, get out of here!"

"Come this way," he said, gesturing to them both and Logan followed, slinking down the staircase, following Ricco deeper into the house. Down two more short turning sets of steps, and he stopped.

"I am sorry for this," Ricco said, armed and to the right of a window.

"Thanks, but I think they came for us," Tessa said.

He glanced back. "No, I am thinking that they mistake your friend," he nodded to Logan, "for *mi patron.*"

She frowned deeply. "Oh, give me a break, he doesn't look a thing like Armando." Except maybe from a distance, same height, hair color, but that didn't answer why the police were *shooting.*

"Go back toward the city," Ricco said. "You may be able to lose them." He held his gun close and nodded toward another staircase below.

Tessa followed Logan as he overtook the stairs, and at the base, threw open the door and searched for a light switch. Fluorescent beams popped on one by one and the ta-da was a line of vehicles, light gleaming off the chrome and waxed paint.

"Yes!" He searched the rack of keys, plucking a set. Logan hesitated, his gaze catching on a large photo on the wall with racing memorabilia.

Tessa didn't move as he inspected the line of cars. "Wait, wait, wait. Doesn't anyone think this is a bit much? If they're after us, why shoot at Armando's house?"

"Armando is an alias, Tessa. This house belongs to Alejandro Carriòn."

"No," she said warily. "*Armando* Cirrada."

"Either way, that man"—he nodded and her attention went to a picture of Armando—"is the head of the Venezuelan drug cartel."

She stared at the picture and didn't doubt him. The man she'd met carried a gun and wasn't jumpy till he left his entourage. "Was it DEA who shot at us?" Her voice rose an octave.

"Hell if I know. Venezuelan version, maybe. Carriòn wouldn't keep drugs or evidence in his house. The man is clever enough to stay far away from his operations. It's the reason he's still free."

Logan knows him, she thought. "That was meant for us?"

"If it wasn't, then they have lousy Intel. They had to know he isn't here. So, yeah, it's for us." *How does this guy get around so fast?*

He bypassed the lemon-yellow Hummer and climbed into the green Jeep Cherokee. Tessa joined him, then strapped in, the garage door already lifting. Her eyes flew wide.

A chopper hovered a couple feet off the ground.

"We can't be this unlucky in one day," she said.

Logan threw it in DRIVE and gunned it, heading straight for the chopper.

The jeep had speed, and less than thirty feet from the nose of the chopper it lifted and they shot under it.

"It's a news chopper. Wait. That's a National Geographic helicopter," she said, ending in a squeak.

"Not exactly."

Tessa twisted in the seat. "It's blocking the other one's path. I'm so screwed if that's NGS but . . ." She frowned. "They shouldn't be here till next year." She looked at Logan as he opened the window and adjusted the mirror to see the chopper. "It's them, isn't it? It's your buddies."

"Yes."

"Clearly there is some bend in that morally straight-arrow spine."

"I get what you mean," he said dryly and turned into traffic. "We have about two minutes before the APB goes out on this jeep." He was certain the authorities had information on Carriòn's cars. Logan looked for a clearing as he drove through a traffic circle, then shot to the right toward a park.

The chopper lowered into the ground, the door sliding open, and Logan yelled, "Get out!" then slammed on the brakes, the jeep fishtailing under the blades. "Go, go, go!" Two choppers in a dogfight he did not need.

Out of the car, he grabbed her by the waist, pulling her over the top of the jeep and toward the chopper. She landed hard on the floor and pushed up as the aircraft rose. The door was still open, wind beating at her clothes and hair. Logan handed her a headphone, and she twisted her hair in a knot and shoved it down the back of her shirt before she slipped them on. She looked at the men, smiling.

They, on the other hand, didn't look all that happy to see her.

"What I'd like to know is," Max said, looking back from the copilot's seat, "just how do you screw the living to pretend you're dead?"

"CIA?"

"Oh, well, that figures."

Seven

Salazar slammed on the brakes outside the estate and threw himself from the truck. He flashed his badge and shoved his way between the officers; some backed out of his way. "Who left this house? Who?" he demanded of the officer in charge.

He listened to the events, feeling the resentment from the drug enforcement officers. Interpol had far too much jurisdiction and he planned to cut it short. Without comment, he strode into the house, stopping near a man bound and facedown on the floor. Salazar drew his pistol and put it to the man's head. "Where did they go?"

The man met his gaze, a look of pure hatred in his eyes. "Fuck you, Salazar."

Salazar's gaze narrowed. "Where is the woman?"

Ricco frowned for a split second, then spat in his face.

Salazar wiped off the spittle and pressed the gun to Ricco's temple hard enough to push his head. Agents swarmed Salazar, aiming at him, and ordering him to drop his weapon.

Salazar pointed the gun to the ceiling, let it dangle from one finger, then showed his badge. Weapons lowered.

He'd given them a tip. False, of course, but it gained him more manpower to search. Interpol was always lingering near drug lords' homes. But they'd assaulted far too soon. The couple was proving to be a challenge.

"You will find nothing here," Salazar said. "Carrión has not been here for weeks. Your intelligence is compromised."

He turned to the doors, but not before an agent brought an armload of damp, muddy clothes and dropped them in a plastic bag. Salazar grabbed the woman's shirt, inspected it, then lifted it, scenting her perfume on the fabric.

The agent frowned at him, and Salazar released it as if it were foul, then strode from the house. Yet her scent lingered, adding to the mystery of her. Once in his truck, he grabbed the radio, demanding reports from traffic control. The response had him peeling away from the mansion and heading east.

He had to have her, for more than his government.

Sebastian flew low to the ground, under radar.

"I bet that's scaring the old folks right out of their jammies," she said. But they weren't listening, busy watching monitors, the sky, ready for anything with a lot of loaded weapons. She looked away, her gaze colliding with one man. Max Renfield. She could feel his animosity and didn't blame him, but she didn't regret orchestrating her death. Her life had been damn good till recently.

The chopper swept inside a property surrounded by stone walls, setting down with a delicate touch. The blades were still beating the air as she left the chopper, and she couldn't help herself—she pulled off the magnetic NGS logo and shoved it at Logan.

"Never again."

He held her gaze. "It's good cover. Saved our asses a couple times."

"They wouldn't approve. Noncombatant, Logan."

"You're going to be a tyrant about this."

She folded her arms. "You really don't want to go there."

He tossed the shield at Sebastian. Max stormed away, grumbling to himself.

"Wait a second," she said and they stopped. "You've got a chip on your shoulder." She moved near Max, her chin up. "Let it out, I can handle it."

Max looked at Logan, then her. "Bitch."

"That's it?"

"I'm being polite."

"You do know that sticking up for your friends is a good thing, right?" she asked as if he were dense.

"Don't make me wish you were blown up," Max slung back, then walked into the house.

"I'll take the silence as meaningful." She looked at the other two. "Any more darts to throw?"

"I'll throw anything you want, lass." Riley looked her over with a thoroughness that wasn't meant for the public. "You're a lovely little deceiver."

"Thank you." If he thought the Irish accent would win her over, he was wrong. She'd heard the best lines in about forty languages.

Her gaze went to the house and she understood instantly why they'd selected it. "You fugitives live very well," she said as she walked inside.

Besides the slick black chopper, they had two vehicles, an SUV with some mean-looking tires and a jeep that had seen better days about ten years ago. Leading to the heavy oak doors was a half-mile-long driveway that wound up a hill, the property surrounded by eight-foot stone walls, and around the two-story house, the lawn spread out like a skirt. They had a three sixty view and could see anyone coming minutes before they arrived.

"A rental," Logan said, guiding her inside. "It belongs to a former client."

He left her side and started pulling black metal cases from the floor, sliding them onto the table and throwing them open. They were filled with electronic gear and computers.

"Well, someone shops at the Costco For Commandos."

Logan laughed to himself, and Riley got busy running cables. They worked like a well-oiled machine, or rather well trained. Sebastian moved slower and Tessa stepped back when she realized he was handling explosives. He gathered them and left the house. A couple minutes passed before she saw him through the window setting the charges around the perimeter. Okay, even if she wanted to leave, which she didn't, escape was no longer an option.

"Smart people would call this operation a disaster," she said. But again no one listened, too busy to stop. Especially Logan. He was adjusting a satellite dish near the window that overlooked the city, and she bet she'd be able to see the VP's residence from the upper deck.

In the corner of the room, Tessa felt like an outsider, the four men working a routine they'd obviously done several times before. When she had to move to dodge some piece of equipment, she headed to the sofa and curled into it, staying out of the way. Within moments, she was asleep.

Max nudged Logan, and he looked, then followed his gaze to Tessa. "What's it like seeing her again?"

Logan continued to work the computers for a secure line. "Like finding out Santa isn't real. I believe her. There is no reason not to. Ramos blackmailed her into coming to him, but he never intended to leave. He gave her this." Logan pulled the leather from his back pocket and tossed it on the table. The rest immediately stopped for a look. Logan gave them a rundown on her story and when he was done, they said nothing, then one by one . . .

"They'd have a lot on her. Photos, prints, DNA," Sebastian said from the kitchen.

"Her real name is Tessa?" Riley asked.

Logan shrugged. "That's the name she had when I met her."

"Ramos is a bastard," Max said. "But what he did to you, he did for her." He nodded to Tessa. "I could see it," he said. "Women like that make you nuts."

More than a little, Logan admitted to himself.

"Where does that leave us?" Max asked.

"Nowhere good till we figure that out," Logan said. "Ramos didn't understand the document, and he's smarter than the average bear. He threatened to expose her, and relied on it to get that in the open. He's got to be desperate because she hasn't been in the game and he knew it. Which means he's not trusting anyone at CIA."

"Well, there's a real switch," Max said dryly.

"We still have to get him out and if it's the key, then we take it. It won't be easy with the Secret Service climbing up our ass."

"Maybe not," Max said.

Logan looked up sharply, scowling.

"Someone they only call "Commander" is giving the orders, and when they apprehended her, they had strict orders not to search her."

"For the document. Then they know it's missing," Logan said, moving faster. "Patch us in, Riley, we need everything you have on Venezuelan intelligence. McGill needs to hear this."

"Yeah and he'll probably be glad we're not prisoners," Max added.

Logan froze. "You didn't contact him! Jesus, Max."

"We thought rescuing *your* tired ass was more important."

For the past forty-eight hours, McGill's living environment was a twenty-foot square room beneath the earth. There wasn't much room to pace and he knew it made his guys nervous, but locked away in an undisclosed location kept noses out of this business. The risk was too high for even the slightest breach in security.

He loathed that he was forced to take desperate measures, but he understood that something was working itself through the intelligence community beyond the usual suspicions. McGill's reaction was to surround himself with people he could trust. While the CIA employees resented a military man commanding operations, he knew his best backup was Staff Sergeant Walker. The young man had a keen eye for detail, and finding it in the most obscure manner. In his pocket was David Lorimer, a CIA satellite expert he'd dealt with before when he foiled an internal plot to kill a covert agent in the field. By his own boss. The intelligence game has gone to hell, he thought. Walker and Lorimer could gather Intel from the driest of sources and both were far more computer savvy than McGill ever claimed to be. And these men were the only people aware that Dragon One was doing this dirty work.

Lorimer turned in his chair, smiling. "Sir, we have a Sat link to Dragon One."

Even the walls seem to sigh with relief and McGill let out a long, tired breath. "Thank God." He left his chair, resisting the urge to rub his numb ass as he stood behind the men. He put on the headset and nodded.

"Bet you thought we were dead or something?" Chambliss asked.

McGill smiled. "Or something. So just how bad is it?"

"We encountered a little trouble."

On the other end of the line, Logan sat before his computer, the webcam giving static feedback as McGill's image appeared on the screen. Logan gave his report, but spoken aloud, it sounded hopeless. "I'm sorry, sir."

"So am I."

The general broke eye contact. It was a fraction of a second and out of character. He'd seen McGill stare down the barrel of an assault rifle without so much as flinching. What wasn't he saying? Or allowed to say?

"We aren't done till he's home," Logan said. "We'll try another route." Unfortunately, if they found one, it was doubtful they could get that close that quickly again.

McGill nodded. "This belongs to Garcia's wife?" the general asked, holding a copy of the document. "She's a childless woman with nothing to do with the government. You can't possibly think she is a threat."

"Ramos did, enough to use blackmail to get it out."

"Yes, the woman. I'm running a match to the photo. But all I'm getting is a closed file on a dead woman, Contessa Petruscu."

Logan's gaze shot to Tessa stirring on the sofa. "Contessa?"

Tessa launched at him, covering the mic and pulling him away from the web camera. "Please don't confirm it, please, Logan. I'm begging."

"We enhanced her photo, though it's vague," the general was saying.

But Logan's gaze was locked with Tessa's. Her desperation was transparent, pleading. Terrified. "General," he said. "I'm cashing in a favor."

Tessa inhaled sharply, searching his face.

"I'm not going to like this," came wary and tight.

He touched her cheek, swept her hair behind her ear. "Bury it."

There was a long pause on the line. On the screen, the general nodded. "Will do."

The call ended, the screen going blank.

"Thank you." She swiped at tears, then looked at the guys. "Thanks."

Her lip quivered and Logan dragged her into his arms, and pressed his lips to the top of her head. "If you want to stay dead, then I'll help you." The threat of exposure was far more than just leaving the CIA. Enough that she tried to do this alone, that she wouldn't speak a word. He'd seen it before, in her and in himself.

Absolute fear for her life, he thought and he dreaded hearing the truth.

McGill stepped back from the console. "Lose it."

"Sir, it was global, U.S. Intel net."

Damn. That meant that anyone in any agency could have seen it.

"Gather everything on her and erase it." He looked at the men. "All of it."

Walker typed, working with Lorimer, then suddenly they stopped and looked at the general. "Sir, we're too late."

* * *

Salazar strode into the VP's residence, taking the stairs two at a time. Word traveled through the house, and a young woman, Eloisa's secretary, rushed ahead of him, blocking his path.

"You cannot, señor, please."

He looked directly at the girl and she stepped back. He continued on his way to the private rooms. He gave her the courtesy of knocking, then pushed through the door.

Eloisa looked up from behind a dainty desk, her brows knitting softly. Her staff surrounding her, she asked them to leave. A couple people cast a glance at him, and Eloisa nodded as if assuring them she'd be fine alone. She closed the door and faced him.

"You have something for me? Give it to me." She held out her hand.

"If I had it, it would be yours."

Her arm lowered. "Then why are you here?"

"For what do I search? Exactly."

"*Madre de dios,* you are too inept for the position," she said, walking to her desk. "The attackers, of course."

His gaze narrowed. "The city is contained. They will not leave it."

She looked at him. "You can't watch the borders, the rivers."

"If I knew what it was, I could get ahead of him." Salazar didn't tell her about the figure in her husband's rooms. Except for a glimpse on a camera, the woman didn't exist until he'd seen her again with the prisoners. He didn't bother to learn how she'd escaped, there were many places to hide in a house so large.

"That is my business."

"And you have made it mine."

"Do not overstep yourself, Commander Salazar." Her hand rested for a moment on a picture of the President and her husband, her point made clear. She had the ear of the President. But Salazar had the Army.

He took three steps nearer, a slow prowl. She stood her

ground, yet the flare of fear in her eyes was unmistakable. "How far are you willing to go for this, madam?"

She smoothed her skirt beneath her before she sat behind the desk. "Do not be obtuse, you know the answer." She signed a note, slipped it into an envelope, then onto the stack beside her.

She'd insisted the attackers had taken something. She wanted it back, but that she wouldn't tell him exactly what infuriated him. He'd performed countless tasks for her and his President, yet he was her confidant in only some matters.

It was time to change that. "Then we are done."

She looked up. "Pardon me?"

"I cannot fight what I cannot see."

Tossing the pen down, she sat back. "I thought you were the most skilled, the most talented."

"You doubt?" He pulled her from the chair and nearly against him. "I have done your work and kept your secrets," he said softly, a lover's whisper. "I have seen them."

Her cheeks darkened and she reached to slap him. He caught her wrist, turning it back the motion forcing her in his face. "Now they have it, and I hold all but one card."

Eloisa stared into his black eyes, his Spanish lineage in his angled face. She didn't trust him. He was a man with few morals. But she needed him. Although, telling him too much was far more dangerous than not having him on her side. She struggled with the decision, against his hold. She had no other resource, and she certainly couldn't go about the city as easily as he could.

"It's a guide."

He released her, scowling. "They will follow it."

Now she smiled, smug. "No. It's a puzzle, written in riddles, they will never understand it."

"Do not underestimate them, my dear." An unbreakable code did not exist. With enough time and resources, they would learn it.

"Ahh, yes, how can we? They've escaped and you still have yet to recapture them."

Salazar ground his teeth and had a flash in his mind: his fingers around her throat before he cut it. He shook it loose. "Surely that was not the only copy."

She put her hand on her hip and gave him a sassy look often seen from the girls on the street. It reminded him that despite the jewels and fine garments, she was not so far from her past.

"Then that was your second mistake. Allowing it to be taken from your own home was your first." Her expression sharpened and while he suspected her husband, calling the Vice President a thief would not serve him. The woman in the shadows, he realized. He could have given it to her.

"Do not chastise me, Diego. You don't have that much power."

She would learn otherwise, he thought, then said, "A maid, your husband?" There were no cameras in her suite of rooms, and her husband despised her puzzles.

"Does it matter now? It's not in *my* possession." She turned away from the desk, and opened a cabinet, drawing out a box. One of her puzzles, he thought, and she motioned him to turn away while she opened it. "Here," she said after a moment. She held the copy over the desk.

He took it, frowning at the jumble of symbols. "You have this, why do you need it back?" He tried to hand it back.

She met his gaze and said nothing.

"Ah, yes, a trail that leads to you. And what is at the end of it?"

She barely smiled, a mere curve of her lips. Only her gaze shifted to his and he'd never seen such a look from a woman. Salazar resisted the urge to cross himself.

"Victory," she said.

The men exchanged glances. None wanted to ask her why she insisted on staying dead.

"I have to know," Max said. "If you hated it enough to die, why the hell did you ever join the CIA?"

Tessa pushed out of Logan's arms, using her sleeve to dry

her cheeks. "I didn't. I was recruited from the State Department. I was a translator. Nothing more, just standing in the corner, repeating words. But I was paid well and had a lot of time off to play."

"All because you looked like that other woman," Logan said.

"That time, an agent had been in the operation for weeks and had been wounded. They didn't tell me that. Ramos did. I refused and they accepted it, then asked me again, put me on the spot as if time was of the utmost and it was all on me."

"Sometimes it is on one person." He pointed between them. "Or two."

"This"—she mimicked the gesture—"is self-preservation."

"Petruscu?" Max asked. "You're Russian."

"Romanian. Contessa"—she made a sour face—"is an old family name. A long line of high-wire artists."

"Trapeze, as in carnival?" Max asked.

"A carnival is not like the circus," she said, hands on her hips.

"I've been to the circus," Riley muttered.

"A circus isn't a bunch of wild eyed performers who decide to stage a show or con people with games. It's generations of performers. My great-grandmother was a Wallenda."

No wonder she got in and out of the residence, Logan thought, intrigued as she moved to Max.

"Or were you expecting this?" She reached for his ear, drawing back a coin. With her other hand, offered him his own wallet. They all checked their pockets. Except Logan.

Tessa laughed, then slid Logan a glance. "You don't know what to do with me, do you?"

Logan had a few ideas and none of them had to do with the mess they were in now.

"Put her to work." Riley smiled at her, then continued surfing through TV channels. "Nothing on the news except the shooting was blamed on street gangs."

"Convenient fall guys," Max said, then sat back in the chair to look at her. "Sebastian's cooking."

"Not anymore," the man said from the kitchen door, carrying a tray. He set it on the table and offered her the silverware.

"For me? Oh wow," she said. Blackened steak and some glazed vegetable thing, but Tessa was too hungry to speculate. She immediately found a spot and tasted the first bite. "Oh God, I love being a carnivore."

Sebastian chuckled, pleased. "So, *cheri,* how did you get to be a location scout?"

"I helped with a setup team in North Africa and it went from there. No one wants the job. It's a lot of living in hotels or in the wild, arranging *much* better accommodations for the film crews. I do location photography, hire guides, get equipment and make the trek to wherever first. Which is the fun part."

"So if you can't do it, it's a bust?"

She nodded and told him about Fiji, paused long enough to eat, then said, "This is fabulous. Is that ginger?"

Sebastian nodded, keeping her company while the rest were studying the document. He told her about his restaurant and she was suddenly homesick. "I haven't been in the U.S. in so long. Every time I meet an American I want to run home to Mama."

"You haven't seen your family since? Ever?"

"I risk it once a year. Only my mom though. We meet at the circus. Big crowds and unfamiliar to the locals. It's usually in Europe." She couldn't let her mom suffer, but the once a year trip always left her looking over her shoulder and scared someone would put a bullet in her head. "The rest of my family think I'm dead."

Sebastian frowned. "That's harsh."

She stopped eating, staring at the plate. "Yeah. Sometimes. My baby sister has three kids now." She looked up, her eyes tearing, and when Logan moved to her, she flashed him a smile and went back to eating. The subterfuge sucked. There was no nicer way to put it, she thought, taking a bite. The food didn't go down as easily this time.

As she brought her plate to the kitchen, Logan thought, she sacrificed her family to stay hidden. Across the room, he met Sebastian's gaze. The Cajun arched a brow and said softly, "We have to fix this."

Logan agreed. "The only way is to finish it. We need to keep tabs on Ramos and find another way in. Or all that is useless." He flicked a hand toward the computer running through a database of symbols and dead languages.

Logan felt time riding his spine. They were desperate enough to kill innocents to get to that map. "Riley, I want every photo, every piece of film and a transcript of anything that came out of Ramos's mouth in the last few weeks."

Riley nodded, then turned to a stack of files.

"Bring all the surveillance on him again. We start over."

They were out of time and now—hunted.

Salazar walked through the house, the walls and surfaces dusted with fingerprint graphite, the house littered with discards from the Interpol agents. They'd found nothing here. His motives were to locate the couple and nothing more.

He passed the long, dark hall, the sunlight streaming from the courtyard, and behind him, his man Juan walked. In the center of the courtyard, his helicopter rested, repaired and gassed. Ending at the last door, Salazar stopped beside the man secured to a narrow table.

Ricco stared at the ceiling, refusing to acknowledge him. Blood dripped off the table edge and onto the cement floor in soft splats.

"Who is the woman? The man? How do you know them?"

Ricco remained silent, his face swollen and bloody. Salazar drew a knife from inside his jacket. The man's eyes flared, but impressively, he didn't finch. Not even when Salazar cut the tendon in his arm.

Ricco clamped his lips tight, his breathing hard through his nose, yet he refused to scream. Not that anyone would hear him. Then Salazar cut him again and Ricco succumbed to the pain, crying out in a short gasp.

"The woman? Her name!"

"Fuck you," Ricco said, and Salazar motioned.

His man grabbed a handful of Ricco's hair and yanked his head back. The knife danced over his throat.

Ricco turned his head slightly, staring him down. "You will regret this."

"How does Carriòn know her?"

"She was just a guest, you idiot."

Salazar's eyes flared. "Then you are of no use to me."

He scoffed. "You won't get anything from Carriòn but his rage, Gutierrez *puta*." Whore.

Salazar sent him an arched look. "You have no idea what I'm capable of, do you?"

Ricco's gaze faltered. "I've heard enough."

Salazar glanced at the blood flowing from Ricco's arm with his heartbeat. He had little time, his eyes already glazed. He dragged the knife across Ricco's throat, just enough to bleed him slowly, then he stepped back and admired his work. Then did it again.

A half hour later, he left the room, the screams silenced and the body already beginning to decay.

"*Commandante*," his man said softly, his hand on his ear mic. "We have activity."

Salazar wiped the bloody blade on the sofa cushion, then returned it to the sheath behind his back. "Finally," he said and headed to the helicopter.

"Sir?" his man asked. "The body?"

"Send the head to Carriòn."

Logan felt her move up beside him.

"Want me to give it a shot?"

He met her gaze. "I thought you didn't like computers?"

She nudged him out of his chair. "Doesn't mean I can't use one. Jeez, get out of the Dark Ages, Chambliss."

"I thought you might want to beat it with a stick, jungle girl."

She slid him a narrow glance. "You are *not* amusing." She

started typing, opening up the Internet and surfing. The system was running through thousands of symbols from different cultures. "You know," she said, "smart people would never have written it down."

"I think this is a game," a deep voice said from the corner and Sebastian unfolded and rubbed his face. "A wild-goose chase."

Logan shook his head. "They killed a man to get to Tessa."

Her shoulders drooped with her smile. "Or you?"

He met her gaze. "Sure. But I'm a fugitive, you're not."

"That depends on the point of view." And which government.

He took a bite of his sandwich, and when the computer nearest him pinged with a match, he practically lurched at it. Out of habit, he glanced at the one running a composite of Cassie's killer. Still nothing.

He tapped the keys, and then leaned into the screen. "Journey. Half a sun. Vision. Words, then something that looks like an eyeball, then the Luna god. River. And it hasn't found the language of the text. Pictish or Celtic, it can't decide."

"Hold up," Tessa said, and they looked at her. "This one is Hunnic." She gestured to the screen and the first words in the map. "It's a dead language. It hasn't been spoken in a few thousand years." Logan frowned at her. "Hunnic—you know, the language of the Huns."

"As in Attila?"

"Yes." She hopped up to get her phone and started dialing.

"Tessa." He put his hand on the phone. "That's not wise."

"I know a guy who might be able to translate this, if he's awake. I'm sending him the first few. He's cool," she said when they started to protest. "We need help." The call went through and she spoke for a moment, copying the text and sending it through email. She chatted idly, then suddenly checked the email. After a short conversation, she hung up and looked at them. "It means 'Upon the center of the eye.' "

"One is an eye symbol. Looks Egyptian," Logan said.

"With Hunnic directions. Dr. Matob can translate the words for us and send it to that email," she said about the computer. "He said some are numbers and he thinks the next one is an age or a date. He's working on it."

"There's a marker with an eye on it. From the Spanish conquistadors. Not on the tourist maps because it's too out of the way."

"How far?"

"Fifty miles east at the Orinoco River."

"We got one!" Riley said, then turned the screen toward them. "The last is old Gael. From a ninth-century manuscript, *Book of Kells*. It means 'hollow of the glen.' "

"No glens here, so it must mean a valley," Logan said.

"Moon river?" Sebastian said.

"I'd like to buy a vowel," Max said and Tessa laughed. "There's a trick, something we're not seeing. She loves puzzles, they wouldn't be easy to decipher." Max turned the map counterclockwise and pointed. "Now it looks Cyrillic."

"You're just asking for trouble now," Tessa said, turning it back upright. "All the rest read upright. We have to take this as a whole, but read individually."

"The moon is full at around midnight, so the Luna god could be seen," Max said. "That's the vision part. But this icon that points directly above it?" It was a broad, short figure with its head back and mouth wide open. A beam shot from the mouth and hit a moon. "Sun and moon, in direct conflict with each other?"

"That's at dusk. Yeah, so here at dusk"—Logan pointed to the first few symbols—"then here at midnight."

"And do what?" Max asked.

"Hell if I know."

"Find the eye," she said. "Journey till dusk, at the river, see the moon and find the center of the eyeball. Makes perfect sense." To a loon, maybe.

"It's not letting me run the next one," Riley said. He tapped the same keys, then left his chair and went to the black duffel. He pulled out a cell phone and turned it on. "We have no signal." He moved around the room with the phone, looking for a signal, then tried the others and got nothing.

Logan turned to the computer and tapped the keys. "Damn. The wireless is gone, too."

Men scrambled.

"We're blown," Logan said. "They've shut down or blocked all the signals in the area."

"What? They know we're here?" She stepped back out of the way. "How was that possible?"

"Better resources." Logan was already turning to the hall-way.

Clever ones, she thought, and the men started packing gear they hadn't really unpacked yet. As soon as one was full, Max rushed to the door with black duffels. Riley was breaking down the electronics. The computers were speed printing.

"What about the map?"

"We have the first few." He grabbed the printer pages, slipped them into an envelope and handed it to her. "It will have to be enough. Max?" He tossed him a set of keys. "Bring the jeep to the front." Max hurried out the door while Logan filled a backpack with God knew what. Then he dug in a smaller duffel and pulled out a prepacked syringe. "Come here."

"My shots are updated," she said and didn't move.

"It's a biomarker, in case we get separated."

"That's not in my plans." Yet she rolled back her sleeve. He swabbed and injected her.

"Max and Riley can track us if we need help. They'll dissolve in seventy-two hours," he said when she rubbed the spot.

"Sort of like those things for dogs?"

He smiled. "Yes." Then with a fresh syringe, he injected himself.

"Did you create this?" She'd never heard of one that dissolved.

"With Max, yes."

God, she was glad he was smart. "Just don't lose me, okay?"

Her tone made him look up. Engrossed in the team removing gear, fear colored her features. He came to her. "Not when you just came back from the dead." She met his gaze, her lips curving. "We'll be okay. This is what I do." He touched her for a moment, then turned and slung gear.

Then Riley was out the door, Logan behind him with Tessa. Riley put equipment in the chopper, the wind forcing Tessa to braid her hair. She tied it off with a scarf as Sebastian lifted off in the chopper. Logan stashed his pack, then hurried to the SUV. They set frequencies on radios and discussed options. She really wanted a bed and some sleep, but settled for coloring her lips.

The men were suddenly fascinated with watching her apply lip gloss.

"Tessa, I don't think we'll see anyone in the dark."

"You never know when a good lipstick will save the day." She smacked her lips together and smiled, then through the window, handed Max an NGS business card. "My satellite phone." Max took it, and Tessa and Logan climbed into the jeep.

He didn't put it in gear, scowling at the other truck. "If you think you're leaving me behind, don't."

"It'll be rough." He'd feel better if she was safe with the guys.

Tessa scoffed. "Just what do you think I've been doing for the past eleven years, getting my hair done? My job is outdoors. What's at the end of that thing is keeping me from a life I really loved and I want it back."

He put the jeep in gear, and they rattled down the drive. "I could just shoot Ramos for you."

Logan said it so dryly she wondered if he meant it. It wouldn't matter. If she was found out by the wrong person, she'd be dead. Instantly.

They had barely reached the city when Tessa's satellite

phone rang and, frowning, she answered it, then put it on speaker.

"We're out of the block range and we have the next one from Tessa's professor," Max said. "You're not going to like it."

"Work on that pessimism, will you?" Logan said. "It's depressing."

Max chuckled. "It's a date. Today's. The full moon is tonight, right now."

Tessa peered out the window. The moon was already coming up.

Logan checked his watch. The silence was telling.

"Yes, that's right, sports fans," Max said like a game-show host. "You have two hours till dusk."

And over a hundred miles to go.

In the distance, a figure sat on the hill and through binoculars, followed the cars rolling down to the street. He watched till they vanished under the cover of trees. Then he lifted a radio to his mouth, climbing down. "They're moving again."

Eight

"What do you mean we're too late? It's been out there for hours." McGill didn't need an answer, he suddenly knew. "Get me everything on this woman, and trace that, find out who's in our business because other than Dragon One, guys, we are the last line of defense."

"I'm honored, sir," Walker said, and turned sullenly to the screen. He glanced to his left at David Lorimer and whispered, "He won't believe it."

"Yes, he will. You got to trust him, bud."

"Sir?" Walker turned in the chair. "I know who had it. Elizabeth Jacobs. She had a lock on the file, so it probably flagged her."

"You broke in?"

Walker cringed a little. "Well, yes, sir. You said everything and the computer includes records of deceased."

"Excellent," the general said. "Can you track her without her knowledge?"

Walker's features pulled tight.

"Last line," McGill reminded. "Even if it's from within."

"Yes, sir."

"Do it." Give her enough rope, McGill thought, and sat back in his chair. "I want everything on this Petruscu woman." He would honor the marker, but he'd be damned if he'd do it without knowing everything.

* * *

The jeep sped farther from the city, the textured walls of haciendas giving way to the barrio of corrugated steel walls and tilting doors. Then there was nothing, fewer people, and abandoned cars peppered the side of the road, stripped of anything useful. They left the state highway and the roads were unpaved, little more than gravel on a path.

Tessa didn't think her butt could slam into a seat any harder. "We need a plane."

"I doubt anyone would fly at night," he said.

"I could."

He eyed her, surprised.

"Bush pilot license helps with the job. I'm just not familiar with this area. But there are airports all over the place on the river, Cessnas to charter."

"We're trying not to be seen. We're wanted, remember."

"Darn, how could I forget that."

"You're not fond of rivers, are you?"

"Not around here. On the Amazon, I saw a man taken down for a dinner roll." A croc grabbed its victim, took them deep and rolled continuously until it was dead, then stuffed the carcass somewhere in its nest. "He kept screaming for us to kill him." Just the thought of it made her wish this would fall through and she could be elsewhere. "We couldn't. No one was armed except him."

They went over a deep rut and Tessa's teeth clicked. Logan shrugged an apology and slowed but it didn't do anything for the rocking. The thick wheels crawled over the uneven ground and they were tipped back so far Tessa thought, *We're falling to Hell*. The jeep front hit and she swore her eyes fell out.

"I think faster is easier on my rear."

"But we're here."

"Oh, good, 'cause I was going to really start whining."

"Start?" Smiling, Logan stopped the jeep, left the head-lights on and got out.

Tessa followed, rubbing her fanny as she looked around. The lights from a town up the river glowed against the purple sky. Logan moved to the front of the jeep and worked a palm-sized computer. The TDS Recon screen glowed, illuminating his face.

She leaned in and could see them as thermal dots. "Pretty soon you won't have to leave your command post."

"It's a handy little thing," he said, working the buttons and tiny keys. It was broad and short with a five-inch screen.

"That one of those Blueberry black-tooth things?"

He looked at her, unimpressed. "You're pitiful."

"That just means my social life is better. What happened to a compass and ka-bar knife?"

"Oh, we still have that. It's for those times when I can't just delete the enemy."

She smiled, then studied the map before he checked the GPS against his wrist compass watch, then tucked it away. He drew out a waterproof packet and slipped out what looked like a hearing aid. He put one in his own ear, then leaned, gesturing, and Tessa held back her hair.

"Another toy?"

"This one is all Max," he said, and she frowned.

"I don't hear anything."

He took several steps away, then said, "You have to be at least two feet away. Max is working on that, but you hear with the vibrations." He kept his voice low. "It's short range, too, only about a hundred feet."

"Okay, this toy I like." Then she reared back when Logan drew out a long machete.

"We have less than an hour."

"And here I thought we'd be rushed." He turned into the rain forest and Tessa muttered, "It would have been easier to fly."

Salazar walked away from the plane, two men behind him. A thin old man came out to check the aircraft, but Salazar ignored him, striding to the waiting vehicle. His men loaded necessary gear, then one climbed behind the wheel. Salazar sat in the rear and opened the laptop. Eloisa had given him the first locations.

She hadn't been difficult to convince since he'd squeezed the couple out of hiding. He hadn't located them exactly, but now he knew where they were headed and why. Yet, like them, he didn't know what he'd find. Eloisa had refused to say. Salazar considered forcing her, but then again he could walk away from this with simply killing them all right now. Like her, he wanted to play the game.

The truck raced into the dark toward the Orinoco River.

Riley drove. Max jammed the adapter into the lighter, then flipped open the laptop. He thumped the side, waiting for the screen to appear. "They made it there." He frowned. "But they're moving really fast."

Riley glanced, heading north. "We shouldn't have split up."

"Logan can handle it." Tessa was no slouch, either, Max thought, and wondered what she was hiding. His imagination easily came up with all sorts of scenarios, but none of them fit her personality.

Max gave him directions to a hotel. They needed to be stationary to track and get them to the next step.

Under the midnight moon.

It sounded like the title of a novel.

Tessa's boots squished in the mushy ground as she hurried after Logan. They had minutes. "What could be at the end?" she asked aloud.

"You'd have to understand her motives first."

"She likes handbags and puzzles, what's to know? Maybe she's stashed her new Vuitton bag out here? Or she wants all the muffins and bagels in the land?"

He looked back at her, deadpan. "You can actually talk and run?"

"Sorry. I'm free associating."

Logan hacked at the underbrush until he found a path, and they took it toward the river. Tessa kept close, their way spilling with moonlight. She heard the lap of the water and hurried with him.

"This is it." He moved faster and they rushed on to the shore, stopping short at the edge.

Tessa inched back a little farther and shined the flashlight but saw nothing except a mass of green. "Could it be any darker? There has to be something obvious here." She handed over the flashlight and walked a few paces, pushing at ferns and palms tightly packed on the ground.

Logan looked at his watch. "It's now," he said, frustration in his tone as he walked the edge of the small clearing that was no wider than a bed. Softly rounded boulders edged along the shore, worn away from the yearly flooding, looking like beached whales in the dark.

"What are we supposed to find? Eyes? Big rocks?" Tessa climbed the dense plants, over a rock, then turned back as Logan pushed at branches, tearing up vines and digging through the vegetation. "It's not here," she said, out of breath. She was beginning to agree with Sebastian. It was a wild-goose chase.

A few feet away from him, her boot hit a stone, and she stumbled. Logan rushed to catch her, holding till she got her footing. Tessa looked back, and Logan shined the flashlight over the ground. She bent and felt the earth, brushed at the leaves, pulling a maze of vines, then she went down on her knees, digging.

"I feel an angled edge."

A small folding shovel appeared in her line of vision and she took it, digging deep and fast. He drew his knife and cut through the roots bordering the area near her. She pushed away the sandy soil and exposed the small pyramid-shaped stone.

She sat back. "Ta-da." The top was flat and carved with the shape of an eye.

"Excellent." He squatted, then compared it to the symbol in the map. The same crude symbol chipped into the stone. The eye.

"It has to be thousands of years old. I wonder if there's more," she said, glancing.

"We don't have time for a National Geographic expedition."

"Yeah, well, you've seen one thousand-year-old marker, you've seen 'em all." She straightened, her gaze on the shore. "There were docks here once." Then she stepped on the marker, and he frowned. "The document said in the center of the eye. Not beside it." She looked around herself, then straight up. The moon was directly over her and it felt almost warm in the darkness, a cool breeze pushing at the treetops.

"No trap, no clap of thunder. I knew it was too good to be true."

Yards before her, the water was mirror flat, the trees reflecting as if from under the surface. The breeze shifted the bushes.

"There must be more," she said softly, and standing on the rock she turned slowly, searching the ground, the trees. Water lapped at the shore, the hum of the jungle sizzling with snaps and chirps. She stopped, then lowered the flashlight. "Stand behind me," she said, and he did. "Look to the center, then left." She shined the beam over the area, then moved it away.

Something glittered from under the brush, an overhang of branches, the roots washed away from the floods. "There. In the water." She pointed left. "There's something under that tree." The banyan hung over the water, the end of the branch dipping the surface.

"Probably anaconda," he said, yet stepped into the water.

She grabbed his arm. "This water is a breeding ground for them."

He met her gaze. "We have to have it. We can't go on because this map doesn't make a damn bit of sense." He handed her a weapon. "Protect my back."

She took it, the gun felt heavy in her hand, almost offensive.

Logan waded into the water, his legs disappearing under the surface in increments. Her heart beat a little faster, and she speared the light over the stagnant water. A soft slosh and she knew he was trying to keep from breaking the surface too much. He reached the roots, pushing up the overhang and ducking under it. She expected to see the curl of an anaconda. They sensed warmth and vibration. *And they eat you whole down here,* she thought. She heard a scraping sound and shined the light on him as he pulled a small canoe from under the drape of Mother Nature.

When he was clear of the vines, he climbed in and picked up a paddle, sweeping toward her. Long and narrow, the Indian canoe was a familiar sight on the river. Flat bottomed and hulled from a solid tree, it had the look of a kayak. The metal was something in the bow, small and near the rim.

This changes things, she thought. It meant that the map was real and each site had a purpose.

Logan neared, and Tessa watched the water for movement, but the only ripple was from the paddle. The hull scraped onto the shore and he climbed out, pulling it higher.

"No motor, just two oars."

"I knew I would have to work this job," she said, handing back the gun, then was beside him, kneeling to see the metal. "It's the next symbol." The river. Three wavy lines scored into a small metal rectangle.

"I noticed. We're on the right track."

"To where?"'

"At dusk, here, at midnight in the glen," he said.

"The hollow of the glen is downriver?"

"Theoretically." Logan drew out the Recon. The TDS Recon was a handheld computer with GPS, wireless net, phone, e-mail—the works. "There's a valley, this river splits into it. A hollow is the deepest point." He stared at the skyline, then at the GPS.

She leaned in. "The water level dips geographically, downhill after the bend. But it is just as wide and shouldn't be too rough."

"Max might have the next symbol deciphered by then," he said.

"And we can't go back." Tessa looked behind herself, wondering when that man would appear. An innocent man killed in the streets meant they were capable of anything.

Stowing his toy, Logan pushed the canoe into the water. Tessa pulled her pack onto both shoulders, then stepped in, the little boat rocking hard until she sat in the damp bottom. Logan was on his knees in front of her less than five inches away.

She took up the other paddle and dug into the water. "Somehow I never imagined you doing this."

"You actually thought about it?"

She stared at his broad back. He was the one man who'd left such an indelible mark on her that she couldn't forget him, or what it felt like to be in his arms. "When you're alone and scared, you think about every event in your life and the choices you made. Or didn't."

"Regrets?" He understood perfectly. "I've done that."

"You? You plan everything, how could you ever make a bad choice?"

He twisted to look at her. "I'm not that much of a tight ass, am I?"

She met his gaze dead on. "A little stiff. But then you're older."

"Hey, I remember you being—"

"A nervous wreck?"

"A little prim." He glanced. "Well, there was that one time . . ."

She laughed softly. "I broke out of my shell. Amazing what a little freedom will do for a girl."

Suddenly he twisted, using his oar to stop her from putting hers in the water. "Croc to your right."

She snapped a look, mesmerized as the hard, uneven scales rolled above the water, then disappeared under the surface. She was glad he was paying attention. "I'll take that gun back now."

"Nunchuck him to death."

"Don't think I won't," she said and adjusted the weapon for easy reach.

Logan chuckled to himself.

It died when the quiet cracked with gunfire.

Paul Ramos stepped out of the helicopter and rushed into the residence, ignoring everyone to find a bathroom and privacy to lose his dignity. He wished Garcia was alive and suffering this crap. It angered him more that he couldn't figure out how they were giving him anything. He bore no markings, his food was tasted by others and his water from bottles.

After rinsing his mouth and brushing his teeth, he stared at the face in the mirror, wondering why he'd prided himself on his looks when he'd grow old with an unremarkable face. The surgeon had done an excellent job with implants, considering a bullet had ripped through his cheek. Countless scars marred his body, and disguising them from Eloisa was his only concern. She was far more interested in keeping him contained away from the public and upset that she couldn't.

The first week he was still feeling the pain of the surgery and getting tossed in the crash that took Garcia and his bodyguards. His recovery was too slow and he figured something else was controlling it. He just didn't know who. Eloisa was his prime candidate. She was absent enough that he could search the entire residence and had found the puzzle boxes. He'd gone to Caracas, had been in Garcia's offices and through his papers. He'd mastered the man's signature, turned funds designated for socialist parties into health care for the poor. Garcia had wanted that and it was the least he could do for destroying his government. He'd studied the man, but his wife was another matter.

He left the rooms, walking into the office. There was nothing left to find. He'd been all over the building, and turned back, walking slowly toward her suite of rooms. Garcia, it had been reported, had taken separate rooms after a year in office. He probably got a taste of her ambition.

Leaning on the cane, he walked slowly through a wide

hallway, and took the stairs, pushing to the second floor. Servants passed him, and he nodded and kept moving. They each looked prepared to catch him should he fall. He hated it. His anger over his helplessness frothing in him, he had to keep from confronting Eloisa. He'd learn nothing if she knew he was aware of her moves.

He stopped in the hall, his hand on a wall, and he closed his eyes, willing his uneven balance to straighten up and fly right. It was another ten minutes before he could take a step alone.

A soft click sounded somewhere behind him and he turned.

The wall was open, the cut seamless and disguised by molding. He pulled at the edge, the glow of screens drawing him inside. Quickly, he sealed the door, then strained to see the systems.

"Well, well, the heartbeat of the house," he said and sat at the console, familiar with the surveillance. He pulled up the last few weeks of video.

Eloisa didn't know of this, he thought, smiling to himself as he watched her climb onto his lap. The stream stopped and he frowned, and all attempts to pull it up failed. Erased. He checked the file's last access and realized someone had recorded it before erasing it. Salazar topped his list.

He watched a stream of himself sleeping and wondered at the camera position. It gave a view of the bed, and he realized the camera was somewhere near the fireplace. He was about to shut it off when Eloisa appeared in the frame, approaching the bed slowly.

She stopped beside it, leaning over him, and she held a swab of cotton in her right hand. She stroked down the right side of his throat. Instinctively he touched the spot. There was no mark, no burn.

Then he noticed she was wearing a latex glove.

The bullet pierced the water to his right, barely missing the wood canoe. The second shot hit the side, imbedding in the wood hard enough to feel the impact. Logan turned the boat, paddling faster. Tessa mimicked, keeping low.

Another shot cracked in the dark, the impact sounding like a hammer hitting wood. "Logan," she hissed, water splashing her knees. "I am not going in that river." She worked furiously. "I'm not."

"I understand, baby, we're not."

He dug to the left. The current grew stronger, the churn of black water boiling.

Tessa helped him steer the boat under the overhang of trees, out of the moonlight, then steadied them. She grabbed a branch to stop the canoe from drifting.

Logan pulled out a pair of night vision binoculars and looked back at the shore. The green glow reflected a vehicle, the edge of the fender and bumper. He could barely make out the figures, but they were moving. "I think it's our buddy."

"Uninvited guests are so rude. How did he find us?"

He kept watching. "He knows as much as we do."

"I figured that. Why?" she whispered, knowing that even with the ear mic, her voice carried over the water.

He met her gaze in the dark. "To stop us?"

Her expression soured. "You must really think I'm dense, huh? No, why him? The wife of the Vice President doesn't give orders to a guy like that. Now the VP could, but me thinks Mrs. Garcia is in cahoots with him, and Ramos is dead-on."

"Probably. But it doesn't change anything. He's here to wipe the slate clean."

Sweepers. "I don't want to be wiped." She surveyed around her, but it was too dark to see anything and they couldn't use the lights or they'd be spotted. "Are we going to ground?" she asked.

He shook his head and whispered, "We'd never have time to get ahead. He knows that. We have to get to the valley at midnight." And so did the hunter.

She let go of the branch and with the paddle, he pushed off, the wood canoe floating swiftly on the current. The water churned harder, shoving them along and Logan steered, the moon giving him little light as they neared the valley. Mountains rose around them, the tree line silhouetted in silver against the black sky. Branches floated past like lifeless bodies rolling on the surface. Logan leaned and dug the wide paddle in, sliding them around the bend as the river split, a tributary blending into the valley between sloping mountains.

Tessa searched the darkness for movement and saw it. "They're on the other side of the river," she said.

"They won't stay there."

"*You* need to work on that pessimism."

Then they heard the rumble of a motor. They both turned, and Logan sighted through the night vision binoculars as they coasted on the water. "He's got a boat. We have to get off this river."

"I'm all for that," she said, digging in, the wood canoe slicking over the surface. She gripped the edge as it rocked hard and Logan pointed it to the bank. Minutes passed, the shore feeling farther away with each stroke till the bottom of the boat scraped the ground. It was a glorious sound.

Logan went over the side, splashing to pull the boat onto land, then reached for her. He gripped her waist and lifted her out, then urged her with him. He moved north on the shoreline, and they climbed over thick fan palms and spiky bushes. He stopped, sighted on their predators. A black Zodiac made the curve, showered in moonlight.

"He's armed better than us, too." He handed her the binoculars and she looked.

The boat had a machine gun mounted in the center. "I count four."

The men weren't the problem, Logan thought. A .50 caliber machine gun could cut through the forest faster than a logger.

"We're at the deepest point or darn close. What's the next icon?"

Ducking back from the shore, Logan motioned for her to

move ahead, and they went deeper into the jungle. The air was motionless, the slightest sound magnified. Logan drew out his palm computer, using his body to shield the glow.

"White orchids?" He shook his head, confused.

"Orchids grow in trees down here. How long do we have?" It was midsummer, dusk was at nine.

"About an hour."

Tessa groaned and walked deeper, but although the moon was bright, in the forest it was nonexistent. "How are we going to find white orchids now?"

The motorboat drew closer.

"Quickly." He covered the little boat with branches, and together they moved deeper into the woods, then Logan stopped and went to ground, watching the water.

Tessa crouched beside him.

The noise of the water covered any sound they'd make but the motor hummed loudly. Logan simply waited. They appeared in his line of vision and while their faces were covered, they were prepared, outfitted with night vision, assault weapons, and then there was the .50 cal.

Logan checked his watch. "They won't give up anytime soon." He looked at the Recon. "We're a couple hundred yards from our target."

"Can we make it?"

The motorboat turned, fighting the current less than thirty yards from them.

"Let's try; we aren't getting back on the water with stalker boy there."

"Agreed."

Logan turned with her, and moved on instinct, keeping the water to his right. He couldn't chop at the underbrush, forced to climb over boulders and use the hanging roots to swing across a creek. On the other side, they stopped and Tessa asked for the Recon, then walked a few more yards and stopped near a tree.

"We're at the deepest point in the valley," she said, breathless. She handed it back, then dragged her sleeve across her sweaty forehead. The tree was just a couple feet from the water.

"That's a big tree," he said. "I've got some rope." He started to take off his pack.

"Don't need it. I can make that branch."

"It's twenty feet up."

She shouldered off her pack, then backed up several yards. Before Logan could say anything, she bolted in a hard run, then spring jumped. She sailed straight for the lowest branch, and grabbed it underhanded. It dipped with her weight and her body shot straight out, level with the branch, and her hips hit the branch straight on. She used the force to push off and like a boomerang, her body in a perfect tight line shot backward and swung up into a handstand.

She balanced for a second, and then slowly bent her lower body till her boots touched the same branch. She straightened, looking down.

"That was amazing."

She blew him a kiss, bowing. "All compliments readily accepted. Been doing it since I was three." She didn't waste a moment and climbed, patting the branch to make sure it wasn't something living, and feeling for the angle before she grabbed on to the next.

Logan watched the river through the trees. The motorboat was moving slowly, making circles on the water. The sound carried and she looked down at him, giving him a *"What's going on?"* look. Logan waved her on, tapping his watch.

Tessa stood inside the branches, and with his night vision goggles, searched for white orchids. The NVGs were state-of-the-art, giving her distance and coordinates, but as she scanned slightly left, she saw it. They'd have seen it from the river, too, she thought. A tree stood taller by comparison, the top branches spread wide and nestled with white flowers as big as her head. In the moonlight, the flowers had a beautiful pearly glow like a strand draped inside its wooden arms.

She maneuvered down, then dropped to the ground and straightened.

He smiled widely and it felt like a bolt to her chest. God, he was so handsome when he did that.

"I saw orchids. They're in a single, very big tree, that way around the bend." She pointed. "In the top. White orchids beneath you. I think we'll have to climb that tree, too."

"Well, clearly, that's your job."

She smiled. He wasn't afraid of heights. The man jumped out of airplanes. "One problem."

He eyed her.

"It's on the other side of the river."

Salazar adjusted the NVGs and waited for the couple to appear. He enjoyed this match, both seeking an elusive prize at the end of the rainbow. He smirked at his own eloquence and zoomed in on the shore. His man threw the engine into REVERSE, and the boat spun like a ball in boiling water.

He pushed the goggles to his forehead, the moonlight stinging his eyes for a moment. His gaze swept to the tree line matched against the sky. They were on foot and he could out-distance them easily, but wasn't ready to end this. Eloisa had told him enough, where they were headed, but not what they'd find. She was growing impatient and it wouldn't be long before she included him in the final prize. Till it was necessary, he wouldn't concern himself.

Until then, he had people working on the guide, but clearly this man had more knowledge. Yes, he thought, moving to the mounted machine gun. This would be a very good game.

Nine

Forty yards behind them, it hit.

Like a barrage from a fire team of Marines, bullets chipped a line through the trees. At the first shot, Logan swallowed Tessa in his arms and rolled with her behind the tree.

He looked down at her, arching a brow. "He's getting impatient."

"I'd hate to see him pissed off." How could Logan be so calm? Just a few yards away, a tree was severed in half.

He shifted to sight on the water, his body still shielding hers. The boat was upriver, the machine gunner masked and ready to fire again. Carefully, he reached for the rope.

She put out a hand to stop him. "We could go up."

"It won't be long before he shoots there too." With a jerk, he yanked, then coiled it.

"This guy is really wearing on my good nature."

He slung the coiled rope over his head and under his arm. "We keep going. He thinks we're back there," he said, nodding behind.

"And he's pushing us forward. Hello? He wants to kill us."

"No doubt." He looked at her. "You're taking that rather well."

"I'm counting on you being smarter than him and, so far, you're doing a fine job." She stumbled, slapped her hand on a branch, and steadied herself. "We deserve it, that's what floors me. We're the bad guys this time."

"Not getting any argument from me."

"Keep talking like that and you'll turn into a Democrat." She looked to the river and could see little more than flickers of movement. Reflections on the water, or boat guy, she didn't know.

"Let's keep moving." Logan angled toward the river, Tessa behind him. Moving in different patterns would give them a fighting chance, and he froze when more gunfire swept back and forth behind them, then suddenly stopped. He could hear only the rush of water, the roar of the motor and he hurried toward the river, then went to ground. Tessa slid down beside him. Through binoculars, he followed the rigid inflatable boat as it motored toward the banks. Then he curled back and from his pack, drew out a small canister.

Tessa smiled, patting him. "Good commando."

He grinned. "Move back and stay low."

She obeyed, hunkered down and watched as he crawled on all fours closer to the water and out from under the shield of trees. He kept himself behind the whale shaped stones and she could barely see him in the dark. Then he lobbed the charge, and scrambled back to her. They ran several yards before the charge dropped into the motorboat, flashlights jerking in search but too late.

The explosion ripped like an orange flower opening, fire boiled in tight clouds, the smoke pale in the dark. The force blew a man out of the boat, the others jumping after him as the machine gun tipped, sinking through the bottom. Tessa was mesmerized.

"Amazing what a little Satchel charge can do," he said, smiling as he gripped her hand, pulling her with him as he hurried over brush and rocks. The river twisted right, widening, and Logan crouched, drawing his weapon again.

The boat sank swiftly. He searched the water for a body, and spotted a figure frantically reaching for the rocks and debris to stop the wild ride. Logan drew back when he spotted the muzzle flash of gunfire from across the river.

"What is that?" she whispered.

"Drug runners, poachers, or just plain folk. It's a distraction and we'll take it."

Logan led the way, using his machete to slice through just enough underbrush to get them farther from the explosion. He didn't talk and she sensed the urgency in him and kept quiet. He seemed to know where he was going and she was all for getting far away from those guys. The area grew brighter from the town lights in the distance.

"We're going there? Won't he be anticipating that?"

"Yes, and I'd rather have him coming at me in more familiar surroundings." And anywhere that had some light, he thought.

"And if he knows the next one and gets there before us?"

"He's playing with us." Logan didn't doubt it. The man had resources. He'd blocked an entire region's cell towers and if he had the next location, he would have just blown us to hell and been done with it. Logan thought for a moment. "This guy knows that shooting at us in the dark won't get him anything but a tough search for proof later. He did it for the fear factor."

"It's working."

"Yeah, well, I haven't been shot at this much in a long time."

"You're enjoying this, admit it."

He smiled slightly. "Making for a helluva weekend." Logan checked his map for a way to cross. "There's a bridge a half mile downriver and a bunch of little tourist towns, camps for river tours. One between us and the bridge."

"Tell me we are not going to try to cross tonight? We don't have the next pieces yet. It won't be hard to spot in the morning."

"We'd probably need more rope this time."

"I'd like rope, rope is good. Maybe a harness?"

Logan felt rather than heard the thump of footsteps coming fast and he looked back, using the night vision binoculars. A man ran at top speed, the mask was gone.

"Fast as you can, baby. He's out for blood."

"Oh, holy crap."

She had to lift her legs high to get over the weeds and she followed close behind him. He reached back for her once yet kept advancing. Then he pushed her to the left, pointing, and she shook her head.

"Use this, go east, then north. I'll meet you, I'll intercept."

He wrapped her hands around the Recon and forced her to go, then turned to run in the opposite direction, leading the man off.

Logan ran, leaping logs and a gully, making enough noise that the man would follow him and away from her.

In a hotel that cost them the equivalent of a six-pack of beer, Max sat at the small table, eating a Cuban sandwich as he watched the screen and the biomarkers move toward the town. A knock rattled the thin door and he drew his gun, leaving the chair. Through the peephole he saw Sebastian and let him in.

Across from him, Riley rubbed his eyes and worked on streams of video of Ramos.

"I'm getting no word," Max said. "They're moving again, and it's erratic. But we won't have it for long." He had to jump off public satellites, but soon the protection systems would block it. "They're being chased, that's for sure."

Sebastian looked at the screen. "Maybe I can stall them with some fireworks. Keep hailing." He grabbed a radio and headset, slipping the earpiece on and tucking away the radio. Then he found a particular duffel. It had a red stripe on the side.

"They're west, near a bridge," Max said, unplugging the download, then handing him a GPS. "It's got all possible locations of indigenous personnel."

Sebastian scraped the keys off the table and slipped back out.

This would give them choices when they had none.

Tessa hurried as fast as she could in the dark, skidding down a slope, then feeling it rise again. Brambles caught her skin, her clothes, as she tried to get ahead of Logan. Upriver, he was somewhere to her right. She saw a brush of movement, the twist of fronds. It wasn't Logan.

Man in black, she thought. Unmasked this time, he was closer to her than Logan. She let him get a few yards ahead, then she went laterally and approached from behind him, drawing out her nunchuck, one pair in each hand. Then the man stopped and went down on one knee. A black chill swept over her when he shouldered his rifle and sighted in on Logan. She moved more for speed than silence, her gaze locked on the man, and for a second she lost him in the dark. She rushed forward and swung, the nunchuck catching the barrel.

He fired.

The shot went to the left, and she yanked downward on the rifle, then turned to swing the other nunchuck. But he was fast, throwing his elbow back and connecting with her chest. She went flying backward, and hit the ground, knocked breathless for a second, then rolled to her feet, crouching. He turned the rifle on her. Oh, shit. Tessa snapped the second nunchuck, throwing low. It caught him hard behind the knee, and he folded to the ground, discharging a half dozen shots into the trees.

Tessa dove for a nunchuck. He rolled to his side and fired. Bullets chipped the ground near her thigh and she flung to her back, a death grip on the pair of wooden rods and rope. He called her a whore and she spun it, throwing hard. He fired a second shot before the solid wood rod cracked against his temple, driving bone into his brain.

Logan rushed to a stop in time to see it.

The man dropped instantly but he wasn't dead, his body convulsing. Tessa sat up, her gaze locked on the man's bloody head.

Logan moved quickly to the man, assessed, then drew his knife. His back to her, he finished him. He cleaned the blade and turned as he put it away. Tessa just stared, and Logan stripped him of weapons, stashing them before he came to her.

"Look at me, honey, come on." He pulled her from the ground, and she met his gaze.

"Oh, Logan." Her eyes teared, sparkling in the dark. "I killed him."

"No, *I* did." He cupped her face. "You did what you needed to do."

She clung to him, squeezing tight. He buried his face in her hair and relived those few seconds when he'd seen the man aim at her head. He rubbed her arms and she cringed. Frowning, he flicked on the flashlight long enough to see blood on her sleeve.

"Damn, Tessa." Instantly, he tore her shirtsleeve at the shoulder and used it to tightly wrap her upper arm. The gash was deep enough for stitches.

"Ow, your bedside manner needs work, Doc."

"I swear, I'll be gentle next time." He cupped her jaw and shined a light in her eyes, did a quick check for more wounds. Satisfied, they headed north toward the town.

"Won't he be expecting us to head to people?"

"There are a lot of tourists here, foreigners. He doesn't want anything reaching the news media or state departments sending someone to nose around." Logan shook his head. "He's a clever little bastard. He'll flash his badge enough to get answers quickly. That's if he's alive after the blast."

"If he's not, I get to dangle him from the high wire or something. No, an elephant standing on his head." She described other circus deaths as they pushed through the woods toward the bridge. When they met a solid road, they both released a relieved breath. Logan didn't stop and wrapped his arm around her waist and held pressure to her wound. She was losing blood.

He was about to treat her when he spotted a lone cab on the edge of town, and he hailed it. Inside he tightened the bandage, then watched behind as they rode into town. Logan stopped the driver, paid him quickly, then left the car with her.

When he wrapped his arm around her again, she sank into him, feeling her lack of sleep as they walked the quiet avenue. Trucks moved with deliveries, but other than that, at two in the morning the streets were empty. The lights of the hotel beckoned and he strode inside as if he were wearing a thousand-dollar suit and not ten pounds of mud and thirty pounds of gear. The hotel was clean and humble. Tessa felt like a zombie and let him help her along. *Screw feminism, I'm tired,* she thought. He paid cash—very wet cash—and took charge. So much for her control issues.

Logan turned to her, offering a gentle smile. She was standing on her feet but looked asleep. He touched her and she woke like a morning glory.

"Almost there," he said and helped her up one flight, trying to keep pressure on her arm until they were inside the room. Logan closed the curtains, then shouldered off his pack.

"I've been awake for nearly three days. We're here," she said, and pulled off her one-sleeved overshirt and loosened her boots. She punched the pillow and drew back the spread. "I want this day to be over right now." She sat and flopped on the bed.

"No, no. Not yet."

He pulled her upright, then prepared the tools to treat her wound. He gave her an injection. Tessa stared at his face as he put a couple stitches in her arm.

"I didn't feel it."

"You won't for a few hours, either."

"This earn me a purple heart?" she asked, and he frowned

at her slurred speech. He opened a power bar and pushed it into her hand, forcing her to eat.

"I'll give you one of mine."

"One of them? Jeez."

"We can compare scars later." He finished treating her arm and met her gaze. "Don't do that again. Follow the plan."

"We had a plan? He was aiming at you." She popped the last bite into her mouth, smiling around it.

"Then thank you." He kissed her and she laughed, still chewing. "But don't do that again."

Tessa sat still as Logan checked every inch of the little room. From his pack he brought out plastic explosives and rigged something on the window. He tucked a chair under the doorknob and surveyed.

"It's secure."

"You sure?" She looked around. "You don't want to set some claymores at the door, a few grenades in the waste-basket?"

He smiled.

"I love it when you go all commando on me." She shivered dramatically.

"You'd be good at this now. You're strong, resourceful." He removed the ear mic.

She shook her head. "It made me too scared to live. That night, me and you." She gestured between them. "Was more for me."

"I wouldn't say that." It was one night when they were in their twenties. Old memories had a way of being better than they actually were. He sure as hell would like to compare notes, but the woman was barely conscious.

She plucked out the mic and handed it to him. "Guys are always horny," she said, waving that off. She looked a little paler just then, and Logan sat beside her.

She bounced on the bed. "Give you ideas?" She said it with a teasing smile that lightened his mood.

"I don't need a bed for that. There's a reason I can't kiss you. Can't stop at just one."

"I know." She fluffed her hair like a prom queen. "I am hard to resist with my big biceps and calloused hands."

"You didn't have those before."

"No." She looked at her hands.

He turned her face toward his. "I like this woman. And I think you're still afraid."

She searched his face. "Logan, if anyone knew."

"Your secret's safe."

She nodded, then shook her head. "I appreciate you calling in a favor for me. I thought I was free and hoped they forgot about me. But this—" She threw her hands up, then let them fall to her lap, unable to put the last few days into one thought. "It's out of my league again."

"I'll protect you."

"It's not that. I want my life back the way it was."

"Happy?"

"Yes. I really don't want to lose my job. It's more of who I am than what I do. If I didn't need money I'd do it for free. I don't mind the boring parts because I get to be outside and travel. Hell, I've got a little house on the beach in Java."

His brows rose. "You're my new best friend."

"You'd love it. Though I've rebuilt it twice after typhoons." She turned toward him, warming to the subject. "I met the most interesting people, like Dr. Matob. He's Syrian. He's a great man, Logan. I'd hate it if I'd missed knowing him. I love the NGS. I love what they mean, the people. What they do. They've explored incredible cultures, made spectacular discoveries, saved species from extinction . . ."

Logan's smile grew wider and she stopped talking.

"What?"

"I haven't heard anyone talk like that in a long time," he said.

"Don't you love what you do?"

He shrugged. "I like medicine more. But with all that's wrong in the world, this is right, too."

"Putting Ramos here wasn't. Why would they do that?"

"I wasn't privy to the details."

"God. Your blind faith is dangerous."

He made a face at her. "I have the least faith, except in General McGill. He can handle what led to this. It's a problem that needs fixing." He shrugged. "We do what we can."

That kind of devotion was rare, and she could never match it and didn't want to, really—not to any government. Politicians had a long history of screwing up. The NGS, sure, they had her loyalty, and Lord knows she'd witnessed terrible atrocities over the past years that went far beyond a man and a crocodile. She appreciated her country, probably more than the average American. Nearly every trip, she saw people without the simplest of freedoms.

"Why you, Logan? Why Dragon One?"

"General McGill asked us and because of inside intelligence leaks."

She rolled her eyes. "That happens all the time."

"If it did, you would have never gotten away."

"That remains to be seen." She started to stand but he caught her.

"If McGill says he'll bury it, he will."

"I love him already." She smiled and inclined her head to the bed behind them. "So can I sleep now?" She folded into her best begging look.

"Be my guest."

Tessa rolled over the bed to the side. Boots and socks went into a pile, and she pulled off her tee shirt, then noticed he was watching.

"I just had a memory flash."

She smiled. "With a lot of speed and more desperation, too." She met his gaze, and shimmied out of the dirty shorts. "I've lived on that night for a long time."

"I refuse to believe you haven't had sex in eleven years."

"Good, cuz it ain't true." She sent him a sexy glance. "Just never as vigorous."

She stood in a bra and panties and all Logan said was, "Jesus, Tessa." Her body was ripped with muscles.

She looked down at herself. "You've seen it all."

He scoffed. "No, not really." Penthouse sexy, she had sleek curves and defined lines that sent his body into overload, blood rushing to his groin. "Get under those covers, now." He was cocked and loaded, and when she smiled and snapped her panty leg, it took everything in him to stay where he was and not jump on her.

Worse, she knew it.

She crawled on the bed, giving him a splendid view of her behind as she drew down the covers, then slid her long legs in. "God, I love mattresses," she said wiggling into the bed.

"As opposed to what?"

"Grass mats, cots, the sand. Once I hung in a sling on the side of a mountain," she mumbled, closing her eyes. She let out a deep breath and quickly drifted to sleep. He stared at her, and wondered just how long he could keep his hands off her—this time.

He moved to the side of the bed, tucked her in, then turned away to contact the team. After a twenty-minute conversation Logan showered and, like any man with a half-naked woman in his bed, he crawled in beside her.

Salazar jammed the wad of gauze into his shoulder, then with his teeth opened the plastic encasing a syringe. He pulled away the bloody cloth long enough to inject directly into the wound. He clenched his teeth and pushed the plunger. He threw it aside and let out a lungful of air, sinking to the truck's door frame. With one hand he patted his pockets, taking inventory. He'd lost his pistol on the river. He twisted, winced, then reached for a case under the seat and loaded another.

He'd lost one man and didn't know if the others survived. He holstered the gun, then changed the gauze, no longer able to feel the torn flesh. Yet he smiled to himself. It had been a good plan and the flaw was his, for not anticipating his opponent. The man would go to ground, hide and in a much larger area to search. Beyond bringing in reinforcements, and doing a house-to-house search that undoubtedly would generate questions, he had to maintain discretion and change tactics. It made him wonder about the man he was hunting.

Salazar knew nothing of him, not even his nationality. Only one of the men had ever spoken and that was with a German accent. He grudgingly admired their resilience. His resources had failed to locate even a name. It hardly mattered. This was no longer Eloisa's little war, but his, and he would not lose. The difficult path he left behind was enough to know what kind of man he was dealing with now. It pleased him.

Suddenly, Salazar raised his weapon, aiming at the forest when bushes and low branches swayed, disturbed. Then his lieutenant, Juan, appeared. He was dripping wet, breathing hard and his pant legs were shredded. They moved to the rear of the truck and tended to the wounds.

"Tomas and Cheuy are dead."

"We'll retrieve the bodies first," Salazar said.

"They are hiding for the night, probably in Ciudad." Juan inclined his head behind him.

"They are miles away, while we are back where we started. They don't care about that." He flicked his hand to the jeep fifty feet away. "He knows how to run to hide." He shook his head slowly. "We wait."

Salazar knew where the man was going next and planned to be there first. He pushed away from the truck and went to the jeep, inspecting it, but didn't find anything useful. He nosed around the car as Juan closed the rear of the truck and jingled the keys. He was at the driver's door.

"Stop!" Salazar darted near but stopped short, motioning to Juan.

Juan backed away from the truck and Salazar pointed to the ground. "Someone else. Big feet."

Salazar put his own inside a footprint. It was easily two sizes larger, and recent. From his position, he looked around, his brows knitting. "Why have they touched nothing?"

Juan followed the prints around the front of the truck and back. "The prints lead into the woods."

Salazar kept shining his light over the area, then stepped back, tapping Juan, and they walked a distance away near the jeep. "Let us be careful with these men." He took the key ring from Juan and pressed the truck's auto start.

The explosion blew him back over the jeep's hood.

When he came to, it was daylight and his truck was still there, minus four tires and rims. Nothing else was damaged. Not even the paint job.

Tessa woke when the sun was setting again. The warm body tucked to hers made her shift gently in the bed. It had been a while since she'd woken up next to a man. When it came to sex, it never happened at her place. She needed the option to leave as soon as it became uncomfortable. Sort of a guy mentality, but closeness wasn't something she allowed herself in the past years. She scooted back and didn't touch him but let her gaze travel down his long body. Shirtless and wearing only jeans, he looked damn good. She noticed a multitude of scars, a couple left by bullets. Her hands itched to touch him, but she wasn't in a position to start anything with him, and quick sex would never be enough, not with Logan. Not this time.

But her body was craving him.

Quietly, she slid from the bed, gathering her things, and went into the bathroom. She showered and as she'd done a hundred times before, she washed her clothes in the tub. Fresh water and soap were luxuries sometimes in the field. She liked her comforts as much as any woman. Slipping into fresh underwear and a tee shirt, she took the phone into the bathroom to call room service. She was halfway through ordering a huge meal when she heard Logan stir. She came back into the bedroom, and something shifted inside her when he reached for her in his sleep. Tessa gave in to impulse, cancelled the order then slipped into the bed with him. He never opened his eyes as he pulled her into the curve of his body. She felt safe and protected, sinking quickly back to sleep.

And tucked close, Logan smiled.

* * *

Nolan Deets's focus was no longer pieces of a charred stateroom, but the accounts that had paid for the trip from Basuo Port, Hainan Province, China, to Miami. There were layers of encryption and routers that took the payment across the cyber waves, siphoning it into various bank accounts before it landed in a Grand Cayman Bank. The Fort Knox of security. Nolan had already punctured a few international laws to get this far. One more wouldn't hurt.

He'd have to write a program for it.

While he worked he listened to sporadic conversations, bits and pieces snagged from the airwaves, communications from a dozen factions and from the military.

Five hours skipped by before he cracked the account. A company and an account, but no name. Yet with the account number, he worked to find deposits and transfers, and when an impressive portfolio came up, spewing a gig of data, Nolan understood that his speculations had just turned into a solid lead.

In a direction that would rock a few more people besides the accountants.

Logan woke with a start, instantly took in his surroundings, then sank into the pillows. Across the room, Tessa sat at the only table, reading, already dressed and eating.

"Hi," she said, smiling. "Hungry? We have coffee." From a carafe, she poured him a cup. "And I didn't even get shot at once."

"Excellent, you're promoted." Logan left the bed and came to her, took the cup.

She nudged a plate of pastries toward him. "They're great. Calories galore."

He took one, biting into it when he wanted just to kiss her, then leaned close to read the papers. It was the map translation printout; he'd forgotten he'd given it to her.

"There is another eye symbol, then water, and I don't know the rest. It's only four more."

Logan grabbed his phone and dialed Max and after a quick conversation he did something with TDS Recon. "Max is sending it here. Dr. Matob translated the last words . . . *Into the hands of the Taipan.*"

"Not Taipei?"

"Max double-checked it."

"Into the hands of a foreign business leader, in China? Because that's what it means. Years ago, it was the warlord of the era, but *the* Taipan is a non-Chinese business tycoon." Centuries past there was a huge competitiveness with the spice and silk trade that usually ended in a sea battle to keep it. "*What* into the hands of the Taipan?" she muttered, confused. She flipped through the printed pages. "It doesn't say what you'll see from the tree."

"If we could figure this one"—he pointed to the eye—"we could skip the next, maybe get ahead of him."

She shook her head. "Not when each one has given us something for the next."

He shrugged, conceding.

"Okay, so we have 'the white orchids beneath you.' The home of Isis? Here?" Her wave encompassed the country as a whole and she shook her head. "That's Egyptian or pagan, which depends entirely on your view of religion and the universe, but Isis? Might as well be an Irish artifact."

"I'm surrounded by pessimists. Think puzzle. Nothing is as it seems." With his coffee Logan went to his duffel, checking his gear. "We need to get some more rope."

"Just be sure you have enough bullets and grenades."

"Don't worry, I'll be packing."

"Honey, you already are."

Her gaze slid over him and the reality of him was far better than any fantasy she'd worked up over the years. Barechested, a delight in itself, he sipped his coffee, his gaze on her, not her body or anything else, but her face. It was intense and she felt it down to her bones. Her gaze slipped to his jeans, the top button open. She wanted to peel those off and get busy with him. His lips quirked, as if reading her mind.

She started to leave the chair and come to him, then hesitated and met his gaze. "I'm really hating these people right now."

Logan understood and carefully set aside his cup. He wanted to cross the room, to taste her again, ravish her like a king to the conquered. He'd been waiting, in a sense, eleven years to do it again, and the sexual heat between them was just under the surface, waiting for ignition. He wanted blast off right now.

"The map," she reminded him, recognizing the look in his eyes. "Bad guys. Ancient symbols."

"You're all business, aren't you?"

Smiling widely, she reached for her pack. "Get dressed, Logan. Before I get you out of those jeans."

He chuckled and obeyed, but the image stayed with him all morning and played havoc on his concentration.

Near the peak of dawn, they were on the road to the bridge. Hitching a ride with a local bringing produce to market, Logan and Tessa sat on the back of the truck, holding on and bouncing. "We couldn't afford a car?"

He smiled as they bounced across the bridge in rhythm with the other vehicles.

When it slowed at the end, they hopped off. Logan handed the driver some folded bills, waved, and then they headed down a sightseeing path. The tour buses moved past, rolling toward the next town upriver.

Logan and Tessa walked off the path, Logan following the GPS to the location of the tree.

"I see it," she said and started running.

Logan kept up with her, passing a man with a cart and donkey moving up the steep hillside.

Tessa stood about twenty feet from the tree, staring up. "I'm glad we have rope."

"Whoa," Logan said. "This has to be five hundred years old."

"She looks good for her age." Tessa dropped her pack and

unloaded, keeping her passport and credentials pouch on her, then pulling together her climbing gear. He realized what a pro she was when he saw how fast she adjusted the harness, clipped herself in, then tested her line.

"You know . . . It's a rare man that gives over the lead to a woman," she said. "Especially in a situation like this."

He smiled. "Honey, you're a lot faster than I am and we're targets. I can't watch your back if I'm watching my hands." The base of the tree was the size of a truck, and the first branch was thirty feet up and nearly ten feet wide. It was spectacular. "Ever tree climbed?"

"Counting this trip?" she asked. "No. But I like new experiences."

Logan stepped back and swung a lasso, gaining speed with each turn. The end was weighted with a flashlight.

"Well, you're just all sorts of hidden skills."

"Sam Wyatt's our usual pilot. He's a rancher."

"Somehow, I think that was a really boring workday for you."

He smiled and threw. The rope sailed over the branch, the weighted end dropping over the side. She grabbed on, dragging enough line to anchor it. The rope was a safely line: Tessa had climbed a lot of rocks and mountains with nothing but a resin bag and some water, but not a tree. It wasn't like it had hand and footholds between the branches.

Logan held the rope and Tessa used the line to climb up to the first branch. When she was on top, she turned to anchor for him. He was beside her without much effort. Logan remained on the branch as wide as a sidewalk and fed her rope. She couldn't use a spring-loaded camming device. There were no crevasses, so she drove in an eye pin every few feet, hooked a carabiner to it and her rope, then continued.

The orchids grew right above her, tucked in the bend of the branches like snow.

"I can see something but it's still too dense. I have to go higher."

"Dare I say be careful?"

"If I couldn't do it, I'd tell you."

Yet she made it look effortless, her tanned arms straining to pull herself up. The girl had some strength, he thought. The branches grew narrower, her khaki shirt and green shorts making it difficult to see her. She stopped, her back braced to the trunk, and after looking around with the binoculars, she did it again.

"Some sort of mound at eleven o'clock."

The orchids were beneath her now, little white clouds like offerings from elves.

"It looks like the same marker back on the shore. Only bigger. A pyramid of stones or grass but flat on top." She gave him the coordinates showing on the binoculars, then started down. "I didn't see a symbol."

"We have a good mile and a half to travel."

With the clink of carabiners and the slide of rope, she scaled rapidly down. When they reached the first broad branch, she sat and mopped her throat and face with a scarf.

"You have to give Eloisa credit. It's a clever map. Granted, it plays to her love of puzzles, and her personal enjoyment."

Logan was too aware that this could be a ruse, and for nothing. "What scares me is what's at the end."

"Try not to be a downer, it makes wrinkles."

He smiled at that.

"I bet it's something stupid, like a pair of shoes." She hoped, but knew it wasn't anything close.

"I'm still trying to wrap my brain around that woman as a threat."

"Hey, she reminds me of my mom. Deal with that, why don't you? I can say with some authority she didn't make this journey." Not in Prada heels and a Givenchy suit. She coiled rope and started down to the ground. "She either wants to ride on Gutierrez's coat tails or run for office herself."

"With Ramos gone, she could."

Tessa held the safety rope as Logan slid down. "She needs him. Without him she's just the ex-Mrs. VP. The fact that she's a woman barely comes into play. The President would appoint someone, or follow their constitution. Gutierrez has a mix of Castro lovers and haters along with the military leaders who were part of the coup." It was a really screwed-up government that kept the traitors on after the betrayal. "He'd probably give it to a general, but not Betty Crocker Garcia."

"That depends on their relationship. She is the acting first lady."

"Acting, not real. She's arm candy." But she's tasted power, and Tessa knew from personal experience that authority in the wrong hands was too deadly to ignore.

Near Langley, Virginia

Before Liz Jacobs left the cab, she adjusted the light-colored wig over her dark hair. She felt ridiculous playing masquerade at her age, but she knew Intel was monitoring her home computer and, she suspected, her brownstone as well. Slipping out at predawn had been simple enough when two brownstones shared a courtyard and it was Sunday. In outdated clothing she'd dragged from the back of her closet, she walked up the wide stone steps, then hesitated to look behind. The parking lot and roads were empty, her cab just turning onto the highway.

Inside the building, she went to the front desk, then found the computers, stationing herself in the corner with a view. Impatience rode her spine as she logged on. She'd been a field operative for nearly twenty years and her hunting skills were sharp. For the next half hour, she broke nearly five federal laws to learn why the file on a dead woman had been accessed.

Ten

Paul Ramos had survived dozens of operations in hostile territory that were far more of a risk, physically, than watching out for the Hillary Clinton of Venezuela. Eloisa had skills. She was seductive in a nonthreatening way to other women, and she could certainly convince the pants off a priest if she wanted. But using the men around her had a faster purpose. The final objective, he surmised, was to kill him and put herself in the VP seat. She had Gutierrez wrapped so tightly, the man didn't know who was squeezing him.

Once Ramos had seen the video, it had taken little to protect himself. Without access to anything substantial, he worked with what he had. A bottle of clear nail polish and a little Vaseline at night. He now slept well and felt his strength returning quickly.

He gripped the iron bar and pulled into a chin-up, his head still spinning a little, but he pushed himself for a dozen more. He did his circuit training, then went to the shower. Beyond the doors were bodyguards and secretaries all vying for his time. His health improving rapidly, it forced him into the role. He wasn't trained to be the Vice President of anything, let alone a country in turmoil, and studying the man had little to do with who he really was. He understood Garcia's political position. Gutierrez had aligned himself with Garcia to sway votes. A figurehead. But Ramos would make this work for him. For Garcia, he clarified. He had his face, and his power. He'd use them to do something worthwhile at least. He had to. This was all supposed to be temporary—and to keep himself from actually participating in the government—but that option vanished when he set off the alarm. He wished he hadn't and if he hadn't suspected Eloisa of anything, he'd have gone with Tessa. He hoped she was all right. He knew Logan and his team had escaped. Even Salazar couldn't keep that information from him, though the man was doing his best to circumvent his own Vice President.

Garcia wasn't a complicated man. Bright and honest, he'd been an officer in the military and skilled. One advantage: his own military training wouldn't be suspect and he knew it showed in his demeanor. Learning who the man really was came from studying Garcia's notes and personal papers. Garcia had suspected internal movement happening around him and feared for not only his own life but for his country. It made Ramos wonder who was really behind the coup that lasted two days.

Killing Garcia wasn't beneficial to Gutierrez. It would rally the people against the President because Garcia had made it extremely clear he didn't want socialism. He was the only person stopping Gutierrez from jumping in the sack with Castro or China. They had succeeded, they just didn't know it. Ramos planned to keep it that way until he learned the truth behind Eloisa's map and what was at the end of it. Eloisa knew it was missing. His mistake was giving the original to Tessa instead of the copy in his back pocket.

To be this close to a source wasn't uncommon, but as to having access to codes, to the real proof of anything, it was a fortress. Garcia's wife's love for puzzles warned him that the truth wouldn't be simple. But then, he had faith in Logan. The man did the *Times* crossword puzzle in ink. Ramos knew. They'd once been friends.

Until a woman came between them.

In her private offices, Eloisa stared at the housekeeper on the other side of the desk. Maria Rojas was older, perhaps sixty, and trusted. The housekeeper oversaw all aspects, but only she was to maintain the private suites.

"Maria, I know you see to his rooms personally, and I would like your help."

Mrs. Rojas was known for her lack of interjection, and never once questioned an order.

"I ask that you keep an eye on him for me. A sharp one. His health isn't good and the doctors don't believe that will change."

Maria's expression fell into sadness, and she crossed herself. Eloisa wondered if she had chosen the right person. But she knew that while she herself despised her husband, many adored him. "I love him dearly, but he'll insist on joining me even at the risk of his health. I am filling in where I can." She gave her a humble look and Maria instantly pepped up.

"*Sí*, and doing a wonderful job, señora."

"Thank you, I try." She accepted the compliment with a slight bow of her head. "But I cannot be near all the time. Our country needs help now. It's like a child without a mother since the coup."

"I understand, señora."

"Please tell me if you see anything unusual also. When he's in pain, his actions are often . . . odd." Eloisa handed Maria a business card with her private number. "I'll expect reports during the day. Can you text message?" She didn't need to speak to Maria, just get an account. But Maria shook her head. "Then just call me."

"Will he be alright soon?"

"I hope so." Eloisa drew near and slipped the woman some money as she whispered, "For your grandson." He was in college, supported by his grandmother, and they were struggling, Eloisa knew. She'd heard it from the kitchen help.

Maria blinked, then looked aghast at the wad of bills. Just the reaction Eloisa was hoping for. The housekeeper thanked her profusely, and Eloisa closed the bargain when she hugged her like a mother. It brought Maria to tears. She stuffed the cash in her apron pocket, straightened her uniform and left.

Eloisa closed the door and smiled, satisfied the Vice President wouldn't be able to even use the toilet without her knowing. Her appearance, without Estavan, of course, was needed elsewhere. She took her seat behind the desk and arranged to leave.

Eloisa didn't see Mrs. Rojas bustle down the corridor and head directly to the other side of the residence.

Salazar's shoulder throbbed, and the twenty stitches and Novocain did little to keep his fingers mobile. He was forced to rely on other people, instead of being in control. He'd changed from his usual black, donning worn trousers a size too big and a faded tee shirt advertising some beer. He felt unkempt in the shabby garments, but in daylight, they would attract less attention. His gaze swung from Juan to their path into the forest, then moved to the tourists. Several people hopped into the small riverboats to tour, but he remained, sitting with a soft drink and watching the area.

His prey was a few yards downriver. He thumb dialed his phone. She picked up on the first ring.

"Yes."

It was all she said and she did it with the arrogance of an aristocrat.

"All of it. Now," Salazar said.

"No."

He cut the line.

A moment later, his phone hummed.

"You dare push me? I will have—"

"Quiet," he snapped, his shoulder throbbing. "I am not interested in your threats. I'm sure several other people would be interested, though . . ." He let his voice trail.

She was silent for a long moment, then spat, "You will do nothing, except bring it to me. Are we clear?"

"Perfectly." Salazar popped a painkiller into his mouth, swallowing it without water.

He listened to her, and Diego Salazar experienced the full force of her conspiracy. He realized her elaborate map was more for protection than secrecy. A terrifying power in her manicured hands.

The path took them south of the river and farther from the town into the countryside thick with trees and brambles. Animals made themselves known in the brush of reed grass, a slither under the water. Logan was moving along at a brisk pace when he heard voices and stopped short. Tessa bumped into him, but he turned quickly and pulled her behind some trees.

"Problem, honey?" she asked softly, brows high.

"Max is slacking on his Intel, there are five squads of troops a hundred yards from us." Through binoculars, he sighted in. In a sunlit field, squad formations of the Venezuelan Army drilled with assault tactics; he recognized the posture and lunge. Several officers were standing under the trees in the shade, and Logan narrowed the focus on one man shouting at the troops.

He glanced at her. "More than meets the eye."

She frowned as he handed over the binoculars. He directed her to one man. "Chinese, *here?*"

"I'm betting this is field maneuvers for warfare training," he said, looking around. "We were involved till Gutierrez started hating the U.S." She held out the binoculars but he didn't take them back. "Make yourself useful. Keep watch."

Smiling, she tucked herself alongside a fat oak tree and focused on the troops in the distance. His shoulder was pressed to hers, as if losing contact right now would hurt. Logan worked the Recon, then hooked on the ear mic to contact Max.

"Have a fun night, did you?"

"Can it, Renfield."

"Ahh, always the gentleman."

"One of us has to be." Logan didn't want any reminders of the sex he was craving, and the woman he wanted was only a few inches away. "Give me something," he said.

"Ramos is still closely guarded, but he's getting out more.

Seen this morning walking the grounds. Sebastian is working on something to get close to him. He didn't elaborate, but he comes back dirty and sweating, so he's earning his keep."

Sebastian had the looks to blend in. Dark haired and swarthy-skinned, his Cajun roots came in his lazy walk and slow talk. But since Sebastian often kept to himself, Logan knew he was following a hunch that might not pan out. "He need backup?"

"Hasn't asked for it."

Logan explained the problem. "It's a low mound, more like a rock pile and there's a flat stone in the top. The location is hazardous."

Tessa leaned, staring at the screen. "I really need to learn some of this," she said.

"I need satellite, Max. As close as you can get."

"Roger that."

Logan thought they had a tail but didn't mention it to Tessa. He hadn't seen anyone, yet the feeling of being watched overwhelmed him. "The rest of the map?"

"Coming through now. Let me get the satellite."

They waited.

"The eye doesn't have anything to do with Isis," Tessa said. "I think it's simpler, the eye means to just *see*."

Logan started to repeat her words, but she held out her hand for the comm link. Logan gave it up.

"Max, how you doing this morning? It's a pyramid shape with the capstone missing. Well, I know it's not Egyptian, but it looks like that. Ring any bells?"

"Not on the tourists' walkathon."

"That's odd. Isis would be a winged woman." She didn't discount that the symbol had more than one meaning.

"With a disc and horn headdress, yeah, I know."

"Ooh, someone needs a nap. Did you get any rest?"

Max sighed through the link. "Not really, thanks for asking, and I'm sorry."

"It's okay, I think we just made a breakthrough, Max."

He laughed and she winked at Logan. "Home of Isis and

the eye, which is different from the first eye on the marker. Then words." She read off the translations. "Euclid? The father of geometry. Not my strong suit," she said, leaning away as if math would be contagious.

But Logan worked the keyboard with a stylus and she leaned in. Figures jumped on the screen.

"It's an equation," he said. "The next symbol is numbers, three sets of them." The numbers were sandwiched so tightly that he paused to run the stylus over the lines so she could see. Then suddenly he stopped calculating. "There's a number missing."

Tessa looked toward the rock. "If there's a number on that rock pile, then someone put it there or there'd be a historical note somewhere." She met his gaze. "The mention of an Egyptian goddess in Venezuela is glaring, and yet numbers were an obsession to the Inca, and the Mayans, for that matter. Inca calculated in groups and rounded up most answers."

"It's got to be *on* that mound of rock," he said.

"We can't get near it without the troops spotting us."

He inclined his head and they backed up and moved farther from the sunlight. "You need to get up a tree and stay there."

"What are you going to do?"

He shouldered off his pack and motioned for hers, then pushed his gun down the back of his jeans. "We need a look at that thing right now. If it's got a number on it, then we're good to go. If not"—he shrugged, sheepish—"we have to figure out something else. Keep the channel open."

He removed anything metallic from his clothes, including his belt and compass watch, slipping that on her wrist. "Up," he said, his thumb pointing the way. "It's the safest place."

She felt like she was being sent to her room. She rigged to climb and was about to attack the lowest branch when Logan pulled her to face him. "Stay there. If anything happens"—he tapped the handheld computer now hooked to her belt—"call Max."

Her gaze rocketed over his face. It was a telling moment

for her. They'd managed this far with someone on their tail, but the thought of separating from him felt like a door slamming shut. She was out of her league with these guys and while she'd been an operative for a short time, none of it had to do with evasion from the enemy. She was scared for him but shouldn't be. He was a cut above, yet nothing had gone in their favor and that little voice in her head wouldn't shut up and let her hope it would.

"Nothing better happen. I have plans for you."

Logan offered a comforting smile as he cupped the back of her head, drawing her nearer. She went eagerly. His mouth covered hers, a brief, hot slide of lips and tongue that drove a thick spill of desire, and she clung to him, forgetting the danger and drinking in his kiss, the feel of him pressed hard to her. God, we're good at this, she thought, and she wanted the chance for more—without guns blazing around them. He drew back, met her gaze, then kissed her again so tenderly it made her throat tighten.

Then he pressed his lips to the top of her head. "Stick with the plan," he reminded her. "Don't come down till I come for you."

"This is making me really nervous."

"Just going for a look, nothing more. But we need this." Logan stashed the packs in the bushes, covering them with branches. He liked her theory of it being simple; the eye meant just to see, because if you could figure out the answer to the equation, then you knew you needed one more number. For the dimensions of a triangle, he suspected. More than one.

He stood beneath the tree as she climbed, her stitches forcing her to go slowly, and he waited till she was well hidden and they had a communications link, then with a branch, he swept away the evidence of their footprints. He headed toward the slab of rock that held the key.

The high-powered binoculars with a stabilizer was her best friend as she watched Logan move farther away from her position. She felt as if she were right behind him, the binoculars that good, but then he crouched out of sight. She caught up with him when he smeared mud over his face. He had clumps of the grasses shoved down the back of his shirt, hiding his dark hair. He glanced back and although she knew he couldn't see her, it was comforting. Still crouched, he moved forward, then she lost him completely.

She searched the stretch of land between the edge of the forest and the open area around the mound of rock, but nothing moved except tall grasses swaying in the wind. She glanced at his watch on her wrist, heavy, like her mood. He'd been gone thirty minutes already. From her position, she had a great view all the way to the troops, but she was confident she was well hidden.

The mound was fifteen or twenty feet high with relatively straight lines. Tessa had no idea how old it was. It wasn't on any tourist map, yet it had been here a while. Asking a local was risky, since neither of them saw the face of any shooters, but they were already a good distance from anything on two legs. On four was quite another matter. Unfamiliar territory didn't bother her—a forest is a forest, forget the location—and she was used to winging it most of the time, but she felt that nothing good was at the end of the map. It was for Eloisa's eyes only, never meant to be found or deciphered. That made it more dangerous, because she'd constructed it with no inhibitions, without restraint and that usually brought out the dark side in people. Yet if they didn't finish this, Ramos would expose her. Of course, that would also expose himself—where he was sitting . . . and who put him there. A whispered word and a secret house of cards would fall.

Her luck, she'd be under it.

The land was less dense, the river widening, fertile earth rising into the Andes Mountains and the border of Bolívar. It offered less cover, sunlight catching through the trees and splaying the ground. On his stomach, Logan inched along the ground. From the tree line, he could see the back side of the mound. There was nothing carved or shaped into the rock, and although approaching was easy, he didn't want to leave a trail, and had to move as if they were watching. It took him ten minutes to reach the rear, then another half hour to inch along the path to the far left of the mound near an outcropping of trees. When he finally reached the left side, he was in an awkward position on the ground to see the stacked stones.

Shaded by the structure, he rose up enough to see and feel the stones. Upriver, the marker had been carved, but as he ran his hand over the stones, they were smooth from the floods and rain. He crawled forward, toward the front, facing the troops, and through the tall grasses he saw trucks and tanks. They weren't hiding, he thought, or they wouldn't be cooking a meal. He could smell it already and ducked into the grasses again.

Tessa saw flickers, like shadows behind frosted glass. She strained to find him, making it a game, but he was invisible out there. Impatience rode her spine and she really hated being up a tree without a weapon. She had good aim with a nunchuck, but not good enough to miss the branches. He'd hidden both packs, but she kept her wallet and passport on herself all the time, mainly because she had this twisted feeling that if she lost them, she'd somehow cease to exist. It was the only solid identification she had. Aside from some pictures in the box under her mother's bed.

The GPS system hummed and she had a tough time answering. The thing was like slapping a brick to her ear. She put on the headset and whispered, "Max?"

"Tessa? You okay?"

"Yes, fine, Logan is looking at the rock."

"I have the troops on satellite. They were under trees or camo netting, but the road is torn up from their convoy."

"I'm just amazed you can see that."

"Give them a wide berth. I saw some rocket launchers."

"Well, I don't want an invitation to that party. The rock?"

"The satellite picked up the mound, but there is nothing carved into the top stone."

"Ya know, finding Waldo isn't even this tough."

Logan had to risk exposure to feel the stones for impressions. The troops were drilling toward him now, yet still a few hundred yards away. Chinese teachers, Spanish-speaking students. Bet that's a lesson in diplomacy, he thought, and gently pushed aside the stiff grasses, prying through them till he found solid wall. He reached, his hand skimming the rocks. They didn't move at all, locked into place like Inca walls. Grass crept up the edge, but not very high—someone had cleared it recently. It was a tall chunk of real estate and on the ground he couldn't find anything that shouldn't be there. Then he shifted back, widening his circle, and wished he could stand.

There was a pole protruding from the mound about eight feet up, the remnants of dead flowers swinging in the breeze. Offerings, he thought, then looked toward the troops. They were in full combat gear and running a makeshift obstacle course. And dying in the heat, too. He backed up several yards, near the cluster of trees, and looked back at the mound.

He whispered her name.

"Oh, thank God," she whispered back into the mic. "Are you okay? Where have you been?"

"Right nearby, shhhh, baby. You're not going to believe this."

"Try me, it's been one of those days."

"The winged woman, it's not carved into the stone, it's the color of them. And if you weren't looking for it, you wouldn't notice it." He told her that the outer stones were bleached white from the sun and the center ones held a mossy green cast to them. "I figure that the channels between the stones must direct the rainfall, and have stained the stone in layers. The wings stretch the width of the pillar, with the hourglass shape of a woman in the center. Amazing. No headdress but still incredible." He wondered how Eloisa Garcia knew of it.

"The number?"

"Roman numerals. Thirteen." The position of the stone shaped it, moss and dirt outlined it.

"How soon can you get back here?"

"Oh hell."

"Yeah. One SUV, black, with black windows and speeding this way."

Logan hesitated, then said, "Well, I guess he didn't die in the blast."

"Damned rude of him, huh? Don't come back."

He froze. "Why?"

"They're right under me."

Logan crushed down the urge to run and moved to his right to the trees hemming the field. With the pyramid on his left, in front of him was more forest, and beyond that, Tessa in a tree about fifty yards or so in. Hidden, he moved slowly, glimpsed the silhouette of the truck through the trees, a flicker of light on chrome.

They really need to vary their vehicle selection, he thought, as two men left the truck. One favored his leg, the other moving more stiffly. *I hope it hurts, pal.* He wished he had the binoculars to see the man's face.

Tessa held still inside the branches and almost didn't breathe. The men left the vehicle and stood under the tree several yards away.

The taller of the two limped, attractive in a hound dog sort of way, but the other would have turned her head in another time and place. This guy had shot an innocent man in the street. She'd be a quick target and silently urged them to move their ass or speak up. The doors were open, and from the darkened interior more than one small screen glowed. She hated to think what was in the back.

She peered down as the men walked toward the pyramid, then, bold as you please, they strutted around it. *Well, yes, of course,* she thought. They aren't being hunted. She sighted through the binoculars to see the troops rushing them, rifles at their shoulders. Where was Logan? She scanned but didn't see any movement. Then the smaller of the two walked forward, something in his hand. A Chinese officer strode near, shouting something, and Tessa was thrown for a loop when the other guy was right back in his face like a junkyard dog. The officer stepped back, bowed and looked as if he were apologizing.

Now there's a man with some power, she thought. Or perhaps just feared.

"Come down."

Tessa looked below, and her eyes widened when she saw Logan beyond the truck. How'd he *do* that? Stowing the glasses, she moved down quickly, casting a glance at the troops before she dropped to the ground. He motioned to her and she rushed to the rear of the truck. He had the packs and pulled her with him into the woods back toward the bridge.

"We could steal the truck."

He scoffed. "Not from this guy. But it's filled with electronics." Some used by NSA a few years back.

There was no telling what this man could do with a single phone call.

Briefly, Salazar watched the troops drill. Some had been his own men for a time, though none would acknowledge that fact in public. These men were trained to root out the anti-Gutierrez followers, guerilla rebels harbored throughout the country. Political fighters had a cause, Salazar didn't. He didn't care who was in power. Services such as his were always in need, if not in government, then in the private sector. He enjoyed the hunt, the risk, and most especially his own secrecy to move without so much notice. The men marching in the open field had loyalty. Salazar's loyalty came at a price. It wasn't always paid in cash.

He turned away from the troops and stepped back from the formation. He didn't need to see the mound, but his curiosity brought him here. He barely understood the map, or Eloisa's reasons for it, other than amusement. Hiding something in plain sight would have been simpler, but she was a woman, she knew nothing of defensive tactics.

He walked the flat ground around the structure, mashing the grasses, but found no evidence that the couple had been here, and he suspected they'd covered their tracks.

Juan stared at the stones, then glanced at Salazar. "We go to the final mark and wait?"

Salazar nodded, and they returned to the truck. He was about to get in when he noticed the right-side tires. Both were flat. Drawing his weapon, he turned sharply, searching for signs, but even prints leading to the truck had been erased. Clever boy, he thought, and signaled Juan. They moved into the thicket. Salazar smiled when he found crushed leaves and snapped twigs, then looked toward the mountains, considering his next moves. He suddenly turned back to the truck and grabbed the radio.

He would have little time to set up an ambush.

Riley frowned at the TV screen. "Ramos is out of the house, at least."

Sebastian moved in. "He looks better than when we went in."

They listened to Gutierrez blast America and Britain with his usual rant. Beside him was Ramos, filling the role of Vice President. Riley leaned in and hit RECORD on the DVR, and watched Ramos, Garcia's wife standing between the men. Somewhere in Caracas, the three stood behind a low wall of a veranda.

"Look at her touch the President, she's almost shoving Garcia, uh, Ramos out."

"That's a fake smile if I ever saw one," Sebastian said about Ramos.

When the broadcast went to another issue, Riley rewound and hit PLAY. He slowed the recording, watching Ramos put his hand on the wall. Riley froze it on the screen. "He doesn't look like he's being forced, but that"—he circled Ramos's hand—"is coercion."

His fist was clenched, his thumb forced between his index and middle finger. Hand gestures and eye blinking were often used by prisoners of war to send messages to the outside. "He's not bound and gagged, but he's trapped."

"I don't really give a damn," Max said.

Riley glanced. "You said yourself Ramos did it for Tessa."

"The bastard knows when to tie off an operation and he didn't."

"Oh, yeah, that attitude helps us now," Riley bit back and went to the computers. He pulled up streams of recent video from newscasts and interviews. Anything with film on Ramos posing as Garcia. There wasn't much. He pulled up three streams, running them side by side, his gaze flicking back and forth, then he froze it.

"You guys," he said, pointing, taping one video after another. "He's been trying to send a message since he got there."

Max moved in, frowning. "You're kidding. Can you decipher it?"

"I'll try but I have to figure out which appearance came first. Man, he was really depending on the CIA to get him out."

Sebastian flipped through the pages in the files. "I don't think they were there to rescue." He handed over a sheet of paper. "There was no out for three men, only for the two going in. No overnight gear. A water escape," he said. "One propulsion torpedo, two tanks requisitioned. That's not enough air or ground power to get three men away safely more than a mile or two, and to stay off of radar they'd have to get to international waters." A hundred miles off the coast. "They never made the pickup. I bet the gear is still there."

"Come again?" Max asked.

"It goes two ways. Gutierrez rants that we're spying and then produces bodies and he's a winner all the way around. It's a smoking gun. But he doesn't use it." He waited for that to sink in. "He's not in the loop. Then we have the opposite, a gag so tight nothing whispers."

"No bodies?" Max asked.

"No, not a peep about the assault in the news. Then there's Ramos refusing to leave?" Sebastian shook his head. "Did it ever happen? This has the stink of conspiracy, and people with their own plan. The rescue shouldn't have happened, not that soon. McGill didn't say who ordered it, but they didn't give a damn about cleaning this up neatly. Well . . . not in a way that didn't involve more options than a bullet."

Max leaned back, hands behind his head. "McGill is lying to us."

That was met with scowls.

"This is too catastrophic for the U.S. to get involved," Max said. "I think it was all outside the loop. It wasn't a rescue, it was a hit."

"That does change that we agreed to sweep this," Sebastian said.

"How clean?"

"Neatness doesn't count." But D-1 needed to cover their backs.

Riley glanced at the video. Deciphering Ramos's blinking and hand signals wasn't his strong suit and he wished he was better at this POW stuff. Logan would know. He was the only one who'd been in a prison. But Riley agreed with Max. Ramos had been sent in for more than as just a stand-in to hold an empty place.

Joaquin Castillo strode through the door and Ramos smiled. He liked this young man and when he embraced him, then shook his hand, his pleasure was genuine.

"No visitors, no phone calls. You were damn near captive."

The rest of Castillo's staff started to follow and Ramos put up a hand. They retreated and closed the door. "Too many doctors and opinions and none of it pleasant," he said, trying to keep his accent in Garcia's tone.

Castillo would not be easily fooled. He was intelligent, energetic and old enough not to be a threat to the rest of the government. The strongest man was always in the greatest doubt because they laid their hopes in him; they wanted assurances. Castillo could do it. A representative in the national assembly, he had no ties to the military, though he'd attended military schools. Oddly, in the United States. He was disciplined, knew how the military did things and was just damn likeable, Paul thought. There aren't many people comfortable enough in their skin that they'd walk into the office of the Vice President in jeans and a polo shirt.

"I've got a proposition for you. Just listen and then decide."

"That's ominous." Castillo's dark brows tightened. "You're distressed. How can I help?"

"Liberate them."

Castillo frowned.

"Use these celebration weeks to get your position heard, to let the people see *your* face and know what you stand for."

Castillo didn't say anything for a moment. He'd heard him, every word, and knew exactly what he meant.

"You're not expecting to be running."

Ramos smiled gently and wished to God that Garcia was alive and in his shoes. "I plan to be running and haven't changed my views, but I have angered the wrong people, Joaquin. I've made myself a target." He touched the still-red scar on his forehead and jaw. "And that means that freedom is a target."

"You know the army is loyal—"

"No army, no force. Use nothing except your words, Joaquin. All we really have is the honor of our word."

That Castillo was not military was an advantage. Lately, no one here trusted the Army, not because they'd helped stage a coup and let it go within two days, but because it was under Gutierrez's control and he was lethal with it.

"You have mine. Yes, I'll do it. Always wanted your job, anyway." Castillo put out his hand. "Though my brothers will think you're insane to tell me to *keep* talking."

Ramos smiled and knew he was right to back this man. He had to correct this wrong he'd done. His own arrogance and his self-righteous views had changed lives. Millions of them. He had to give the people the chance for true democracy. It was in this man.

Stage One begun, he thought.

Later that same day

He could feel it building. Like the crescendo toward the last wild bang of a Van Halen jam session, the strings were tightening. It left a stark chill in his bones. It no longer mattered that he wasn't Estavan Garcia. He was using his face.

Ramos walked down the grand hall of the Presidential palace—which had connotations of dictatorship written all over it—and a man rushed to open the door. He entered the equivalent of the Oval Office and smiled at the President. The man couldn't hide his shock fast enough and Gutierrez glanced at Eloisa. She straightened from leaning over his shoulder and frowned at him.

"You are not too ill to travel?" she asked.

"Apparently not." He enjoyed her shock.

He moved to the President and they shook hands and talked quietly for a moment. Eloisa didn't shift a muscle, yet her gaze flicked to the beautiful young woman who stood a few feet behind him and to the left. Anna was a secretary, someone he'd asked to join him to record events, and though she was a bit intimidated, she'd jumped at the opportunity. It snagged Eloisa at the vanity level, and Ramos could almost feel the claws sliding out. Woman to woman, Anna was suddenly Eloisa's competition and the slim, sexy girl of no more than twenty-five had two degrees and spoke more languages than a UN interpreter. Eloisa would see herself for a brief moment as only the wife.

Ramos handed Gutierrez a document folder, the Vice President's seal on the cover.

"What is this?" The President waved at the press stationed at the door.

"The new hospital. The funding needs your signature."

"I vetoed this." He pushed it away.

It was Garcia's baby, the *Asamblea Nacional* had approved it.

"I'm asking you to reconsider and sign it. Our people in this area are the poorest and they need help, especially when the annual basin flooding starts." He raised his voice an octave, enough for the press behind him to hear. Putting the President on the spot was the only way to get anything accomplished when the Vice President was no more than a figurehead. When the President simply glanced over the proposal, then closed it, Ramos leaned in.

"Sign it, Manuel."

Well away from the cameras, Gutierrez leveled him an even stare, but Ramos saw the heat beneath it. He didn't want anything pushed forward that didn't benefit his pocket. Socialism was even distribution of wealth, and Ramos knew that Gutierrez would never give up his shares of Venezuelan oil to the people.

"This is a large portion of the budget," Gutierrez said.

Eloisa inched closer to the President, declaring her allegiance.

"And the poor are large portions of our country. Have you seen the recent polls?" Ramos asked for his ears alone. "You haven't the opportunity to turn this away."

Ramos had studied both men, and while they'd never seen eye to eye in the press nor in the office, Garcia was an Indian and had a distinct advantage with a large percentage of the people. Probably why someone had assassinated him. Garcia was loved, an icon of hope, and Ramos could only speculate from the man's personal notes what he could have done for this country if he'd been elected to the presidency. Or alive.

Water under the bridge, he thought, and pushed the document closer. The press crowded inside the door, snapping photos. Ramos could feel Eloisa's gaze on him with the power of a drill into his brain. He stepped back, let the press knock off a few shots and started to turn. Gutierrez flipped open the folder and succinctly whipped his signature across the page, then handed it to him.

"Thank you, Mr. President." They shook hands, then he moved to Eloisa.

Her eyes flared as if he'd entered her personal space, but he kissed her softly, throwing in a hint of passion. She gravitated toward him, her hand gripping his upper arm and taking control. Inwardly he smiled, but as he drew back, Gutierrez was scowling. It left enough doubt to spoil the rapport between them.

"I'll expect you to be at my next press conference." Ramos's voice was cordial, but decisive, leaving no question. His wife would be at his side. He almost smiled at the venomous look only he could see. She didn't like even the suggestion of an order.

"She's attending the independence celebration." Gutierrez laid the challenge.

Like a husband defied, his gaze narrowed with warning. "Of course, but remember, Manny, she is *my* wife."

Then Ramos turned to the press and lavished praise on the President for his generosity as he showed the document. Flashes blinked rapidly in the dark-walled room. It would be on CNN within hours. Stage Two executed.

Ramos strode out with the press, herding them like a classroom of children.

Eloisa almost touched her numb lips, but didn't, watching as he left, his posture the same military erect. She still couldn't fathom his audacity to strut in here without informing them. While the shock had worn off, she wondered why wasn't he in bed or at least a wheelchair? Maria had failed her—quite easily. The old bitch would suffer for it.

The doors closed and she looked at her President. "He won't last long."

"You had better be correct, my dear. We cannot have him gaining favor. Or pushing costly projects like that!"

She frowned. "He will be dead, then, after the mourning, you will appoint me."

Gutierrez's thick, bushy brows rose high in his forehead. "You are so certain?"

Her gaze snapped to his and she had the urge to slap him. Men were such fools, she thought. "If you want me to bring his people"—she nodded to the sealed door and her husband beyond it—"to your side, yes, I am certain."

Gutierrez rose, towering over her. His square face was flat and bore his mixed heritage. She stepped back, affronted. "I wonder," he said, "what you would do if you weren't?"

"That should be enough of a motivation not to betray me."

Yet as she said it, she slipped close, resting her hand on his chest and pushing her body into his. He was an old man who'd been without his wife for enough years now that he depended on her. For more than just a lover.

Or running his presidency.

David Lorimer was leaning back in a chair and stretching when a stream of data infiltrated his system for the second time in three days, and then vanished.

"I keep getting these short bursts," he said to Walker. "A blip, then it disappears."

Walker leaned to look at David's screen. "Sneak attack to see if they can infiltrate the encryption?"

He shook his head. "It's not doing anything, just sorta butting heads with the firewall, but when the program tries to lock on it, it vanishes."

"No trace?" Usually it left a signature of some sort.

"Not a one. Like a fly buzzing into a window." David thought of hackers who did a mass send. Sometimes junk got caught in the airwaves, especially if it hopped a satellite feed, and from this facility, they were dancing across several birds.

"What's the problem, guys?" McGill asked from behind.

David glanced over at McGill and thought, *The general is showing his age, or just the burden.* Maybe it was the civilian clothes. He looked like he'd slept in them. He held a mug of coffee in one hand, two others by the handles. He set them down as David explained.

McGill's expression changed instantly. "Can you track the source?"

"Difficult but not impossible. It's not cohesive, sir. It's fleeting, just a stream of letters, numbers and symbols. No program association—nothing."

David started to access an encryption program when McGill asked for a printout.

"Sorry, sir, it doesn't hang around that long, but I remember most of the stream."

David pushed off, the wheeled chair sliding before he caught the desk behind him, grabbed a sheet of paper and wrote. He slid the paper across to McGill.

McGill looked at the series of numbers and letters, then sat down with a pencil. David frowned at Walker, then watched as McGill crossed out random figures, exchanging numbers for letters. He stopped and sat back, a little paler, scowling before he folded the paper and pushed it into his pocket.

"It's not just lost bytes getting caught in the satellite stream?" David asked.

"No. Watch it, see if you can trace the source. Give me anything ASAP."

"Yes, sir," David said and glanced at Walker.

Apparently, there were some things only a general was supposed to know.

Eleven

They couldn't use the chopper with the Chinese and rockets in the area. That was fine with her, except the sky that woke without a cloud was fast filling up. Miles away, the sky was nearly clear and morning-yellow, but over them, gray as spoiled pâté. Tessa stopped to pull out rain gear.

Logan backtracked to her. "No time."

"Oh, yes, we do." She worked the poncho on, expertly flipping it over the pack. "Wet, this thing is unbearable and unbalanced." Above them, the black clouds bumped. "Let's find a place to ride this out."

"We have a little head start and have to take it."

"He's got a truck, Logan."

"Not with four wheels."

She wouldn't have thought of that and smiled, waved him on. "We need a vehicle, too."

"Already ahead of you. Sebastian is recovering the jeep. We get wheels on the other side of the bridge." Logan set an even pace.

She was accustomed to hiking, just not at this speed. He veered through trees to a road, then he slowed to a walk. She moved beside him, hitching up the pack.

"Tired?"

She untied the bandana from around her neck and swiped it over her face and throat. "I'm sufficiently motivated. I just want this over with." She glanced behind again, half-expecting men with guns to come chasing after them. It had been the norm since she'd climbed in Ramos's window.

"Don't like my company?"

She grinned. "Boy, are you fishing for compliments," she said. "And let's be honest here, till now all we knew of each other was the job and one night of trying for something more."

"Delicately put." He leaned in to say, "I like what I see."

She glanced, going pink from the inside out. It shouldn't mean so much but she hadn't been complimented as a woman in a while. It was always for her job, her athletic skills. She missed having a significant relationship with anyone. Andrew was about the only person she knew well. Enough to know that he saw sleeping with her merely as some "do it with the older woman" goal to achieve. But the men in her life her age wanted more, and she couldn't tell them the truth. That usually pushed them away. It shouldn't matter so much. People had relationships without revealing *everything*, but a false identity—that was pulling the trust factor a little too tight.

She looked down at her boots. He didn't know it all, her conscience reminded her. Hiding behind the classification would work for him forever, she supposed, considering his background. When this is over, she'd tell him the truth. She trusted him and owed him that much. The man had risked his life for her enough already this week, but bringing him into her past would put the same burden on him. She could barely think on it, and had never put it into words. The images were enough to live with.

"Tessa?" He said it like he'd called more than once, and she met his gaze. "You okay? You were somewhere else." He stopped her.

"I was," she said, then forced a smile. "I'm back now."

He held her gaze and seemed to dispute it inside, then just smiled. "We're near people."

She looked around, and moved with him as they continued, puffs of sandy gray dirt punctuating their steps.

"I need a minute to redo the equations. I've got a hunch." They rounded a curve, the first sign of civilization in the gravel spread on the path.

"Share."

"That's the thing about hunches . . ."

"I think they're longitudes and latitudes."

He looked at her sharply.

"Okay, your surprise is almost insulting. Or are women with brains rare for you?" Tessa laughed to herself.

He had the good grace to look chagrinned. "Apparently my standards have dropped."

"I bet their *ages* did, too," she snickered, nudging him, briefly forgetting the killer somewhere behind them.

The gravel spread to a parking lot that wouldn't hold more than three cars. The tour bus was a short, fat, jeep-like thing rusted to dark orange. Two men stood near the dock, launching a boat, a guide at each end, and each of the passengers wearing a life vest. It looked silly out here in the vastness of the jungle, but then she didn't want to go in that water, either. Logan found a bench behind the bus and sat to work the equations twice.

"It's three triangles, all the same size and overlapping." Logan loaded the longitudes and latitudes into the computer. "If I use this country as an enclosure . . . all set north and south . . ." He did something with the stylus. "The point where all three meet and, well . . . X marks the spot."

She rolled her eyes. "It's got to meet in a couple places."

"Yes, but those coordinates are in the sea or the river. This is the only one on land."

"Rats. I was in the mood for some diving," she said, leaning over. "I trust you, but I need to see it."

Using the Recon, he drew.

"That's Nordic."

His brows rose in that "well, well" manner he had lately.

"Once again, stretch your mind *really* big." Only his smile grew wider. "And imagine that I've been around the world several times and in the last eleven years, I've set foot in every country on the planet, except the North and South Pole and the U.S."

"Okay, it's stretched."

"It's Odin's Knot, the heart of Vale, heart of the slain."

"They bisect over a Spanish monk's grave."

"That's about the most sense this thing has made since we started this. So we dig it up?" That had a gross factor she didn't want to imagine.

He shook his head. "The body was moved to Caracas years ago. But these are the coordinates." He tipped the screen toward her and she shielded it to see.

There was a map of this section of the region, and as he pressed a key, it kept narrowing down the focus. He punched the priest's name into the computer and said, "It says it's a burial site. A Spanish missionary was slain by Indians, but his body was moved to some church in the Plaza Bolìvar."

"Every town in this country has a Plaza Bolìvar; it's the center of town."

"The coordinates are very exact."

"I was actually hoping for another puzzle." As she said it, she shook her head.

"There is. Before the '*into the hands of taipan*' is a symbol Matob couldn't figure out."

Tessa scowled at it. "Looks like one of those IQ test things. Which symbol doesn't fit?"

He rose and followed with the group to the boats.

"Where is the gravesite?"

He looked to the mountain looming like a wizened old man slumped over dinner. "Up there."

She grabbed his sleeve, tugging. "I hear a vehicle."

"He must be riding on the rims." Logan looked back at the narrow spot where civilization ended and knew there wasn't enough time to get into the boat. People were still loading and short of pushing them all aside, attention he didn't want, and with the police behind him, they had no choice.

"He's got to go around, we don't." He led her into the forest again.

Climbing the steep hill, Tessa glanced back and glimpsed the chrome of the truck. "I hope you know some shortcuts. He's gaining."

Salazar slapped his hand on the dash as the truck rolled over the uneven ground. His bruised ribs burned up his side, his shoulder wound throbbing hot, and he grit his teeth against the pain. "Why don't they pave these roads?" he growled and didn't expect an answer.

"We should come out near the docks." The SUV burst through the trees, smashing foliage, the rims sparking on rocks as it slid sideways, spitting gravel. People lurched back, yet the owner pushed in front of the customers, giving orders to paddle out.

Salazar was out of the car, his arm stretched as he aimed

his pistol. "A couple, where did they go?" he shouted, advancing. Pain scratched up his ribs, and his aim faltered.

No one responded, and he shifted the weapon slightly and fired. The bullet went into the water, the threat clear as he aimed again at the owner, a tall man in stained clothing and a frayed straw hat.

"Put away your guns," the man said, staring Salazar down. "They went north on foot."

Salazar lowered the gun and turned away. The tightness in his chest slowed his walk back to the truck and he climbed in. Juan drove, and Salazar watched the ten-inch screen fastened to the dash as they closed in on the location. The slope was not steep, the roads passable. The couple stopped hiding their trail, but he didn't need it. Several minutes later, they passed a jeep parked off the road. The same one from the riverbanks. The truck jolted, rocking, and he grasped his shoulder as if to halt the pain. His stitches felt hot, his skin tight, and he popped another pill.

The radio cracked with reports. While he didn't want anyone involved in their capture, he had men moving in the northwest, narrowing the field. The mountain at their backs, the hills were low, the snow runoff adding to the pressure of the river and waterfalls. The sky rumbled black, sitting like an angry child working up to a tantrum. Storms didn't linger here, but with snow melting on the peaks, a four-hour storm could drop enough water to flood and push several feet over the banks. It was already sliding over the roads.

The truck engine strained, the rear fishtailing, and they could go no farther. Salazar climbed out, grabbed his pack. Juan took it, shouldering the weight, and together they went into the forest. Salazar pressed hard. They needed to reach it first and speculated what he would do when he found them. The woman's face bloomed in his mind. He'd caught only glimpses of her, but the collection made a lovely picture. He knew he would have to go through the man to have her. He counted on it.

*　*　*

At the gunshot, Logan turned back, but couldn't see through the trees. "Damn that bastard."

"Hey, *hey*," she said again when he kept studying the field. "The map is a priority. Right?" God, he was such a superman and it was a habit she needed to break. "He's got no reason to kill. Those people won't cover for us."

He held her gaze for a moment, then nodded shortly. "I hate it when you're right."

"I never get tired of hearing that." She pushed on, glancing back once and hoping no one else died because of this. The tally was racking up.

The sun was blackened out by the clouds by the time they reached the bridge and hurried across to the jeep. It was nearly nose down in a ditch, the impression that it was abandoned, and Logan threw open the door. The keys were inside, but Sebastian was nowhere in sight. She slipped off the pack and pushed it to the backseat. Logan scowled at the car's position, then climbed in.

"They'll be looking for this car, won't they?"

"Probably." He turned over the engine and slowly eased the jeep out of the gully. "We work with what we have." He pulled onto the road.

Tessa leaned to see the sky. "He definitely has more choices."

Logan ducked. A chopper swept in from the west. "He's getting desperate. Good."

"Good?"

"I can expect the worst."

That kind of thinking just escaped her. "He's going to beat us there."

Max had tuned the engine, added some enhancements, and Logan knew the rusty bucket would give Andretti a run. "Surrounded by pessimists," he muttered and gave it some gas.

In shabby clothes, Sebastian fell in line, signing a false name and taking a tool belt with the other day laborers. Aside from a quick trip to leave the jeep for Logan, he'd been at it for a day now, and after the instructions were given, the men assembled into groups for specific tasks. Sebastian kept an eye on the building: the summer residence. It gave him the creeps to be this close. The beatings and dunkings were still fresh in his memory. Getting some payback kept his mind occupied as he worked.

Sebastian slammed the hammer, sending the nail into the wood with one hit. He positioned another nail and kept hammering. His broken thumb started to throb. On either side of him, local Indians labored to construct a viewing stand. At least he *thought* that's what it was; he hadn't seen any plans. The contractor was a nervous little man with thin legs who bustled around like a wedding planner at the marriage of the century. It was annoying, but Sebastian understood the guy needed a flawless performance from his crews. They were, after all, building for the Vice President. It was the reason he'd joined this crew, for the chance to get close to Ramos. When and if he did, he wasn't sure what he could do, but he'd seen the man twice. Venezuelans were celebrating their Independence Day. Coincidentally, it was the day after America's own Independence Day.

Getting anywhere near Ramos was impossible, yet too close and he risked recognition by the troops who had bashed on him for ten hours. His broken thumb was forever mangled from both that and hammering. But the truth was, he was enjoying the hell out of himself.

He went to the stack of wood and, with another man, lifted a plank, then marched it into position for securing. They hammered like machines, smiling when they raced, then he stepped back, giving his partner's shoulder a shake and smiling so hard his face hurt. He'd missed the joy of building something by hand. Sebastian made bombs, and each time he created a close-quarter detonation he knew someone would die horribly. He understood all that "getting the bad guys before they get us" motive, yet it still made him almost hate his skill for it. Probably why he enjoyed cooking so much. Everyone was always happy when he did that.

Beyond his partner he saw Ramos appear and leave the residence, flanked by bodyguards and Eloisa Garcia. The woman didn't look all that happy as they crossed the lawn to board a chopper. Along with the workers, Sebastian watched and he could tell that Ramos was recovering well and quickly. Sebastian moved from behind the piles of lumber and with the workers merged forward. They shouted at Ramos, and he looked up, waved high and smiled back. Reporters started to rush him and Eloisa. Sebastian chuckled to himself when Ramos refused to let Eloisa speak, handing her into the chopper first.

The look on her face was hot enough to fry bacon.

Ramos addressed the crowd, thanking them for their hard work, and Sebastian moved closer. Ramos spoke briefly about freedom, jobs and his appreciation. The workers surged, the guards stopping them from getting too close, yet the people lapped up Ramos's words like a treat. They loved him, Sebastian thought, for the simple reason that Ramos spoke Garcia's words, phrases he'd heard the Vice President utter more than once.

Suddenly, Ramos's intention gelled firmly in his mind as the man scanned the crowd and Sebastian stepped forward, standing out because he towered over most of the workers. He knew the instant Ramos recognized him, but he didn't acknowledge it. A young woman rushed to his side, said something in his ear. Ramos nodded, said good-bye to the crowd and turned to the chopper. Before he stepped on, Ramos searched and found him in the crowd again. He nodded, resolution in his expression.

Snatching him out of the hot seat was impossible. The only choices were to get close enough for verbal contact or to kill him—and Ramos knew it.

McGill thought of the covert intelligence facility as "the little house on the prairie."

Although ordinary on the outside, after you got past the front porch it wasn't. Then it was a series of scans under the scrutiny of cameras. No one visited unless invited, and McGill waited as his first guest passed through the outer checkpoints that were completely automated. Only then did he open the door.

For a moment, he let his gaze slide from head to toe. Blond hair, black suit, nondescript face—although his momma might debate that—Deets was unassuming. He held out his badge and McGill inspected, then referenced it. He didn't trust anyone today and NSA agent Nolan Deets was no exception. McGill had been informed of his arrival by the director of NSA, an admiral he'd known when they were just baby officers, but this operation was too delicate to let anything slide. He handed back the badge.

"What can I do for you?" McGill asked, sitting in a padded chair that was a hell of a lot more comfortable than the ones two stories below ground.

"It's we who can do for you, sir." Deets set a small tape recorder on the desk and McGill frowned. "We intercepted a call to your theater recently, and we're just getting voice pattern references. I thought it might be . . . helpful."

Then he hit PLAY.

"You haven't finished. You didn't do your job."

Elizabeth Jacobs, McGill thought, and his gaze snapped to the agent's.

"Screw the job, get me out of here."

A voice McGill recognized as Paul Ramos's, and he sat forward. Ramos was whispering.

"You're insane to think we can salvage this now. I shouldn't be here still, we shouldn't, and you fucking know it!"

"That's moot now. We finish this."

"Just what do you think I can do from this position?"

"More than you are now! Did you let something slip under drugs?"

The viper rears its head again, McGill thought. She didn't care about the dead nor that Ramos wore a target on his forehead. Only the intelligence she could get.

"It's not my first time, you know."

"*A rookie could do better. How did they intercept them?*"

The rescue team, McGill assumed.

"*Christ, give that up. They're getting suspicious,*" Ramos said.

"*What? You're just paranoid and making this difficult.*"

"*And you're a bitch. A first-class hard-ass.*"

McGill smiled to himself. She didn't miss a beat. "*Thank you. But you're letting that* weak spine *get in the way of duty to the country.*"

"*Whose? The U.S.? She's the one you should worry about.*"

"*Then deal with her quickly, too.*"

Too? Something settled over McGill as he waited for the response.

"*No.*"

"*Excuse me?*"

He could almost see her face, her features sharpening, one brow arching so high she looked like a witch ready to ensnare children.

"*You heard me. He's impossible to reach now and eliminating her won't solve anything,*" Ramos said. "*She's been planning for a very long time. There are more players in this and my feeling is—*"

"*You don't get feelings, you get orders!*"

She talked right over him, pressing hard, refusing to admit failure. Then she mapped out steps to a crime that stunned McGill.

"*Wake up, woman!*" Ramos nearly shouted. "*It's over. Let the chips fall.*"

"*Really? Then get yourself out of that country.*"

The line went dead.

The call confirmed McGill's suspicions. Jacobs had sent Ramos in with an agenda that was her own. He lifted his gaze to Deets, then waved at the opposite chair.

"How long have you known about this?"

McGill would withhold everything he knew until NSA gave over more information. Jacobs hadn't been formally charged with any crimes, yet she was under house arrest. But using CIA resources for her own personal agenda was big enough to keep her away from any intelligence.

"Long enough to know this isn't the first time she went off the reservation."

"Then why isn't she in jail?"

Deets unbuttoned his dark jacket and sat in the chair. "I'm afraid it's a little bigger than that, sir."

McGill put up a hand. "How did you intercept this call?"

"I'm not at liberty to say."

McGill couldn't stop his burst of laughter. "You have no liberties, Agent Deets." He'd find out and had just the men to come down on this agent. "Where are you going with this?" He nodded to the tape. "Elizabeth Jacobs has had a commendable record for twenty years." Till now, he thought, and while he felt no moral obligation to defend Jacobs in any manner, he wouldn't air dirty laundry.

"Scrutiny shows otherwise. Jacobs forced a woman who was merely a lookalike to do the work of an experienced agent," Deets said. "She was killed."

McGill kept his face impassive. He'd already read the file. There was little here, short and to the point. Originally with the State Department, she'd participated in a half dozen operations with success. Except the last one. He knew the woman was alive and well, but he wouldn't compromise his promise to Chambliss.

"Give me the particulars," McGill said. He hadn't been at this job long enough to know what was hidden in every closet.

"That's just it sir, we don't have any more than a Serbian government report and a news account. Neither of which are dependable. The Operation report was thin, but also deemed black."

Sealed and locked. It would take the consent of the President and several others to open it. "An eleven-year-old case and you don't have it closed?"

"People lied under oath, sir, or KIA. Proof of any wrongdoing on Jacobs' part died with Ms. Petruscu."

He didn't have anything, he thought. Ramos was whispering, a voice pattern couldn't be matched, and he needed to learn more of what the NSA was hunting before he would compromise this operation. Snatching that call out of the airwaves said they were nosing too close already.

McGill tossed the file on the table between them. "Then you'll have to find something else."

Deets held his gaze. "Sir. We know she's alive."

"No, you don't." Steel-gray eyes targeted Deets. "Because you're digging into a classified matter."

Deets was affronted. "I have the clearance, sir, and—"

"Not in this. We're immune to the loop," McGill cut in, "and you had better move out of it very quickly, Agent Deets. Have I made myself clear?" Leaks would break this operation.

Deets sighed hard. "Yes, sir." He rose and tossed down his card. "If the dead rise from the grave and want to tell the truth, have them call me . . . or just hold a séance."

McGill toyed with the card bearing only a phone number, and when Deets was gone, he turned back to the console, pulling up Petruscu's old State Department ID photo. The young woman reminded him of his wife thirty-five years ago.

That NSA had an alert on Jacobs wasn't surprising. Every aspect of her life was tagged and under full investigation. But Logan's woman was classified as KIA, so why was NSA hedging that she was alive? Did NSA pay attention to the file transfer?

He stood and went to the rear of the house, grabbed the plate of sandwiches he'd made before Deets arrived, then stepped into the closet. He felt like the dumbwaiter as the two-man elevator lowered to the underground rooms. He stepped out and Walker and Lorimer nearly charged him when they saw food.

"We have a potential leak." McGill held out the card. "NSA," he said to their curious looks. "He's in our business. Circle the wagons on him."

Walker took it, chewing fast and swallowing to say, "Yes, sir."

When he went to do just that, McGill put up his hand. "Sit down and finish, son." He reached for the secure phone and hit speed dial to the NSA director. "I'm not done with my resources yet."

Behind him, the young men exchanged a small smile, anxious to see McGill bring down the hammer.

Logan remained hidden, watching the burial site.

It wasn't difficult to spot. Someone had tended to it in the last month, yet the cross carved into the stone above the entrance was clear enough. The opening to the cave was narrow and smothered in moss, trickles of water dripping on the ground, the overflow streaming to a small pool a few yards to his left. Near it was a stone obelisk about four feet high, a sign they were near something sacred. The rain had eased up a little, yet the sky was still dark, clouds hovering in a hard stall, ready to unleash again. There was no sign of a vehicle or two-legged life anywhere near here. Below, on the side of the mountain, the town sold trinkets of the dead priest, but in the rain, most were busy trying to keep their homes from slipping down the hillside.

He looked at Tessa. She was in a squat, her back against a tree, her pack still on. Water dripped off the poncho and pooled around her. She looked asleep again.

He nudged her. "All clear to go in."

"Without the packs." She slid hers off with a grateful moan, leaving the poncho covering it. She helped him disguise them, then he shifted past her and led the way. Neither spoke. They'd gone about a hundred yards when he stopped.

"The entrance is ten feet ahead, but down there." He pointed to the slope below.

They'd rappel. It would put them less out in the open and closer to the entrance. "Smart commando," she said with feeling. Logan just smiled.

Going slowly put a time lock on every move and like drugged monkeys, they rappelled down slowly, using the blanket of vines for rope, then switched to all fours, hands and boots digging into the muddy earth. At the bottom, they moved cautiously, nearing the entrance. Secluded from view, Logan inspected the surroundings. Vines clung to trees and bushes, a green shawl thrown over the land and draping to hide the underworld. Other than the soft patter of rain, it was painfully quiet. Logan didn't trust it a damn bit. Nothing had gone right on this mission and he didn't expect it to change. He moved to the entrance.

"We did it." Tessa felt a strange exhilaration. This was the end of the hunt and while they hadn't figured the last symbol, she was sure the answer was inside. She started to duck and Logan clamped down on her arm, avoiding her stitches.

"Do you *always* rush ahead without thinking?"

"Life's too short to waste, but fine, go on, be a cautious fuddy-duddy."

"I think I'm insulted." He pushed past her and shined the flashlight inside. It illuminated the cave walls, water trickling steadily and feeding the moss. The ceiling was low and Logan entered, inspecting everything on his way till Tessa tapped him, shooing him on.

"Hurry, it's going to really open up out there."

She was right; they didn't have time to lag, but the soft mud floor was already sucking at his boots and it wouldn't take much rain to fill this cave like a bucket. A few steps farther the ceiling rose. The narrow corridor was less stone than packed earth.

"The air is colder," she said behind him.

"We're going deeper."

"I guess this isn't a good time to mention I'm not fond of closed, inescapable, could-flatten-you-to-a-pulp-at-any-moment places. Although diving doesn't bother me in the least. How weird is that? I guess because I can swim away."

She was rambling, and frowning, he glanced back. She stared at the ceiling as if it were already falling.

"It's sloping here, careful." He pushed against the cave walls for stability and they crumbled.

Tessa whispered a quiet chant for the walls to remain standing just a little longer. "Then you can collapse," she whispered, patting the walls. "When I'm out, you can rest."

Logan smiled to himself, but it vanished when he lost his balance and landed on his rear. The momentum didn't stop his slide, and slick mud carried him swiftly to the bottom, tumbling him into a larger room. His shoulder hit hard and he winced, expecting Tessa to come flying after him. She didn't.

"Gee, I'm really glad you're the cautious one." The laugh in her voice had a shaky edge.

"No choice, honey. I'll catch you."

She didn't appear and he pushed up, looking toward the hollow in the wall. She bent to the slope.

"Heights, no problem but, oh, hell," she said and started down. When he could reach her, he grasped her by the waist and swung her from the tunnel. "Don't let that little fear destroy my image." She flexed her arms like Popeye.

He smiled widely. "Nothing could do that." He already knew her soul, he thought, and whatever she'd done in the past that made her stage her death was meaningless to him. A couple times he'd caught her with a look of such extreme sadness it was like a white glare in the dark. Whatever she was hiding, he'd wait to hear, but while his mind came up with scenarios that chilled his blood, he couldn't wrap his brain around Tessa doing any of it. Not willingly.

He searched the mud for the flashlight and smacked it against his palm a couple times before it came on, then shined it over the space. Bursts of blue and pink crystals shimmered from the cave walls. While Tessa *oohed* over the colors, Logan inspected the circumference. The only way out was the way they'd come.

"Now there's something you don't see every day," Tessa said.

It was an altar. Four feet tall, and its six-foot width spanned the small chamber. She and Logan had enough room to take three steps in any direction except toward the back where the altar filled the space. It wasn't carved; there were square stones set in place, moss growing between them. The floor pooled with a little water, but it slowly drained off somewhere under the altar.

"The stones are stacked like the ones in the mound," he said. "They fit tightly together."

"Does that mean pull one and they'd all go?"

"Only one way to find out. But which one?"

Tessa dug in her back pocket for the folded papers. She studied the last symbol. "It's shapes, that's a definite, but they're so close, it's hard to tell where one ends and the other begins." She put her thumb over the center, turning it sideways and back while Logan drew his knife from his hip, and started scraping moss, flinging chunks. One hit her boot and she shook it off into the puddle. The moss floated in a clump, then separated. Tessa looked from it to the symbol and inhaled sharply.

"It's pagan."

He frowned.

"It's a pagan altar, look." She showed him, her thumb over the center. "The lower left is a triangle, that's fire, the right is water, and center is the earth. Then these two, the dots on the upper left and right, are the goddess and the god."

"You're kidding."

She shook her head, still thinking. "It wouldn't be a Catholic altar. That would be too easy. Lots of religions have certain positions for the ceremonial tools." She shook her head as if explaining it to him would make her lose her train of thought.

"The woman is a staunch Catholic."

"But look back at all the other parts of this map. Celtic, Hunnic, Viking, Isis? All considered by scholars to have pagan roots." Excited now, Tessa forgot all about the confinement and crouched near the altar. She plucked at the moss, and they cleaned off the stones. "The ground here is mushy," she said.

Logan gripped the edge of the stone and shifted it. The one above it tilted and he stopped.

"They'll fall. There are more that move," she said on his right. "None of them are marked with anything except mold." She sat back. "Pull one, they fall. Don't pull, we can't end this."

They stared at the stone blocks, then Tessa stood and stepped back till she was against the opposite wall. His look questioned.

"I figure if Isis was the color of the stones, this might be similar."

He backed out of her view, but she didn't see anything special in it, then knelt and in the muddy ground, she drew the same symbols but spread them out a little.

She pointed left, then right. "The God, the Goddess." Then she did the same at the bottom of the rectangle. "Fire and water, and the center, spirit."

"Spirit?" It had been a grave.

She shook her head. "You said understand her motivation. This map has been all about confusion and enigma. Nothing has been the norm."

"I'll say."

"But it's all about *her*. This proves her intelligence, her cleverness. How she did any of this while being the wife of the Vice President is a mystery. She's proving a point to herself and now to us." Though Tessa was certain that was never her intention.

"So it's about her authority? That's a bit surreal."

"Think big ego and giant size hunger," she said almost distractedly as she studied the blocks and the representations. "Pull this one." She tapped a square. "It's the Goddess stone."

He hesitated. "I'm just not going to ask how you know this stuff anymore."

"I've got a pal who's a witch."

He looked at her, taken aback.

Tessa returned it deadpan. "I see we're going to have to work on broadening your outlook on several levels." She waved him on. "Give it a shot."

"Get ready to leap to the entrance in case anything decides to collapse." Then he muttered, "This is really stupid," before he pulled.

The stone slid out with little effort. The instant it cleared the edge of the others, he let out a breath, waiting for the world to go south. He ducked to look inside the hole, then, smiling to himself, he handed her the flashlight.

She frowned and bent, shining the light. Her brows shot up high and she looked at him, grinning. "Well, I guess there's no question it's really all her doing, huh?"

Logan reached into the gap and pulled out the small handbag.

Rain fell softly, the wind pushing leaves as Salazar slipped back behind the cover of trees and boulders. Well hidden and protected from the rain, they kept a line of sight on the cave.

"She is taller than I thought," Juan said softly, offering a bottle of water.

Salazar shook his head as he motioned Juan to take off the pack. They'd been here for nearly two hours, and he considered taking care of these two the instant he'd seen them, yet instead, lingered back to watch. His patience had paid off, and he admitted his surprise when they appeared from above the cave. The couple were without packs or weapons of any consequence, and stepped cautiously. He noticed a certain agile grace about the woman, and although she shadowed the man, it wasn't without her own confidence.

"Why do you wait?" Juan asked, his tone disgusted. "Just blow them up and be done with it." He plucked a grenade from his belt and pulled the pin.

Salazar's hand clamped on to Juan's wrist. "They die when I want them to die."

Juan frowned, then threw Salazar's hand off. "You're obsessed with a woman you've never met." He replaced the pin, then the grenade.

"Don't you want to meet her? She infiltrated into the very center of the house, and escaped without notice." He opened the pack, sliding out a metal case.

Juan pointed up. "She was on the roof."

"Intriguing, eh?" Salazar said and popped the locks, opening the case.

"You forget that bitch killed Cheuy?"

His tone challenged and Salazar's gaze narrowed. "No. I did not." But that she could do the same to him drove a curious rush through him. Strong women were uncommon to him and while he could easily take her body by force, that wasn't his interest. Willing, she'd be an adventure. "I'll avenge them, in my own time." From inside a case with a bed of foam, he removed the Dragunov rifle stock.

"You lost track of the purpose."

Salazar's gaze flicked to Juan. "I have but one." He assembled the sniper weapon with care, each click locking in place, then loaded the long bullets that would take his head right off. He'd allow the couple to find the final piece for him and bring it out. It was easier to search a dead body, he thought, smiling as he shot the bolt home.

"Liar," Juan scoffed, and Salazar glared. "You do this for money, not the cause."

Salazar pushed the pack into position and used it to brace the weapon, then focused through the scope. "Causes rise like the sun, Juan, and change with each politician. Before this day is over, they will change again." Weekly, his President angered world leaders, while Eloisa was fickle and power hungry. It mattered little to him unless it was in his personal interest to do so, but he'd never discount that Eloisa was the more dangerous of the two. She was a woman on constant PMS and unpredictable. "Money has no politics."

"You'll never get what you want from her."

"Then I'll take it." Inside the cluster of trees, Salazar sighted in.

The entrance was several yards ahead, the rain washing the earth and stone, sending thick streams of water off the hill and down into the cave. They would have to leave soon. There was no other way out.

* * *

"I've got slacks that color." Tessa couldn't be more stunned.

"She's insane." Logan handed it to her like it had cooties.

"This isn't just any handbag either." She inspected it, holding it by the crystal handle. Small, in lavender silk, it was heavy with beading depicting a swan; the beads so finely matched and intricate that you couldn't tell where the beads met fabric till you touched it. The specks of mold were inevitable but that told her it hadn't been here long. She peeked in the square, then reached inside. "Only a woman would try to protect this." She pulled out a scrap of muslin left to do just that. "It's custom-made or maybe Vera Wang. *Very* pricey." Just seeing this in the wilderness was unreal. "About four grand, maybe."

He made a sour face. "The impracticality of that is just sad."

"Not to a woman. The right accessory is like the perfect shade of lipstick. Unbeatable." She flipped the silver catch and pulled it open. She dipped her hand inside, scowled, then held out a wooden sphere the size of a plum. "It looks like a croquet ball." She shook it near her ear, then shrugged. "Solid, with weight." She tossed it up, caught it, then handed it to him. "It's nothing."

Shining his flashlight on the surface, Logan peered. "It can't be. You don't expend that much manpower or kill for a wood ball."

She leaned in as he passed the light back and forth over the smooth, polished surface. There were no seams that she could see and the grain of the wood was continuous as if honed from the center of a tree, but it was heavier. There was definitely something inside it. "Considering her puzzle fetish, there has to be a trick to opening it. If it opens at all. Which would really bite."

Logan twisted the sphere as if it would unscrew, but it didn't budge. "We need to see inside it. I've got an X-ray machine on Dragon Six, but that's in Caracas."

"Nearest clinic or hospital?"

"About thirty miles west."

"I'm all for getting out of the jungle." And doing it alive, she thought as her gaze dropped to her boots. Water rushed over them. From the entrance, more poured inside, filling the chamber. She grabbed at Logan. "Time to go!"

Logan dropped the sphere in the bag and Tessa stuffed it down her shirt and started up the slope. She jammed her boot toes into the mud and clawed, nearly on her stomach. Rainwater sluiced off the hill from above and flowed inside. She struggled to get up the muddy incline and used her nunchucks like spikes. The water washed away any leverage.

"Wait, let the water help you." He held her still, the water speeding past and thigh-deep already. "Let it take you up to the slope. It's not going anywhere else very quickly." It drained somewhere or it would still have more water than just puddles till now.

The water nearly to her chest and her shirt billowing, she felt her feet leave the ground. She knew she'd have less buoyancy in the narrow tunnel, but the water lifted, splashing her face, flowing around her shoulders. She kicked and climbed, digging her nunchucks in, the lift giving her enough momentum to move up. Then Logan was behind, underwater and pushing her. She felt vines and grasped them, pulling hard to get outside, and when her legs cleared the water, she turned for Logan. On her rear, she braced her feet wide apart in the mud, leaned and grabbed his shirt.

"Put some effort into it, you're heavy!"

He thrust out and landed on top of her between her thighs with a solid grunt. He met her gaze, pushing up. "I planned this." He smiled.

"I'd like to see what you can do with some real time on your hands." The hard rain created pools of coffee-colored water around them.

Logan pulled her more firmly beneath him. "Gimme a minute," he said and lowered to take her mouth.

"Would you two like to be alone?" a voice said and Logan instantly lurched back, aiming.

He didn't expect an Indian. Nor the six or seven guerrilla fighters who aimed their spanking-new Type 81 Chinese assault rifles. A bastard of the AK-47. Complete with grenade launchers.

Who says this isn't a fun country?

Twelve

Sebastian was hammering so hard he almost didn't feel the vibration of his cell phone in his pocket. Discretely, he glanced at the message. *Cutter has company.* The thermal readings were off the map. Logan could stave off a couple, but they were surrounded. He glanced in their direction, toward the river and the mountains. The peaks were surrounded with black clouds and dumping rain so hard it created a white mist in the lowlands.

He put away the cell, and hammered furiously for another three minutes before he pretended to stagger from the heat. He knew what they would do: they escorted him into the shade, gave him water and left him alone. He drank, then stood, heading toward the portable bathrooms set up past the private grounds. Then he walked right past and quickened his pace.

Getting to the chopper was going to be tricky, getting it in the air even tougher.

Christ. Shitty odds again, Logan thought, wishing he could catch a break. He rose slowly, his hand out to Tessa. He pulled her off the ground, then motioned her behind him. He stepped back. An instant later he heard the decisive *thip* of suppressor gunfire to his left as the shot whizzed past, leaving its stroke across his hair before it struck a tree.

He hit the ground with Tessa, scrambling back toward the

cave as the fighters returned fire in the direction of the sniper shot. Birds chased to the sky, the squawk of animals unequaled to the gunfire and Logan joined in, firing four rounds in the direction of the first shot. Return fire left a trail toward his feet, chunking wet dirt and water, and he backpedaled until they were tucked in the underbrush. He sheltered her with his body, feeling her flinch with each crack and report.

She muttered into his chest, "If I weren't a really stable person, I'd get a complex about this."

"People just don't want to enjoy our company," he said dryly, and cracked off four more rounds. "I don't get it. We're nice people."

He saw movement to his far left deeper in the forest. Escaping, he thought, and Logan pulled her back with him, physically pushing her where he wanted her to go, and they dug into the drape of vines, climbing the hill. Tessa moved like a crab ahead of him.

Muddy earth spread between his fingers as he dug for a hold, clinging vines pulling at his clothes and boots. They crested the ridge and burst onto the flatter land. They paused long enough to get their bearings, then ran for a half mile without stopping, bashing through the forest, and crossing a dirt road, then higher into the hills.

"Right, go right. To the packs."

"But they'll follow—"

"I have about seven rounds left."

"I told you to pack more bullets, honey."

"I know, dear," he said in a dull tone. "You were right."

"Never get tired of hearing that." She raced after him.

His boots thumped on the mud-soaked road, and he made no move to disguise it. They didn't have time. He could still hear the exchange of gunfire, though it was fading off. All that meant was that it was time to regroup to hit again. Reaching the spot, he uncovered the packs, glad for Tessa's poncho, then emptied the ammo into his pockets. He unhooked the Recon from his belt, sweeping aside mud and grass from the screen, and punched in the codes. Rain fell through the stand of trees, drenching them.

He read off numbers that had nothing to do with longitudes and latitudes. More military speak, Tessa thought. He tried to contact Max, and when he reached him, he'd barely said a word before gunfire sounded closer. Tessa dropped down beside him in a squat, double-checking the bag inside her shirt, and then slipping it inside her pack. Logan thumb typed so fast it was scary and it told her he worked his gizmos in tight situations a lot. He practically quaked with an odd energy, like an uncapped wire you weren't certain was live.

"Want to try this?" She held out her satellite phone. "I'm chuckless."

He glanced, smiled, water dripping off his hair and chin. Then the gunfire suddenly stopped, and he looked in the direction, scowling.

"Were those drug dealers or rebel fighters?"

"They don't inform us of their affiliations before they shoot."

She made a face.

"As far as I know, there aren't any suspected drug fields or factories in this small area, but the cartels aren't in the habit of making that public." He loaded bullets into a magazine. "There's no reason for rebels to tangle with us. We aren't a threat." So why was everyone so damn trigger-happy? What pushed those guerillas to come out of hiding for a couple of tourists? He popped the magazine in and chambered a bullet. "Follow this ridge. There's a stream to the right." He had one arm in the pack strap as he urged her with him into the woods, off the paths.

"Max will be going nuts, and this will just set back our relationship issues."

Logan's lips curved. "He's going to meet us. I gave him a rendezvous point."

Getting the hell away from gunfire was his only concern

and Logan could only assume that the shot came from their personal hunter. He had had plenty of time to set up the trap.

"We can't go to the car." He swung the blade, cutting through plant life. "They had to have seen it. Probably impounded or rigged to track, anyway." Or to blow up. But he kept that to himself. "This guy's no slacker, covering all the bases before I can think of them."

Great, Logan was about the smartest person she knew. "He's hunting fugitives," she said dispiritedly. "Yet he knew where to look for us so he obviously had the coordinates to the cave. What I don't get is, with all that authority at his fingertips, like the chopper, why didn't he just jump ahead and stop us at the cave?"

Logan didn't have trouble understanding this guy. "For him, it's the hunt, the risk. He's not interested in capture, either."

"I'm not comforted by that."

Neither was he. But their hunter had a lot of opportunities to kill them and didn't. That told him they really needed the map and orb back. "Till he gets what he wants, he'll play with us." He didn't think that would actually stop this guy. "You just keep that sphere close." Logan had the map.

The Recon vibrated and he grabbed it. "Air traffic is denying Sebastian clearance for the flight plan to this location. Damn." That just proved his assumptions again. The man had influence. "No choice but to drive." He directed her to the river. It was the fastest method out of there.

They didn't slow down. Hidden behind clouds, the sun started to set, the rain coming down hard, and making each muddy step a challenge. Logan could smell the river and pushed on. They could see a clearing in the distance and headed for it, then stopped suddenly, his gaze moving around the woods. He grabbed her close, weapon drawn.

"Was it something I said?" Oh, she hated it when he got that look, a current of awareness running through him.

He looked down at her, resolution in his eyes. "We're not alone."

"So right," a voice said; familiar with its teasing lilt. From the shadowed woods men emerged, but Logan's gaze went to the Indian in the center. Wearing black pants rolled up to midcalf, the man was bare-chested, a necklace of what looked like bones hanging between massive pecs and a red cloth tied around his forehead. His feet were bare and muddy, and he held a large elephant palm leaf like an umbrella.

And the T-81 rifle, of course.

Logan let his weapon dangle from his fingertips and lifted his hands. Outnumbered, he knew when not to fight back. If he fired, they'd return it and Tessa would die with him.

Salazar refused to leave the area.

Guerilla fighters were a surprise Salazar hadn't anticipated. Nor the bullet that grazed his thigh. He was lucky; the Chinese rifles could have taken his leg off at the kneecap. He tied a bandana around it, cinching it tightly and rushed with a staggered gait back toward the truck. He hated retreating, but he was outgunned. He radioed for the troops in the north to remain in their location. This man was *his*.

Juan moved up beside him with an expression of curious disappointment. "We cannot get to them. Give it up for the night."

"Night has little to do with this."

"The roads are blocked sufficiently and there's a wall of fighters between us. What do you think to accomplish and keep this covert?"

Salazar whipped around. "They have the map and orb, now the fighters do. Do you really think we can go home and sleep?"

Juan still wondered what was inside the sphere—then again, he probably didn't want to know at all.

Salazar pressed on, and Juan followed dutifully, mulling over this foray for the female he considered no more than a target they should eliminate. He suspected they were Americans and if so, Juan didn't want to kill them. The USA would hunt them unrelentingly, forcing them underground to escape retribution. But Salazar didn't see that. He thought he was immune to anything and anyone. Safe in his ugly stillness. It was the mental picture Juan always associated with Salazar. He rarely reacted to even the most grave of crises with little more than a sharpening of his features. He would not be denied success. While Juan had been at his side for three years, he wasn't always with him. Nor was he privy to every detail. Salazar cosseted information like an old woman and it reminded him to watch his own back.

The charges went off yards behind them and Juan turned sharply, the jungle on fire. "That was unnecessary, but effective." He hurried just the same. "The man will die to protect the woman."

"That's my plan. He's escaped our custody, and taking away his freedom and his woman will suffice."

They rushed the road, and Juan slowed his steps, but didn't offer Salazar any help. He wouldn't take it, anyway, despite that blood still dripped off his fingertips.

"They're captured. So we get them back tonight?" Juan jutted his chin toward the town, the lights in the low valley soft from the distance. Snatching them out wouldn't be easy and they'd need more men.

"We keep going." Salazar's tone was tired, the loss of blood affecting his speech.

It won't be long before he passes out, Juan thought, then glanced behind, walking backward for a few steps. He aimed to the trees. "Faster Diego." He could hear them coming.

Juan pushed him ahead, but his wounds hampered every step. Then Salazar tripped, going down on one knee before falling to his side.

Juan walked to where he lay and stared down, unsympathetic. "Now will you see reason? Before you die and leave this shit in my lap?"

Salazar struggled to stand, glared accusingly at Juan. "Your dedication to mission is disgusting."

Juan leveled him a look of warning. "Kiss my ass, Diego. I

can keep going. Admit that you cannot." Juan walked toward the truck parked down the road, and opened the door for him. The man limped, his bloody fist clenched. "I know a doctor."

Juan didn't mention he was tribal, and when Salazar was inside, he climbed in and put the truck in gear. Within minutes, Diego passed out and Juan hoped he stayed that way long enough for him to search him. It wasn't that Juan distrusted, but Salazar hadn't offered enough information and Juan was tired of seeing his friends die because the man played the game so guardedly. He didn't doubt it was a sport to Salazar. His entire life was a game of manipulating his surroundings to his advantage. He always remained on the edge looking in. No family, no friends. Only this. A sad existence.

Salazar's phone hummed and Juan glanced at the number. It was the seventh call from the same number, no name. He was tempted to dial it and for this reason, he memorized it, then let it go. Their assignment was to retrieve the map and a wooden ball. Salazar had told him little else, but Juan was not without recourses.

He pulled onto the road and the guards barely glanced up, the only light from the fire barrels between them. They were posted on the outermost roads near the highway. A pointless act because all the troops could do without raising suspicion was to question the comings and goings. They had no authority to pursue, and their paycheck wasn't enough to push them for more unless ordered. The Army would follow his orders out of fear, not respect. A time would come when Juan would be one of them, a knowledgeable threat. If he wasn't already.

Elizabeth Jacobs plastered on a bright smile as she opened the garden gate, her anxiety softening with the woman's sweet smile.

She really didn't have a problem with using Alice, and before she closed the gate, she glanced into the street, and found them easily. Two men sat in a parked car a block up the road. She looked to the building across the street and on this lovely summer day, the shades were drawn tight. But she could see the black rim of a night scope lens hidden behind the fern on the sill. They had a perfect view into the courtyard and her bedroom.

Hope you're getting a show, she thought, then closed the door behind Alice and led her into the brownstone. Liz didn't have many friends, the price of her job and being an admitted workaholic, and right now, the only one who came when she called was Alice. They'd met at a State Department dinner and were instantly comfortable around each other, mostly because Alice didn't pry. She was the wife of a diplomat and knew better.

"Are you all right? You sounded frazzled and on you that's a little scary."

Liz smiled. "I'm going stir-crazy in here alone and needed a friendly face."

Alice flashed her a cheesy smile, then walked around, tsking at the dead plants.

"Want some coffee?" Liz asked, heading into the kitchen. She paused long enough to turn on the radio, then poured coffee for them both. It was easy to get Alice to talk and Liz knew the right questions to ask. It was her job to know, and as they took their coffee to the living room, she was aware of the listening devices planted in the rooms. She'd found them the day after her operation fell apart and had moved two so they wouldn't get much on tape that she didn't want them to have. It would frustrate the surveillance team and she liked the hell out of that. They chatted about Alice's life, her kids. It made Liz see more clearly that they had nothing in common. While Alice could keep a conversation going, a diplomat's skill, she was concerned with party planning, schools and the upcoming holiday celebration. Liz's world was clandestine operations on foreign soil for national security. A social life didn't exist unless she was ordered to go have one.

They sat close, their voices low as Alice curled into the corner of the sofa and talked about her family.

Liz waited for the drugs to kick in.

Alice took another sip, and Liz watched her fade out mid-sentence, completely unaware that she had. Liz pried the mug from Alice's fingers and set it aside, then stripped Alice out of her clothes. She tossed a blanket over her before she went for the toolkit. On the floor at the end of the sofa, she worked to remove her electronic cuff, keeping pressure on the catch so her watchdogs wouldn't know it was open, then quickly transferred it to Alice. Liz didn't need to ensure Alice would stay put. She'd be long gone before anyone realized it.

She dressed in Alice's clothes, thinking she needed to lose a little weight if a woman with three children was thinner than she. She crossed to the living room to the end table, pushed it aside and flipped back the carpet. She pried up the wood floorboard, exposing the safe. It was a slender steel box, bulletproof, and designed to slide into a compact space; this time, the floor joists. She'd moved it before this op fell apart, before they searched her home and should turn it over to her boss, then thought, *fuck them all.*

She had the guts to do what should have been done. Needed to be done. Gutierrez was a threat beyond democracy. He'd already gathered more than the socialist Bolivian President and Fidel behind him, and was aligning himself with the Chinese and with very unfriendly Middle Eastern countries. He was a walking time bomb ready to start a war. Openly defying the UN, his fascist attitude alone denied his country's admittance into the Security Council. Not that the man could contribute a damn thing, she thought. If he wanted to live like Castro, fine, but shut the hell up and stick with the Cuban.

Instead, Gutierrez backed nuclear testing by democracy's enemies and offered to put their weapons on his soil. That was the real clincher. Iranian missiles within striking distance of the U.S.? He needed to be taken out. The coup had gone sour because the Gutierrez supporters got between the switch and shot Garcia in the head. Undisciplined idiots. Gutierrez alive was still a threat.

She hit the keypad. The safe popped open with a soft *shush* and she collected false passports, money, but no weapons. She'd get those later and added another grand to her mission funds. She dumped Alice's huge handbag, filled it with her own things and then headed to the door.

She stepped out and called back into the house before closing the door, then climbed into Alice's car and pulled onto the street. No one followed. She'd leave the car at Alice's house and take a cab. This was her last option. She'd failed to learn what McGill had on Tessa, or why her photo had been accessed. McGill was working her operation, too covert for her contacts to know anything about it, or maybe they saw the writing on her walls and refused to help. She was a pariah now, under house arrest, all her privileges revoked. She'd be in jail in a month or less, if she was lucky, and as far as she was concerned, there was no way of salvaging her career, but there was of her life.

And to do that, she had to make certain parts of it stayed dead.

Eloisa felt her breath punched out of her lungs with each heavy push of his body into hers. Mentally, she begged him to climax and be done with it. The niggle of annoyance brought some sympathy for his dead wife—enduring this for twenty-five years must have been revolting. His final grunt came blessedly swift with a passionate kiss. She responded wildly, insisting she needed more from him. It was what he wanted to hear. They all wanted to know when the next piece of ass was coming. He chuckled and rolled off her, flopping back, and a moment later he was in the bathroom. She grabbed the remote and flipped on the TV. The large plasma screen showed news footage, world leaders coming to meet and the uninvited were complaining. Then there was a flash of her husband with field workers, sweating in the heat, his sleeves rolled up.

She'd have to go home again and slow him down. She preferred him gone but couldn't be too hasty. He might be necessary.

Manuel came out of the bathroom, and she turned it off. He motioned, and she stifled a snarl, turning it back on.

"Your husband is making himself known when I recall a promise he wouldn't be saying a word."

He slid her a look that reminded her to tread carefully. "He's become overcautious, inspects everything. It's been difficult."

Impossible, she wanted to say. Estavan wouldn't touch her unless he was in front of a camera, and how he was guarding himself, she didn't know. As far as she knew, he never slept. She rolled toward Manuel and pulled the sheet over herself just enough so he didn't forget what he'd just had.

"I have argued for the general in the cabinet," he said, "because you said it would bring solidarity. It hasn't. I don't trust him. It's not good that I cannot trust my own people."

God. Why did men whine when they felt cornered? Defensive, ready to fight. The longer he talked, the closer the conversation led to the Americans. "Shut up, Manuel."

He went still, scowling at her.

She'd do anything to get him off that subject. "What do you want the general to do?"

"Agree with me. In public."

She laughed to herself, her hand sliding down her thigh, then up the inside. He watched her every move. "I can arrange that."

He scoffed. "It has no meaning if he does not say it willingly."

"You want the public to hear that or is it just for yourself?"

He scowled.

"Haven't you learned? We are in the eyes of world. Give the press a morsel, they will eat it and want more."

She waited for it to register, and he finally nodded. "You didn't want to know the details." She leaned back against the headboard, the sheet drawn between her thighs and barely covering her breasts. She tipped her chin down, her gaze on him as she let her legs part a little bit more. "I'll speak to the general." She exposed her breast a little more and when he didn't move, she forced her impatience down and prowled toward him.

He simply watched her with an odd fascination.

This will take some convincing, she thought, her hand wrapping his flaccid penis.

"Manny," she whispered, stroking him. "The general is away from his power, the army, and his duties are few. He's retained enough staff to order around and is content."

"His own don't trust him."

"But they trust *you,*" she said. He'd rewarded them for their loyalty with land and money like a feudal lord. She didn't think it was wise, but they could pass off the payments easily. "They're peasants. They've rallied behind you after the coup, and the rest will come around at the celebration."

That amused him, and she enjoyed it, playing to his belief he was a chosen leader, a man destined to change the world's opinion. He was as corrupt as the general, skirting international laws and outright breaking them in front of the world and from behind his desk. It gave her the advantage. When it came time for what she wanted, he'd capitulate. She'd made certain he'd have little choice.

None of them would.

The pounding rain eased off to a constant drizzle, and their boots squished in the mud as the men led them north. Tessa was close at his side, hands bound like his. A quarter mile along the ridge, Logan could see the town. It wasn't small or quaint but filled with color and movement, settled on the edge of the stream in a shallow valley. The next rolling hill, the next rise beyond the river and the mountains rose to white peaks. They either were too far away for anyone to notice the chain gang of people or no one cared.

They were surrounded by trained soldiers, not a group of rabble looking for a fight. Just about every signal and gesture was familiar and he deciphered enough of their language to confirm it. It was easier to think of them as professional soldiers and put them on equal footing.

He and Tessa had been stripped of everything except their clothes; all of it was in the packs and carried by a man a few feet ahead. No one spoke. Logan tried to maintain his sense of direction as they took them through a winding path, and he glanced to the mountains. Still at the same altitude.

They herded them toward it and that raised his hackles. They couldn't mean to walk them through town? Then their guards veered left, taking a narrow road around the circumference of the town. They passed behind homes and shops, and between the buildings Logan saw signs for riverboat rides. Their path curved before the land widened under the cover of trees, the ground grassless and muddy from the rain. His gaze swept their surroundings: the paths, the vehicles and their care, the possible weapons stash, then he noticed the children near a doorway, a mother behind them with a weapon in her hands. They felt threatened, he realized, and looked more closely at his surroundings.

The homes were individual with a designated property line and didn't resemble the humble buildings they'd seen since leaving the river. A couple hammocks were strung between trees, but it didn't have the poverty-stricken look of the small villages. It had the look of an assembled command post. Men were armed and roaming, but it was the ones he didn't see that kept him on edge.

Well fortified, secluded and decently far enough from the town, Logan suspected there were some strategically placed traps nearby. He and Tessa weren't a threat. So what made them all so aggressive? These people weren't hiding, at least not from the townsfolk. Yet Logan knew that whatever offense they'd committed, if their captors wanted it, they'd never get out of here alive. They had to convince them they weren't a threat.

He glanced at Tessa, expecting fear and saw only open curiosity. It reminded him again that what he expected from her wasn't what he'd get. He nudged her, and she met his gaze.

Tessa tried to smile, but with a rifle prodding her back she was all out of grins and giggles for the moment. She bit down the urge to talk to him, each step feeling like a dead man's walk. Logan was right; they were tourists to these people. They could be just locals defending their territory, or drug dealers doing the same. If the fighters were anti-socialists, they were well equipped, and had the capture routine down to a science as the outer rim of men split off from the group, narrowing it down to four and keeping them surrounded. The men led them like prizes, silent and armed.

Homes sat on the sloping hills, chickens and pigs penned under trees. That the men could walk the streets openly with weapons told her that either they had control or the people wanted them there. She couldn't tell. Everyone looked on with suspicion and animosity. Drug dealers would kill them or use them for ransom. Since no one would pay a penny, the clarity of "the rock and a hard place" actually stung through her chest. She glanced at Logan.

He didn't have that confident we'll-get-out-of-this look she'd come to love.

The soldiers stopped them at a long wood table outside one of the larger homes, and dropped the packs on the table. She felt like a kid waiting for the principal and peered into the house. The stucco was painted a soft orange with white trim, with curtains, furniture and a porch with rockers. After seeing a KitchenAid mixer in the middle of the Java jungle— actually running on a generator powered by fermented co- conut milk—nothing shocked her. But while the ratio of armed men to women was drastically lopsided, everyone ignored them as if there were some unspoken rule not to acknowl- edge them.

Yet Logan did the opposite, taking in everything, every face. From his position beside her, he let his gaze travel over the village, his neck craning, but he never moved his body, only his head, his eyes. It made their captors nervous enough that one poked him with his rifle barrel and told him to look at his feet. Logan didn't and turned his head, leveling a stare so chilling she felt the bite. The man didn't retreat, but his cockiness was certainly punctured, and Tessa smothered a smile, her fear ebbing a bit more. In a situation like this, Logan was the best weapon to have.

The hunter didn't expect the rebels, the only reason they were still alive, and if they got out of this unscathed, then *he* waited for them. The odds were getting slimmer, and she was about to say something to Logan when a sable-haired man pushed past another out the front door, then stopped on the porch, drying his face and throat with a towel. He tossed it to a woman heading inside, then looked at them as if he were sizing them up for auction.

Six foot at least, and in jeans and a mud brown tee shirt, he had huge shoulders, and she realized it was the same guy who had interrupted the start of some great foreplay at the cave. Even with the deep scar on his temple, throw a suit on him and he was easily corporate exec–ready. He ascended the three steps and stopped on the opposite side of the table. Someone brought him a chair, and he motioned to one of his men. The man came to Tessa and reached for her waist.

She stepped back. "Whoa, pal, no, no, no. Personal space." She batted his hands with hers. He obviously didn't consider her a threat and grabbed her waist belt. She twisted in his grasp, ignoring Logan's warning, yet before she could knee him in the nuts, he unbuckled it, sliding it free. Tessa went still and didn't utter a word, trying not to panic as that strange *lost* feeling swept through her. The soldier handed it to the *jefe* behind the table. He just laid it aside. Her gaze stayed locked on it.

"You'd better have a good reason for shooting at us," Logan said, and Tessa cringed.

"Brave talk from a man with no weapons."

"I don't need them."

Tessa rethought her position about the best-weapon thing

and tried not to gawk at him. He was drawing a line in the sand. *Now?*

"Do you get much done with this attitude?" the man asked.

Logan scowled, studied him. The man sounded more American than he did, but his features said otherwise. Then the man answered for him.

"I was educated in the U.S."

That didn't surprise Logan. "Who are you? Why would you waste your time with us?"

"I'll be asking the questions . . ." The man opened Logan's passport. "Logan Chambliss."

The man didn't offer an explanation and instead stood, drawing the packs in front of him. He didn't go through them and instead, held the Recon. He pulled out a penknife and snapped open the blade, then pried off the back.

Logan moved to stop him. A guard yanked him back by the arms and held him. If he removed the battery it would erase everything on it, but instead, he flicked the knife against a small square, the global positioning chip, and it popped out. He put it back together and did the same to Tessa's satellite phone. He crushed the chips into the mud. The idea was reasonable, Logan thought, but the ability to know and locate that particular chip was not.

Under the tarpaulin, the leader opened the packs, unloading everything. Some interesting lingerie rolled out of Tessa's pack and he glanced at her. She had her attention on her waist belt as if it would grow legs and walk away. The man examined each piece until he came to the handbag with the sphere and the map. He unfolded the latter, studied it for a second or two, then positioned the map on the table facing Logan. The leather had been in a plastic bag and was the only bone-dry thing for miles.

"This means what?"

"It's complicated." And explaining where it came from would get them killed, Logan thought, and stared at the map. The wind kicked up, snapping the tarp and sprinkling water.

Heavy drops hit the right corner of the map, just past the last symbol. Water flowered a stain on the leather, and Logan's breath locked when another symbol appeared. *This gal doesn't give up easy,* he thought, and something about the symbol pinged familiar.

"Try me." From the handbag, the man removed the sphere. He tossed the ball, caught it, then set it down.

Logan's gaze flicked up. He offered enough to keep him happy. "It's a map."

"For what?"

"We're looking for artifacts," Tessa said quickly. "I'm National Geographic Society. Look in there." She nodded to her waist belt beside him. He obeyed, unzipping the flat compartments, but his demeanor changed only slightly.

"You're a reporter," he said, suddenly angered.

"No, no. I'm a location scout. We're thinking of doing a show about the area. We're not a threat."

"Everyone is a threat," he said, opening Logan's wallet. "You're a doctor?" He looked up, "We need medical help." He gestured to the people moving in and out of a large tent a few yards away.

"No."

Tessa swung a wide-eyed look at him.

Then the man behind the table drew a gun and stuck it in her face. "You were saying?"

"Hurt her and you get nothing. *Nothing.*"

Logan's tone sizzled with outrage as Tessa stared down the barrel of the gun and wondered how far Logan would take this. When the man pulled back the hammer of the old .45, her reaction was instant. Every muscle locked. Sweat blistered her upper lip, and the only sound was her heartbeat pounding in her ears.

Oh, Jesus.

The tracking light on the screen went dead and Max cursed under his breath as he drove. The truck bounced over the uneven roads, and he could almost hear it sigh with relief when he hit something paved. He tapped the screen, bringing up the biomarkers. The two green dots blinked in unison. They had about two hours of time left before they'd dissolve and fade completely. He gunned the engine, the headlights flicking wildly over the mass of green and an occasional swinging monkey. The signal was good within a hundred feet and he headed higher toward the light in the distance.

Ahead, he spotted fire barrels, the silhouette of troops with rifles clear, and he slowed.

"Oh, shit." Immediately he turned off the headlights, downshifted, then in the dark turned back the way he'd come. "No one is taking that hill today." No one was getting off, either.

He pulled to the side of the road and carefully worked the truck into hiding with an easy out, then turned off the engines. Removing the loaded pistol from his holster he laid it on the seat beside him. He glanced at the screen. Except for the biomarker, he had no signal from the Recon or Tessa's satellite phone. Even the GPS tracker on Logan's belt had stopped sending. It had to be on him to activate. The biomarker would be gone by morning and locked on their last location. Logan and Tessa were farther up the hill and surrounded. Thermal readings were off the map.

On the wireless connection to the command post—a humble hotel he was already missing—he checked in with Riley and Sebastian, and relayed his situation.

"I tried going around the no-fly zone," Sebastian said, "but the tower ordered me back with some really creative threats."

"Troops on the road, threats to shoot you out of the sky? This just snowballs. Those are Garcia sympathizers in that town. I wish something would go right this week."

"It has," Riley said. "I figured out what Ramos was saying with hand signals. He's said quite a bit, actually. The first was coercion. He's being poisoned, or he was. So the shitty face was for real. Sources unknown. But at the first appearance the other day he was saying, *Protect Tessa,* over and over."

"You think he's got a thing for her?" Sebastian asked.

"Not a chance, he's a self-centered bastard," Max said, having a long dislike for Ramos he'd probably never get past.

"No," Sebastian said. "You didn't see him. He's Garcia. Gracia's words. Garcia's platform."

"And being seen," Max said. "He's made it impossible to get him out cleanly. He can't walk away or it will be a nation-wide search. How do we get him out now?"

"Ramos solved that part, too." Riley's tone was softer.

In the car, Max scowled. "What does he want us to do?"

"Kill him."

The sudden silence punctured that.

"That's just not funny," Max said. "It's a ringside seat to Ramos's death, and a quick execution for the shooter. The man's crazy."

"Oh, you bet, because he even gave us a deadline," Riley said. "Three days from now. The fifth of July. Catchy, huh?"

Tessa couldn't see anything except the gun barrel a few inches from her face.

"You have taken a Hippocratic oath," Cero said.

"Not for a murderer."

The man did a "so be it" shrug, and Logan stepped in front of her.

"You don't want to play this game with me," he said care-fully.

After a moment that stripped her nerves, the man tipped the barrel up and Tessa stumbled back. Getting shot at from a distance wasn't nearly as bad as staring down a barrel and seeing it coming. Enough to make her fold to her knees and fight the urge to vomit on the nearest pair of shoes.

Logan reached for her, but she shoved him off and stood on her own power. She glared at him. What was he thinking? She rubbed her face and exhaled slowly, then looked at the leader.

"Now. If you two are done measuring testosterone levels, how about we talk? Hi. I'm Tessa Carlyle, National Geo-graphic Society." She held out her hand, both still tied with rope. When he just looked at it, she wiggled her fingers and said, "You shake it."

The man chuckled softly. She wanted to belt him.

"I'm Cero," he said as he stood. He still held the knife and when he grasped her hand, he sliced the rope. He looked at Logan, and a little more warily, severed his. The guards didn't move from their position behind, weapons ready. Before she realized it, Logan drew his arm back and punched the guy.

Rifles cocked as the leader sank back into his chair.

"Geez. You *want* to get us killed today!"

Logan ignored her and leaned over Cero to say, "That's for putting a gun in her face."

They stared each other down like desperados on a dusty street.

Cero rubbed his jaw, the sting still exploding up his cheek. *Jesus, the man packed a lot of anger in that hit,* he thought. The man needed to protect his woman, he understood that, but he didn't believe their story.

His gaze shifted between them. Both looked like swamp rats in need of a bath.

Capturing them was more for information than as hostages. After the casualties they'd suffered, his men wanted revenge— on the wrong party, of course, but he needed to know why someone would fire on these two. It wouldn't keep their operation solvent if anyone knew. The troops lurking close were enough to increase protection around the town. Keeping this couple contained till he learned why was his only goal.

He met Chambliss's gaze and nodded.

Tessa let out a long breath. "Now, if you ask nicely this time I'm sure *Doctor* Chambliss will agree to help."

Tessa looked at Logan, her expression bland, but her eyes told him, *"Screw this up with me as a pawn and I'll find a nunchuck and beat the stuffing out of you."*

"Will you?" Cero asked.

"Will you guarantee our freedom?"

Cero didn't answer because a man rushed from the tent.

There was blood on his clothes and hands and he spoke to Cero in hushed tones.

Cero looked at Chambliss, his face distraught. "I guarantee you can leave."

"Show me," Logan said and hurried after the man toward the tent. But Logan didn't go inside and stopped short, looking at Cero. "She comes with me."

Cero shook his head.

Logan started walking back toward her. "We can go at this all night. You need me."

"*Jesùschristo*, there's no bargaining with you, is there?" Cero waved her to go with him.

Tessa followed Logan, but remained outside the tent. It was hard to tell what Logan was doing, there was so much blood. People helped him with instruments, but it was little more than battlefield triage.

"This man needs a hospital." Logan didn't look up from what he was doing.

"The nearest one with a surgeon is thirty miles."

"Do you want him to live? I can stop the bleeding, but he needs blood and surgery. You're not equipped." The last time Logan saw wounds like this was in Iraq. The man would lose his leg, he thought, and worked to save it. When the patient stirred, moaning, Logan issued orders to the nearest man. But he just stared blankly and he looked at Tessa. "Tell him more morphine."

She relayed the orders and dose. "Can I help?" she asked and he shook his head.

Blood crawled up his arms, his overshirt gone and his water-stained T-shirt already bloody. Her stomach rolled. Logan swabbed and injected the bleeding man, pausing for a moment to whisper to him and squeeze his hand.

Logan looked up. "A hospital, now. Or he loses that leg."

Cero flicked his hand and men obeyed.

The rev of engines and, moments later, a van appeared. Tessa stepped back as Logan helped load the man in and it rocked away. He watched it go for a moment, then turned back to the triage tent. There were three people waiting, all hastily bandaged. Logan checked each one, then looked at Cero.

"I need to wash up properly if you want me to continue." Cero inclined his head to follow, and Logan grabbed a fresh towel and some gloves before he glanced at Tessa, motioning to her. Cero hurried him into a house, and to a kitchen sink. Children and a woman moved out of the way, horrified at the blood on him.

Logan scrubbed his hands and arms. "We're nothing to you."

"You are steps ahead of several squads of troops."

Logan scowled. The troops they saw in the field? Or more? he wondered, and felt Tessa's gaze on him, asking the same thing.

"They were, until that fun time at the cave, working their way toward this area," Cero said. "We needed to know why."

If they'd tracked the troops' movement, then maybe this guy knew what was really going on. "Did you learn it?"

"You and the lady." He nodded to Tessa who was on the floor with the kids and apologizing to the woman for her muddy boots.

Logan leaned to rinse and Cero shook out a towel and handed it to him. "What makes you say that?"

"There's no one else in that area. The terrain is too rough for sightseeing and we are connected, Dr. Chambliss." He held up the TDS Recon. "How well do you know this man?"

Logan glanced at the picture on the Recon, one of nearly two dozen in an ongoing reference search to match the composite of the diver. He went through hundreds a day but Logan's description from a speeding chopper, fifty feet above him was anything but solid. "I don't."

Then Cero worked the Recon, the fact that he had it and all the information was a threat in itself, but then Cero showed Logan's composite and next to it a matched photo that looked ten years old.

"How about now?"

Logan grabbed it, forgetting about his sterile hands and stared at the face.

Tessa rose from the floor and came to him. "That looks like the guy who's following us." She cast a quick glance at Cero.

Logan's gaze snapped to her. "You saw him? Clearly?"

"Yes, though from up a tree."

Logan met his gaze. "Who is he?"

"Diego Salazar. *Commandante* Salazar," Cero said.

Logan looked at the old ID photo, taken at age twenty-five, maybe. It had a generic look about it, and if Riley hadn't sent it, he'd have thought it was PhotoShoped.

"He answers to no one but *el Presidente,* but the truth? He has more power than him and most of the Army is loyal to him."

"An Army?" Tessa said. "We'll need more bullets, then."

Logan wasn't listening and scrolled the pictures. There were three photos of men whose appearance was so close to Salazar they could be related, yet none with a Venezuelan background, nor was any information on them blocked. He could find it out, use the Recon like a cell phone, but at least he knew who was chasing them. Discreetly, he erased several files, but he wasn't dumb enough to put anything classified on the computer in the first place. He tried to send a message to Max, but Cero took it back, tsking politely.

"I'll be getting that back before I go," Logan warned, then returned to the sink and washed again.

He almost couldn't think, words rolling through his mind over and over . . . *Was Cassie's killer within reach?* Or was he just seeing a resemblance because he wanted the chance to bring in her murderer? He shook his head with a self-deprecating laugh. Revenge, he thought, admitting his outrage still ran deep.

The last images of Cassie's life flashed in his mind. The blood, the spilled champagne, the bridal gown still bearing the creases from her wedding day.

No question about it.

Capture was not an option.

Thirteen

Nolan Deets had never been nervous in his job. It was a calling of sorts and a comfortable fit. But getting on the bad side of a three-star had the potential for a quick career ruin. Explaining why he was monitoring his operation, even if McGill refused to release any information on Petruscu, he needed to have some of NSA's pieces.

The locks engaged behind him and McGill was waiting, his arms folded and looking like a bear roused out of hibernation.

"You're not here to cause me more indigestion, are you, Agent Deets?"

"No, sir, and thank you for seeing me again."

"Tell me why I should."

McGill didn't have much doubt about Deets's security, but he did about anyone near him. If he could trust more, he wouldn't be here in said undisclosed location, in a fake Frank Lloyd Wright house that didn't quite get it right.

Nolan held out the CD.

McGill recognized the label markings of the spy satellite and sighed tiredly. "You're mine till this is done. I'll arrange it."

Nolan only nodded.

"I'll say this once, Agent Deets. Liz Jacobs and her crimes are secondary. Security cannot be compromised. If you're the cause, don't worry about your job, because I will *personally* come down on your ass so hard you'll feel lava, got it?"

"Yes, sir." Oh, hell. What was he getting himself into here? But he had to know the truth and if this was the way . . . "Agreed."

McGill didn't explain further and led him to the elevator. On the lower level, he introduced Deets, then handed the CD to Walker. A large flat screen mounted to the left played the video.

"Satellite imagery. Very focused. China?"

Deets nodded. "Basuo Port, Hainan. It's a modest—"

"I'm aware." McGill kept his attention on the three trucks lined up outside the dock area, then on the dock. A small ship, he thought, nonmilitary, a hundred fifty feet, maybe. From the east, trucks approached and stopped on the pier, then men boarded the ship.

"They're searching, obviously," Deets said. "Our sources say it was chemical. The ship sailed with the morning tide and made port in Miami. I got a notification ping on it along with Customs and Homeland Security. It was inspected, then released for loading."

McGill whirled his chair to face the man. "If you have a point, make it."

"The same ship was attacked and nearly sunk off the coast of Jamaica."

McGill frowned, raking through his thoughts, then his features went taut. The yacht with Logan's friends aboard. "They were all murdered on international waters. Interpol has the case."

"And Dragon One," Deets said.

McGill arched a brow.

"Chambliss and I were grad school roommates. I asked to be assigned to the yacht investigation. I backtracked the ship and anyone who got near it. The original voyage was from China to Miami. No passengers. No cargo except the standard staples for the skeleton crew and added fuel tanks. That's a lot of fuel to pay for with no one aboard. I traced the payment to a Grand Cayman account, and to the owner, Eloisa Garcia."

Walker swung around in his chair. "Her?" He pointed to the smaller screen with Venezuelan TV showing Mrs. Garcia opening some center.

Deets nodded. The look on the general's face said he understood what led him from a murder on the high seas to Jacobs's phone call. "She's wealthy in her own right. A hundred million easy, enough to buy anything, and most of it from private deals with the Chinese for oil. She owns 12 percent of the country's oil reserves and the acreage where they're drilling for more, despite their own deforestation laws. There's no telling what she bought or why."

McGill didn't look surprised. In fact, he hadn't appeared any more than curious.

"Sir?" Nolan asked quietly. "You know what the Chinese were looking for, don't you?"

"Unfortunately, yes."

They weren't allowed privacy, nor hot water. She wasn't going to complain. Anything was better than the grass and mud itching her skin, but the outdoor shower was no more than a troop shower, a box with a partition of wood between her and Logan. An armed guard stood less than ten feet away, and didn't have the decency to turn his back, so, being naked with Logan in the dark wasn't as exciting as she'd like. She stepped under the water to rinse her hair and flinched at the cold slap.

Logan stared across the partition. "You're mad at me still."

Her gaze slid to his. "Hell yes, I'm mad," she said, yet with little venom. "What were you thinking, using me as a pawn like that? I've never been so scared . . . damn it." She huffed, scrubbing harder. "I want to slap you so bad right now."

"If it will make you feel better." He leaned his face in, icy water splashing his back. "Slug away."

"Don't think I won't, Chambliss." She put her hand over

his face and shoved him back, smiling. "I'm over it now, and you really just wanted a look at my breasts."

"There is that, and your tight little butt, but my skills were our only bargaining chip at the time, and I'm sorry he scared you."

"The punch in the face counts for something." She dragged the rag over herself, keeping eye contact with him when she really wanted to jump over the partition and go from there. "He got what he wanted."

"So did we."

"That would entail trusting him to keep his end of the bargain."

"Trust is not a consideration." He waved at the shower and their clothing on posts nearby. "But we could be in a cell somewhere or dead." Cero had already returned the packs and clothing, though without their IDs, weapons and phones—Tessa's didn't work at all without the GPS chip to bounce off the satellites—Cero also kept the map and orb.

"There was another sign on the map."

Her gaze snapped to his. "How can there be? We have—had—the sphere. It's over."

He told her about the water bringing it out. "It's familiar, but I can't place it."

"Try. This woman is nutsy cuckoo, no telling what it could mean."

"I don't care if it's a tip to shop at Macy's, we can't leave without it." He really didn't want to fight to get it back, but Cero was overly paranoid about their presence.

"Who are these guys, you think?" she asked, leaning near enough that he got a perfect view of her muscled body, soapy-skin slick in the torch light, and Logan thought, *Who cares?*

She flicked soap at him, and when he looked up, she said, "Try to stay focused."

"Too much fun losing it," he said with feeling, then lathered his face and picked up a disposable razor. "They're not drug manufacturers. We'd see the waste evidence or something to hint at it. They could just be protecting these folk from the army Cero said was in the north. No one trusts them after the coup, then switching sides." And now trained by Chinese.

"I don't know," she said thoughtfully and looked around, the darkness lit with torches and farther toward the town, with streetlamps. Other than the guard, there was no one milling around.

"You get the feeling it's more like keeping trespassers out than us in?"

She looked at him sharply. "Yeah." She hung over the partition, her voice low. "After he got a look at your Bluetooth PDA thing, he changed his tune. One minute a gun in my face, and then next, telling you about Salazar?" She shook her head.

"Knows a lot about him, doesn't he? Adversaries, I'd guess. He didn't have to tell us. He's making sure Salazar isn't aware of this." He inclined his head to the guard and Cero's house. "The photo match is just a computer-generated guess. It matches general physical, but not exact bone structure. We'd need an expert and pictures of both, DNA, prints, something more."

"Or a dental record," she muttered. "Preferably charred to death and that's after we light his ass on fire and shoot him out of a cannon."

He just arched a brow, amused. "Salazar is real enough, and he's clean-up," he said, then noticed her go still. "He could have taken that map at any time since we left the Isis mound. Playing with us, remember? That has me wondering, Who is Cero and what's his game?"

He looked around as if some clue would jump out at him and Tessa thought, *There goes that superman thing again.* "Please don't look for more trouble. We're involved in enough."

He met her gaze. "They're connected."

"How's that our problem? Salazar's a badass, and we all hate him, yeah. But he's out there waiting. Or will he try to get us here?"

"Only if he brings the Army, and he won't. We're actually safer here for the night."

She nodded, then suddenly disappeared from his sight—scrubbing somewhere interesting, Logan thought—before she popped back up a moment later.

"Cero's got my passport and ID."

Her face looked strained at the mention of it. "I'll get it back."

"Promise?"

Logan frowned at the hope in her face. "I can get you another anyway." He shaved.

"I know, but I need that one. I feel like a nobody without it."

"It's fake."

"Only the last name," she defended. "And I know my attachment to forged documents ranks right up there with admiring a paint-by-number Mona Lisa, but that's the way it is." Her last words were muffled under the pour of water as she rinsed.

Logan shut off the water and reached for the towel thrown over the crooked bat-wing doors. He met her gaze, drying. "What's really going on here?"

Tessa twisted her hair, wringing water. "You have records, mine are in the archives somewhere with KIA stamped on the front. It's got to stay that way. Cero's got my identity and I *have* to control it. I can't rise from the dead."

Logan had every intention of rectifying this problem and bringing her back from the dead after this was over, but that would mean she'd have to confide in him, and she still wasn't ready to do that. Exasperating, but he was patient and nothing could be done now, anyway. "I'll get it back if I have to steal it."

She eyed him.

"Trust me?"

It struck her again, had almost daily for eleven years, that other than her mother, Tessa didn't have anyone she *could* trust.

Till now. It was a strangely euphoric feeling, like a long-held breath finally exhaled. "Without a doubt."

He grinned for the first time since he'd realized they were surrounded, and crooked a finger. She moved to the wall separating his naked body from hers.

"I'll make this right for you, I swear it."

She tipped her head. "I know you'll try, Logan. It's the only thing I can count on." He'd already asked a three-star general to bury her files. But neither of them knew what they were up against, or rather *who*. She'd lose everything and while it wasn't much, this moment would wither and die beneath the cover-up of the century. Her throat tightened and she hung on the edge of the door, and when Logan leaned in and brushed his mouth over hers, she made a sound in the back of her throat and sank into his kiss.

He took more, deeper. "Damn this wall."

"Come over to my side and play."

He met her gaze.

"We're already naked in the wilderness, what's the problem?"

He smiled, loving her frankness. "Witnesses?"

"Wait till I get you alone." She slid her tongue over his lower lip and his breath hitched. "I've learned a lot since last time."

"God. I didn't need to hear that." His muscles tightened in a ripple down to his heels and he deepened his kiss.

"Wake up, Logan, I've been trying to get you in the sack since Carrión's."

He grinned against her lips, yet the sudden slide of a bullet into the chamber separated them. The guard aimed, yet behind the sight of the loaded weapon, he grinned.

"We're naked. What threat could we be?" she asked in Spanish.

The guard spoke, and Tessa looked at Logan.

"He said there are children here and we're X-rated." She peered over the edge, arching a tapered brow. He was wrapped in a towel, dammit.

"Not yet," Logan muttered, putting his hands up.

Tessa laughed to herself, and Logan reached for his clothes, dressing, though stuffing himself in his jeans was a chore.

Dressed and her hair wrapped in the towel, she sat on a stump to put on her boots. She didn't bother to tie them. Logan stood beside her, his look daring the guard to comment, but the guy kept his mouth shut, smirking when he led them to the end of the road, under the trees to a humble A-frame tent. It was positioned away from the road and yet in perfect view of the tents housing troops. No escape. Three men sat near a campfire a few yards away and glanced up, nodding to the guard.

The troops had better accommodations, but that they gave them *any* consideration was due to Logan and she was grateful, and suspicious. It was as if they were trying to soften their capture, yet still cautious. Then why didn't Cero just let them go? The only threat to either of them was Salazar.

Tessa ducked under the flap, the guard remaining outside, a short distance away. Inside were a couple of rusty iron beds, each with a lumpy mattress and blankets. A lantern sat on a wooden box. "Wow the Ritz of the jungle."

Tessa found her comb, then noticed the tray of food on the wooden box. She immediately sat down and opened a water bottle, then tore off a hunk of bread. The bed creaked with every motion and worse when she worked off her boots. The other bed was no better. Logan closed the flap, then sat beside her to inspect her stitches. She held out a bite of bread for him and he ate it, then probed the wound enough to make her wince.

"Ow. That's all you can think to do with me?"

He met her gaze, loving the dare in her eyes. "You've already filled my shower fantasies for the year." Then he bounced on the cot. It shrieked loudly. "That's a siren to our neighbors, dear."

"That white-hat Southern gentleman is annoying," she said, playfully pushing him away. "And my ego will only take so much rejection."

He made her look at him. "I'm not rejecting a damn thing . . . Jesus, it's been painful to keep my hands off of you, but I don't want them having a ringside seat in shadow puppets." Which is exactly what they'd see.

"You're thinking of my modesty?" She smiled, touched, actually. "After bathing in front of five of them?" She fed him a piece of spicy meat. "I'll just torture you till you see things my way."

She licked her fingers and Logan grabbed her hand. "You don't have to make an effort." Then he leaned in to whisper, "I remember what it was like to be inside you."

Tessa moaned, sinking into the memory, and turned her face toward his.

He didn't stop there. "And the taste of you on my tongue," he began and dragged his tongue down her throat. Her head fell back. "All of it," he said darkly and scraped his teeth over her skin, then took her mouth in a heavy slide of lips and tongue that only fueled the need.

"Oh, yeah, now that's what I'm talking about."

His chuckle was dark, so masculine it slid over her skin, waking the core of her.

Her hands moved down his chest and closed over the bulge in his jeans. "Think of something, Logan."

He easily drew her across his lap, his hands molding her thighs and under her shorts. "Yeah, we need to finish this."

She tipped her head back, exposing her throat. "Ravish me. Quick."

"I'm trying—God, you taste good." He wanted to eat her alive.

"Dressing was such a waste, huh?"

He nipped at the curve of her shoulder, her collarbone, but when she wiggled closer, the bed creaked.

Logan leaned back, breathing a little fast, then reached for his pack. He found a Chem-Lite, ripped it open and bent the plastic till it cracked and glowed green inside the tent. He put out the lantern, throwing them in pale darkness. He reached across to the other cot, gripped the straw mattress and dragged it to the ground.

"Clever."

"Improvise, adapt . . ."

"I thought that was the Marines not SEALs." Her tongue found his ear, her teeth tugging his lobe before she ground her lips to his throat.

"I was Marine first, then qualified for the teams . . . ahh, jeez, I can't think when you do that."

"Good. I plan to use all my womanly powers on you." She moved with him to the straw bedding. "We're not kids. No guessing, no wondering, 'Will she?' I will." She stripped off his shirt, his skin still damp from the shower, smelling of homemade soap.

"Thank God." He worked her shirt and bra off in one effort and Logan nearly swallowed his tongue.

"Go ahead, say it. Nice rack."

He met her gaze, sheepish. "Well, it is."

She laughed to herself, shaking her head. "The whole guys-and-breasts thing, we've got you over a barrel with no effort." She brought his hands to her breasts and the instant he cupped her, wild sensations started coiling out of control. She moaned his name, covering his hands and dropping her head back. He massaged, smoothed, and she leaned back, offering herself, and he loved the breathless sound she made when his lips closed over her nipple.

He worried the tight, hard peaks, then took one deep into his mouth, the hot pull of heat driving a bolt of heat to her center. She went liquid inside. God. No one else made her want like he did. Just looking at him brought a primal hunger to have him closer. She didn't need a seduction and yet wanted it. His hands spanned her rib cage, pulling her near and on her knees, he opened her shorts, pushing them down. His fingers playing over the skin he exposed. She was bare beneath.

He arched a brow. "My erotic fantasies just reached a new peak."

"Told you dressing was pointless." Her mouth played over his, her tongue sliding. He mapped the curve of her behind, his stomach flexing when she opened his jeans, working them down, easy, since they'd taken his belt. She tossed his jeans on the bed, looking her fill at ropey muscles and wanting him more. Then he dragged her into his arms, his mouth devouring hers till kisses weren't enough.

They'd never be, Logan thought, and sampled the underside of her breast, his teeth raking before his lips closed over her nipple again. She arched into him, her fingers combing into his hair, holding him right there.

"I feel like we're in the back of Daddy's Chevy."

"Something to be said for age and patience," he whispered, dragging his tongue down the taut line of her stomach, and then he noticed the lack of tan lines. It made him harder. Her hands went to his shoulders, heat rolling off them and musty in the tent.

He met her gaze and felt something shattering between them, pieces cut, a few falling away, and when she reached between them, he stopped her, catching her hands.

"That still works really fast around you," he said with a self-conscious glance. "I wanna play."

He didn't give her a choice, and he kissed her with slow deliberation, drinking in more than a kiss with a woman he thought he'd lost forever. His arms closed slowly around her, drawing her in, and she could feel his heart in it. Something was different. The heat between them steadily grew, and he stretched her over his arm, tasting her flesh, his hand slipping and diving. She was an adventure in contours and he explored her with the persistence of a man who knew what he wanted, and enjoyed the journey.

His hands rode her thighs to her toes, a soft brush over her center, and she said something in Romanian. He smiled, moved lower, finding the curve in her hip especially sensitive and making her squirm.

Tessa didn't have a thought in her head. Not one. Well, maybe the constant shriek of "Oh my God, that's good," but when his hand slid between her thighs, parting her so gently, the anticipation spiraled through her with the rush of dampness. He pushed a finger inside.

"Oh . . . God."

He dipped and played with exquisite skill, her skin tingling with a hot pulse, damp under his hand. Then his mouth found her, his tongue slicking over soft flesh and Tessa watched him, fascinated, then was lost in the swallow of sensation fighting for her attention. He circled the delicate bead of her sex, and she flinched with pleasure, the impact snapping down her body, circling her hips, and diving lower. She twisted in his arms.

"Come here."

He didn't. "Control freak."

"Nah, leverage," she said with a smile, leaning up. She pushed his shoulders, forcing him back. She straddled his thighs, his erection a gauntlet between them, and she encircled him. He let out that wonderful man-groan, deep and scraping, and she smoothed her fingers over the tip, molding him as she inched up higher. She rocked, her wet center slicking him, and his eyes flared.

He gripped her hips. "Oh God, be still."

But she kept touching him, circling, sliding. His breath hissed through his clenched teeth and his "Jesus" was barely audible. She rose, her thighs flexing as she guided him. Her gaze locked with his, she sank down.

His hand swept over her hair, holding her face. She smiled, her eyes a little teary. She'd been alone so long. Not just the solitude of her job, but in her soul, she'd felt abandoned. She clung to him, arms locked tight.

"I really missed you," she whispered.

His hold tightened, and he buried his face in the curve of her throat, his hands soothing her spine. She kissed his throat, his shoulder, then her mouth found his, the stir between them heavy with the pulse of desire, an ache pushing beyond the heart. They moved, and Tessa couldn't drag her gaze away from his, didn't want to, and loved the patience neither had eleven years ago. They weren't all about the lust of the moment, and staring into his eyes shadowed in the dark, she wanted this to be more than sex and satisfaction, and with each gentle push of his body into hers, she felt her blood move slower and pull in her soul.

Logan held her, something inside him unraveling as his hand swept her spine, his touch light on her body. She had a roundness he liked, and it felt ripe under his hands. She was unafraid, like she was in life, seizing what she wanted because she denied herself any connection to stay hidden.

"I've thought about this a lot."

"Me too."

"Yeah, but you thought I was dead."

"That didn't matter." His words whispered over her lips. "I never really let you go."

Tessa's throat clamped like a fist, and his kiss soothed it, their bodies pushing into each other. Her fingertips followed the lines of his face, her breath shuddered, and she clutched him, fused with him with each slippery stroke. Nothing mattered, not even the evil outside the door. Inside here, she had Logan and didn't imagine beyond this moment. Everything intensified; the taste of him, the slide, and the sound of skin to skin, the feel of his mouth, the roll of his hips. Tremors racked her body, and he cupped the back of her neck, his forehead to hers before he kissed her. Her breath panted and she quickened, whispering erotic details that drove him quickly to the edge. He pushed her legs around his waist and lowered her to the mattress.

The scent of straw rose around them. Stone hard, his hips pistoned in a pace he couldn't control, and she welcomed it, clamping herself around him, and he kissed her. Long and lean, she kept thrusting, throwing a heat wave at him, and the power of him pushed her across the mat. Her body quaked, her gasps filling the dim tent. He was lost in her, tension low in his stomach, each motion thickening him, making every tiny sensation raw and primal. Tendrils of pleasure wrapped him, riding his spine, impatient for the friction that would put him over the edge.

Then she did it. He felt her climax around him, the wild flex of muscles, the squeeze, and he never lost sight of her as he joined her, the savage peel crashing though him. She grabbed his face, kissed him wildly and refused to let the moment fade. They were suspended for long, glorious seconds, fused before muscles started to relax again.

When he could catch his breath, he met her gaze, sweeping her hair off her face and kissing her softly. God, her body was still shaking.

"We do that really well."

"Oh, hell yes." He grinned. "I'd like to say something profound, but . . ." He shook his head. "Nope, nothing left in the brain."

"That's okay, I wasn't after your brain."

Logan laughed quietly, and they wiggled into the sagging mattress. The scent of straw and dirt reminded her of the circus, of home as she drifted into sleep, and for the first time in eleven years, she felt truly safe.

Juan drew on a thin cigar, exhaling and blowing on the tip as he propped his feet on an old crate. He listened to the sounds of the night. Behind him was a shack on stilts half-submerged in the river, and ahead a floating dock stretched beyond the banks. The water rolled and swelled for a moment, and he glimpsed the jagged scales of a croc. There was enough brackish water and fallen trees that he'd bet there was a carcass or two shoved under a dam of debris.

A noise made him twist to look inside the shack.

Salazar lay stretched on a grass mat, stripped naked and sweating profusely. A good sign. The tribal shaman worked over him. It was a lot of rattle shaking and chanting, the ribbons of scented smoke curling into the small space, yet Juan had seen the man work miracles without modern medicine. Once on himself. Salazar's shoulder wasn't in too bad a shape. He just kept breaking it open, and the shot to his thigh was little more than a deep scratch.

The Yanomami Indian brushed back the drape that served as a door and stepped out. Sopai met Juan's gaze and nodded. Juan didn't speak his name out loud. It was an insult to pronounce it in front of the owner. Narrow and hunched, Sopai was fit for an old man, his body tattooed with tribal markings across his forehead, cheekbones. Blue dots and shapes colored his chest and arms, the symbols reminding Juan of the map he'd only glimpsed. The copy was in his pocket. There was no reason for it now, though he had to take Salazar's word for it. Salazar hadn't said where his orders had come from, only to retrieve the map and orb. They'd go after the couple at daybreak.

Salazar would want him to continue, but Juan didn't have the information nor the incentive to keep going. He wasn't devoted like Salazar, who believed in his soul that what he was doing was right and correct. For the money. It was someone else's agenda, and Juan saw no way it would benefit Salazar other than a paycheck. Which was the only reason Juan was still here. Money had a way of blurring duty. Learn the real truth, the reason behind the orb, his thoughts nudged. He had a feeling even Salazar was kept in ignorance.

He dragged on the cigar, then from his pocket handed another to the shaman. The man's wrinkled face split in delight, and he bit the tip, spitting it aside before he accepted a light. His tattooed cheeks puffed hard before he sat, his necklace of beads and shells clicking as he moved. His head was banded with a faded scarf, his pierced ears dangling with bright yellow and red Macaw feathers.

"He'll live," Sopai told Juan, his voice surprisingly mellow. "His soul is black."

"So is mine." Juan had lost count of the sourness of his own life.

Sopai shook his head. "He cares for nothing. Not even himself." The shaman twisted to look into the hut.

Salazar wasn't aware of his surroundings, under the influence of the fever and whatever Sopai had given him. Salazar didn't know how lucky he was because Sopai, at first, had refused to treat him, insisting his arrival was a bad omen, and Sopai wouldn't touch him till Juan dumped him in the river first. Even then, it had taken some convincing and a few gifts. It was all Juan could do for Diego. Anything more would expose them. Juan smoked leisurely with Sopai, both enjoying the rare breeze, and waiting to see if Salazar survived enough to finish this hunt.

Sitting up with her arms wrapped around her legs, her chin on her knees, Tessa watched Logan sleep, not really amazed at how contented she was to do just that. Being near him shaved away doubt and fear. Well. Let's not go too off the wall. Though if he kept up that Superman thing, she'd have to adjust or find a nunchuck. Her lips curved, and she tucked the threadbare blanket a little higher on his chest. He looked so relaxed, the lines between his eyes that always showed when he was in deep thought were gone, yet there was nothing boyish or innocent about him, even asleep. Pushing forty, a few scars and new bruises, Logan was effortlessly a *man*— strong, skilled and sexy—and he made her more aware of herself as a woman. But then, that was the reason she went to his room eleven years ago. That, and to say good-bye.

She believed if it were possible to keep her presence unknown, he could do it. But she was a realist. It was a mess that couldn't be fixed, and she felt as she had years ago . . . breakable. She didn't like it and managed not to think about what being near Ramos meant. People who knew him, knew her. Yet things were different now. Not just between her and Logan. Ramos wasn't a threat, he was trapped. She'd come here to do whatever it took to end this. Blackmailed, sure, but she'd just wanted to do what needed to be done so she could go back to her job without ghosts. There was a comfort in being reborn, in starting fresh, just as there were supreme drawbacks. Like guilt over those she'd hurt. Even her mom got in a couple well-targeted potshots. But then, that's a mother's gift. Guilt us into growing up.

Stop hiding and do something, played in her head and she pressed her forehead to her knees. She didn't sign up for the intelligence field, although it would probably be exciting now, with some training, but three years before she was keeping secrets for her government—she was partying with frat boys at Nebraska State and chugging a beer bong. *Okay, quit justifying yourself. It's done.* It was time to see if she could salvage her life. She lifted her head and found Logan awake, and wearing nothing but a smile.

It fell slowly and he sat up, frowning. "Talk to me."

Tessa's mouth went dry, and she felt like the coward he'd once called her. She inhaled and on the exhale said, "Elizabeth Jacobs. The tactical operations chief. She's most of the reason I staged my death." Her shoulders tensed as if awaiting a blow.

Logan searched her upturned face and the impact of her confession clutched at his chest. He grasped her hand and she squeezed back. "You sure you want to tell me this?"

"I have to. I—" She started a couple of times, then closed her mouth.

"Take your time." She looked on the verge of a scream.

"I haven't said this out loud, ever. And I think it's only fair to warn you, I'll make your life worse."

"I doubt it."

She scoffed. "Think about the worst thing you've ever seen in your entire life, Logan. A scene that haunts you with the slightest provocation."

"You, blown up."

Her eyes watered, and she leaned, kissed him. "I'm sorry."

She sat back, cross-legged, then pushed her hair off her shoulders. "I was sent into a refugee camp in Serbia about a hundred miles north of Bōr," she said, staring at her manicure. "There were a lot of tent villages like it. People just trying to stay out of the crossfire. It was a mess in one city and untouched in the region near the Romanian border. I posed as an aid worker to search for weapons of any kind and, well, bad guys." Her voice was flat, weary. "It was summer, beautifully green, cool weather, but all very makeshift, no established help or order. There were three of us with the medical staff. We were inoculating, so I got around. I met some great people and the children were incredible." Her tone lightened. "They had nothing except their clothes and their families, but you'd never know it. They made me forget I was spying on them. A little boy, Sammy, attached himself to me and was my guide." She smiled to herself. "He'd complain he was sick just to hang around with me while his mother worked." Her voice broke. "He was only five."

Logan didn't interrupt, the torture of her emotions flowing in her words.

"We found some weapons, old and barely usable, but nothing like the *new* government expected. I knew because I'd been there for longer than any op. I'd already done the paperwork, everything. It was my last one, Jacobs agreed." Tessa shook her head. "I believed the bitch. Which makes me first-class stupid instead of your average village idiot."

"Would you like a whip?"

She met his gaze, frowning.

"You're beating yourself up so much I figure you'd want to leave some marks."

"Point taken," she said with a half smile that held no humor. "So we're done. I—we report and information is turned over. I'm going to leave the country, go back to the base in Hungary like a normal person, right?" She shook her head. "I was on the road to the airport when I realized Jacobs had my passport. She'd collected them before the operation. We had aid-worker fakes." She was quiet for a second, thoughtful, then smiled sheepishly. "Okay, so the ID fetish is a latent neurosis."

She scooped up a handful of pebbles from the dirt floor and spilled them from hand to hand.

"Getting back in that area wasn't easy, but I didn't have a choice. Jacobs wasn't answering her phone. It took a while with all the checkpoints and I still had the aid-worker credentials. I get there and they're formed to leave, three all-terrain-type trucks lined up. But they're not moving. I walk up behind Jacobs and then it gets surreal. I was standing on a hill. The grass nearly hip high, purple wildflowers everywhere, so serene. Then I see past her."

She looked at him, quiet for a moment, and Logan saw the horrible memory in her eyes.

"It sounded like popcorn in a microwave." She stared at nothing, the images flying through her mind—not like ghostly specters, but with a clarity she'd never allowed to materialize. "I can still remember the sound of a bullet hitting bone and flesh." She cringed and swallowed the bitterness in the back of her throat. "The troops started in a wave from all sides, firing at anyone that moved. A sweep. God, I hate that word. It's too clean when it really means kill everything in sight. The only thing they're sweeping is lives."

Logan didn't think she realized she was crying so hard, her shoulders lurching with nearly every word.

"I ran. I ran into the camp, and begged for them to stop. Then Jacobs was there. I must have been screaming. I don't know, but she hit me and I fell. It gets hazy then. I remember Ramos pushing me in the back of a car. He held me down. I hit him and kicked and was nearly out, then Jacobs pointed a gun in my face. She just kept watching. I didn't know what to do. They were the real professionals, but they did nothing!"

Good Lord, Logan thought.

"I was so mad, so heartbroken." With a flat hand, Tessa patted her chest. "All those people, they trusted us, and we backed out on them. Oh, God." She shielded her forehead, trying to control her sobbing.

Logan's skin tightened as she described it, her voice fracturing with every word.

"The tents were red. They didn't just kill them, they massacred. No one was left alive, not even the infants. A baby? What threat is a *child*? How could anyone do—?"

She didn't finish, sinking miserably.

"The Serbian soldiers killed thousands of people and we didn't stop it. Know why? Do you know? The people were terrorists, they claimed. It was a training camp." She shook her head, pushing her fingers through her hair. "They weren't anything but scared. I was prepared to scream to Congress and Jacobs threatened to silence me—permanently."

Logan smelled a setup, Jacobs using the incident to her advantage.

"She didn't come out and say it, but she told me if I opened my mouth she'd make me *deathly sorry.*" Tessa sniffled and swiped the back of her wrist across her cheeks.

Logan handed her a folded handkerchief that was a little muddy on the edges.

"It was effective." Tessa cleaned up and clutched the cloth. "She kept a guard on me till we got back to the base. Ramos came to my room and said he knew I was running, and it wouldn't work. Foreign country, close-knit group, people who notice details. As far as I was concerned, he was just as guilty, but he convinced me that faking my death was the only way to get clear of Jacobs."

"He arranged it."

"I know what you're thinking, he could have set me up to die. I didn't trust him, but I didn't have a choice, either. My place had already been searched. No passport, no money. I was packing when he showed up."

She didn't have to tell him more. At the time, he was serving with a detachment in Hungary. Special Operations covered a large umbrella with SEALs, Special Forces, Marine Recon, along with allied forces and NATO. His team was on alert to get any Americans out of hostile areas, mostly US diplomats. He was housed in a hotel, on a twenty-four-hour break meant for sleep and mission review, till she showed up at his door. They cut loose on each other and yet before dawn, she was gone, and he was heading to the base for duty.

A couple of days later, his team was sent to get her and two others out. Ramos had been attached to Jacobs's team, and from the investigation he knew that Tessa had planted some listening devices inside a suspected training camp. When he saw her, it was through binoculars while he floated in the water. She was dressed like a hooker.

Ramos was the primary contact to get her from the transportation to the dock and into the boat. Logan would take them from there to a secure location. The instant she neared the dock, shots rang from beyond the Danube River. Instead of hunkering down till he got close enough to reach him in the boat, Ramos sent her ahead. She'd taken a couple steps onto the dock when the explosion ripped the darkness. All he saw was the orange flash, then the dock sinking into the water. A part of him died that night with her. He'd never wanted to relive the experience, and reached for her, lying back and taking her with him. She curled around him.

Tessa didn't say it, but they both understood that an operation needed money, and her fear of Jacobs's discovering her—was secondary to whoever gave Jacobs orders.

Eleven years ago the head of the CIA was Mitchell Avers.

Two Presidential terms later, he was the Secretary of Defense.

fourteen

Elizabeth waited under the bridge with the rats.

Rainwater streamed off the causeway in sheets like torn curtains, offering an odd privacy in the low-slung tunnel. Inside the confines, rodents scavenged for food they'd already picked clean. He was late. Not surprising. His arrogance was always a problem, but if she could stand under here with the rats, he could damn well get his ass here on time.

She worked her neck, then adjusted her clothing, discards from the Salvation Army, and she thought her toe peeking out of the old boots was a nice touch. A car rolled to the deserted street, the lights from nearby buildings flashing on the polished black hood. Headlights shined on her and she turned away, pretending a drunk-walk. She heard the car stop and the door open but not close. She looked back. He stayed in the shadows behind the car lights. Another man got out of the passenger's side and stood, facing the other direction.

He just couldn't let go of that ego. He'd say it was for protection. She knew he'd brought his own witness.

She approached the car, shuffling her feet. She stopped before that one step that would take her under the glow of the streetlights. He walked around the door and as he neared, she stepped back into darkness. He didn't have to ask her if she knew the risks or why she was here. He understood.

"Give it to me," she said and held out her hand, the fingertips of the gloves cut off and frayed. He handed her the crumpled paper grocery bag. She tore it open, pulling out the bundles and stuffing them in her pockets, but not before she fanned and checked each one. She tossed the empty bag at him.

"I'm insulted," he said.

She scoffed. "You're the one who taught me not to trust anyone. I know how to tag items."

"You'll just make this worse."

"I'm going to jail, and so are you. Now it's all a matter of how we go. And when."

He didn't respond and she took a step closer and thought, *He shouldn't think too deeply about these things, just stay behind his desk.* "Don't do a damn thing, I'll handle it."

He frowned. "It's too far gone."

"I said, I can take care of this, but if I go down, I won't be lonely."

He straightened from his hunch. If he thought that disguised him, he should have left the bodyguard behind with the DC license plate.

"I've got four million if you shut up and take it."

"Take the fall, for everything?" She scoffed and loved the meanness of it. "I'll disappear and you'd never find me."

"You really think that's possible?"

"I know it is." When it came down to it, he was a politician. He chose not to see that she'd survived twenty years of Black Ops work, mostly following orders from people like him. Politicians could talk it to death, but in the end, they had no skills, no true sense of what it was like in the field. "Betray me, and you won't like the results."

His shoulders pulled back, his gaze tight on her. "Is that a *threat?*"

"God, you're quick." She turned away.

She'd gone several steps before he said, "What do you think you can do at this point?"

"What I do best." Her voice was hollow under the bridge. "Sweep."

* * *

Juan felt a kick to his ass, then twice more when he didn't move. He squinted into the sun, and from his position on the ground, stared up at Salazar as he fastened his belt, then checked the load of his gun.

"You had a good time, I see." He nudged the bottles of corn liquor the Indians made and usually only drank during festivals and celebrations.

Juan sat up, rubbed his face, then put his boots on. "You're feeling better?"

Salazar only nodded. "You did this. Brought me here." He looked at the shaman as if he were a bug in his water glass. "What did you do to me?"

"Let you see the morning sun," the old man said, and Juan heard the sarcasm in his tone. The broken-English talk was for the tourists and he sensed an unaccustomed anger in Sopai.

Salazar scoffed. "Where are they?" he asked Juan.

"Still in the town, I suppose."

He looked up, the old scars on his face a little redder than usual. "You didn't search?"

"In the dark? Don't be a fool, Diego. No one has left." He held up the radio, wiggling it. The sun was just cresting the horizon.

Salazar grabbed the radio and demanded reports. It was another five minutes before anyone responded, infuriating him further. Juan stood by, unaffected as Salazar issued orders, checked with his spies.

"They're still there." Salazar stormed to the car, then glanced back when Juan didn't follow. "You drive."

Juan said good-bye to Sopai, the man's sharp, angry eyes following Salazar as he went to the truck.

Juan frowned back at Sopai, then saw him make a slash across his throat. His scowl deepened. There was no word for distrust in the Indian's language. It was Sopai's way of saying, *Watch your back*. Juan already was and as he climbed behind the wheel, he wondered what the witch doctor knew that he didn't.

* * *

Though Logan didn't expect it, Cero was as good as his word. Their belongings were on the same table, the Recon and Sat phone without the GPS chips but workable.

"There are troops blocking the roads here, north and southwest toward the Orinoco and Ciudad. You'll have trouble getting past them."

Logan nodded as he inventoried his things, sliding his knife back into the scabbard. He glanced at Tessa as she pushed the map and orb into her pack.

"Salazar will not—"

"Give up, I know," Logan said. "He's a prick and I should watch out. Sound about right?" Logan didn't think the guy was suddenly going to go all home-boy friendly on him, and connecting the *commandante* to his composite was far too watery to consider as official, but these men had seen Salazar, recognized him. *Works for me.*

Salazar was an entity who couldn't be caught. He'd left a trail of bodies that didn't raise suspicion or a mention in the news. While Logan had hoped he'd get careless, it was doubtful. Drawing Salazar to him was out of the question with Tessa near. Though there was nothing less appetizing right now, avoidance was the only solution.

"I think you understand him more than you realize." Cero crossed his arms over his chest, keeping the table between them.

Logan's gaze flashed upward. "Are you *trying* to insult me?"

"Caution." Cero put up a finger. "Just a caution."

Logan wouldn't learn why Cero was paranoid and while he had his suspicions, his brain was still fuzzy. He glanced at the reason why.

Tessa checked through her ID, then strapped on the belt. "As accommodations for imprisonment go, it was decent."

Cero chuckled. "You slept well, señorita?"

Tessa's blush was endearing, Logan thought, and she moved near him. "Surprisingly, yes."

Cero smiled. "You're free to go."

They didn't shake hands, only nodding to each other. Cero looked to add something, then didn't, and Logan and Tessa walked away.

She glanced back once to say, "If you see Salazar, shoot him, okay? One bullet."

Logan gripped her arm, steering her away. "Jeez."

"Never hurts to leave on an empathetic note. Salazar's been consistent. He wants to kill us all."

"He always has." He met her gaze. "But now he *needs* to kill us."

"Needs? Serial killers *need* to kill, Logan. We've consorted with his enemy, you mean," she said, inclining her head back to Cero.

Logan thought for a second, then shook his head. "He has to finish on top. And we don't want to be around when this ceases being a sport to him, either."

"Wow, I'm feeling so like . . . I don't know, a deer in the headlights? And what happened to being surrounded by pessimists?"

"I'm not ready to let him win."

"Good. How many bullets do we have?"

He gave her an odd look.

"I swore an oath to not pick up a gun. Doesn't mean I don't want to fight back with a little more firepower in our favor. God, I feel almost naked without my nunchucks."

"Yeah, I'd like to know you can beat the shit out of something if they get too close."

"Doesn't stop a bullet." And Salazar was fond of those.

The soldiers led them out in a different direction. Though, this time, it wasn't secret. Trucks and cars moved around like in a normal city, and their guards, weapons concealed, dropped back when they came to the Plaza Bolívar.

"Oh, God, nirvana," Tessa said, then rushed to a coffee vendor perched on the street corner.

Logan smiled, followed as he turned on the Recon. The walkie-talkie feature was too risky, anyone could listen in, and without the GPS to link with the satellite, he used it like a cell and dialed Max. If there were any towers, they were in a good position up the mountain to get something.

She blew on the hot coffee and sipped quickly, then ordered one for him.

He frowned at the Recon. The line was busy and he just let it ring. Inserting the earpiece, he was hooking it on his belt when he noticed a stone pillar much like the one near the cave. Flowers draped the crude stone obelisk, candles scattered at its base like a skirt. But it was the picture pinned in the center that made the hair on his neck rise.

Estavan Garcia.

Was it a display to honor a hometown boy? Or an altar to honor his death? Because with the exception of a select few, supposedly no one knew Garcia wasn't alive and running the show.

If they did, they were in a world of hurt.

Cero felt the man move from the shadows under the trees and come up to his left. The couple were already far down the street.

"Make sure they get away safely," Cero said, then glanced to his left. The man remained under a tree, a mug of coffee wrapped in his big fist. "We cannot afford more coming that close."

"You realize this could bring retribution."

Cero understood and feared that the most. Each day grew more delicate, the balance threatened by overzealousness, himself included. "Hopefully Chambliss will be the solution to our troubles."

"You're counting on him to eliminate Salazar? He's just one man."

"Salazar is a butcher, he was as a child. And now he leaves his trademark on anyone he can." Mutilation. "I'll deal with him when it's necessary. For now, his moves give up information."

The man scoffed rudely and when he stepped to follow,

Cero blocked him. "If you want this to end well, all loose ends have to be cut," the man said.

Cero scowled, disgusted. Was that his solution for everything? "People have died unnecessarily already. Leave them be."

The man watched the couple shrinking in the distance. "Just checking your conscience, Cero." He met Cero's gaze, his expression as if fighting the urge to speak, but he only turned away, silent.

Cero eyed the man's back as he slipped into the shadows where he lived. An uneasy alliance, he thought, and prayed it helped his country.

Tessa handed Logan the coffee, frowning when she had to wrap his fingers around it, then followed the direction of his gaze. She stepped closer. "Oh, crap."

"I'm liking how we think alike." He gestured between them, then looked at the display. "Impressive."

Tessa addressed the vendor and asked him about it. "It's a tribute," she translated for Logan. "This entire area is Estavan Garcia's hometown."

The vendor was all smiles and praise for the display of flowers and candles. "Garcia lived here?" she asked him. The vendor pointed and she met Logan's gaze. "Down there on the Orinoco River."

Their elevation was higher than the main body of the town. Though the township rose from the river into the mountains, there was no uniformity to it, homes dotting the roads as well as the slope.

"Forgive me," she said to the vendor. "But it looks like a memorial. A grave."

The vendor looked back with an uneasy expression, as if gauging his response, then said, "How can that be when he is only a few miles away?"

She just smiled, hoping her expression hid her sympathy as she moved beside Logan, his touch on her spine comforting and a reminder of last night. Though she didn't need it.

He was imprinted all over her body. In *such* a good way. For a breath, he met her gaze and understood where her mind went to play.

He smiled, leaned and brushed his mouth over hers. "Another impressive piece of history," he murmured and she went soft inside.

Then his gaze flicked back toward town. The guards were still watching them at a distance and one spoke into a radio. Gutsy guy Logan was, he waved and smiled at them.

"I like pushing the envelope as much as the next person . . ."

"Just letting them know we're not a threat."

"We haven't been, ever, especially against that kind of firepower, Logan. They helped us by capturing us. This stinks, all of it." She looked back at the exhibit and at the coffee vendor relighting some candles. "I don't think it was a memorial. He was too happy about it."

"Hometown hero, not surprising."

"It's giving me that 'they know more than they're saying' feeling again."

"Yeah, but it doesn't change anything. Ramos is making it more difficult." He referred to the messages stacked up from Max, and she leaned to read off the Recon. "A ruse of this magnitude is bound to be flawed somewhere, and every moment he's in office is a risk. It locks him in and the only exit is a bullet."

Tessa swung her gaze to his. If anything, Ramos understood that.

"From the information we have, it happened very quickly. The attack on the real Garcia was by troops loyal to Gutierrez and likely thinking, or being told, he was the instigator. He wasn't. The coup was in Caracas, while Garcia was near his own residence. I think when the coup occurred, he was clueless."

Her expression soured. "Stretching it thin, aren't you? He's the Vice President."

"Maybe, but if he knew it was coming, he would have been heavily protected and certainly not out in the open. It validates that he didn't know and likely tried to mediate the attack, but was killed for it." Ramos was there for the switch.

"If they were trying to oust Gutierrez, why attack Garcia? He would be the reason for the coup."

"It was staged, a ruse."

She was already shaking her head.

"Hear me out. The general was loyal and the coup was all done with troops. When the troops loyal to Gutierrez learned of it, they attacked near Garcia." Probably believing he instigated it. "Unfortunately, it just happened to be the moment when Ramos was there to assume Garcia's position."

"Okay, I can buy that for the simple reason the areas are separated by a couple hundred miles. But with communication handy, you're saying they did it on their own?"

He nodded.

"Witnesses?"

Logan hesitated. "I think Cero was one of them."

She nudged him. "How about voicing that speculation next time, huh?"

He smiled sheepishly. He kept forgetting she could handle just about any crisis. "It's the scar on his temple that made me think of it. I'd need to review the crime photos."

"It's amazing that we have their photos. We are such snoops."

"No argument here, but then, with stuff like this, we should be."

She was inclined to disagree but didn't have much of a soap box to stand on. She was in this just as deep, and staying an outsider was weak-spined. "What's Uncle McGill say?"

"Not enough."

She frowned, looking up from reading the messages from Max, each one a little more stressed out, the poor guy.

"He's concealing some details, but he's ruled by his superiors and orders. He's also CIA this month, and need-to-know goes without saying." They'd gone a couple steps before he added, "I hate to think a man I've trusted let us walk in without all the Intel, but stranger things have happened." Like the rescue team going in, when right after an attack, security would be airtight. They'd come to kill Ramos.

"Would he?"

"He'll keep the promise to me or he wouldn't have agreed."

"He owes you, doesn't he?"

Logan glanced. "At one time or another, the whole team served with him."

"That's not what I asked."

"Yeah, he owes me. Just as much as I owe him."

Tessa ducked under a branch. "Logan, honey, that no GPS thing a problem?" They were off the road.

He glanced, his smile crooked. "I can read a map, dear."

"Me, too, and this ain't the way home."

"We head to Garciaville." He pointed down the slope that was just giving them trouble. "We'll get a boat and ride the river down to Max." He checked the Recon's phone mode, still ringing. "Salazar will have blocked the roads, and Cero said the troops had drawn near during the night in the north. That's the only place he won't flex his muscles, at least not too much."

It took them a half hour to get down the hillside, avoiding homes and working their way through the woods about a half mile. The road grew more populated with small cars, flatbed trucks. A woman leading a donkey passed by them without a glance. Mostly because she had a basket on her back, supported from a strap across her forehead. It looked painful and with the donkey loaded to the swayback, ass-dragging level, it was difficult to walk side by side.

Tessa followed him. "I was hoping for a leisurely morning."

"I was hoping for a repeat of last night."

She smiled to herself. Weeks of that would be good for her.

"Maybe some breakfast," he added. "And not getting shot at, yah, that would be good, too."

She gripped his pack, making him stop, turn. She kissed him ruthlessly, onlookers making noise over it.

"You're just teasing me now."

"Oh, good, I got myself a smart one." She kissed him again, smiling at his little frustrated groan when they parted. "You were great last night."

"I like playing grown-up with you, too," he murmured, leaning in for another kiss and laughing when the donkey pushed between them. Head-basket woman tooled along as if they didn't exist.

Then Max's voice came through the earpiece, making Logan flinch.

"Jeez, you guys, scare a person, why don't you?" Max said.

"If you'd get off the phone . . . A little pillow talk, Max?" He flipped the speaker on low so Tessa could hear, then glanced around to make sure no one else did.

"With McGill? Oh, hell no. The man's going ape. He's ready to tie it all off, Logan."

"It's a bit hopeless." Tessa shrugged.

"Pessimists again," Logan muttered.

"I'm about a mile downriver," Max said. "You have a checkpoint between us. You both okay?"

"Max, another breakthrough, wow," Tessa said dryly.

His chuckle was diabolical, and she glanced at Logan, smiling. Logan reported all they'd learned: Cero, the guerrillas and Salazar.

"Salazar? Intel believes a member of the *commandante*'s squad was killed at the attack on Garcia."

She exchanged a "how about that" glance with Logan. "It answers a lot," she said. Like why Cero was so concerned about Salazar and their association. A Garcia loyalist like Cero was protecting his own and hiding them from his enemy to do it.

"He's as Black Ops as it gets, gang. A nasty boy. We need to get you guys in, now." Worry laced Max's voice. "Sebastian's ready to pick up."

"Negative, by vehicle. Trust me, this guy didn't leave the

area and he will shoot." He looked at Tessa. "This is where that NGS logo comes in handy."

"Yeah, well, I'd fold on that if it will get us away from the death-squad dude." She walked briskly beside him.

"We're at the river," Logan said and they moved off the road. "I can see the checkpoint." Through binoculars he viewed the troops. "We'll cross here and then meet you south at the big bridge." While the men loitered before, now they were at attention, barricading the road. "The boss is coming." *Or had made contact,* Logan thought, scanning the terrain for a way around the checkpoint.

He plotted a route to the bridge, then with her started moving, leaving Garcia's town behind. The river flowed on their left, winding down the steep hillside in tiers.

"We cross that bridge and follow the river southwest on the opposite side."

"They'll cover the roads with checkpoints."

He pointed to the boat rental on the other side of the bridge. "That's our target." They used the crowd for cover.

While they did, Logan relayed all they'd learned, then pulled out the map and sphere from his pack, and handed the ball to Tessa. He paused long enough to fold back a corner of the map to expose the symbol. Tessa wet it with bottled water, then he used her phone to photograph the symbol, loaded it to the Recon and sent it to Max on the cell. They kept moving. The roads grew more crowded, locals taking their goods to market, and the morning rush hour was like cold syrup, a lazy shuffle of the masses. Half the roads were blocked by troops and the locals avoided them.

His gaze went over her right shoulder. "We're spotted."

Two of the three soldiers from the checkpoint were leaving their posts. Logan and Tessa were halfway across the bridge when the soldiers rushed toward them, pushing people out of their way.

"Max, a ride would be great right about now," Logan said.

"I'm coming."

They shifted around the people in bug shaped cars or pulling handcarts, then ducked under a slat of wood on some guy's shoulders with baskets dangling like ornaments. Logan was off the bridge first and he turned back for her, but she was sandwiched behind a small truck that was chugging black smoke into the morning air.

His gaze flicked between her and the soldiers till he pressed between the crowd, reaching for her pack strap. He grabbed it, pulling. People balked, and when he had her near, she held out the sphere.

"Take it. I almost lost it back there."

He didn't, gripping her wrist. The sphere had collapsed a little.

"How did you do that?"

Tessa frowned, hurrying off the bridge with him. "I'm not sure, I was just tossing it." She held the open wood sphere, running her finger over the paper-thin slices, loose, but not enough to separate more than a sixteenth of an inch. Yet when she cupped the bottom and turned it upside down, she heard something catch. The mechanism pulled them all into position, tightly closed.

She looked at him. "Oops."

"Do what you did before." He ushered her along.

She batted the wood ball between her palms in a span of just inches, then caught it and pressed both ends at the same time. It opened, pinching her skin. "I did that a dozen times before and it didn't work." She shook out her hand, looked at her palm, then held it up.

The bright red pinch of skin was painfully obvious. His gaze snapped to her other hand.

The wood ball was open, the slivers of wood sandwiched so tightly it created a curved fan effect. This time it was completely open, like a flower, yet the uniqueness of the sphere didn't compare to what was inside. A small silver metal vial, one end elongated less than a quarter inch and blunted off.

Blunted said corrosive to him, and he inspected further. There was a small glass tip; half was broken off. He grabbed her hand.

In the meat of her palm, glass fragments sparkled in the morning sun.

"Oh, shit."

"Logan," she said, panic in her voice. "What just happened?"

"I don't know. But it launched something when you opened it." Quickly, he pulled her off the road, using a stalled car as cover, then dropped his pack and brought out a small kit. He swabbed with a sponge saturated in some reddish liquid. It stained her palm orange, then he injected her. "Charcoal. If it's a nerve agent it will neutralize it." He inspected her pupils.

She reared back. "Nerve agent! Jeez, you're kidding, right? And if it's not?"

He met her gaze. "I don't know." He hailed the team. "Max, Max! How close, man? We've got a problem."

Logan wrapped the vial, stored it in a plastic bag lined with the metallic paper that waterproofed some of his gear. He lifted his gaze to hers.

"Man, this bites." She stared at her palm. "I don't want to die for them."

"I won't let you."

"You're making a lot of promises you probably can't keep," she muttered.

"It didn't puncture the skin that I can see." He hoped not, anyway.

Then he clutched her to him, her pack making it awkward, but he held her, kissed her. The ground softened under his feet as he searched his gear for the mini comm links.

"Damn, Cero kept the comm links." He forced her around to shove the sphere and map in her pack, yanking the zipper. His gaze went to the soldiers. They were stuck on the bridge, the locals refusing them passage. He hurried her along with him toward the tour boats.

"Max, where the hell are you!"

"There's a jam at the bridge. Fruit rolling everywhere. I can't get through."

"It's an all-terrain vehicle!"

"But not amphibious. I'm stuck *on* the bridge."

There were several spanning the narrowest points that were too few to accommodate the population.

"We're getting on the river."

"Keep coming, I've got a mark on you."

Tessa hurried behind Logan till he paused and made her go ahead of him. He was at least armed but somehow she knew he wouldn't shoot around civilians. Closer to the river the ground was mushy, the spray wetting their clothes and packs.

Logan rushed to the tour boats, the attendant scowling till he shoved enough bills at him to buy the boat outright. Logan pushed the raft off the bank and it slid into the water.

They climbed in, Logan grabbing the oars, but the vendor kept chattering.

Logan looked at Tessa. "Is he questioning my ability?"

"Yeah, and he wants us to sign a no-suing type of thing." Tessa grabbed it, scribbling her signature, and then looked back toward the bridge.

The troops were almost off the bridge, less than forty yards away. Now the soldiers were yelling at them to stop, aiming rifles. The vendor cursed at the troops and Logan used the oar to shove off.

The rubber raft was meant to hold about eight people and it spun in the churning water. Tessa held out her hand and he passed her an oar. They sailed downriver, the ride smooth for only several yards. The troops stopped on the shore and fired. Logan and Tessa dug in, pushing the raft close to the shore. It widened, more boats on the water, yet tethered to the docks. It was too rough for anything but a rubber raft.

Tessa was in front, Logan steering the raft, and she glanced back and smiled, enjoying the bucking ride. Logan tried to raise the team.

"Max? Max?" He shook his head and yanked out the earpiece. "He's out of range."

Juan drove. Salazar switched on the computers and tracking devices, and Juan suddenly longed for the disconnection of Sopai's house. "Answer that," Juan barked when Salazar's phone kept beeping. "The same person's been calling you all night."

"You answered?"

"I want nothing to do with your plots."

Salazar hit SEND.

"Where have you been? How dare you not answer my calls." Eloisa, impatient as usual, Salazar thought.

"I'm busy."

She didn't care and launched with, "Do you have it? Do you?"

Salazar glanced at Juan. "An hour good enough for you?"

"Bring it to me, *today*, Diego. Please," she added after a moment.

His brows shot up. "I love it when you beg." He cut the call before she could respond, then pocketed the phone. He decided then that before he handed over the items, she needed to pay a price for treating him as if he were inferior.

Salazar listened to reports on the couple and when they were spotted, he ordered his men to shoot.

"Killing them, Diego? In public?"

Salazar scowled. "Shut up. They cannot escape."

"You and your fucking games. You should have killed them before now."

"I'm taking care of that today."

The vehicle bounced along the jungle roads, and Juan knew it would open Salazar's wounds, but the man didn't care, his eyes on a target. He glimpsed through the trees, saw the couple riding the river, but when he ordered Juan to pull over, then drew a launcher from the rear of the truck, Juan knew Salazar had slipped over the edge of his obsession.

Before Juan left the truck, Salazar fired, the rocket propelled grenade streaking an arc toward the water.

Logan heard the sharp whine, looked to the sky, then shouted, "Tessa, jump! Now!"

She glanced back, then up, and lunged over the side as the RPG barreled downward. Tessa struck the water as the RPG hit, pulling the boat down like paper stuck in a sucking drain before it exploded, throwing them like leaves onto the river.

The impact sent a percussion through the water, stunning her so hard her limbs felt liquid. Yet the rolling current took over, dragging her farther downriver, the weight of the backpack making it impossible to keep her head above water.

Max heard "RPG," then yanked out the earphone when the explosion nearly shattered his eardrum. Oh, Jesus. He put it back in and hailed Logan several times, then radioed Sebastian and Riley.

"Heads-up. I lost them. No contact. They were hit, I think they were hit!" Max drove off the bridge and made record speed toward their last location. "Coonass, get in the air. They're in the river!"

"Riley's got a lock on the GPS tracker on his belt, he's on the west shore. He's not moving."

"Man, this is not good," Max muttered, then slammed on the brakes before he threw himself from the car. People gathered, gawking, and he pushed between them and ran to the shore. He called for Logan, scanning the surface, then the far shore. The boat was snagged in the rocky shallows, a shredded rag of rubber now. *Salazar's a ballsy little bastard.*

"God, please don't be this mean," Max said as he hurried closer to the river. "Not today."

Water poured and knocked boulders, splashing a fine

mist, but there was no sign of Logan or Tessa. Max's stomach churned as he radioed Sebastian.

"Make a sweep of the river, comms open. Coonass, come get me."

"Roger that," Sebastian said. "I'm on you in three minutes."

Through binoculars, Max scanned the water as he walked the bank. The grasses were tall in the still areas where the river widened, but this tributary took the flow of melting snow off the Andes, and the force had torn the bank.

Then Riley's voice came over the headset as Sebastian flew toward their last location. "That symbol Logan just sent? Where was it?"

"It was on the corner of the map, why?" Max asked.

"It's Chinese, a warning." They heard Riley draw a breath. "A hazmat symbol, for a bioweapon."

Tessa didn't know which end was up. The water carried her swiftly, the speed turning her upside down. Her waterlogged pack dragged her down but she couldn't reach the clips to get rid of it. Air was more important.

She kept swimming toward sunlight, got her head above water and caught her breath just before the current smacked her into a rock, then twisted her under the water again. She couldn't grab anything, felt weightless, and she really didn't want to die today. Not after all this. After Logan.

Her lungs screaming for air, she kicked hard and shot to the surface, spitting water and sucking in air as she struggled toward the rocks. Her fingers grazed a boulder and slipped. *He doesn't get to win,* she thought as she swam harder.

Then Logan was there, on his knees on the edge of the rocks, stretching a branch out to her, and she caught it, held tight.

"I've got you." The current flowed over his knees. "Lose the pack!"

"But the map, the ball!"

He shook his head. "It's going to break, lose the pack!"

Holding on to the branch with one hand, she dug into the water to unhook the clips. She didn't have to struggle to get it off, the force of the water took it away. Hand over hand she worked to get closer, and Logan leaned out on a cantilevered rock to grab her.

"Come on, baby. Just a little bit more."

There was no fear in her eyes, only the determination to beat the river. She levered onto the edge of rock, water rushing past and fighting her hold. He reached to grab her shoulders.

He didn't make the mark. The rocks and ground gave away underneath him, tossing him forward onto her, a hundred pounds of dirt and rock right behind him.

Tessa shrieked, arching her body away from the boulder. It would be so her to be crushed by it. The force tore at her clothes, her hair obstructing her vision. Her feet never touched bottom and she swam toward the surface, the spill to a waterfall only about fifty yards away. It forced her to swim against the current, then she saw debris coming toward her. She ducked deeper underwater to avoid it and it scraped by her cheek. She saw rocks and grabbed on. Water rushed over her head, she clung, her lungs straining for air as she tried pulling herself above the surface.

Then a broad hand plunged into the water, gripping her wrist and she grasped back. Thank God. He yanked hard, pulling her onto the bank. She scrambled onto the rocks, coughing up river water.

"That was interesting," she said and coughed again. For a second, she just hung on, water flowing off her. "Thank you." Then she looked up.

It wasn't Logan.

Fifteen

Salazar.

His grin was wide and oily as he pulled Tessa to her feet. Great, just great. She pushed his hand off and looked at the man. Up close, he wasn't any better looking. Dark skin, hair, and eyes that were soulless black.

"We finally meet."

Her brows drew tight. There was something creepy about the way he looked at her; like a teenager looks at a *Playboy* poster.

"I've been waiting for this moment."

"Can't say that I've been." She glanced around, hoping to see Logan and his big gun. She was a half mile from where they'd gone in, but he'd fallen with her. So where was he? She searched the water, but the bend in the river was too sharp to see much.

"Your life belongs to me now."

Ugly and delusional. How nice. "Oh, in your dreams, pal." Salazar grabbed her arm and Tessa bashed it away. "No touching!" It didn't do much good. He grasped her arm in a vise grip, dragging her close, his face in hers. His breath smelled like spices and not in a good way.

"You have nothing."

"Except you, *mi belleza.*"

Okay, that's a little disturbing.

"What's your name?"

She didn't answer.

"Soon you'll scream it for me." His thin smile sent an icy sensation down her spine.

Oh, God. He's got plans.

Logan dug his fingers into the earth, pulling himself out of the water, then looking for Tessa. He shouted her name, but the noise of people gawking and the water drowned him out. Unaccustomed panic plowed through him as he climbed to his feet and rushed the bank, searching for her body. She was nowhere in sight.

Please no, he thought. *She's strong, she'd have made it.* Yet his search gave him nothing except the TDS Recon. It was cracked, waterlogged, and he tossed it on the bank and kept looking. He'd lost his gun and the pack, and then he checked his boot and found his knife gone, too. He still had the vial, though, wrapped and in his back pocket. He called out as he watched the current, but kept moving downriver, searching, his heart breaking little by little when he didn't find a trace of her.

Then he heard his name, long and loud. He scanned upriver.

Tessa emerged from the woods, and Logan smiled widely, relief sinking his shoulders until he saw the man behind her, pushing her along. *So this is Salazar.* At this distance, it was hard to be impressed. No more than an inch or two taller than Tessa, he was just . . . dark.

Tessa stood on the pile of rocks, out on the edge, and behind her, Salazar held her upper arm, ready to shove her in.

"Bring it to me!" he shouted.

Logan gestured to the water. "It's in there!"

Salazar looked at the river, his fury in his features magnified as he pulled her back against him and pressed a broad knife to her throat. "Find it! Or she dies!"

Logan understood his desperation, more so when he stretched back, forcing her off balance. If she fought him, he'd cut her throat open.

"Bring it to the stone mound!"

Logan clenched his fists and nodded.

Salazar wasn't finished torturing him, and nuzzled Tessa's jaw like a lover, then dragged his tongue up the length of her face. She elbowed him, but he only kissed her cheek with enough force that her head tipped. He laughed to himself.

What a prick. Across the river, Logan met Tessa's gaze.

"Don't let him have it!" she shouted and Salazar smacked her.

She stumbled, then rounded on him, crouched to strike back.

Calm down, baby. He hoped she didn't push the envelope with this guy because he wasn't long on patience and pointed the gun in her face. She put her hands up. He motioned her with the barrel and when she didn't move, looking at the water, Logan thought, *Don't you dare jump in.* She'd never make it. Not matter how strong she was. There was a water-fall about fifty yards ahead.

Salazar forced her away from the river, and before they melted into the forest, he looked back and grinned smugly.

Logan recognized it.

That smile was imprinted in his mind, and he felt a chill in his soul when he comprehended what he was seeing. Cassie's killer. He was sure of it, though it made less sense than ever right now. Later, he thought, and let his emotions drive his speed as he ran back up the shore to the narrowest point to cross.

The nearest bridge was a half mile upriver, and he waded in at a wider point, then swam to the other side. He was climbing out when he spotted a mass in the water upriver a few yards and he ran to it. It was Tessa's pack, and he whispered thanks as he stripped it of the sphere and map, then took the nylon ropes she had coiled with a couple carabiners. He grabbed a disposable lighter from the bottom, and left the pack on the bank as he raced to the point he'd last seen them.

He found footprints and tracked. Salazar was overconfident and leading him along toward the mound. He found a spot where they'd scuffled. He'd known she wouldn't make it easy for Salazar, He stopped to set a smoke pile. Sebastian would understand it. A marker and confusion. Smoke cascaded up to the sky, black and sooty, but Logan was already running.

The forest was dense and wet, the coolness of the river left behind. The air grew thicker with each step. Salazar was behind her, their pace quick, and if he shoved that gun in her back again, she was going to have to hurt him. Which was her bravado speaking. He had bullets and knew how to use them. From what she could see of Logan from across the river, he was unarmed.

"He loves you?" Salazar said from behind. "That man?"

"What? No . . . I don't know." She loved him, and in that instant, a lot became clear. Without Logan, she did not want to breathe.

"You'd better hope he does."

"So he'll come for me?" She stopped and gave him her best "you stupid asshole" look. "He doesn't have to love me to do that, Salazar."

His eyes flared when she said his name, and his gaze moved over her with a hunger that made her skin crawl. She'd hit a nerve and hated that it had anything to do with her. But apparently, this was her lucky day.

His head tipped. "You have been a mystery, little one. A shadow." He grabbed her document waist belt, pulling the zipper, then diving his hand inside. When she tried to take her ID back, he put the gun barrel under her chin. "Tessa. Pretty name."

He didn't keep it, shoving it back in her pouch, but took his time zipping it closed. He reeked of old blood.

"What business have you with the Vice President that has you sneaking in at night?"

Damn. The cameras must have caught her. "I'm just a tourist, mister."

He scoffed. "One who sleeps in Carriòn's home? Escapes Interpol and runs from the police?"

Well, he was on top of things, wasn't he?

"Carriòn's a killer."

"Then you two ought to get along well, huh?"

He leaned in to say, "Not after I sent him Ricco's head in a basket."

Tessa reeled. "You bastard! He never hurt you!"

Salazar shrugged. "He is dead because of *you*."

She couldn't help herself. She punched him, knocking his head to the side. When he only rubbed his jaw and smiled at her, Tessa packed her anger and let it loose in a fist to the nose. He went backward, stumbling and nearly falling, but kept his ground. She was already running hard and headed south, listening for the river, but all she heard were footsteps behind her. And coming closer.

He threw his weight into her, hitting her back, and the impact snapped her head back before she fell hard. Then he was on her, crushing her into the wet ground. She tried shoving him off and wrestled for a moment, his laughter infuriating her, and she went girly and bit his arm. He howled, then whipped out his knife, pushing it in her face so close that if she moved, he'd slice her cheek open.

"Keep playing, *mi belleza*. I like them with plenty of defiance." He laughed as he backed off her.

Pervert, she thought, and rolled over, shaking out her hand, her knuckles burning. She stood as another man entered the clearing.

Salazar shoved her toward him. "Tie her up."

She glanced between them. *This guy was with Salazar at the mound.* Tall, slender, and decent-looking, whereas Salazar was a little dweeb with big guns. Fit, but nothing to write home about. And he looked a little frazzled right now. His lip was bleeding, oh, joy of joys.

"Give it to him," the partner said softly, tying her hands. "You might live."

She met his gaze. "You won't." Another cocky moment she'd regret, but what options did she have left?

His shoulders stiffened.

"You have no idea who you're up against, do you?"

He glanced at her, his features sharp. "Do you?"

She wished she had her nunchucks. "I've seen his work."

Juan scoffed, shaking his head as he made the last knot. "No, *chica*. You have not." He pushed her to the ground, then walked away.

Max heard Riley clearly enough. "This shit just doesn't end," he said.

"They can't know," Riley said, then added, "he would have alerted us."

Just one more crisis, Max thought, then over his head, Sebastian lowered the helicopter over the river, then followed it.

"Drac, there's a couple people looking and pointing east," Sebastian said. "They're south of your location."

Max climbed back into the truck, his tires spitting gravel as he headed back. He ducked to see Sebastian in the chopper bearing the NGS logo. *She'll be pissed about that.* With Sebastian directing him, Max stopped, and then raced down the bank. There were several people, mostly children, standing on the shore.

"There's something in the water."

"I see it." He motioned to Sebastian to fly the chopper higher, then Max followed the shore downriver toward the fruit bridge, as he'd come to think of it. He spied the lump in the water, his heart pounding as he raced toward it. Closer to it, he stopped short. It was snagged on a jut of fallen trees and rocks. Like an island, it was in the middle of the rushing current, and he couldn't reach it without dislodging it. He looked to the trees, then shimmied up one about ten feet. He didn't have time to cut a branch so he swung out, using his weight to break it. He fell to the ground, then wading out thigh-deep, he stretched it to the mound. A backpack. He hooked it, drawing it in.

"Thank God," Sebastian said from the air.

Max twisted to look up. "Anything?"

"Negative. No body, no clothing. Just an oar."

Max carried the pack to the bank and dropped it. "It's Logan's, and from the look of it, he's unarmed."

Tessa watched the two. At Salazar's feet were a couple black bags like Dragon One's. They spoke too softly for her to hear clearly and she learned only that the tall guy was called Juan.

"You're mad, Diego." His partner looked her over from head to foot. "She's useless to us now because you fired on them. It's gone. Let it rest in the river."

Salazar shook his head, kneeling to dig in a pack. "We must have it back."

"I don't want to be near it." Juan pinched the plastic wrapper sticking out of Salazar's duffel, the sterile white hazmat suit showing bright.

Salazar barely spared it a glance. "They came into our yard and took a shit. They don't get to live."

"Then just do it. Because I do not trust her to control something this deadly."

Tessa put on her best confused look as if she didn't understand the language. But she did. Logan was right, it was a game to him.

"I'll safeguard it." He lifted his gaze. "But it has its own luck. If they try to open the sphere, it will launch."

Tessa heard that, looked down at her hand, and thought, *Oh, damn.*

She rubbed at it, trying to see if her skin was broken, but then with it getting into pores, she was probably going deadly just sitting here. This bites. She looked the way she'd come, hoping to see Logan with lots of loaded guns. She never doubted he'd find her. She patted her pockets for anything to help herself but found only a soggy Chiclet and her lip gloss. So much for evening the odds.

"You can't help him, he will fail." Salazar pulled her off the ground.

She wrenched her arm free, her stitches stinging. "You keep saying that like it will make it true. How's the nose, by the way?"

His temper engaged like a striking match and he raised his arm to hit her.

She moved out of the way. "Oh, yeah, be a man." She was so ready to kick his ass, but Juan lurched between them, grabbing his hand.

"She already got in one shot." He jutted his chin to Salazar's swollen lip. "And her man will shoot first. Prepare."

Tessa frowned. What was going on here between these two? A battle for control?

Salazar threw him off, swiping his bloody nose and lip, then looked at her. *If looks could kill* came to mind instantly and Tessa thought, *Probably not a good idea to antagonize him.* He'd kill her if she wasn't useful.

He pushed her ahead, sandwiching her between them as they headed back to the cave. The sun barely reached here, the ground loamy with decaying leaves. The sound of a chopper sweeping the area had them running faster.

Her boot caught on a root and she flew forward, bumped a giant tree before she landed on her side. She felt the stitches in her arm pull, then smelled something awful as she pushed back on her haunches.

"Jesus!" She scrambled back, her gaze on the giant tree.

"Get up!" Salazar grabbed her by the hair, yanking her and expecting her to take a swing at him again. But she didn't.

"There's a body in there."

Juan approached quickly, then followed where she pointed. His features pulled so tight he looked like a different man.

A body, savaged by animals, was shoved in the base of a tree. The roots were already growing over it and any clothing had been stripped from him or torn by animals. Juan stepped closer. The body was folded, knees to chest. Not an Indian. A gold glimmer on the ground caught his eye, and Juan reached for it, then froze. The skeleton bones were broken. Each finger, both hands. His gaze flicked to the toes. Missing. He recognized the marks and looked at Salazar.

He wore a bland expression, and then shrugged.

"You did this!" Juan suddenly grabbed the gold and found a ring, the remnants of a life left behind. One of his teammates. "Benito was supposed to be at his mother's bedside."

Salazar's gaze lowered to the broad roots curving toward the sun. There wasn't a shred of emotion in his face.

"Someone put the sphere in the cave," Juan ground out. "No one knew but *you*. Because Felix took it to his death. Tomas and Cheuy are dead because of her." He flicked a hand at Tessa and she lurched back. "You did this." He nudged the body, then met his gaze. "Is it my turn now, Diego?" Juan's expression was absent of sorrow and brimming with pity. "You have killed all who were loyal to you. For what? That bitch used you, uses you still."

Salazar scoffed. "I use her."

"Then you know what they have? In the sphere? You know the damage it will bring?"

"Certainly. Canned death."

Comprehension dawned quickly. *"Madre de Dios."* Juan held his pistol at his side, his fist working the grip. "You go too far!" He shook his head as if that weren't enough. "You'll kill us all."

Juan raised his weapon, but Salazar fired first, the bullet planting squarely in Juan's forehead, his expression frozen on his face as he fell.

Tessa screamed.

"We'll meet again," Salazar said and crossed himself before he took his weapons and left him to the buzzards.

Tessa stumbled as he dragged her away, pushed her ahead, but the image stayed.

Elizabeth was skilled.

She hadn't lasted half her life as an operative not to be.

She knew what to look for, who'd be watching, and their checklist. Rookies—anyone with under five years in covert operations—were easy to spot. They talked out of the side of their mouths toward their mics. She'd made the same mistakes herself once. She blended in now, hiding her assets, plain Janed up. Camel jacket and T-shirt, black slacks, low-key jewelry, her hair pulled back in a barrette. Pulling her carry-on, she looked like the average woman rushing home to kids or the next meeting. She didn't make eye contact with anyone, and walked as if a little rushed, like a thousand other passengers.

Alice would have woken by now. Elizabeth wanted to get out of state long before they found out about the switch. She'd taken the train to North Carolina, then a rental car and now back to the train.

Getting out of a country was easier than getting in. Her last leg into Venezuela would be the toughest.

She walked briskly along, and felt that spool of adrenalin, the wonderful sensation that came with more than success: success without raising a single suspicion. It left her more options. She hadn't spotted anyone suspicious and she reminded herself she was only halfway there.

I missed this.

She approached the counter. Minutes later, she smiled at the young man as she took her ticket, then wished him a nice day before she turned toward the platform. She glanced around casually, picking out the mother with two twin boys in matching clothes. What? Like you won't recognize them otherwise? Her gaze flicked to the porters, the people waiting to board.

The sound of the engine in the near distance was loud enough that people spoke loudly or moved closer to each other. Three men loitered near the trams to the parking lots, and the longer they stood apart and alone, the more suspicious she grew. Then one man smiled and rushed to a woman half his age, then together they departed. It was a few more minutes before another hurried to an elderly woman, then took her bags as they left. The last man hadn't moved, his gaze searching each face, his surroundings, then back again.

A porter approached her and she waved him off, checked her ticket and found her car, then glanced at the stockstill man before ascending the stairs. Inside it was warmer, and smelled of fresh-brewed coffee and pastries. Something sweet, she thought, and it made her smile.

She had a private cabin, small and easily defendable. Avoiding contact with too many was essential. She stepped inside the compartment and slid the pocket door closed. She didn't lock it. The conductor would be coming. Stowing her bag, she kicked off her shoes and then leaned on the seat to look out the window.

She spotted the dark-haired man. He was rushing the length of the platform, trying to see inside the compartments. Before he came near, she sat back, but the temptation to watch him was great enough that she flattened to the wall adjacent to the window and peered. She didn't see him and then switched sides. He was getting on the train—alone and still looking. She glanced around the small berth for a place to hide, then heard a rumble in the passage. Figures passed in front of the frosted glass doors. She shut the shades, leaving a spot so she could see anyone approaching. Then she went to her bag, bypassing the new magazine and going to the Walther PPK. Small, powerful and excellent for distance shots. She screwed on the silencer.

Someone tried the knob, then knocked.

She opened the door a foot. "Yes?" Behind her back, her finger slid over the trigger.

The man stared at her for a long moment, then glanced to someone to his right. "Move on. Sorry ma'am." He closed the door.

Liz turned away and went to the padded sleep bench. Gripping the arm, she sank slowly into her seat and let out a long breath. She was still for a moment, enjoying the rush, then reached for her bag, sliding the gun to the bottom.

* * *

Ramos stepped into his suite of rooms, then stopped and put up a hand to the guard intent on following him. "Thank you, Enrique."

The guard wished him a pleasant rest, and stationed himself outside the doors as Ramos closed them. Quietly, he flipped the lock and let out a long breath. A long day being a fake, he thought. He was gaining respect for politicians. Talk, shake hands, eat fancy dinners till your cholesterol is hurting, then try to pass legislation. Then there was corruption. He'd gone over special committees, pork projects, budgets and outlines. It all looked fine on paper. But there was no distribution of wealth to anyone outside the cabinet and national assembly. Trails led close to Gutierrez but never quite reached him.

He went to the wet bar and knelt, unlocking the safe inside the lower cabinet.

It was the only spot Eloisa couldn't reach. He'd cracked it his second day here, but it was empty. That meant Garcia had another somewhere more safe. He removed a small box of tea. He prepared tea, although what he really wanted was a shot of bourbon. But he'd done that last night and regretted it when his symptoms returned.

Eloisa was getting clever. That she didn't have him killed outright said she had other plans for her husband. He already had a smoking gun on a CD full of video streams, but he wasn't her biggest concern or she'd be watching him 24-7. Garcia had known his wife was dangerous. Before the coup, he wasn't looking so hot, and Ramos sympathized. Garcia would have had backup. Documented.

He took the tea to the desk and lowered himself into the leather chair, then relaxed back. He tried to think like Garcia. It was a supreme arrogance that he even tried to know another man's mind. One thing he knew: Garcia was far wiser than he. The man had detailed plans for changes he'd wanted to implement, and Ramos noticed right off that Gutierrez had shot down most of them. Garcia had written everything down. Ramos never did. Good memory aside, to him, it was evidence for another to find and use against him.

A truly pathetic way of living. He watched the vapor coil into the air, then picked up the tea. He didn't experience that almost-chilling sensation when he recognized his flaws. It was recent, this honesty shit. When the doctors had removed the bandages from his face and he held the mirror, he knew he couldn't ignore the deep-seated neurosis even before they'd altered his face. He was torn up pretty bad, anyway, but the excuse didn't matter. Ten years ago, it was a personal rush to know so much classified material, to be in the middle of changing the world. Now it was just a burden.

Ugly things I've done, he thought, sipping. And not done.

Tessa's image rose in his mind—his hands clamped on her arms as he held her in the backseat of a truck while thousands were murdered. She'd fought savagely, spat in his face when the gunfire went silent. She shouldn't have been there, but she was a witness that could destroy them all. A viable threat.

Jacobs wanted to train her, make her a hitter. Tessa's exotic looks and grace were primo assets to getting in close to the big-league players, and Liz wanted to use those assets almost desperately—as if she saw herself in Tessa and the chance to make a better copy. Tessa wasn't having any of it. When Jacobs recognized defeat, she told Ramos to tie it off. Sever all ties, get out, leave no evidence to follow. Tessa was innocent, unwilling, and manipulated by Jacobs from the first op where she was a fill-in. He didn't know what it was about Tessa that put stars in Jacobs's eyes or what had driven the plan to pull her in so deep she'd never get out, but he suspected Jacobs had the hots for her. Whatever. It was an ego trip all her own. If he had refused Liz, she'd have done it herself.

He had had ten hours to plan Tessa's death. It had to be flawless, and the witnesses credible. Blowing up the dock without hurting Tessa was easy; lying and letting Logan take the heat wasn't. If they'd probed too deep a lot more would have come out in addition to why he rushed Tessa on the dock. Chambliss shouldered the responsibility, but he would have regardless. Giving orders to another man that might cause death or injury was, like everything else, a serious matter to Logan.

They weren't best pals, just friends. He respected Logan, but eleven years ago, Tessa's life meant more to Ramos than his friendship with Logan. Still did. It was his one shining moment and he hadn't seen many since.

He glanced around the suite he'd searched thoroughly.

Garcia would have had more of a reason to bypass the UN Security Council and come to the U.S. However, Garcia didn't frequent any one place beyond this house, except the government offices in the capitol and the Presidential Palace. Garcia had kept it locked, something Ramos understood when the guards reminded him and seemed surprised he hadn't. This was the only group of rooms inaccessible to anyone except Señora Rojas, who'd already proved her trust.

A few feet away on the wall over the hearth was an oil painting of Garcia's great-grandfather in full Indian dress. Garcia's private suite had a considerable collection of artifacts gathered from his childhood and Ramos understood that Garcia's pride came from his ancestors. Ramos's eyes narrowed on the painting and the bag the chief wore, then his gaze flicked to each piece Garcia had collected, ending on the slinglike sack hanging on the wall. Made from animal skin, the long strap fashioned from tree bark, the bag had once held weapons and poisons. The tribal chief kept guard of the precious venoms and a blowgun that was no more than a piece of hollow reed, but the darts were still tipped.

He left the chair and went to it, carefully lifting it off the hook. It didn't weigh more than a half pound and disappointment made his shoulders droop. He set the fragile sack on the desk and carefully slipped the hemp loop from around a polished stone that served as a clasp. Avoiding the darts hanging in loops on the outside of the sack, he opened it and looked inside. Quickly, he drew out the thumb sized flash drive.

"Oh, smart boy, " he muttered with feeling, then went to the computer, inserting the flash and opening the files.

Documents uploaded, and Ramos sank a little. Cargo manifest? Shipment orders for supplies to the Army? Then he looked closer at the model number and realized that the order was for an older model of AK-47s no one used anymore because one round cost a dollar U.S. The new model expended twelve cents a round bullets, which was still pricey, and the Army used those.

So why were there records of sales for weapons the Venezuelan Army didn't need?

He read further. That wasn't the real cherry on the sundae. Gutierrez had also bought up all the ammo. There were warehouses full of dollar-a-round ammo. There was paperwork on the shipment of the AK-47s to the Colombian FARC guerillas. He armed the FARC and had a strong hold on the ammo, forcing them to buy it from him.

Arming a rebellion in a neighboring country to incite unrest in Peru. Jesus. The FARCs were crossing the border and doing damage there, armed by Gutierrez. Profits went right into the President's personal accounts. No wonder no one learned of it. A President knowingly interfering in another country's policies violated the UN and NATO policies and countless international laws. Gutierrez wanted South America behind him. Only Bolivia was biting. Peru's government had refused to align with Gutierrez and he retaliated by arming the enemy. There was a small file named IMD. He opened it and saw a proposal to install Iranian missiles on Venezuelan soil.

He reached for another flash drive to make copies. A lot of them. Garcia had come to the U.S. for help with proof, and we'd refused him. Jacobs had not.

Stage three, on its way, he thought, and contemplated how to reveal this information—and to whom.

Sixteen

Dragon One's chopper was a redesign, the outward appearance of a normal chopper, yet it was armed to the teeth. Unfortunately, they couldn't use any firepower without starting an international incident. It was a last resort.

From the copilot's seat, Max watched the screen and the GPS dot as it progressed. "He's alive and moving."

"Good, cuz I promised his grandma I'd watch over him."

"He's headed toward the training grounds."

Sebastian hit a switch, and from the nose, the gun ports folded back in layers of honed black metal, revealing dual .50 caliber machine guns.

Max scowled.

"Just in case," Sebastian said, shrugging.

"Let's hope this thing can outrun a rocket." He pointed to the thermal screen that showed heat and movement. "Someone knows we're here."

He kept pushing her as if his overdeveloped legs moved faster than hers. Behind her was a man who killed his friends, not that anyone would actually like him, but she understood damn quickly that she was nothing to him beyond amusement and maybe a little vendetta on Logan. Weak people like that overcompensated.

The forest thinned, sunlight finally touching the mossy

earth as they neared the mound. She watched her footsteps. She'd already fallen twice with a little help from the dweeb with a gun, and her hands itched for a nunchuck. She stole a glance at the tree she'd hidden it in. The rope was still there and she tried to think of a use besides strangling him. But he hurried her toward the mount, pushing her again. Tessa spun, her bound hands up.

"Perhaps not?"

Tessa stared down the barrel of a gun for the second time and damn near wet her pants. Then she saw a shadow move behind Salazar. He caught it, too, and whipped around, aiming at the jungle. The breeze stirred and he fired twice. The movement darted right, and Salazar spun with it. Tessa tried to back away, but he grabbed her, pulling her in front of him like a shield.

"Coward," she said.

He stiffened. "I'll eat his heart when I'm done."

"Then you need fiber. No wonder you're cranky."

He thrust her forward, sandwiched to her back, his gun arm over her shoulder. A flicker of movement and he fired. The shadow passed right and without a choice, Tessa spun with him. She prayed no one fired back. The movement went left, and she realized it couldn't be Logan. It was in two different directions. Who else was out there?

Salazar pushed her toward the open land and the stone mound, forcing her to stand in front of the Isis symbol. Tessa grabbed for his gun, and in the grand scheme of things, it was stupid, but he backed away, wagging a finger at her, then roughly grabbed her tied hands and slid the ropes over the iron rod protruding from the mound.

It pulled on her arms, forcing her to balance on her toes. He inspected her with his hands, and took his time, and then he grabbed her to him, humping her like a rodeo rider, laughing to himself and copping a feel of her breast. *I need a bath now*, she thought, but didn't dare voice it. She was so done with this guy smacking her. Then he pulled a small round object from his leg pocket and peeled off the back and stuck it to her shirt. She looked down at the little glowing red button, then to him.

He wore a twisted, self-important smile as he unclipped his hand radio. He met her gaze and said, "That's a laser dot. To track you." He gestured to the squads of men about two hundred yards away. Troops trained, assembled as they had been days before.

Then she remembered they had rockets—just before Salazar ordered them to lock on the target to fire. *Oh, crap.* She looked down. *That's me.*

Salazar just grinned. "Now he will show himself."

A thousand vile things ran through her mind in that instant and instead of spewing them at his ugly face, she drew her legs up and punched out, hitting him in the chest. Stunned, he went flying back, landing hard enough to lose his weapon. The guy was solid rock and she swore he never bounced. But he jumped to his feet and searched the tall grass for his gun. When he didn't find it, he looked at her.

Uh-oh. Maybe that wasn't so smart.

Then he charged.

The tracking alarm sounded inside the chopper.

"We're painted?" Max said. "We're painted!"

"No. She is," Sebastian said.

Sebastian swooped over the valley, heading north over the trees and kicked the streamlined black chopper into high gear, gun ports open.

Logan bolted from the woods, hit Salazar and took him to the ground. Then he grabbed his clothing and rolled over with him, then he jammed his feet into his middle and tossed Salazar over his head. Logan leapt to his feet. Salazar was just as fast. Upright and ready to charge him.

"Hi, honey," she said.

He didn't look at her, his complete attention on Salazar. "I'll just be a second."

"Go for it. Please."

Salazar drew his knife, tossed it from hand to hand. "I'm going to enjoy this."

"Oh yeah? Me too."

Logan waited for Salazar to strike, blocked it, driving his fist into his rib cage, then gripped his wrist and forced it backward. Salazar pounded on him, trying to loosen his hold, but Logan peeled the knife out of his hand and threw it aside. Then he went to town.

But Salazar was trained and Logan understood how well. Salazar spun, his left foot shooting out and hitting Logan's knee. He went down and Salazar chuckled, rushed him like a bull, but Logan rotated on his knee and blocked, then executed a half dozen successive hits. He heard ribs crack under the pressure. He didn't let up, but Salazar was mindless with rage, and each hit Logan delivered angered him more, throwing off his balance.

In the back of his mind, Logan heard the scrape of a launcher moving into position.

"I will fuck her till she is dead." He spat blood as he spoke.

"She'll kill you first."

Logan quickened his speed. One strike breaking Salazar's nose, the next relieving him of a couple teeth. It cut open his knuckles, blood wetting each punch. Salazar landed a right cross to Logan's jaw, snapping his head to the side. Blood flew in a spray.

Tessa felt the dots of blood on her cheek and was amazed Logan was still standing after all the punches he'd taken. But he was a reckoning force of anger. Salazar kept getting back up, bloody and smiling as he lunged for Logan. He grabbed his hair, then drove his forehead into Logan's. Logan stumbled back, dazed, sinking to the ground. Salazar approached and Logan swung his leg out. The man jumped, laughing. But he didn't expect him to use the momentum to come to his feet.

Logan gave no quarter. He pounded the man, chasing him when he staggered out of range. Troops started to rush from the training field, but Logan kept hitting, turning Salazar's face and body to mush.

Tessa tried pulling the pole out of the stone, but it wouldn't budge, the ropes cutting into her wrists. Her strength was weakening rapidly, yet she got busy, gripped the ropes tightly, then twisted, her back to the fight. She extended her legs, boots barely catching a layer of stones and she used them to push herself up. Every inch she forced the rope closer to the mound. Parallel to the rod, she gained balance, then swung till she had enough momentum to curl around the bar. The motion tightened down the ropes, turning her fingers blue as she came upright, her hips against the bar. She stretched a leg and caught the stone, straining to slip the rope free, then pull herself onto the stone mound.

She stood, feeling a little dizzy, and used her teeth to work at the ties, but they weren't budging. Then she saw the rocket launcher move into position, its point rising toward the sky. She plucked at the laser marker, then stuck it in her mouth. At least it's not shining, she thought, then realized it didn't stop the troops. Then she knew. They'd already found their target. She spat the marker as far as she could, then yanked at the ropes.

"Logan! The rocket!" He didn't hear her, and dragged Salazar off the ground, ready to finish him. *"Logan!"*

He froze, fist raised, then saw the launcher. Instantly, he dropped Salazar and rushed to Tessa. Her vision swam and when she jumped down, she crumbled to the ground. Logan untied the ropes, then helping her up, he ran with her toward the tree line.

She leaned into him, her legs collapsing. "Oh, damn," she muttered and looked at him.

Logan's heart clenched. "Hang on, baby." He glanced to the sky as the black helicopter crested the trees.

Sebastian lowered the chopper, the blades beating the land nearly flat. "I see them."

"Come in behind it, low to the right." Max slid back the

door and shouted to them, waving. "Come on, come on! They're lighting the fire!"

Logan ran toward the chopper, his arm around Tessa, helping her along.

Max leaned out to grab her. "We're hot, we're hot!"

She reared back when she saw the white containment suits, but Logan hurried her inside, then threw himself aboard. The chopper lifted off as Logan grabbed a pistol and turned to his adversary. Logan fired, and Salazar stumbled, shouting. "Incoming!" he shouted as Salazar emptied the rounds at the chopper.

"Hold on tight, people, this will get a little rough." Sebastian pulled back on the stick and went high at a steep angle, the force throwing them against the rear of the craft. The chopper sped over the mound, and Logan tossed out the sphere and map, then slid the door shut and sank to the floor.

Tessa moved to him, and he pulled her into his arms. "You could have kept it."

"No point." He checked her pulse. "Wouldn't have made a good souvenir." Right now, he didn't want any reminders of this moment.

"You could have killed him, too."

"He wasn't worth it." She was more important than punching a hole in Salazar. The bastard could wait to die.

"You're such a superman," she said, and he chuckled weakly.

She was showing signs, her skin damp, pale, and without knowing the traits of the bioagents—or even if it was one— he'd no idea what to expect. Or whether he was infected, too.

Sebastian flew above the trees, troops on the ground ready to fire, but didn't. He headed north toward the airport. "Dragon Six is on the tarmac." Sebastian radioed Riley to start the engines.

"Hurry. Please." It would be precious hours to get to help and Logan was afraid Tessa didn't have that kind of time.

He touched her face, pushed her hair aside, and with his

thumb swiped at bits of blood. Her skin was hot, her pulse rapid. When she went soft against him, he knew she'd slipped into unconsciousness.

Tucked inside the jungle, he sighted through binoculars and followed the helicopter as it rose high. *Salazar got his ass creamed,* he thought, smiling. The pleasure was short-lived when the ape stood and readied to fire. He drew his own pistol, sighting in on Salazar. Then the chopper swept across the mountainside and headed north, but not before they tossed something out. That weird map and ball, he thought, wondering what that was about, then dismissing it. His attention slid back to Salazar and what he'd do next.

He'd already found two bodies, one fresh. Killing his own men made Salazar more than lethal—a serial killer in his own right. *This guy needs to be taken down,* he thought, yet understood Chambliss had given up the chance to finish the twisted puppy for the woman. She did look a little paler than this morning. But then, the RPG probably had something to do with that. It was a helluva show he couldn't stop.

Salazar limped toward the Venezuelan troops marching north. *At least he's outta my theater.*

Tessa stirred when they loaded her into Dragon Six on a stretcher.

She lay still and white as the massive cargo plane lifted off. Logan had already inserted an IV and monitored her vital signs. He'd injected her with something, but she was beyond caring. Her body was on fire from the inside out.

"This is worse than Fiji in July," she moaned, and he soaked her with cool packs, then drew blood, tapping a drop on a slide and viewing it under his microscope. The cells were normal, and he frowned. Her body temperature was rising, but if she was infected, he should see something happening. He wasn't.

*   *   *

Tessa opened her eyes and found Logan sitting next to her, his head cradled in his palms. Her heart clenched at the sorrow on his face and she reached, touching him. He looked up, grasping her hand. The others were in hazmat contamination suits, Logan wasn't.

"Don't ask me how I feel. I don't know. One minute I'm fine, the next it's like needles are trying to come through my skin from the inside."

"We'll have help soon. Hang in there. We're only an hour away from it." He blotted the perspiration on her face and throat.

"Your bedside manner is improving."

"I've got other techniques up my sleeve I'd like to try on you later," he said for her ears alone.

"Playing doctor? I'm so game for that and then some." She smiled, wiggling her brows.

He grinned and realized that he wanted to see that face for the rest of his life. He'd been falling for her again ever since he saw her in the residence, but for a different woman. Tessa was under his skin eleven years ago, and never slipped completely away from his mind. Now she was stuck there. Nicely. He couldn't even think beyond this moment, and keeping her alive, but he wanted more. Lots more.

He leaned in to kiss her.

She reared back a bit. "You'll get infected or whatever."

"I'll take my chances." He took her mouth in a slow, soft kiss and her hand slid to the back of his head, her fingers sinking into his hair.

He groaned and pulled back, pressing his forehead to hers. "Tessa, I—"

"I know," she said softly, running her hand over his hair. "I know." Her voice broke. "Once again my life is in your hands. Don't screw it up."

He smiled weakly, his throat tight. The next hours were too uncertain and Logan knew he didn't have the skills to help her.

Fort Buchanan, Puerto Rico

"We have a problem," Sebastian said.

Logan moved into the cockpit as he brought the jet in line for landing.

"A reception party." Humvees with .50 caliber machine guns waited for them.

"Get McGill on the wire, something's wrong."

Max hailed him as they touched down, the jolt making him lose the handset. He grabbed it, hailing McGill, and got Walker.

"Sir, he was called away."

"Get him, Walker. We're in deep kimchee right now."

"How is that, sir?"

"There's a squad of soldiers outside this plane and we have a big medical emergency." He glanced at Tessa, so still and pale. "Really big."

Sebastian radioed the tower and got orders to remain inside the craft. He relayed the warning of a possible exposure to a bioweapon. They kept telling him to remain in the aircraft.

Sebastian repeated one last time. "Buchanan Tower. Hazmat Alert. Do not come near us without protection." Then he shut down the aircraft and hit the hydraulic lift switch. The back of the jet opened like a yawning mouth.

Logan did his best to keep any hazard contained, dressing Tessa in a hazmat suit, then wrapping her in a silver thermal blanket. She complained of being hot and Logan pulled on his containment suit, then secured her for transport. Between the barriers he met her gaze. She nodded and he leaned to press a kiss, then rolled out the stretcher.

Twenty rifles trained on him. A uniformed army officer walked near.

"Logan?"

He patted her and she slipped her hand out to grasp his. "Please. Don't come farther."

The captain smirked and kept coming. "Commander Chambliss, you and your team are under arrest." Instantly, they were surrounded, the click of chambered bullets chilling.

They wore only gas masks for protection.

"On what charge?"

The Captain held a paper bearing Logan's face. Above it the words WANTED BY INTERPOL. TERRORIST WATCH LIST.

Oh, holy shit. "This is wrong. We're Americans." His voice was muffled through the suit and hood.

"Then they'll go harder on you." The captain gripped his arm, pulled him away from Tessa.

"Logan!"

She looked scared and his heart ached for her. He tried to get to her, but two troops dragged him back. Soldiers relieved them of weapons, searched each. Logan strained to see her. They left her on the concrete, strapped to a stretcher as the soldiers dragged them away.

"Hey! Listen up, you Army pukes!" Max said. "You think we're wearing these suits for the fashion statement!" They cuffed him, ignoring the obvious, "This is *Hazmat*." They didn't stop. "When you all start dying, you'll wish you'd listened!"

Several soldiers stepped back and looked at their captain. "They're terrorists." He ordered them gagged.

Dragon One knew the military personnel were not to speak to any terror suspects. It was the FBI and CIA's job to question.

"You're going to lose those bars, Captain," Max said before they put a cloth over his mouth. The captain kept to his duty as American troops escorted them toward the buildings.

"Quarantine!" Logan shouted. "Quarantine her! I'm a doctor, you fool. She's been exposed to pathogens!" Logan fought them till a soldier hit him between the shoulder blades and he went down.

Personnel moved the gurney toward a waiting ambulance—the medics in full protection gear, thank God. Logan caught a final glimpse of Tessa as they lifted her into the ambulance before the security detail led them away.

Staff Sgt. Walker looked at Lorimer with wide eyes.
"No," David said. "That's not possible."
"Man, this week, anything is possible."
Walker was trying all resources to contact McGill. "He's in DC, but nothing's going through."
"He's one of four places: NSA, CIA, the Pentagon or in the White House."
"But it's his private number."
"White House, definitely," David said.
"We gotta do something. I don't want them getting a Gitmo Bay treatment again."
"I can break in. Your call, Staff Sergeant."
Walker thought for a second. "Do it. I'll get a plane." He took his seat at the computer.
"How?"
Walker typed. "I can requisition anything. And for a three-star?" He scoffed. "You want military transportation or a Lear?"
"A Lear, he'll be pissed."
"After what they'd asked D-1 to do? He'll be breathing fire."
Both men worked, smiling to themselves and wishing they could witness General Joseph "Mac" McGill go ape shit on a bunch of Army guys.

He was inflamed by the American Fourth of July celebration and Eloisa wanted to leave, disgusted with his rants.
"Your temper is talking now. Save your passion for something worthwhile," she said, a ghost of a smile on her lips. "You must control yourself."
Gutierrez eyed her, the ruthless side the country rarely saw showing in his eyes.
"I'll do no such thing. Not for them." He stared at the

television, at the meeting of the American President with the French. "They chose the wrong time to be in my waters."

"They aren't," she said testily. "Nor are they going to invade. Fight the Americans? Why? What purpose? You're mad if you think the Americans would, and even worse to believe we could win. If America wanted Venezuela, they could take it. You know this."

"I would have all of South America behind me."

That was his ego talking, she thought. The Bolivian Revolution wasn't as strong as he thought. But it would be. "There are simpler ways to deal with them."

He looked at her, arching a brow.

A summit on global warming was convening, the British hosting it on their islands off the coast. For security, no specific island had been mentioned and all were preparing. However, Manuel hadn't been offered an invitation. Nor had any other Latin American country. It had been mentioned in the press that it was a clear snub to the people of Venezuela.

Eloisa saw it as an opportunity.

Sebastian, Riley, Max and Logan were each in an eight-by-five-foot cubicle, handcuffed, ankles secured to the floor. It had recently been hosed down, the floor was still wet.

Between each man was a wall of heavy iron mesh you'd need a hacksaw to get through and it was sharp as hell.

"This is a new low," Max said. "Imprisoned twice in one week? Nothing like getting slapped for all the hard work."

"It's better than torture, right?" Riley said, groaning as he stretched out his sore leg.

Sebastian said nothing, dozing in the corner of his cell.

Logan tipped his head back, his anger suppressed only by his helplessness. He had no idea where they took Tessa or if they'd accepted that she been exposed. At least the medics weren't stupid. They needed CDC experts, scientists, to get this analyzed. They didn't ask him about the vial, and he hoped no one tried to open it. Knowing Eloisa, it was another puzzle.

"How'd we get on the *Watch* list, for crissake?" Max asked.

"We failed to get Ramos out. Disavowed." Logan snickered to himself.

"I didn't sign up for this shit," Max said, standing and pacing the small space. "McGill did this to us. I can't believe that."

"He was hiding info from the start," Logan snarled. He didn't want to hear speculation. Not now. He couldn't think of anything except Tessa and what she was going through. The doctors here were good but no one had come to them to ask a single question, and the guards were afraid to look them in the eye. But it was the lack of immediate response that infuriated him. All precautions should have been taken for the unknown. They'd given them fair warning.

Logan didn't worry too much about getting out of here. It would happen. When, was another matter. He was desperate to see Tessa. Riley didn't have time to alert McGill in the past twelve hours, but keeping them off the Most Wanted was sort of part of the bargain.

"Terror Watch list, my ass," Logan muttered. Someone connected to this operation was flexing their muscles. If it wasn't McGill, then who?

McGill closed his cell phone and rubbed his hand over his face. There was no safe way to close this operation without a lot of lives being destroyed, but he'd be damned if he'd let his guys take the fall.

"Do I need to know?"

He shook his head and lifted his gaze to the man on the other side of the desk. They were alone for once.

"I have your authority to take this to the mat?"

"Yes."

"When it's done, we'll talk. Not till then."

"I agree."

McGill nodded and turned away, then heard, "God speed, Marine" as he quit the oval office.

Seventeen

Tessa had so many wireless leads tacked to her body, she felt like a stripper in pasties.

She knew nothing. No one would speak to her.

They just kept sticking her with needles and watching the machines that monitored everything. They could at least be chatty. She was out of it when they landed, and drugged until she slapped the last guy for sticking her with a needle without asking. She'd heard them say that the men were incarcerated and that brought all sorts of images, none of them good. But in the windowless room, she lost all sense of time and place. She didn't even know what country this was, not that any of it mattered.

Lately, nothing was as it seemed. If she was infected with something, she should be breaking out in sores or something equally disgusting, yet she wasn't. She felt fine; occasionally hot as hell, but then she lived in Java so heat wasn't much of a problem for her.

However, the pinpricking feeling she got from the inside out was no picnic. It was like needing to scratch her liver. Impossible to relieve. It made her jittery, and she hopped off the bed and paced. They'd confined her to a white-tiled operating room with a drain in the middle of the floor. It was creepy, but then, housing a leper wasn't in the manual, she supposed. Almost immediately, a doctor's voice came over the speaker, telling her to please get back in bed.

She looked up, glaring through the glass at the guys in hazmat suits that made them look more like fat white lab rats. "Find out what it is?"

"We're running tests."

"You keep saying that. Maybe we should get someone else in here?" Someone smarter?

She moved to the glass. There was a little desk on the other side. A lot of charts and paperwork. It was all meaningless and she was going stir-crazy. Not from the confinement but from her fear that her last days on Earth would be in this sterile room, alone. Where were Logan and the team? She'd heard the stories out of Guantanamo Bay.

What would these people do to former U.S. military they thought turned traitor?

General McGill flexed his stars the only way he knew how—with big strokes. When the Learjet landed in Puerto Rico, he was already issuing orders. The commander of the base was more than willing to hand over the matter to the U.S. Army Medical Research Institute of Infectious Diseases, USAMRIID. McGill kept close the horrible realization that something else was in control of thousands of lives right now.

His last report: the scientists were still studying the vial's contents. It was bad enough that it existed at all, and he truly didn't want this young woman to suffer. She was as innocent as they came. McGill had the duty of telling them what he knew. It wouldn't be a cheery conversation.

Within fifteen minutes of touching down, he stood before the row of cells. "Release them."

Logan was on his feet the minute McGill entered the building. The doors swung open and as a soldier unlocked the shackles, Logan stared at McGill. "Do I need to beat the shit out of you, sir?"

"Probably. This is far bigger than we thought."

Max shook his head. "Figures."

"Why didn't you clue us in?"

"I was hoping you'd succeed."

Logan walked out of the cell. "Don't count us out, sir."

"Never did. Take him to her," he said to the guard.

But Logan was already running toward the exit. The young soldier matched his pace. "Get quick on the step."

"Yes, sir . . . uh, sir, sorry for arresting you."

Logan glanced. "You were obeying orders."

"Sometimes, you just know when it's wrong."

Logan wasn't listening, his attention on the quarantine corridor. Outside it, he put on protective gear, then grabbed the chart. The other doctors protested.

"This facility's police action on the tarmac probably infected the entire base and you want to bitch at me? Talk to him." He tossed a thumb to the door. McGill stood on the other side looking every bit the three-star mustang general.

Logan pushed between them to look into the glass. Tessa was flat on her back, hooked up to IVs, and the entire area encased in protective plastic. He glanced back at the doctors. "Any signs?"

"Nothing has registered so far."

"Nothing?" That was odd, there should be cell reaction to a foreign body in the bloodstream. "Elevated white cell count?"

"High, her body is fighting it."

"Is there an antidote?"

The doctor's expression was sympathetic.

"We're working as fast as we can."

Logan nodded and lifted his gaze, feeling the weight of uncertainty as he moved to the glass. She saw him, swung her legs over the side of the bed and rushed to the glass.

"Logan. Oh, thank God." Her voice was tinny through the speaker. "I didn't know for sure."

"We got arrested," he said sheepishly.

"There goes that by-the-book rep you're so proud of."

"How do you feel?"

"The same, not as hot, and other than them sticking me every ten minutes . . ." She showed him her arm. It looked like a pincushion.

"Christ." Logan twisted. "Get me a *Navy* medic. I'll do it till then." He looked back at her, aching to hold her. "I'm coming inside."

"You just want to see me naked again."

"Never miss a chance, my dear."

She laughed gently. His Snidely Whiplash impersonation just cracked her up.

He asked for a tray and Tessa stepped back as they unlocked the quarantine doors and let him inside. Instantly she rushed him, clinging. Logan held her, setting down the tray, then crushing her to him. His protective suit crinkled between them.

"I'm scared. They aren't telling me anything."

"That's because there's nothing to tell." He hated the bulky suit separating them. This one had an air tank. Tessa had nothing. "Sit down, let me do this."

Logan flipped back the cloth covering the tray and put on the tourniquet, then tapped for a vein.

"That one."

He glanced up. "You NGS, me doctor."

"Most doctors stink at this."

Gently, he inserted the blood collection needle, then pushed in a tube. "Try doing it under hostile fire." She inhaled and he met her gaze. "Sorry."

"I have a pretty good idea about it, and after my baptism"—she said it on a little trembling laugh—"nothing would shock me." He filled another tube, then slid out the needle. "You're good at this."

He didn't speak, his brows tight as pulled the tray close to label them. His handwriting got darker, heavier with each stroke, and she thought, *He'll break the tube.*

"Logan if this is as bad as I think, then I have to say something—"

"Don't, baby, please. I don't want to hear regrets, we have enough of them between us, and it doesn't matter." His fingers tightened on the tubes and he set them carefully aside, then met her gaze. "It never mattered. The moment I saw you again, I was angry, but the simple fact was . . . missing you never got easier."

Tears blurred her vision and she blinked. God. She *loved* him. He made her feel whole again. Before, she was drifting, a hobo life searching for the elusive anchor when she knew she couldn't have it, couldn't pull anyone into her odd life. Then there was Logan and change. Even the danger seemed minor against that.

"Does this mean you don't want to hear what I have to say?" she asked on a hint of a smile.

"Not unless it's 'I love you madly and want to spend every waking moment with you.'"

"Yes, sure I do."

He blinked.

"Not exactly romantic, but what did you think I'd say? No? Go away, handsome Doctor Commando Superman. Oh, yeah, sure." She grinned. "I told you I got smarter."

He smiled for the first time since the sphere had opened.

"I see we still gotta work on that 'women who think first,' huh?"

He grasped her hand, then defiantly he pulled off the glove. She immediately laced her fingers with his. It wasn't enough.

"I'm in love with you."

His deep voice trembled over her skin, and her heartbeat staggered painfully. "It's the muscles, right?"

Logan shook his head as he pushed a curling strand of hair off her forehead, then slid his touch down the side of her face. "It's your soul I recognized."

Her lower lip quivered and she drank in the moment, the man. She got lucky so fast, she was terrified of losing him. Her grip in his tightened. "I love you, too."

He smiled widely. "Whew. That's a load off." For a second he forgot about the hood and leaned to kiss her, then stopped and sighed with regret.

"We'll have to do this all over again later," she said. "Not naked, though, you have no concentration when we're naked. Well . . ."—she smiled—"no *brain* activity, I should say."

His shoulders jiggled with a silent laugh. "Deal."

Next to him on the bed, she leaned her head on his shoulder. They couldn't talk of a future, of tomorrow. There might not be one.

"This bites," he said and she chuckled. There was a tap on the glass and they looked up.

Max waved, then said, "News flash."

Logan nodded, then slid off the bed. He didn't leave.

"Go on, I'm fine, just bored. Tell them to get me a book. Video games just annoy me." She flicked at the stack under a TV. "I'm not good at them."

"Want something to sleep?"

"Oooo, my own personal drug pusher." He smiled, pressed a kiss to her forehead through the plastic face barrier. "I'm fine, go."

Then he did, and Tessa felt like she had in Serbia. Though she wasn't wet, cold and alone, she felt just as isolated.

Logan had to go through a series of wash downs to get out of the quarantine area. The team waited outside.

"So who feels like a patsy?" Logan asked and didn't expect an answer. Expressions were good enough. Together they strode out of the hospital building and into headquarters to a conference room where McGill waited.

Logan pushed inside and started to ream McGill a new orifice, but McGill put up a hand.

"I deserve it all, but I have higher orders. I had no choice but to conceal."

"Who?" Logan asked.

He scowled. "Not that it's any of your damn business—"

"Let's get one thing straight, McGill. We took this on *for you,* and if you can't cover our ass on your end, what's the point of trusting you now to finish this?"

The team stood in a defensive posture and McGill's shoulders sank a little when he realized he'd lost some of their trust. "You're right. But I had orders not to divulge certain aspects. The Watch list, I was supposed to have twenty-four hours' notice."

Logan didn't give a damn. "This mess belongs to Elizabeth Jacobs, just like it did eleven years ago. Who do you think gave her orders?"

McGill tipped his head, and frowned.

"Your predecessor had to get funding somehow. This op is two weeks old. You've been in the job for a month."

"If you're insinuating . . ."

"See how easy it goes down the tubes?" Max asked, his arms folded over his chest.

McGill looked at each man and wondered when his last line of defense started cutting out the people he trusted most. Like any soldier, even he had the right to refuse an order that would bring harm to others. McGill hadn't and he was disgusted with himself.

"I apologize. Juggling secrets like this isn't a familiar talent." He looked at Logan directly. "Elizabeth Jacobs has escaped."

The air was blue with cursing.

"She has a twelve-hour head start."

"Well, kiss her spying ass good-bye," Riley said, sitting down and pulling a chair close to prop his leg.

"You can hire us to find her later," Logan said. "Talk."

McGill started laying out the missing pieces and Logan listened, to the journey a lab-created substance took to end on Cassie's honeymoon yacht.

"We had surveillance on the chemist for months, but the Chinese were on it. They didn't want it made any more than we did. It's a designer virus."

It was a strain the CDC had never seen before, and too diverse to respond to an antidote for another virus with similar qualities.

"We thought they had it all. Six vials total, five accounted for at the seizure. Yours completes the set. Intelligence believes there is no more, though any documentation from the Chinese doesn't exist. Originally, the chemist had created a bioagent for eating oil spills that wouldn't destroy the eco-system. It needed first the oil and saltwater to activate. The Chinese tested it on the spill in the Yangtze River."

Logan frowned, remembered Tessa saying she'd photo-graphed the view a few years ago and was arrested by Chinese officials. He watched the recording play on a flat screen.

"The Chinese missed him. But while they weren't watching, the British were." McGill tapped a key and the screen lit with a new video. "A chemist, worse than Hussein's Dr. Germ, was at the yacht earlier, just at shift change. And as you can see, not a suspicious threat."

"Aren't they always," Logan said.

The grainy video showed a hunched man, shuffling his feet and carrying a fishing pole and bucket, nothing else. Clever, Logan thought. The chemist stepped onto the yacht, returning topside a moment later, but instead of leaving, he sat on the dock for a couple hours and fished.

"That's ballsy," Max said.

"MI6 was prepared to capture when Chinese Intel arrived." He stopped the tape before the assault and retreat showed. "The Chinese took out the target themselves."

"I want specifics." Logan wasn't dicking around with history. He wanted something to defend Tessa's life.

McGill drew a stack of papers in front of him. "It needs a second component. It has to mix. Like two binary agents, this is harmless on its own."

"That's good, right?" Max asked, but knew it wasn't.

"The element necessary to activate it is human blood."

The room went pin-drop quiet and Logan's heart sank. *Oh, Tessa.*

"Christ, who thinks this shit up?" Max asked.

"Once that happens, it incubates for a few hours before it becomes deadly. Then it's transmissible by human contact."

"Skin? Transmissible by skin? My God," Max said. "A simple handshake could kill millions." Max held out his hand for the reports and McGill gave them up.

Sebastian leaned forward to add, "That's provided the

carrier doesn't travel, then it would multiply, increasing the strength of the strain. Merely breathing would kill, slower, but it would."

When his voice went silent, the room itself seemed to hold its breath.

Logan left the chair and went to the bank of windows. The blinds were shut, and just for the hell of it, he rolled them up and stared out at the island of Puerto Rico. A delayed-reaction designer bioweapon. He and Tessa had brought it out into the open.

"How close have you gotten to Ramos?" McGill asked.

Logan was barely listening.

"Close enough for a handshake, but not. Ramos acknowledged me," Sebastian said.

"We have to go back for him," Logan cut in.

"Impossible. We were hunted before, now we'll be shot on sight."

Logan waved that off. "We can get in, you know it."

"And do what? Logan," McGill said quietly, "there is no winning solution."

He jerked around. "We better find one. Now. Or I swear to God, I'll start a mess you'll never clean up."

"Is that a threat, Commander?" McGill asked, scowling.

"Oh, hell yes. Everybody get their ass wired together because I'm not letting her die"—he pointed to where Tessa was being fed a dozen different antidotes in the hopes one worked—"without taking this out."

"You heard the general, it's harmless until contact. It's done, Logan."

Logan spun around, glared at Sebastian. "We came to take Ramos out of here. We didn't do the job. This is still a threat." He grasped the now-empty vial, held it out. "There has to be more. It was too difficult to reach if they wanted it quickly." Pessimists, he thought.

"Ramos is the priority. Agreed?" Sebastian asked.

Logan felt the sting of that and he looked at McGill. He

wanted to take Tessa away from here, get her help, but he couldn't and McGill knew it.

"You want me to do it, Mac? Put the man in my sights?"

"You may have to," Max said, sliding off the end of the table as he glanced between two papers. "This says that the vial you found is almost five milligrams less than the others." He handed the papers back to McGill. "There is some out there, a few drops."

It took only what was on the inside of the glass to infect Tessa.

"So . . . we have a plan, maybe?"

Ramos smiled and came to Mrs. Rojas with his hands out. She grasped them warmly, her skin dry and smooth. She reminded him of his grandmother, and feelings he hadn't experienced in a while flooded him around this woman.

"Your grandson?"

"Very well, thank you, señor." She looked up expectantly.

Ramos didn't want to involve her in any danger. She was backup. Not for him, but for this country. So few could bring such ruin, he thought, ashamed of his part in this. Here, for once, he had no ego; perhaps because he knew he would die here. There was no viable solution for the US to come out smelling like a rose, and he'd never see America again. But he could salvage what Garcia had wanted. Before Garcia had trusted him and Jacobs. Garcia was a good man; there were few like him, and Ramos had been humbled by the knowledge.

He stepped back and dug in his pocket. "Do you know what this is?"

"A flash drive, yes, sir." She held up her keys and one dangled from the ring. "This is the household accounts. Five gig."

He grinned widely. God, he adored this woman. "I want to give this to you for safekeeping, Mrs. Rojas. If you don't want to do it, please say so. I'll respect that."

She simply held out her hand. He gave it to her, oddly moved. It was Garcia she loved, he knew, he wasn't whacked about this. Yet the experience was the same.

"Should anything happen to me—"

She inhaled.

"I'm being very careful. This is a reminder to be vigilant." He swept his fingers down the side of his face, a jumble of burn scars, faint but noticeable. "But should the unforeseen occur, give that to Joaquin Castillo. Only him."

She nodded and clipped it to her key ring. "I'm never without these."

He held her gaze, then moved closer, and lightly grasped her upper arms, then pressed a kiss to her forehead. "Thank you."

Stage four out the door.

Then, because he wanted it so badly himself, he hugged her.

Port Kaiser, Jamaica

Liz felt the pump of adrenaline as she left the cab and slung the bag on her shoulder. She'd taken great pains to disguise her gender, though she knew she couldn't mask it completely, but she kept her face shielded by a hooded sweatshirt, and her figure toned down in baggy pants and a ratty jean jacket helped. She walked with more of a stoop to throw off anyone watching her. Surveillance was at a distance, and shape and size came into play frequently. Facial ID wasn't as difficult as the populace thought. Wireless search connections were being built into the smallest equipment and they could snap a picture and have it analyzed within minutes, provided Intel had the information on the subject. The enemy numbered in the many. She was considered one of them now.

She'd be in Venezuela by morning, on her way back by nightfall.

Walking two more blocks to the deep-water dock, she approached the gangway, her heart pounding with excitement for the game. Less than an hour to exile, she thought, and saw the massive tow lines drop from the ship, heard the tugboat engines rev to push the giant out to sea. But before she stepped on the plank, a stout man with huge shoulders blocked her path. She showed her identification, false, of course, as was her passport, but the captain of the tanker didn't care if she hitched a ride. She paid him enough for his silence.

The sailor inspected it and her, smirking at her clothes, then stepped aside to let her pass. She mounted the steep plank and onto the deck, then she adjusted the bag on her shoulder as her gaze swept over the dock, touching on vehicles with the engine running, or a man alone and unoccupied. A familiar rush of awareness surrounded her. Details like a pulsing flash. She plucked and catalogued them, even as she turned away. She counted eleven men on this side of the ship, and smelled the recently greased pulleys. The sailors must eat breakfast up here often, she thought, noting the wrappers and a ring stain just to the left of a thermos. Sea salt and tar lingered in the air; machinery loaded cartons netted and dangling from a crane—and she memorized anyone who noticed her, then headed down the narrow passageway.

Salty dampness clung to the wood and steel, and she barely noticed the paint peeling off in strips. She reached the small cabin, pushed inside and closed the door. She had two steps in each direction. A bunk, a desk, a locker, and a bathroom that looked like something ejected from a 747. She dropped the bag and sat in the only chair, listening for the engines to start, to be under way. A few hours and she'd be back in the arena again. She'd counted too much on Ramos. She never thought he'd be a gutless weenie, but then, most men were more talk than walk.

She'd have to finish it herself and although she was going on sparse information, she'd made good with less before. McGill had flagged Tessa's photo, and since he'd taken over the operation investigation, she knew he'd sent in another team. The risk of leaving Ramos there was too high for

America. He knew it going in, and without Garcia, there was no way out. Hell. He was dead the minute he entered the country. A bullet two weeks later would be uncomplicated, especially during a celebration. Easy pickings from the crowd.

Liz didn't wonder about Tessa and what part she played in this. She couldn't get any confirmation one way or the other. Her past was being dredged up and with it came the picture.

The ship trembled as the engines grew louder. She pushed back the hood, then pulled off the jean jacket and tossed it on the bunk. She released her hair from the barrette, rubbing her scalp, then rose and sat on the bunk with her bag. She unpacked, laying everything out, then assembled the rifle. In under a minute, she was sighting down the scope.

A knock startled her and she threw a blanket over her possessions and went to the door. She didn't open it. "Who is it?"

"The captain, ma'am."

He probably wanted more money, but he wouldn't get it till they made port in Caracas. She flipped the lock, glancing back once to check that nothing was displayed, then opened the door. Incredibly tall and narrow, the Kenyan hunched in the passageway, his pale gold eyes a little downcast.

"Yes, what is it? I've paid you. We had an agreement, Sola." Then she realized his expression was frozen.

In an instant, she knew it was over.

She took a step into the corridor and saw the men on either side of him, weapons drawn. Beyond those were more, rifles trained on her head. The dark blond man nearest her flipped open a black billfold. Her gaze flicked to the badge, then to his face. NSA.

"Sucks, doesn't it?" he said, then had the nerve to smile.

Presidential Palace, Caracas

Another piece had fallen into place two minutes ago.

Ramos stared at the British ambassador to Venezuela and wanted him to repeat himself, but he'd heard just fine.

The summit on global warming or some tree hugger event was being hosted by the British on the Caribbean islands. As a gesture of brotherhood, they'd invited Gutierrez. The same man who had viciously slandered the U.S. President in the press since he took office and the most recent, just days ago. It was all that was broadcasting on CNN. But Gutierrez refused the invitation.

They were all looking at him again, shocked.

His gaze went to Eloisa and he couldn't tell if she was pleased or not. "The man has denied me entry into the Security Council."

The British ambassador frowned. "You mean Venezuela, correct?"

"Yes, yes, of course."

"This has nothing to do with the Security Council, Mr. President," the ambassador said. "It's a chance to talk. The United Kingdom offers a hand in friendship. To meet with us and, yes, the U.S. President as well as Germany's President."

Gutierrez was shaking his head like a petulant child. "Estavan will go."

The ambassador reared back, then tried to recover from his surprise. It wasn't an insult per se but it was close. The offer was not extended to the Vice President.

"I will have to consult, Mr. President."

Gutierrez barely acknowledged him and he was escorted from the room for privacy.

"Don't do this, Manny," Ramos said. "If you're trying to save face, it won't work. It's an insult."

"Good. A slap for a slap."

Ramos resisted the urge to bust his chops. The man wasn't a leader, he was a manipulator. He looked at Eloisa, but she wasn't paying attention, staring out the window intently. There was nothing beyond except a spectacular view that was closely guarded.

He called to her and she looked at him, glanced between the two and came back into the conversation. "Yes, you should go."

"No."

"Then there will be nothing for this gesture," Eloisa said.

"If Manny didn't shoot his mouth off, this wouldn't be a big decision," Ramos said. "You anger the wrong people."

"They cannot touch me," Gutierrez said.

"They don't have to. One word and you fall."

Gutierrez pointed at Ramos. "You need to keep Castillo quiet."

"Afraid of real democracy? Afraid there might be a credible working congress, representatives? A balanced budget that doesn't line your pockets?"

"You cannot change our ways to theirs."

God. He didn't even deny it. "It isn't our way, not Venezuela's way. That's your problem, Manuel, you don't *think* democratically. It's worked for centuries and people flee to countries like the United States. Everyone wants in. They risk their lives to be citizens. What have you risked for this country?"

"My work has helped us prosper! You will attend." Manuel turned away, his glance at Eloisa so subtle that Ramos almost missed it.

The message was clear. They'd get him there. The question was, why were they so intent on sending *him?*

Eighteen

Puerto Rico

Everything depended on remaining invisible.

Inside a hangar at the end of the runway, the Dragon Six cargo plane was locked and chocked, but not useful. Though it was armed with a rotating gun mount and Angel Decoys for heat-seeking missiles, risking landing it in Venezuela again was out of the question. There were plenty of other means to get the three men inside and close to Ramos.

McGill sipped coffee and thought about Elizabeth Jacobs going through a strip search and scrub down. He'd let her stew in a cell for a while, get used to those four walls, but right now, she wasn't stepping on U.S. soil. Interrogating her would have to wait.

He stepped back when Riley Donovan shifted under the table, rigging electrical lines to help Walker and Lorimar set up the command post inside the hangar. He'd had three mobile surveillance computer operations units airlifted in, the white cubes filled with operation computers that needed only a generator to be up and running. He needed all hands on the ball. Timing was everything.

He poked his head into the ten-foot-tall box. "You good to go?"

"This rocks, sir," Walker said. "Ready when you are."

"You track that stream yet?"

Walker's expression fell. "No, sir. It's hit us twice more, too. Sorry, sir."

Nolan walked close by. "Problem?"

McGill eyed him, desperate. "Just how good are you, Deets?"

Deets glanced at the others, his brows knitting slightly. "I don't need software to make a computer work for me, sir."

"You're hired." McGill handed him a folded piece of paper. "I need him to talk to me. ASAP."

Nolan nodded and unfolded the sheet. It was a jumble of letters and numbers that had been crossed out and replaced. "Who do you think it's from?"

"If I remember the codes correctly . . . Truman."

Nolan's features pulled tight and he looked down at the paper again. Truman, Harding, Eisenhower, Taft—he always went by names of dead Presidents. No one had ever seen him, that was the rumor. Not even those who had done similar missions. Truman's identity was buried, and up until this moment, no one had ever admitted to his existence. Speculation as to who gave him orders was rampant. Like a bedtime story, Truman was a legend.

"I'm certain it's him, but—" McGill shook his head for a second. "There was no rescue. It was a hit. You heard the call, Jacobs just cut him off. Someone else sent Truman in."

Nolan's brows shot high into his forehead. "How does the deputy director of the CIA not know a guy like this is in his operation?"

"Come into the job a month ago and see how well you float."

Nolan smirked as he stepped inside one of the large white boxes housing surveillance and computers, and shut the door.

McGill turned back to the tables lined with more computers, maps and gadgets.

Riley wiggled under the tables, then suddenly all the screens lit up, the computers booting. He struggled to stand and McGill rushed to hand him his cane.

"Thanks, sir." He stood. "You're all set. If it's all right, I'm going to sit with Tessa for a bit."

McGill's expression turned grim. "Carry on."

Hot, wet air snapped at his clothes, brushed his face as the charter fishing boat sailed into the bay off the coast of Caracas. The boat would have to wait to unload, but Logan wasn't wasting that kind of time. While Ramos was his target, he needed to be with Tessa, her physical absence almost painful. She was sleeping when they left and he'd wanted to touch her, say good-bye, but had to be satisfied with just looking. She'd grown paler. The doctors were working as fast as they could, and McGill had seen to it that they had everything they needed. Logan felt powerless to help her.

Beside him, Max sat checking dive gear. Sebastian was flying a charter Cessna to an old CIA airport northwest of the VP's summer residence. Once he reached the residence, he'd try to contact Ramos. But Logan counted him out of the running. It would be simpler if he'd just walked away and they'd deal with the repercussions, but he was in too deep. Logan drew the line at killing the man. Intercepting his motorcade on the return trip would have to do. It's the only time they could pinpoint his location. He had ceremonies to attend and the chance that Eloisa had more of the bioagent was a viable threat, but it was no longer their problem. Venezuelan CDC would be warned, but it was out of their hands.

The trawler slowed and the captain swung it around, idling for a moment. He nodded to them, patting his pocket filled with a few thousand American dollars. This was as far as he was willing to go. Entering the country illegally wasn't a big deal, but Salazar wasn't in the grave and Logan didn't doubt he'd keep hunting. A welcoming committee would make this tougher.

Max turned on Logan's air, and he returned the favor, then breathed through the scuba regulator. He pulled down his mask and crouched below the railing. Then he rolled over the side of the boat and sank into the water.

Max followed, and they rode the propulsion torpedo toward shore.

Sebastian couldn't get near the residence.

The area was filled with people, remains from a ceremony he'd just missed scattered around the giant dais he'd help build. He scanned for Ramos, hoping to see him, and hating to think all this rested on his personal habits. Ramos was scheduled to leave for Caracas within the hour. Sebastian wouldn't be able to get close enough to touch him. It might get him shot by the police, but he had to try. But last week's events in this place resulted in more than just the roads locked down. The airwaves were monitored and certainly the calls to the Vice President.

He was about to call Nolan to see if he could reroute the call to look like it came from Washington DC, in the hopes it would bypass some secretary or Ramos's aide, when he heard a helicopter. It flew over the estate, landing on the lawn, the blades destroying the decorations. He looked through binoculars as the passenger left, then he called McGill.

"You'll never guess who just landed."

The unexpected noise sent guards running as a helicopter landed on the lawn.

Eloisa leaned toward the window and watched it shut down. Guards aimed to greet the intruder, but when the door opened, they lowered their weapons. She recognized Salazar and sighed in relief, trying not to get overexcited. He was late but it was good enough that he'd kept his promise.

She walked briskly, her heels clicking on the mosaic floors. Her aides started to follow and she waved them back. She was alone in the wide corridor as he stepped onto the landing. Her eyes widened. He was a bloody mess, his face swollen and blood dripping off his chin. He limped toward her.

"You're mad to come here like that."

He didn't speak, grabbed her wrist and slapped the orb and map in her hand.

Immediately, Eloisa examined the water-stained map, then tucked it under her arm and clutched the sphere, smiling. "Excellent." She turned away, then looked back. "Clean up, you smell."

He didn't let her leave, grabbed her arm and pushed her into the nearest room. She struggled, slapping at his hand, but he held on, giving her a little shove before he closed the door.

"It's done. Pay me."

"The ones who had it?"

When he didn't answer, she looked up. He shrugged.

"Alive? You can't be serious, Diego. They must be eliminated."

"They know nothing, woman, and control yourself." He moved in, swiping at the blood itching his skin. "My money, all of it, right now."

She set the map and ball aside, then went to the sideboard. She removed a vase of lilies and a crystal sculpture from one end, then lifted a false top and flipped a switch. A false drawer popped out on the end and she waved elegantly. "There you are."

"Aren't you going to open your prize?" he asked as he gathered the bundles, stuffing them in his cargo pants leg pockets.

"That's not necessary." She started to put the sphere and map away, but he stopped her.

"Yes, it is." Salazar tipped his head, thinking how nice it would be to snap the bitch's neck.

"Fine."

His gaze lowered to her hands as she opened the sphere. He raised a brow at the mechanism, then frowned when she swore.

Her gaze snapped to his. "It's gone."

It was open to nearly flat and he peered closer. "So . . . You no longer have control of it." He tsked softly. "Pity."

Her expression turned ugly. "Find it. Do you know what that cost me? Millions! Find it!"

"They are gone. We let them get off the ground."

"We?" She scoffed rudely. "You did. Your only job was to get it back and you've been gone for days and look at you! You come here where everyone, including my husband and the press, can see you like that? You're a disgrace."

Salazar stepped up to her, and she retreated. This time he kept coming until she was sandwiched against the bookcases. "I'm no longer your puppet. I have done the unthinkable for you."

"Oh, you have not. Not for me. You did it to line your pockets and you enjoy it. That's why you're a success. Till now." He pressed harder, his hands on her hips, and she shoved his chest. He wouldn't budge. "I'll scream."

"Wouldn't be wise." He gave the knife a push and she gasped as it pricked her ribs.

Her gaze drifted past him, but Salazar didn't take the bait. He just grinned wider.

"There was a woman with him that night, did you know that? When the attack came, he was with a young, beautiful woman. I've seen her, tasted her skin."

"I don't care if there were ten women with him. If they opened it, then they're dead already, and you should have cleaned your mess neatly. If you think we aren't watched by the world, you're wrong."

"That's a clever phrase. How many times have you said it?" He shook his head, rueful. "You are no better than me, Eloisa, you like control, and you use what you have," he said with a glance down her body, "to get it." Then he whispered close to her ear, his strength imprisoning her. "I have watched you fuck him . . . so beautiful when you come."

Eloisa closed her eyes, hating him. He was a professional killer, his touch was foul and at the same time, she antici-pated it when he bunched in her skirt, pulling it upward. He would be big and powerful.

"If the poison wasn't inside, then they have opened it."

"Impossible."

"They probably know exactly what they possess, too. It leads right to you." He tipped his head. "Ask yourself who took it from you." He snared a handful of her hair, twisting it in his fist until she winced. "Eh?"

She met his gaze, her eyes sparking with anger. "You're a barbarian, Diego."

"And you have not really left the streets, *puta*." Whore.

He leaned in slowly and kissed her, not hard or fiercely but gently, his lips playing over hers. He kept on until she softened against him, grinding to her just enough for her to know he was hard.

She responded with spreading herself for him, and he wedged between her thighs, and kissed her ruthlessly. "It's not all gone, is it?" he asked. Bloody hands sought her breasts, her round ass.

Her gaze slid to his, a mean snarl on her lips. "Hardly."

Ramos listened to the conversation from his suite, the earpiece tucked neatly as he slipped into his jacket. He'd been alerted of Salazar by Mrs. Rojas. He'd bugged Eloisa's offices and suites when he'd found the surveillance room but had to remove them frequently whenever security swept the house for listening devices. Salazar had a nice array stashed in his closet and he hadn't been back since Ramos had found it, either.

He paused to listen. She'd never spoken to Salazar so openly. At least Logan had whatever was at the end of the map and, as he had suspected, it was deadly. But when all he heard was heavy breathing, he easily stepped into the role of outraged husband, leaving the suite and rushing across to her wing. Though no woman should be manhandled, no matter how greedy and manipulative, he hated this prick. He had no conscience and it was like looking into a mirror and despising what you saw.

If Eloisa wanted to screw him, fine, just not in Garcia's house. At one time Garcia had loved her enough to marry her, and the man deserved respect. Ramos stopped at the doors, then abruptly threw them open. He let a moment pass, his presence registering, then he let out a deep growl as he charged inside.

With both hands, he grasped Salazar and yanked him off her. She shrieked and rolled away, pulling down her skirt as Ramos drove his fist into Salazar's face, advancing and making him step back.

"He tried to rape me! Arrest him!"

Salazar's expression went black with rage and he lunged for Eloisa. Ramos blocked him, shoved him back, and he stumbled. Ramos noticed he was bleeding from his side.

Salazar glared at Ramos. "Who was the woman, your lover?"

Ramos frowned before he understood. Tessa.

"She's probably dead from *her* poison." He jutted his chin at Eloisa.

Anger flooded Ramos and he laid a right cross to Salazar's jaw. Aides and staff ran down the hall, guards behind them as Salazar threw a hard punch, but Ramos caught his fist, squeezing as he twisted right, forcing him to his knees. He hit him in the throat, once, twice, then he delivered a two-fisted slam to the back of his neck that dropped him to the tiled floor.

Ramos stepped back suddenly. He wanted to kill him, could do it so easily.

More security filled the hall, aiming at Salazar and looking confused that their *commandante* was in hot water.

"Lock him away. No one talks to him. And for the sake of my wife"—he pinned each with a hard stare—"no discussion of this." He pointed to the guards. "Bring me the key."

The men nodded, rushed to pick Salazar off the floor. He roused as they led him out, but he stalled, throwing a murderous stare over his shoulder at Eloisa, full of vile retribution. Ramos almost smiled when Eloisa snarled back. Salazar was still frowning when Ramos accepted the damp cloth from Mrs. Rojas.

"Where did you learn to fight like that, señor?" Mrs. Rojas asked.

"Around bastards like him." He touched her shoulder briefly, meeting her gaze, then turned into Eloisa's rooms. He closed the door.

Eloisa was looking at him oddly.

"You're a liar. He wasn't doing anything you didn't want."

"You saw him! He's disgusting."

He gripped her arms, nearly lifting her feet off the floor. "You didn't even fight him." He thrust her away. What a tramp.

She stumbled, righting her clothing, then rubbed at the bloodstains on her blouse. "I need to change."

"It won't do any good," he muttered under his breath as he glanced around the room. He spotted the map and grabbed it and the wooden ball. His gaze lifted to her. "What poison?"

Eloisa stepped back, frightened by his expression. "You took the map." There was no question in her voice. "You hate the puzzles."

"What was inside it?"

When she didn't answer, he advanced.

She stammered, flustered. "How did you know there was—?"

Understanding came like a hammer. It was inside the wood ball and anything that small was dangerous. "Why would you do this?"

Her chin lifted. "He's tired of waiting for the scales to tip."

"He? It was all you. Manny's ambitious, but not stupid."

"Stupid? We have the backing of Iran, Syria, Cuba and China. We have oil, weapons and textile contracts because of me! I initiated it." Eloisa gave him a dirty look. "You've underestimated him, you all do. He had a chance to bring this country together after the coup, instead he hid away like a frightened child. He didn't use that to his advantage and expel the disloyal."

A failed coup d'état to put him in a stronger position. Kill her husband in the process and get awarded the vice presidency? Christ, did she think she was some Evita clone? "You want this job? Is that where this leads?" Recognition dawned and his skin tightened on the back of his neck. "You instigated the takeover."

No one would give up the real leader, he recalled. Not after Garcia was attacked on the road. It had frightened the troops into silence and backfired enough to keep her out.

"Why do you think it only lasted two days? General obeyed me and, of course, he had control of the troops. Reinstating Manny was simple. You shouldn't have made it home."

Ramos felt a pain in his chest for another man so deeply betrayed. Garcia had wanted only good lives for his people and he was stabbed in all directions. No wonder democracy had a hard time staying afloat here, when so many inside the government were working against it. This had to end now.

"This won't solve anything, they'll elect more to take their place. Those leaders are fanatics. Cuba is a poor country. You want to see ours go that way? Where the President owns the country and the people have nothing?"

"The people will have what they need."

"And you will have more." He flicked at her handbag, proclaiming its name and cost. "You are a greedy woman, Eloisa, and foolish." He shook his head. "And using this poison?" He held out the ball. "You will start a war that cannot be stopped."

"No, darling. You will."

He scowled at her, recognizing the slyness of her smile. "What have you done?"

She leaned in. "You're a gift to them."

As her hand slid off his, he looked at his forearm and the scratch he had thought was from her bracelet. His gaze snapped to her, and then to the celebration beyond the windows. My God.

"A poison that kills like a cancer. I didn't know how I wanted to use it, really, it just felt good to have it." She preened with her own power. "Then the chance presented it-self."

Oh, Jesus. The summit.

Ramos racked his brain for a way out of this. He couldn't be touched, hell, he couldn't step on that ship. He rubbed the spot and thought, this is bad, really bad. He was infected with a bioweapon and was about to step on a ship that would carry him to the President.

His President. And he would kill them all.

He rubbed his face, driving his fingers into his hair. He couldn't make a deal, couldn't even mention it. If he started screaming bioweapons, Venezuela would be seen as a laughing stock. Especially since it came from here. Whatever it was, it couldn't get out in the open.

He looked at Eloisa, a woman more dangerous than Salazar. He grasped her hand. She fought him like a cat snagged in a net, and he tightened his grip as he dragged her through the house.

Mrs. Rojas stood at the base of the stairs, hiding a smile.

"Your public is watching," he said, then pulled her from the privacy of the landing.

She shut up, and he thrust her handbag at her stomach. She scrambled to grab it, and when the cameras flashed she slapped on a bright smile, her arm tucked in his.

"I'm not invited, I cannot go. You will join them, Estavan, and I will be the Vice President."

He sent her a sly look. "If you wanted my job, honey, all you had to do was say so."

She frowned. He'd spoken without an accent.

Ramos stepped into the waiting helicopter, with her beside him. Just to make it interesting, he held her hand.

Perched on the edge of the bed inside the tent, he nursed a cup of coffee. He should be accustomed to waiting. When his satellite keyboard phone hummed, he grabbed it, flipping open the computer phone like a mini laptop. No one knew he was here. No one. Then he saw the garbled message, and put it through the encryption.

Falcon is listening.

Excellent. Time to blow this Popsicle stand.

He typed, glancing up once at the man on the other side of the room. Less than five hours to critical.

Max was a decent swimmer, but he swore Logan was half fish. While he was winded, his quads screaming, Logan was pumped and moving fast. With his fins in his hand, Max walked out of the sea and onto a shore populated with beachgoers. Some were packing up for the day, the sun low on the horizon. Other divers were onshore and waved as he and Logan hurried to the dock.

"Did you see those bikinis?" Max asked, trying to run and look at the same time.

"Half of them were topless."

"My point exactly. Microkinis. What's left to the imagination? There's the cabanas with the blue shade awnings." He'd found the hotel easily with a quick search online.

At the cabana, they pulled off the tanks and hurried to change out of the wetsuits. Max contacted the CP. "Bad news. Ramos left by chopper with Garcia's wife to Caracas. Sebastian has to follow by car, can't land the Cessna that close. It's a no-fly zone for the ceremony." Shot out of the water before they began, he thought.

"So much for intercepting the motorcade," Logan said. "We have to wait till dark, regardless."

Max looked at the sky, calculating the time. "McGill and Nolan are trying to come up with something."

"Something? We need options *now*."

"I'm just the messenger, bud," he said.

"I know." Logan's face was creased with worry, and Max knew he was thinking of Tessa as he stared toward the docks a half mile away. "Ramos has been signaling at every public appearance. To kill him."

"Yeah, today."

Logan shook his head in thought. "Why? He knows that an assassination will make a bad thing worse."

"He should just do it for us," Max said, slipping on the light backpack. Logan scowled and Max met his gaze head-on. "We won't be able to get close to him. It's next to impossible."

"Then we make enough chaos that we can."

"Assassinating the Vice President of Venezuela in public is a death sentence for all of us, and I like living, thank you."

"I didn't say anything about killing him."

Max was still frowning when they left their dive gear behind for some lucky schmuck. Rigged up with transmitters, they hurried to the street, looking for the arranged transportation. If it was coming, it would be too late. The streets were packed, colorful banners and flags hanging from windows and doors. People danced in the streets with the band players.

"You remember how to ride?" Logan asked, then rushed across the street, pushing between sweaty dancers to the motorcycle rental.

Overpaying to cut in line, Max swung his leg over the bike and started it. "Don't crash this one," he said.

Within minutes, they were speeding toward the city.

Salazar paced like a caged animal inside the stone cell. His body sizzled with rage, his hands burning with the need to wrap her neck and squeeze. She betrayed him. Even when she lusted after him. In public he was a peasant to her. Unworthy. For that she would pay as well.

They'd taken his money and weapons, stripped him and cleaned his wounds. His cracked ribs throbbed, the bullet wound in his side burning with several shots of painkiller, and he could move some teeth with his tongue. None of it mattered, his body numb, and he glanced around for something to pick the locks, but the cell had been swept clean. The prison was under the main floor, a boiler room. Days ago, he'd thrown the men in here.

He stopped, staring at his feet. He had to get out of here. But his own troops had orders not to speak to him, or touch him. Anyone who would miss him was dead and he ignored the fact that most were dead by his own hand. He'd done as she'd asked, he thought, and laid the blame for failure at her feet. He backed away from the cell door when he heard footsteps.

A young soldier appeared in front of the cell with a dinner tray. "*Commandante.*" He set it aside and moved closer.

Salazar took the two steps to the bars, frowning at the young man, a child, really. Barely whiskered. He held out his hand in greeting. The young man hesitated, looking on with a little awe. Salazar said nothing, waiting. When the young man grasped it, Salazar yanked hard. The soldier's forehead hit the bars with a resounding *thunk,* his eyes rolling back as he started to slide. With his arms through the bars, Salazar clamped his head and twisted hard. The crack of his neck was soft in the damp basement and he let the body drop.

Salazar squatted, searched the kid, then unlocked the cell. He pushed the door, the body sliding across the cement, his head at an odd angle. He exchanged clothing, took his weapons and kept the keys.

Then he headed to the arsenal.

Tessa didn't think she could be this angry. Her life was slipping away and all she had to look at was a sci-fi nightmare of men in white suits. She felt the aspirator go over her face, the warmth of the drugs in her veins as they injected the IV.

Dammit. *I should get to win this time.*

She didn't listen to the doctors, their voices muffled. But their expressions were grim enough. Her body was on fire, a heat radiating up through her skin. They covered her in ice packs and she barely felt it. Then there was nothing as she sank into a drug-induced haze. Her last thought was of Logan and the life with him she'd lose.

Nineteen

McGill was watching the screens and the markers showing them moving away from the Venezuelan coastline. Sebastian Fontenot was working his way back toward them, but by car, the going was damn slow. So far so good.

Behind him, Nolan burst out of the cube. "Contact!"

McGill swung his chair around and stood.

"I have him, it's Truman."

McGill snatched the message and read, then looked at Deets.

"I confirmed it twice, sir." Nolan swallowed, out of breath with excitement. "It's a go? We can do this?"

McGill wasn't nearly as hopeful as Deets. "Get Chambliss on the wire. We may have a way out of this."

Caracas

Horizontal bands of yellow, blue and red colored the bunting and streamers hanging from street lamps and sky-scrapers. The Independence Day celebration spread through the country, focusing on the capital and, more importantly, the docks.

He carried a slim black briefcase, walking briskly as if he'd be late. His wounds hampered him, and he felt blood seeping from the bandage in his side as he maneuvered through the vendors selling food and souvenirs. He pushed aside a man dressed in period clothing for some presentation; his mind was on the building ahead to the left.

The dock stretched for a quarter mile, the area normally for dry-docking and repairs. It was chosen for its security because it was less populated with longshoremen and cargo being lifted off the ships. The portion secured for this grand meeting was at least fifty yards wide, flanked by a warehouse due to be torn down, the new face of the docks already showing in a chamberlain's offices.

The building was bright white in the afternoon sun, three stories high. Grandstands and celebrators were relegated to the street side, behind security and medical vans, yet all faced the water and the ship that would bring the Vice President to the islands.

Salazar shifted behind the crowds of people waiting for the celebration to begin. As he suspected, Garcia had not alerted anyone of his incarceration. Outside the residence and that suite of rooms, he had control. It was a mistake they'd regret.

He flashed his ID and bypassed searches and checkpoints, entering the building, then turning sharply into the stairwell.

Few paid him any attention, all more interested in gaining the perfect spot to view the docking of the ship that would carry Garcia to the summit. He'd be in the company of his President's enemies. The perfect targets for Eloisa's venom.

It would find its mark. She would not.

The limousine moved down a road between the crowds. People waved flags and shouted at the car, but the windows were blackened. Beside him, Eloisa sat quietly, smugly. She hadn't said a word on the flight here, but she didn't look the least distressed.

Ramos rubbed the back of his hand. When a bodyguard opened the car door, Ramos got out, then turned back to offer his hand to her. She wouldn't take it, snarling at him, and stepped out on her own power. She smiled, waved to the cheering crowd and with his arm around her, he ushered her into the platform. She stepped away and he caught her hand and squeezed, forcing her with him.

"Smile because the press just caught that ugly face on camera."

Her expression changed and she looked up at him lovingly. He thought, *What an actress.*

They walked toward the gentle archways of the building. The viewing grandstand was to the right and left of the pier and when Eloisa tried to disengage herself from him, Ramos kept a hold. If she tried, again her struggle would be obvious, and no matter what, the woman was all about her public image. If the country knew she was a first-class slut, they probably wouldn't be throwing flowers right now.

He stopped and greeted dignitaries, the cut on his hand swelling and red. Ramos glanced at the crowd, searching but seeing no one familiar.

Eloisa leaned close to whisper as if sharing a secret. "You have been a good husband, Estavan," she said with little love in her voice. "In an hour you will be a weapon."

Delayed reaction, Ramos thought, resigned. But when she tried again to walk away, he swept his arm around her and ushered her with him to the podium.

"You've been a lousy wife," he said softly. "And, Eloisa, I'm not your husband."

Salazar finished assembling the rifle, glancing around the chamberlain's newly decorated offices on the top floor. He was secure in here, everyone below stairs celebrating. He'd slipped in so easily up the fire stairwell that he'd have to speak to the Presidential guard about the lack of security. Today it worked for him. He screwed on the suppressor, then he moved to the tall, narrow window. He didn't open it. He positioned himself, sucking air through his teeth when he bumped the wall. He felt the dampness on his side, his wound only lightly stitched, but the exit wound was large. He was losing blood.

He peered down at the crowd, his position perfect, and he lifted the rifle to his shoulder and sighted it. The podium was

328 / Amy J. Fetzer

in the center of the area. She would be standing behind him or to the right. The band played again, streamers and confetti blowing in the air, obstructing vision from the ground. Salazar watched his marks. He saw the vehicle arrive, heard the cheers growing louder.

Garcia left the car, his hand on Eloisa's arm.

The speeches began and Salazar listened, and would wait until the noise would cover the gunshot.

Riley sat outside the quarantine room while Tessa slept. He listened with one ear to the radio broadcasting the speeches, the other turned and listening in on the team.

But his attention was on Tessa. She'd fallen asleep, and the latest antidote hadn't worked. Her vital signs were dropping. Behind him, doctors talked, a centrifuge spinning with the next antidote to try.

He pushed on the earpiece, listening and trying to translate. His Spanish was rotten and he wrote what he caught, singling out familiar words. He frowned at the paper, then shot off the chair, yanked out ear mics, and rushed from the room and out of the building. He cleared the door and dialed McGill, then hopped a golf cart and drove to the hangar.

"Sir, listen to Ramos's speech, listen to the words he's using. *A feeling of contagious unity. Under two hours* we will greet our guests." Riley slammed on the brakes, parked, then ran inside, still using the phone till he crossed the large hangar. "*A simple gesture of friendship* would change lives. He's warning us."

Riley closed the phone and rushed to McGill. He found the general staring at the TV broadcast. "That's the same signal. He's begging for a bullet," Riley said.

"If he moves near anyone, we're all dead."

McGill stared a second longer, then reached for the phone and spoke on a secure line to the President's Secret Service detail, informing them of the crisis. The President's chief of staff got on and McGill explained.

"Rick. We have to stop this meet."

"It would be a diplomatic nightmare. And a huge slap in the face to Venezuela and a President who holds 18 percent of our oil purchase and hates our guts. That he's allowing this is a step forward."

"Now it's about oil? Jesus, this could kill millions, you included."

"We can't turn back."

"I'm telling you," McGill said. "The threat is imminent. Stop him."

"General, if we send in any aircraft or ships that were not prearranged, Cuba and Gutierrez will take it as a threat. It's a powder keg for war. I can't authorize that without absolute evidence that Vice President Garcia is a carrier. I'll inform the President, let him decide."

"Then I want it on record . . . *The red scorpion is in the sand.* I say again, the red scorpion is in the sand."

"Understood, Mac."

McGill hung up. It was up to the Secret Service and the advisors. They will evaluate the threat, but by then, it will be moot. He'd gone through the proper channels.

Now it was time to break some rules.

"David, start hopping off any satellite you can." He held out a plastic card. "Here's my authorization." Lorimar was wide-eyed when he accepted it. "Share." He motioned between the two. "Send this till you get a confirmation." He had to reach the President. "Riley, get on the wire to Logan, tell him the news and keep it open. Right now it's all that matters."

Snatching out Ramos was no longer an option.

The celebration was like a tailgate party for a Packers's game. People were everywhere in clusters, dancing to music, cooking on minigrills and drinking. Logan inhaled the wonderful smell of searing beef and tortillas, and bought a taco from a vendor.

Max had already downed three of them as they edged through the crowds, staying near the dock and water.

"You sure about this?" Max asked.

"Not like we have much choice. McGill thinks Ramos is infected, too. He can't get on that boat."

"This mission sucks," Max muttered as he veered off closer to the celebration.

Logan walked toward the building. The old, lower portions had already been torn down, dozers and cranes ready to sweep the shorefront clean and build new. *Condos, probably,* he thought as he lingered on the edge of the crowd to check his surroundings. The mass of people was chaotic, vendors every few yards and small bands cranking up the tunes. People danced in the street and it was hard not to smile.

He moved farther away, turned and darted to the heavy equipment, slipping behind it. Watching his six, he went to the far end of the building on the seaward side. There were hundreds of ships and naval vessels in the water, surrounding the Presidential yacht to protect the heads of state awaiting their guest. He heard the band strike up and the crowd cheer. But Logan focused on climbing. Inside the rusted walls, he moved to the far right corner, the wind off the ocean whipping the steel walls and hiding any sound.

From his pack, he gathered rope, a small grappling hook on the end. He swung it over his head and lassoed the steel girder. Funneling line till he could reach it, he unclipped the hook and fastened the end to the harness under his shirt. In a few pulls of the rope, he hoisted himself up to the beam and stood. He stowed the rope and kept the harness, then maneuvered to the wall and the crossbeam below an air vent shaft. Climbing another crossbeam, he hunched, the expanse to the roof not enough to accommodate his height.

He tried the vent but the screws were rusted in place. He shifted, his back to it, and thrust his elbow into the vent and it popped. He threw the pack onto the roof and then hoisted himself into the open. He didn't stand, sliding across the roof on his stomach. The building was higher than the brand-spanking new chamberlain's offices, and he had a bird's-eye view. He hoped they didn't send police choppers to scout or this would be for nothing. Salazar could still be out there, he knew, and he figured that was one piece of shit he'd have to let go.

From the roof, Logan had a view of the platform and the wood pier. The end of the dock was empty, the space reserved for the yacht coming for Garcia. News reports were better than Intel for tracking the movements of the Venezuelan Vice President.

Ramos would be greeting the British Prime Minister and French Ambassador, then stepping on the yacht and going out to sea. The ship would be surrounded by armed crafts in the water and sky. If they didn't get Ramos right now, they would lose this chance.

There should be a shooter sitting here, Logan thought, then pushed aside his instincts to protect.

This had better work.

He assembled the compact sniper rifle as the sound of the band came to him. He locked the stock in place, loaded bullets, then slid the bolt home. He swung the weapon over the edge and sighted in. Its range was 900 yards. He was half that from the platform. Max was nearer to Ramos's position, sitting in a line of emergency medical teams.

"I've got a mark," Logan said. He focused on the podium.

Max's voice came over the line. "You really think this will work?"

"No."

"Some optimist you are."

"I'm counting on you getting closer, bud."

Logan sighted down the scope, his body flat on the roof. He had to be accurate so no one would get hurt. Trouble was, to be accurate he had to be seen. A catch-22.

He sighted on the podium, following Ramos as he left the limo and made his way toward the podium.

The line made a puff sound as someone came on. "Chief to Cutter. Do not fire."

Logan released the trigger, and instantly drew back and lowered to conceal himself. He pressed the mic close and said, "Jesus, I had a shot. Are you nuts!"

"He's alive. Garcia is alive. Brain-dead. No function. The bullet injured the cerebellum, he's paralyzed and on a respirator."

Logan absorbed that for a moment.

"How does that help?" Max's voice whispered through the transmitter.

"I'll shoot him," Logan cut in, his mind churning fast.

Squawks piled on the frequency. "Repeat your last?" McGill asked.

"Listen up. I can hit where it won't kill him. Like in Serbia." Graze him for onlookers.

"No, it won't work," Max said. "The timing, the police to get past, and what if someone steps in the path?"

Pessimists. "Trust me. Where is Garcia?"

"Truman is on the other end with him."

"I guess he's not just a rumor, huh?" Max said over the line.

Logan scowled. That's what they were hiding in Garcia's hometown. Jesus. It could have ended quietly if he'd known. His gaze went to the ceremony still going on, then to the walkway to the pier where the yacht was making port. Ramos walked to the podium, Eloisa beside him. One speech and it would be over.

"Max, can you get to an ambulance?"

"Yeah," he said carefully.

"We can do this. Patch me to Truman. Now."

Max didn't like beating up on people who didn't deserve it. The poor guy was just having a coffee break, uninterested in the ceremonies going on a few yards away. The noise from the bands and crowd muffled his movements as he came up alongside the ambulance driver.

"*Hola*," he said, and the guy looked at him.

Max punched him in the face. The man instantly slumped and Max opened the door, pushing him over, then maneuvering him to the back of the ambulance. He stripped the man of his uniform, then gagged and tied him, leaving him wedged in the corner. He couldn't be discovered. A little nitric oxide would keep him quiet.

Pulling down the blue cap bearing the private ambulance service, Max settled in to wait for trouble to come to him.

Inside the back of a dark van, Truman told the driver to stop, then he looked at Cero. "This is where you get off, pal."

Cero scowled. "I'll stay to the end."

"No. Your people are in place. If we're successful, you cannot be involved. Go to Joaquin and stay with him. He'll need you."

Cero looked down at Garcia, then leaned and kissed his cool forehead. Then he opened the back of the van and stepped out. Truman said nothing and closed the door. They were moving again. He prayed these Dragon One guys knew their stuff. The ride would probably kill Garcia. They had to pump blood into him constantly—internal bleeding. But Truman didn't know about that—only that it was time to end this with some dignity.

Logan stared through his binoculars and saw Ramos leave the podium and approach the decorated path to the ship. The British prime minister and the French Ambassador arrived on a hail of music, balloons and a flurry of confetti. Streamers shot across the areas, soldiers lined the right side, ready for inspection. Guests of honor sat erect and brightly dressed in the grandstand. Ramos and Eloisa crossed the cement. They paused and waved to the crowd. Logan warned the team of the coming shot.

Logan aimed.

Before he could pull the trigger Eloisa's chest exploded, her body flying back into Ramos. Logan swung the barrel left in the direction of the shot and through the scope searched. Then he saw him, just drawing back into the building.

Logan fired, caught Salazar in the chest, and he flinched wildly, reflexes pulling the trigger and spraying the air. People screamed, scattered, and Logan fired again and found satisfaction when it hit Salazar between the eyes. His head snapped back, and he was frozen for a moment, then slumped forward, the rifle sliding from his hand and down two stories.

At the first shot, guards returned fire, people scattered in a stampede.

Logan rushed to the side of the building, snapped on the rope line to the harness and rappelled down. Hitting bottom, he released the belay device and unslung the rifle, hurling them into the sea, then ran toward the ambulance and radioed Max.

"Drac, Drac!"

"I'm in, I'm in, number nine. The one ahead of me has the Mrs. Where are you?"

Logan saw the ambulance ahead and bolted, pushing between the people racing away.

Troops surrounded him. "I'm a doctor." They let him pass. Personal physicians were on staff, but were spectators, and Logan counted on them not showing up right now.

Max was pulling a stretcher out of the back as Logan rushed to Ramos. Men were pulling Eloisa off him and onto a stretcher. Logan didn't have to check for a pulse. A hole the size of his fist had replaced her heart. But Ramos lay on the ground in a pool of his own blood.

Logan knelt, examined him and then realized that the shots had gone through her and into his neck and chest. Logan grabbed gauze and blood clotters from a case, quickly injecting him. Max rolled the stretcher close and men gathered to lift him on.

People screamed prayers for their Vice President, begging to know if he was alive. Some openly sobbed. Guards rushed to clear a path for the truck.

Ramos looked at Logan, coughing blood. He frowned, then recognition dawned.

"Time to go home." Logan put the oxygen mask over his face as they pushed the stretcher in the ambulance, then he hopped in and pulled the doors closed.

"Go! Go," Logan said, and Max gunned the engine, lights and sirens going as he sped across the wharf.

A line of Venezuelan Secret Service hot on their heels.

"Truman, we have him." Logan stuffed wads of cloth against the bloody wounds.

"Come south to the Plaza Bolívar."

"We have Secret Service and cops on our tail."

"I'll take care of it. Keep coming."

Ramos gripped Logan's hand, his body convulsing with the loss of blood. "Tessa?"

"She's alive."

His tortured expression eased a bit. "Why did you come, Logan? Why did you try?" Blood bubbled from his lips as he spoke.

"They asked."

Ramos tried to laugh but only coughed blood. Logan worked to stop the bleeding.

"An hour. She infected me. She said it will go in an hour."

Logan injected him with a high-level dose of antibiotics, hoping to slow down the virus. His wounds were another matter.

"She did it all, Logan. She instigated the coup, hoping they'd kill her husband for it. She wanted his job."

Logan told him about Garcia. Ramos just softened on the gurney. "He will be buried with the honors he deserves." He made a sound, blood bubbling, and Logan knew he couldn't save him. The wound to his neck hadn't nicked the artery but it had hit some major veins. He was bleeding too fast.

Ramos choked, arching to get a breath.

"Don't you die, Paul, God dammit! Don't!"

"Lots to make up for."

The ambulance swerved, and Logan grasped the inside bars for balance.

Ramos gripped Logan's wrist, stopping him from helping him. "Don't . . ." he said on barely a breath. "Don't bury me with this face." His weak grip tightened. "Promise me."

Logan did not owe him a damn thing, but he nodded just the same.

"We got trouble," Max said. "Rendezvous in ten seconds and we got beaucoup police behind us."

The line of cars following toward the hospital spread out, some inching closer, one taking a side street. Then a fruit truck rolled after them, then from the right another truck full of chickens exited a side street. They collided, toppling crates and fruit. Another ambulance slid in front, almost taking its place, then sped south. A decoy.

"We only have a minute," Logan said.

Truman came on the wire. "I see you, slow down. We're ready."

Logan saw the van, black and rusty, remembering it from Cero's camp. It had taken the wounded man to the hospital. Max braked to a short stop and Logan threw open the rear doors. The van was opened, two men pulling a similar gurney out.

One of them was Truman. "Hurry, that decoy won't last."

Like playing fire drill at a stoplight, they pushed the brain-dead body of Garcia into the ambulance as Max and another man secured Ramos into the van.

"Chambliss. How's your lady?" He was big and dark with a quiet voice.

Logan's expression pinched. "In a bad way."

"Sorry to hear it."

"You were in the town?"

"All the time." Truman just shrugged and yanked a strap. "Saw the whole thing, got a bit of a conscience after this." He gestured to Garcia. "Knew someone would come to take the fake out of there. I just hoped he stayed alive and under wraps long enough to do it."

Inside the ambulance, Logan gave Garcia a quick assessment, then palpated the man's throat and neck. He could feel the pool of blood beneath the skin. "He's hemorrhaging, he won't last more than an hour." Logan climbed out.

Truman nodded and was still, and Logan realized he had an ear mic and was listening to the radios. "The roadblock is clearing." They traded places, Truman reaching for the door handles, and with the other hand holding out a slip of paper.

Logan frowned as he took it.

"The first two? They were there to kill him, not rescue," Truman said.

Logan's features tightened, and he looked at the list of coordinates.

"That's where I buried them. They didn't have a chance." Truman shook his head. "Salazar slaughtered them."

"I double-tapped him."

"One less scumbag." Truman smiled and started to close the door.

"Who sent you in?"

Truman's lips quirked. "Need to know," he said, fitting Max's ambulance cap down tight, then slammed the door shut.

"Logan," Max shouted. "We be popular people!"

The ambulance sped toward the hospital as Logan climbed in the back of the van with Ramos.

Max drove toward the east, away from Caracas, away from the pandemonium, while Logan tried to stop the bleeding, but the bullet was a hollow point, exploding inside Ramos's chest. There wasn't much left of his lungs and without surgery, Logan couldn't stop the hemorrhaging.

"Hurry, Max. I'm losing him." He gave Ramos oxygen, continually checking his vital signs. His heart rate slipped rapidly.

Max drove, cornering the van on soft wheels. He headed to the airport and raised Sebastian on the radio. He hailed McGill.

"The package is secure. In transport. We have company still and no way out of this country!"

Sebastian borrowed, stole and hitched his way back to the city in time to see the chaos erupt. He pushed his way between the people running past him. The ambulance tore off, police cars and troops rushing.

Logan hailed him. "We need an out and fast, we have cops chasing anything on wheels."

Sebastian spied a chopper on the pad, and rushed to it. "I'll see what I can do."

"Hurry, pal, we need some backup."

Sebastian threw open the chopper's door and climbed in as troops surrounded him, warning him to stop. Sebastian flicked the switches, then the blades started to spin and the troops backed off.

One man grew balls and aimed, prepared to fire. *God. He was such a young kid,* Sebastian thought, yet aimed his own weapon out the window and just shook his head. The soldier lowered and Sebastian lifted off, banking the chopper north.

At least the guns were loaded.

Sebastian hailed Logan. "I'm in the air."

"With what?"

"I stole a chopper, apparently it's Salazar's. I'm coming up behind you and you've got roadblocks."

"Get us past them!"

"Roger that." Sebastian shot ahead, banking the helicopter and facing the roadblock. Beyond he could see the lights of the truck nearing.

The troops blocked the only exit. Over the loudspeaker, Sebastian ordered them to stand down, and the troops recognized the helicopter. The windshield was too dark to see who was inside. When they didn't move, he hit the guns, sending a double stream of bullets across the ground. Men ran, scattering as the rusted van crashed through the gates and sped on. Sebastian covered it, and when the van stopped, Sebastian started his descent.

Logan opened the back of the van as Max came around to help him. Sebastian set the skids on the ground. Logan and Max pulled out the stretcher, then ran across the rough ground, forcing it toward the chopper. Max threw open the door, jumped in and they lifted Ramos off the stretcher and into the aircraft.

"How is he?" Sebastian asked.

"Dead." Logan covered his face and climbed in. Sebastian lifted off as Riley's voice came over the radio.

"Can't talk now, bud."

"Cutter, get back here. Fast. The circus is leaving town."

Logan closed his eyes, his chest aching for air as the helicopter shot toward Puerto Rico.

Twenty

McGill sat back in the chair and closed his eyes, the burden sliding off.

Holy Mary, I've got to retire.

His relief wasn't over.

They might have gotten away with only a little dirt left behind, but the U.S. had some trash to deal with. He left Walker and Lorimer having a beer and guiding the chopper in while he headed to the brig with Agent Deets. The MPs brought her out for him, her chains rattling as they ushered her into an interrogation room.

Liz Jacobs looked like a vagabond in a jumpsuit and no make up. That she'd made it all the way to Jamaica without notice was a feat, but then she was an expert at being a ghost.

"Save us time, tell the truth, or is that foreign to you?"

"Kiss my ass, McGill."

"No thanks. My housekeeper takes out the garbage."

She flamed at the insult.

"I've got enough evidence to charge you with treason."

"No, you don't." She'd made certain of it.

"Contessa Petruscu."

Her eyes flared hotly.

McGill continued to smile and let her think what she wanted. It was only a few seconds before she understood. If they knew about Tessa, then it was over. She was looking at life in prison.

She sent Deets a bitter look. "What do you want—my entire career or just the last month?"

"Let's stick to your most recent. Sing from the beginning."

Liz looked at the space between her shoes as the harsh truth came out.

"Garcia had evidence on cabinet members, military, all the way up to Gutierrez on petty international crimes. We brought this to your predecessor. He consulted the President, and the joint chiefs felt it wasn't a fire we wanted to step on, so Garcia would have to handle it himself. We could not help him, they said. It was too close to instigating a coup."

"Then it happened. How convenient for you."

She snorted. "We didn't have anything to do with the coup d'état. That was all internal."

"Ramos was to take out the President?"

"Initially, and make it look like it came from his own people. But the coup changed the atmosphere. He was supposed to just slide into the role, then slide out. Garcia being shot by troops wasn't expected." She flicked her head to get her hair out of her face. "Garcia didn't trust us. He had the documents, but without a lead directly to Gutierrez, we weren't getting anywhere. Evidence stopped before it reached him. So he was right, it was his wife?"

McGill didn't answer that. The internal workings of Venezuela were never a concern. The USA had denied Garcia help without clear evidence. He wouldn't give it without help. The matter would have gone directly to the UN, regardless. Jacobs had decided it was hers to fix, with Ramos's face.

"What made you do it? What made you go against direct orders from your commander and chief? I'm just curious."

"Gutierrez was allowing Iranian missiles in his country."

"And you don't think we could shoot them down before they even launched?" He was dead certain the instant they crossed international waters to the USA, they'd be nothing but a blip on a screen.

"That's just the start. He's a bad President. Don't you see that?"

"So are a lot, but democracy was working, and will work still," McGill said with supreme confidence. Or he wouldn't be wearing the uniform. "What did you see?"

"Nothing." She frowned as if he was the village idiot and she was the mayor. "It was supposed to be a private switch. But that the army was there meant all secrecy was lost or they knew his schedule, which was not public. I wasn't that close. I heard it by wire. When I got there, Ramos was in the sedan, Garcia was shot. The witnesses fled, then returned to tell a story that implicated the pro-Gutierrez troops. Got a little messy."

"You say that so casually. Does sanctity of life mean anything to you?"

"Sure. Mine, yours. Free people."

"Gutierrez was elected democratically. What more do you want?"

"*Good* democracy."

"You practice dictatorship."

"One man's dictator is another man's freedom fighter."

Her one-track fight for freedom was no more than an excuse to manipulate the situation. She didn't deserve a fair trial. She hadn't given one to her victims. There was no point in talking to her. Disgusted, McGill ordered the guards to escort her back to her cell.

She stopped outside her cell and held his gaze steadily. "You hate me."

"Yes, I most certainly do."

She shrugged. "I'm necessary."

"A necessary evil? No, Lizzie," he said just for spite. "You just don't know when to butt the hell out." He pitied her. She believed she was some one-woman crusade for democracy. Yet she was nothing more than a troublemaker . . . a user. How she convinced Ramos to alter his face for her was incomprehensible.

Suddenly, he ordered the guard to bring her along and McGill led the way. She didn't know where she was going, but she wasn't afraid. She probably never was, and couldn't comprehend that others still had that nerve, that feeling of the unknown. They walked through the quarantine area and into the rooms where Tessa was lying in a bed under an oxygen tent. He pushed Liz toward the window.

She looked at him. "What's your purpose for this?"

He forced her head around. "See what you've done? This is what your crimes have cost."

Liz stared at Petruscu. *She would have been a great spy, if she could have gotten over her fear and morals.* Liz looked back at McGill. "You want me to feel bad? Why? She was dead before. This is just the same thing, eleven years late."

McGill stiffened, then stepped back. "I feel dirty near you."

She shrugged.

He waved to the guards. "Put her in solitary confinement, bread and water. No contact with anyone without my orders." The guards nodded, gripping her by the arms. "No exceptions."

"My lawyer?"

He smiled thinly. "You're charged with treason. A Federal crime against America, Lizzie," he said with relish, then leaned down in her face. "However, on behalf of the Director of the CIA, I'm charging you as an enemy combatant."

Her eyes widened as she understood. She'd be treated no differently than if bin Laden were in the cell with her. She had no privilege unless McGill said so. He turned away, walking the narrow, sterile hall.

"I'll get out of this. I know the secrets. I'm too valuable!"

"Don't tempt me to shoot you myself." He paused, looked back. "I'm taking this as far as I can."

In the hall, Elizabeth watched McGill retreating back and wished she had a knife to throw. "I got the information, McGill. Now we know what he's doing. The Colombians, to Peru, and with Iran!"

McGill turned sharply, striding back like a madman and while the guards didn't budge, she stepped back.

"I've never wanted to hit a woman, ever, but I do now.

You're a pig, Liz, the kind that feeds off the garbage of others. And you forgot one thing, he was freely elected. It was *his* country to govern."

"There's a difference between democracy and good democracy, McGill, or haven't you figured that out?" She was still shouting when he passed through the next security checkpoint, then out the door to the waiting car.

It still wasn't done.

Logan was off the chopper before it touched down, and inside the building, shouting, "Make a hole" as he ran. He made a corner, sliding to a stop. At the far end of the hall, McGill and Riley sat on a bench outside the quarantine room. Riley looked up and stood.

"No. No." Logan rushed to the door.

Riley grabbed to stop him but Logan pushed him off, ripping open the door.

"Is she alive?" No one responded fast enough. "Is she *alive!*"

"Yes, sir. She's alive. We administered an antidote made from the substance, but she slipped into a coma."

Logan dressed in protective gear and went inside, ordering everyone out. He looked back to see Riley and he made a cut across his throat. Riley went to the console and shut off the microphones and speakers. Then he barred himself in front of the glass door.

Logan approached the bed. His heart hadn't shattered or broken, it was whole, beating and hurting so damn bad he could barely breathe. He touched her head, her face, checked her pulse and the monitors. She had brain activity. Her vital signs were not good but getting better. He pulled a chair near the bed, then instead, sat on the edge.

For the first time in his life, he hated that he was a doctor. It would almost be better not to understand the bluish tint to her lips. She was not producing enough oxygen. Her liver would shut down.

He slid his hand into hers and held it, his head down as if it would make a difference.

"Tessa, baby, I want you to squeeze my hand. Give me something." He watched the drugs slide into her veins. "Something, baby." He kept talking, rubbing the back of her hand, then he leaned close to her ear.

"It's over and the winners are you and me, but you still have to fight."

He glanced, the monitors reading the same. So he talked, anything to keep from screaming to the heavens. He spoke of his family, about his relationship with Cassie, and how a knobby-kneed ten-year-old had brought him back after he'd watched Tessa die. He told her how small the world had gotten this week and that he would have found her, someday he would have been at the right place at the right time. The words came stilted, his throat tight.

Logan knew if this antidote was going to work, it had to show signs within minutes. He looked to the window. They shook their heads. He continued talking, telling her that Jacobs was in jail and Ramos had given his life to right a terrible wrong. He laced his fingers with hers, his head bowed, and still wearing the clothes stained with Ramos's blood.

This he couldn't fight. There was no assault. No code to crack. For all his skills, he was useless, powerless while Tessa suffered.

He leaned in to say, "Come on, tough girl. You need to wake up. We need to start a life together and I'm ready." His voice broke. "I need you."

He felt the movement, just a flex of her thumb across the back of his hand. His gaze snapped to her.

It was several moments before her eyelids fluttered and she said softly, "I hope I don't have to be dying again for you to say those things again."

Logan choked, smiled, then scooped her off the bed and crushed her to him.

Beyond the walls of glass, he heard muffled cheers but he simply squeezed her tighter, his hand driving up her spine and pushing her into him. He couldn't speak, his throat burning, and he felt as if he'd received the greatest gift when her arms slid around him. He held on tighter. Then she tipped her head back.

A smile ghosted her lips. "Hi, handsome. Get the bad guys?"

"Yes."

"Knew you would."

He laid her back down and she released a long breath. Logan checked her vital signs, grabbing a penlight and checking her eyes. She pushed his hands aside.

"Stop playing doctor and kiss me."

He smiled and did, leaning down slowly, loving when she met him halfway. He kissed her slowly, the single touch speaking volumes.

His soul had awakened the day he had seen her hiding in the shadows. Tessa hadn't slid into his life; she came rushing like a storm, dragging emotions from him he'd thought were buried too deep to revive. But they were there, on the edge of his skin, in his words, and while Tessa wanted her life back, it was Logan who found his way home.

Maria Rojas was a woman on a mission as she marched down the hall toward the master suites. The rooms had been sealed, but that didn't include her. There were no secrets from her, not in this house. She ripped back the tape on the door and unlocked it, pushing her way inside. She closed the door lightly and for a moment was still.

Afternoon sunlight fell in soft beams on the wood floors, the breeze moving the sheer drapes. She crossed the room and went to the tall cabinet, opening the glass door. Her gaze traveled over the puzzle boxes she'd dusted a hundred times before. Mrs. Garcia thought her too uneducated to open them. She'd seen inside each one. The dragon, a particular favorite.

She held no love for Eloisa, the woman slapped her staff for the most minor offense, working them harder than they should for a woman of her stature. But then Maria knew Eloisa. She'd been no more than a hood before Garcia—she crossed herself—had fallen in love with her. She came from nothing and wanted everything, and she likely would have succeeded, had she not slept with half the cabinet. Maria tended her clothes, her linens. There was little Eloisa could hide from her. Señor Garcia deserved better than Eloisa and Maria was ashamed that she was a little pleased the woman was dead.

She selected one box, then another and, her arms full, she walked to the fireplace. Setting them on an ottoman, she lit the gas fireplace. Then, one by one, she opened each puzzle. Most were filled with diamond jewelry Maria knew her husband had not given her. In one, she found the stars of the commander of the Venezuelan Army. She tsked and set the items aside, then tossed the puzzles in the fire. She opened one and found a small glass tube.

At first, she thought it was perfume till she noticed the open metal sleeve around it. She looked from it to the fire, then tossed it in, stepping back when it flared. She gathered the jewelry, dumping it into the woman's jewel box, then surveyed the suite.

If anything should happen to me, she remembered, and her throat tightened with grief. She held her keys, the flash drive dangling, then she pocketed them and huffed from the room. *Señor Castillo will be wanting his property.*

Through a two-way glass McGill stared at the woman who'd done her best to screw it up for the good guys. A pain in the country's ass. His hatred for the woman and people like her told him he had to step back. There was no place to be objective. She would escape any penalty with the deaths of the first team, they had no body or corroboration.

Nolan Deets had arrested and questioned her. She wasn't budging an inch. She didn't want a lawyer. She was an attorney herself, and she didn't look the least bit frazzled.

"She'll never give him up. The woman married a diplomat to spy. She was a captive three times in her career," McGill said.

"We could give her some other . . . therapies."

McGill's gaze snapped to his. "Don't go there. You know we can't."

Nolan shrugged. "Fine. But the only thing we can do is lay it out and hope she realizes we can get a grand jury indictment."

"No."

"Sir?"

"She knows she'll never be exposed. We can't afford it— the U.S. can't. One of our own going this far off the map? We'll be crucified."

"Then the past rests on Petruscu."

"There is no statute of limitations for treason. No again."

"Your loyalty is impressive, sir. But while I will get to the bottom of it, that doesn't mean anyone else will."

McGill looked up, his brows knitting.

"I'm certain I can keep my end Class A."

"More than that, Agent Deets."

"Sir?" The single word was an acknowledgment and a plea to be taken into his confidence.

McGill glanced at the camera. Without a reaction, Deets immediately left the room, ordering another agent inside, then he walked with McGill to the courtyard outside.

McGill gathered his thoughts. "We have to safeguard this inquiry."

Nolan agreed.

"She had orders, and eleven years ago they'd come from the deputy director of European covert operations."

Nolan frowned for a moment, then his eyes went wide as coins. The Secretary of Defense. The same man who sent Dragon One into the lion's den.

McGill dipped inside his jacket and handed Deets an envelope. Inside were the internal papers the President had given him. The proof that Avers allotted the funding, and authorized her. Proof McGill was allowed to find without impediment.

"She goes down, Deets, quietly. But she doesn't go alone."

Logan was debriefing the general while Tessa was recovering from the load of drugs they'd pumped into her. She looked up from her novel as the door opened and she knew the visitor wasn't a doctor. He didn't have the "what the hell is this stuff?" look she'd seen constantly. She pushed up on her elbow as he entered the room, smiling.

"Hello, Contessa Petruscu, I understand you want to come home."

Tears welled at the hope.

"I'm here to make it happen."

"Seriously?"

He nodded.

Tessa lost it. She cried. Once it started, she couldn't seem to stop the torrents of emotion, and buried her face in the pillow. "I'm sorry, I'll just be a minute." She reached for tissues and he pushed them into her hand.

"Take your time, you've been away a long time." He laid a laptop on the wheeled tray, then opened it.

For a moment, he met her gaze, then Nolan Deets stretched his fingers and typed.

Maximum Security, Federal Prison
Fort Leavenworth, Kansas

Elizabeth Jacobs stumbled into the cell and turned just as the door slammed shut. The sound of the steel frame and iron door echoed in the long, hollow corridor. On the other side wasn't a guard, but a good-looking man she'd never seen before. Through the slot in the door for passing food, he leaned so she could see him.

"Enjoy your new home."

"Who are you?"

He said nothing, smiling too much for the moment, and she peered into the slot.

He turned the heavy key. The clunk of the gears rattled through her bones.

"Answer me! At least I have a right to know who's locking me away."

He tipped his head back slowly, meeting her gaze. "America is locking you away, Elizabeth Jacobs. I'm just turning the key."

"What the hell do you have to do with any of this? Who *are* you!"

"I'm just the messenger."

"Whose?"

"Contessa Marianna Petruscu gave me a message to pass."

"Like I care?"

"You should. It will be the last time anyone speaks to you."

"So what did the little weasel have to say?"

"That jumpsuit makes you look fat and old."

Logan grinned, relishing the full impact. Her confusion, her bitterness, then her resolution. It was all he needed to take back to Tessa. His smile grew with each step as he left the penitentiary.

Sometimes, he thought, justice was damn *sweet*.

CIA Headquarters
Langley, Virginia

McGill watched the night news report with a jaundiced eye.

Garcia's funeral was a long event, the President declaring it a national mourning and showing a sad face for the country. But McGill was interested in the charges lodged by Joaquin Castillo. Gutierrez followers were dropping off like flies and either hiding from the press or accusing the President. Peru's government had already lodged charges with the UN. The elections in a few weeks would reveal the truth. Not a shred of accusations toward America and her people. The satisfaction wasn't worth the mess.

The Secretary of Defense was resigning his position in the morning. McGill turned down the offer of his job as quickly as the President suggested it. Avers was confronted with his crimes and while the people of the United States would seek charges for Serbia, they could do nothing for this matter. Media attention would make every effort thus far a waste of life. But let's just say Avers wouldn't be on the lecture circuit. It had to die a quiet, unmourned death. He was thankful for that small measure.

The intercom buzzed and McGill hit the button. "Major? I thought you went home."

"He did. It's Truman, sir."

He frowned. This was the last place he should be. He tapped again. "Come in."

The door pushed open and McGill felt a childlike anticipation as it swung wide. Truman stepped through and closed the door behind him. He would have blended in on the street and probably scared a few people. *About six two,* McGill thought as he came closer. He was light-footed for such a big man and he extended his hand. McGill went to shake it, but he held out papers.

"I'm done."

McGill didn't take them.

"After all this time?"

"That just about says it all, doesn't it?"

McGill took the papers and nodded. "Can I at least know your real name? I won't repeat it."

He hesitated for a second, eyeing him. "Quinn."

"Army, Navy, Marines?"

"Does it matter?"

This man had evasion down to an art form. "No." McGill tossed down the papers. "You're sure—"

"Yes."

"What will you do?"

"Do you care?"

McGill stiffened, offended. "Yes, son, I do."

There was a hint of a smile, but nothing more. "This job paid well. I was always on it. You'd be amazed how well off you are when you don't have a real life." He started to move away, then stopped. "Good-bye, sir."

Truman offered his hand and McGill thought, *I'm damn proud to shake this one.* "My friends call me Mac." He smiled. "And thank you for your service."

Quinn nodded as he drew back, turned and left.

Joe let out a breath, then reached for his brief case, anxious to be home. The new deputy director would arrive in the morning and it couldn't happen fast enough. He just wanted to go home, kiss his wife and sleep for a couple days. He'd enjoy his retirement, teaching at the local college and watching his grandchildren grow up. The thought of it made him move faster and he was at the door when he glanced back and gave the room a final inspection. His attention caught on the desk. He crossed to it and smiled widely.

On his blotter was a substantial pile of medals. Purple hearts, bronze and silver stars, but it was the Navy Cross on top that had him reaching.

He turned it over to read Quinn's full name. Yet, all it said was, UNKNOWN SOLDIER.

Tessa left the car and grasped Logan's hand in a pinching grip. He patted it and winced. She smiled an apology, then was still for a moment, looking around the neighborhood. Manicured lawns, balls and tricycles in the driveways. Middle America, she thought, and missed it.

They started up the front walk, but Tessa stopped before they met the steps and looked at the house. People were waiting. People who'd loved her and lost. People she'd hurt.

She didn't know what to expect. They'd been warned, her mother had helped. Tessa looked at Logan. He'd gone with Mom, held her hand while they'd told her sister she was alive. For Mama, Logan was forever endeared to her, and Tessa loved him more for it, for his strength and his gentle heart. For the integrity it took to heal the sick and fight the wars.

"Tessa." He squeezed her hand. "Ready?"

She nodded, blew out a breath, but still didn't move.

"Your sister's great. Loves my Snidely Whiplash imitation. They'll love you," he said tenderly.

"Logan, I know I'm not the softest peach in the basket . . ."

He smiled. "You're the sexiest. And the one with the biggest biceps, too," he added.

Her smile bloomed slowly, brightening down to her soul. *I love him.* "So arm wrestling is out of the question, huh?"

He brushed a kiss to her cheek and she mounted the steps, and when she reached the top, the door flew open. Tessa stared into the eyes of her baby sister, a child before, a mother now. She waited, her heart pounding so hard she could scarcely draw a breath.

She's beautiful, Tessa thought, and waited.

Then Katarina flew to her, throwing her arms tightly around her and Tessa clung. Tears flowed and she squeezed, sobbing softly, then faintly she heard her sister thank Logan.

Katarina leaned back, crying, smiling. Then there was a shriek of her name, and three little kids came running out, a tall man behind them. The kids clamored for her and she sat on the porch steps, getting warm, tight hugs from her nieces and nephew. She glanced up to see her sister leaning against the porch post, watching with tears in her eyes while Logan and Kat's husband made introductions.

But when her two-year-old niece crawled onto her lap and settled in, she kissed the top of her head, then looked at Logan and said, "Okay. Now I'm really home."

Java

Tessa walked across the sand toward the open tent. Torches and a generator lit the area, the balmy breeze soft and soothing. She watched Logan tend to a little brown-skinned girl and couldn't help but smile. She was looking at him so trustingly. Then he vaccinated her and she cried over the sting, but Logan rubbed it, kissed the top of her head and surprised her with a lollipop. The child hopped off, running to her mother, and Logan snapped off his gloves and stood to discard the mess of the day. In cutoffs and a Hawaiian print shirt, he didn't look anything like the commando elite who'd rocked her world.

She wouldn't say it was in his past, but she didn't care, as long as she got to love him, she was okay with that. Loving Logan was like breathing; it was easy and she couldn't live without him.

He looked up as she came near and smiled. A lifetime of those, she thought. He'd saved her life in more ways than just helping her duck bullets and a virus. He'd brought her back to the people she loved, the freedom she craved, and a new life without secrets and lies. Such a superman.

She came over to him, smoothed her hands over his hair, then plowed her fingers in as she bent to kiss him. "God, you taste good."

"It's the salamander stew," he said.

She laughed a light giggle and it made Logan grin. She had energy to burn and he was enjoying every second of it.

"Are you done being my bodyguard?"

He pulled her closer, enjoying the kiss, then said, "Not till the benefits run out."

She asked him that almost daily. The NGS employed him with her, as her protection, and he ministered to the sick as best he could. It was a great compromise. She didn't want to be a part of Dragon One or lose her job. Logan understood. The pressure of lives on your hands wasn't easy to carry.

"They never will."

"I'm counting on that."

"There's more." She pulled him toward the little house up the beach.

"Don't you have to work?"

"I have enough." She let him go and walked ahead.

Logan's gaze traveled over her, the tanned skin, the sarong wrapping her hips and hiding the yellow bikini.

She stopped, tossed a sexy look over her shoulder. "Come on, Logan. Go native with me." And just to entice him, something she had to know wasn't necessary—she slipped off the sarong, giving him the best view on the planet.

He followed her, thinking his family probably thought he'd marry a debutant, someone with old Southern lineage and a list of proper qualities. But Logan never wanted proper, or reserved. Heck, he'd never even thought about it till Tessa. But he did now and had exactly what he *needed*—a strong, resourceful woman, comfortable in her own skin and deep under his.

She paused on the porch of her little island house and looked back at him. "You can't move any faster, commando?"

Grinning, Logan jogged to her, overtaking the steps and pulling her into his arms. "I love you."

"Oh, don't I know it," she said, with a smile hot enough to melt glass. "Wanna see how much?"

She pulled him inside, her pale blue eyes speaking to his soul, and Logan dove into his new life, his only love, trapped on an island with his jungle girl . . . no bad guys or nunchucks for a hundred miles.

Don't miss Kathy Love's
ANY WAY YOU WANT IT,
available next month from Brava . . .

"I had a woman read my tea leaves today, too." As soon as the words were out of her mouth, she knew that wasn't comfortable.

And unfortunately, Ren's interest was piqued.

"Oh yeah. And what did you find out? Something about having a wild fling with a long-haired, white-eyelashed musician?"

From her violent blush, Ren realized his flirtatious joke had been dead on. Well damn. He had to find that tea leaf reader and give her a big kiss.

He studied Maggie. Had she revealed she wanted him to the fortune teller? There was something thrilling about the idea that she'd made it clear to someone else that she wanted him. Even after his brush off. He didn't deserve that, but he was damned glad he was getting a second chance with her.

And a wild fling was exactly what he wanted too. Man, this all seemed to be falling into place so easily. There *were* brief times in his existence when he didn't feel quite so cursed. This was definitely one of them.

Of course he still sensed some reservations in her that would need to be worked around. Actually two distinct feelings swirled around her like a cocoon. One real and one manufactured.

Her announcement had her embarrassed, and she'd also drunk too much. He could take care of her embarrassment.

She had nothing to be ashamed of, period. But he did not want sex with this woman to be the drunken variety. He should have realized in his presence alcohol would affect her more.

Humans always got more drunk, more tired, more over-whelmed in his presence. A side effect of his nature. Even when he wasn't trying, he still stole some of a human's energy, which brought their natural tolerance down. It was part of being a lampir that he couldn't totally control.

He did not want Maggie drunk when he was with her. He wanted her fully aware of him when he ran his hands over her soft skin, kissed her and entered into her curvy little body.

His cock pulsed against the material of his jeans as if cheering at that idea.

And Maggie was so worth cheering about. Her energy snapped between them. So alive, so powerful. She had a wholesomeness to her that radiated from her and filled him. He liked that feeling. Wholesomeness. When had he ever known that feeling?

He started to reach out to tuck one of her flyaway waves behind her ear, but stopped himself. She was too uncomfort-able now. He needed to give her time to settle down again be-fore touching her, even in the most innocent way.

Instead, he pushed away her drink. "I think you've had enough Impaler for tonight." God, no double entendre there. Although not in the direction he wanted to go.

She didn't argue. "I think you're right."

"Do you want to get out of here?" he asked, needing to take her someplace where he could touch her. Not that Sheri would think twice if he decided to make out with Maggie right where they sat. Hell, he'd done more than that at this very table. But Maggie so wasn't like the women he was used to. She needed seduction, not the usual inelegant groping he'd simply gotten accustom to.

"I think that's a good idea," she said.

He noticed that her eyes tracked the features of his face as if they were moving. Oh yeah, she'd drunk too much—and he'd taken too much of her energy too. It was so damned hard not to.

"Fresh air might be good," she said, still looking a little disoriented.

Ren nodded, and immediately regretted the action as she nodded in response, trying to focus on him.

He waved to Sheri, thanking her. Maggie thanked her too, her voice sweet and only a little slurred.

"Maybe we should walk around for awhile," he suggested.

"I think that's a good idea." This time "that's" was only slightly slurred.

He took her elbow. She allowed the touch, even leaned into it. He liked the feeling of her against his side, warm and soft. He focused on giving some of his energy back to her. Another trick a lampir had. He constantly took energy from those around him, but he could also give it back. That didn't make him so much of a leech, right?

They stepped out of the bar, and he headed left onto Bourbon, only to take the next side street off it. The smells of Bourbon were not even close to the equivalent of fresh air. Between the smell of beer, trash and other disgusting things, it was not the place for sobering up someone who was a little tipsy.

He walked slowly, not pushing her into conversation, in case she didn't feel quite up to it. But once they were away from the music blaring from within the bars, and the air was mildly less aromatic, she spoke.

"I already feel better. Thanks."

"Sure. Not like I haven't been there." It took him a lot more than three tumblers of wine and a half an Impaler to get there, but he did understand. And yes, he had been counting her drinks. He'd been aware of everything she'd done since she'd walked into the bar tonight.

They reached Jackson Square, and he gestured to benches lining the outside of the wrought-iron fence. "Want to sit?"

She nodded.

Once they were settled, she turned to him, her big gray-green eyes regarding him solemnly—and more focused.

"I'm sorry I told you about the—thing at the cemetery and the tea leaf reading."

He wasn't. He liked both announcements, a lot.

"Well," he said slowly, "technically you didn't tell me anything about the tea leaf reading. And I really liked what you had to say about the cemetery tour."

The dim light couldn't hide Maggie's blush.

"That was a really good story," he added when her gaze dropped to her hands folded on her lap.

"I don't think blurting out that I wished to have a wild fling really constitutes a story."

Ren smiled at that. "Oh, I don't know, I think there's a story there. And frankly, I'm really hoping that I get to be an integral part of it."

Her head popped up, surprise clear in her wide-eyed expression. How could she possibly be surprised by that? Did she still doubt that he wanted her? Silly woman.

"Ren," she started, and the slow way she said his name didn't make him think he was going to like what she had to say after it. So he did the first thing that came into his mind.

He kissed her.

Tensions are running high
in Charlotte Mede's
EXPLOSIVE,
out next month from Brava . . .

"What exactly is the nature of your agreement with de Maupassant? Is it money? The promise of notoriety?"

Devon turned her head sharply to look up at him, absorbing the stark lines of his face, the wide mouth above the strong jawline. She pivoted gracefully in his arms, holding herself stiffly as though more conscious than ever of a confused upsurge of unwelcome sensations, of fear and desire. Blackburn felt her invoke her steeliest reserve.

"My relationship with Le Comte has nothing to do with us."

"He has everything to do with us," Blackburn muttered. "He's thrown us together quite deliberately. And he's prepared to give you access to the "Eroica," despite your denials," he said just as the orchestra struck up a lively minuet.

"It's not that easy." Her mouth was set in a firm line. "I don't want or need your offer of money, or anybody else's for that matter."

"Don't take me for a fool, mademoiselle. And I won't take you for the innocent that you pretend to be," he said in a softly uttered threat. "You know how to play Le Comte for a puppet, and you know exactly how to convince him to relinquish the score to you."

The confusion and embarrassment clouding her eyes was a fine bit of acting, he thought, looking at her drift away from him a few steps, in perfect time with the music's rhythm.

"Tell me, is Le Comte sparing with the purse strings?" he continued ruthlessly as his strong arms propelled her back toward him. "One should think those emeralds around your lovely neck would keep you satisfied. Or are you trying for diamonds?"

"Stop it," she whispered under her breath, then in the next instant lifted her gaze to him boldly as though changing her mind. "Rubies, actually," she said with a brittle voice. "I'm trying for rubies, if you must know."

He didn't like the answer or her bravado. "Then perhaps we should turn up the heat."

She gave him a mockingly sweet smile, for his benefit or for their audience, he wasn't sure. "And how do you propose we force Le Comte's hand?" she asked.

"With the utmost discretion, of course," he said fooling neither her nor himself. "As strategies go, you of all people must know how potent the combination of seduction, jealousy and deception can be, mademoiselle," he explained, his voice rough velvet as he led her from the center of the ballroom to the protective shadows of a grouping of leafy plants.

She was a tall woman but he still towered over her, backing her into a corner. In the wavering candlelight, he thought he glimpsed uncertainty and fear in her eyes as she refused to lower her gaze, staring steadily, courageously into his face. Vulnerability was difficult to feign and for a moment, Blackburn questioned his own powers of observation. He watched the tip of her tongue slide from her lips, the gesture deliberate, he didn't know. All he knew was how his body reacted with a blast of heat.

As if to make it easier for her, his shadowed face moved fractionally closer as he slid his fingers deep into the mass of her hair to tilt her face upward. It was just one way to fight the battle, he persuaded himself, before taking her face in both palms. Her mouth trembled beneath his, moist, pliant and intensely female.

The tension eased out of her by slow degrees as his lips brushed lightly against hers. Instead of drawing away, Devon drew unconsciously closer, her lashes lowered, closing her eyes. He teasingly nipped her lower lip, his tongue licking inside. She surrendered her mouth, opening to the voracity of his deepening kiss while the strains of violins and the protective covering of fronds receded in the distance.

More insistent and demanding, the pressure of Blackburn's lips increased in a velvety heated stroking as his tongue suggestively explored, caressing her sweetness, tasting her mouth with a lazy greed. Slow and inexorably consuming, his mouth devoured hers until she gasped for breath. He heard her groan as she pressed her breasts against him, oblivious to the sharp edges of the pilaster biting into her back, sighing against the succulence of their hot, ravenous play.

"We should have done this from the very first," Blackburn whispered roughly, and plunged again for her pliant tongue as his hands stroked their way down her back and to the sides of her breasts.

Against his mouth, she whispered, "This makes no sense . . ." But she wound her arms around his neck, shuddering at the feel of his palms molding her breasts. She sank into his kisses, long, leisurely, wet incursions that left her so weak he had to hold her up in his arms.

As if he had all the time in the world, and as if a good number of Le Comte's guests had not spied their impromptu rendezvous, Blackburn traced a voluptuous trail along her parted lips, her smooth cheek, the curl of an ear, the highly sensitive, he discovered, curve of her neck. He moved his mouth to the softness of her shoulder and felt Devon shiver at the touch of his mouth, his teeth, the soothing stroke of his tongue.

No longer distant nor in complete control of the encounter, Blackburn felt himself become harder, tauter, his body contemptuously mocking his attempt at detachment. Her skin was like rich cream beneath his lips, her body sinuously lush as it melted into his. She drew a shuddering breath and, against his will, his hard fingers slid from her breasts to the back of her head where they tangled in her thick hair. His mouth, a hot brand, closed over hers once again.

His eyes closed in self-defense and he immediately saw her naked beneath him, warm and soft and ready. He groaned against the tidal wave threatening to overtake them both. Her open and ardent sensuality startled him like nothing had in a very long time, and he had drunk from the very depths of decadence, manipulating, controlling the most sophisticated of carnal games.

He forced his eyes open, pulling back and releasing her by slow degrees with small kisses, erotically tugging at her lips, willing himself to ignore the clamoring of his heated blood, willing his erection to subside. She was just another of de Maupassant's women. His pulse slowed, he tensed and ice water began to replace the blood in his veins.

The objective was to have her secure the "Eroica," at whatever cost.

Keep an eye out for
THE BLACK SHEEP AND
THE HIDDEN BEAUTY
by Donna Kauffman,
new next month from Brava . . .

Elena backed down the ladder from her loft apartment over the outer stables, yawning deeply and wishing like hell she'd remembered to set the timer on the coffeepot the night before. The sun was barely peeking over the horizon, and last night the temperatures had dipped down a bit farther than they had recently, making for a chilly late spring morning. She shivered despite the long underwear top she'd donned under her overalls this morning. Teach her to be a smart-ass and offer up a dawn class. But then, she hadn't really expected him to take her up on it. He struck her as more night owl, than early bird. Serve her right if he stood her up. Her luck, Rafe was probably still tucked in his nice warm bed. Which was where she should be. Well, not in Rafe's bed, but . . .

No way could she stop the visuals that accompanied that little mental slip. It wasn't a shot of warm coffee, but it did have the added benefit of getting her blood pumping a little faster. Of course, if she were in the same bed as Rafe, she wouldn't need any coffee, just . . . stamina.

"Morning."

His voice surprised her, making her lose her footing on the last rung. An instant later two strong hands palmed her waist and steadied her as both feet reached the ground. She could have told him that putting his hands on her was not the way to steady her at the moment, but she was too busy trying to rally her thoughts away from imagining him manhandling her like this while they were both naked among tousled sheets.

Then he was turning her around, and she was getting her first look at a scruffy, early morning Rafe. And whatever words she might have found evaporated like morning mist under a rising sun.

Goodness knows her temperature was rising.

He had on an old, forest green sweatshirt and an even older pair of jeans if the frayed edged and faded thighs and knees were any indication. It was standard weekend morning clothing for most men, but, until that moment, she'd have been hard-pressed to visualize it on him. Of course, on most men, that combination would have given them a disheveled look at best. In fact, she was feeling incredibly disheveled herself at the moment. Rafe, on the other hand, without even trying, looked like he'd just stepped off the pages of the latest Ralph Lauren ad. She'd resent the ease with which he made scruffy so damn sexy, except she was too busy fighting off the waves of lust the look inspired.

"So," she said, her tone overly bright. "You ready for lesson number two?"

"As I'll ever be."

She led the way down the aisle toward Petunia's stall. "It's been a while since your first lesson, so keep in mind that you'll probably need to reestablish your rapport with Petunia."

"Check." He said nothing else, just followed behind her.

She stopped at the tack room door and went inside. "I haven't set anything out, so we need to get her saddle, pads, bridle, everything."

He followed her into the smaller room. "Just point to what we need."

She could feel him behind her, her awareness of him as finely tuned as her senses were to the animals she worked with. Except with him, there was all that sexual energy jacking things up. She cleared her throat, maybe squared her shoulders a little, then made the mistake of looking back at him before reaching for the first of the gear.

Something about the morning beard shadowing his jaw, the way his hair wasn't quite so naturally perfect, made his eyes darker, and enhanced how impossibly thick his eyelashes were. And she really, really needed to stop looking at his mouth. But the ruggedness the stubble lent to his face just emphasized all the more those soft, sculpted lips of his.

Her thighs were quivery, her nipples were on point, and the panties she'd just put on not fifteen minutes ago, were already damp. The morning air might have been head-clearing, but her body hadn't gotten the message at all.

"You take the saddle there," she said, trying not to sound as breathless as she knew she did. Dammit. "On the third rail," she added, pointing, when he kept that dark gaze of his on her.

"What else?" He didn't even glance at the rack.

"Grab one of the pads. Same kind that we used last time. I'll get the halter and bridle."

"Okay."

She waited a heartbeat too long for him to move first. He didn't.

So they were officially staring at each other now. The silence in the small space expanded in a way that lent texture to the very air between them. The room was tiny, the temperature warm, with little ventilation. The sun hadn't risen enough to slice through the panels on the roof, leaving the room deep in shadows, with thin beams of gray dawn providing the only light. There was a light bulb overheard, but she'd have to reach past him to get to the switch.

He stepped forward. "Elena—"

"Rafe—"

They spoke at the same time, both broke off.

He paused. "Yes?"

She really wanted to know what he'd been about to say, before she potentially made a very big fool out of herself, but went ahead before she lost her nerve. "I can't—I mean, not to be presumptuous here, but I can't—don't—mix business with pleasure."

"Are we?"

She didn't back down. She might not be the most experienced person in the world when it came to relationships, but she knew the way he was looking at her wasn't of the innocent teacher-student variety. "It feels like more than a simple riding lesson to me." *There. She'd said it.*

He took another step closer, and her breath suddenly felt trapped inside her chest. So much for being brazen.

"It is a simple riding lesson," he said. "Not a corporate merger. So what if there is more? I don't really see a conflict of interest here."

"You're a close friend of my boss."

He stepped closer still. It was a small room to begin with. He was definitely invading her personal space. Again.

"And you're not planning on staying here long-term anyway, right?"

"What is that supposed to mean?"

"Meaning that as potential conflicts go, that one is temporary at best. As is anything that may happen between us. No commitments, right?" His voice was all just-rolled-out-of-bed rough.

"What are you saying, then?" she asked, tipping her chin up slightly as he shifted closer. She felt the bridle rack at her back. "What is it you want?"

"I just want to learn to ride." His lips curved then, and her thighs—or more accurately, the muscles between them—suddenly felt a whole lot wobbly.

His eyes were so dark, so deep, she swore she could fall right into them and never climb back out. And that smile made it dizzyingly clear that horses weren't the only thing he was interested in riding.

It was too early in the day for this. She couldn't handle this kind of full out assault on her senses. Or on her mind. Or . . . hell, what part of her didn't he affect? He muddled her up far to easily. Muddled was definitely not what she needed to be right now.

But when he lifted his hand, barely brushing the underside of her chin with his fingertips, and tipped her head back a bit farther . . . she let him.

"I think about you," he said, his voice nothing more than a rough whisper.

Her skin tingled as if the words themselves had brushed against her.

"Too often. You distract me."

"And that's a bad thing?"

"It's . . . an unexpected thing."

She wasn't sure what to think about that. And his neutral tone made it impossible to decipher how he felt about it. "So, this is . . . what? An attempt to exorcise me from your thoughts?"

His smile broadened as his mouth lowered slowly toward hers. "Either that, or make all this distraction a lot more worthwhile."

She had a split second to decide whether to let him kiss her, and spent a moment lying to herself that she was actually strong enough to do the right thing and turn her head away. Who was she kidding? Her body was fairly humming in anticipation, and it was all she could do to refrain from grabbing his head and hurrying him the hell up.

Like he said. It was just a kiss. Not a contract.

His lips brushed across hers. Warm, a little soft, but the right amount of firm. He slid his fingers along the back of her neck, beneath the heavy braid that swung there, sending a delicious little shiver all the way down her spine at the contact.

He dropped another whisper of a kiss across her lips, then another, inviting her to participate, clearly not going any farther unless she did. She respected that, a lot, even though part of her wished he'd taken the decision out of her hands. It would make all the self-castigation later much easier to avoid. Given his aversion to commitment, somehow she figured he knew that. They were either in it together, or not at all.

He lifted his head just enough to look into her eyes, a silent question in his own. *Will you, or won't you?*

She held his gaze for what felt like all eternity, then slowly lowered her eyelids as she closed the distance between them and kissed him back.